SCARCITY

Robert Calbeck

SCARCITY

Original cover art by Wyatt Strain

ASIN: B07T86L8RV (e-book)
ISBN: 9781074850661 (Paperback)

First Printing: June 2019

Acknowledgements

The book you have in your hands has been in the works for almost a decade. I've had to rewrite sections more times than I can count because events that were supposed to happen 20 years in the future happened too early. At another point my laptop was stolen and I lost a year of work. Aspiring authors note: back up often! I've had to balance a challenging job as a math teacher, volunteer work, and now a baby to get this bad boy finished. Completing Scarcity has truly been a labor of love, but not all of that labor has come from me. There are many to whom I owe far more than a paragraph on this page that I'd like to thank for helping make Scarcity a reality.

I would be making an egregious error if the first person I mentioned wasn't Andrew Lance. Andrew is one of my best and oldest friends and was the one who helped me get into this writing mess in the first place. Over the course of several years we wrote a novel together, *Flame Bearer*; and no, you can't read it because honestly, it was bad. But we learned the craft and discovered the joy of building a world. Lance is a far better writer than I have ever been; I hope to see a novel of his on the shelf someday. Cheers to you, Lance!

I also must thank my impossibly patient wife, Kristi. Not only is she far lovelier than a nerdy math teacher obsessed with rockets deserves, but is patient enough to encourage me to finish. She has read and edited many of my drafts and frankly deserves any and all royalties I earn—but don't tell her I said that!

My friend JT has also been hugely influential in helping

Scarcity see the light of day. Not only was he one of my best beta readers, but after publishing his debut novel, he walked me through the minefield of the publishing industry. Without him I would certainly have been lost and probably metaphorically blown up.

I've got to give a shout-out to my awesome students! A number of them have read early drafts of Scarcity and given me great feedback on how to improve. So if you are at Nine Mile Falls, Mahomet-Seymour, Douglas County, or Heritage High School, thank you so much for being the best students a lame dictator, err...math teacher could ever hope for! Hope you enjoy my "lit" novel.

Thank you to my long-suffering parents and my brother Cam for always being there. Wyatt, the cover is awesome. Thank you for the incredible design. To the rest of my friends, family, and neighbors I don't have room to mention here, thank you for enriching my life. There is no scarcity of friendship or love in my life thanks to you.

And I thank you, dear reader, for buying this book. Thank you for taking a chance on an unknown author, thank you for your time, and for the questions this novel may plague you with.

To my son, Luke:

May you grow up in a happier world than I have envisioned.

PROLOGUE

Phone call: United States of the West

"You aren't taking this seriously enough."

"You're taking it too seriously. What harm could a physicist do, for carbon's sake?"

"It will be clear once you hear the rest of the conversation."

Over the highly encrypted satellite signal, the two men listened to the same tapped phone recording despite being on opposite ends of the Atlantic Ocean. It had been recorded two days before, then forwarded and emailed a half-dozen times before it ended up on each man's digital desk.

The man on the European side pressed the play icon and both men heard the recording simultaneously.

"You are talking about perpetual motion."

"Not at all. Perpetual motion is impossible."

"Is it? You seem to have discovered it."

"Perpetual motion violates the laws of thermodynamics. You know as well as anyone that makes it impossible. This is different. My device uses a trick of relativistic geometry to create a situation where an object is continuously falling. It is—" The recording stopped abruptly.

"Did you hear what he said? I am not overreacting."

"I was listening. This guy thinks he found a way to break physics."

"Maybe."

"I have heard other recordings of crackpots dreaming up perpetual motion machines, and we ignored them. You aren't ignoring this particular crackpot, so I assume this is more than a *maybe.*"

"It is a *probably.* I have strong reason to suspect that this could be real. Both of these men are high profile scientists: Luthor Tenrel from Fermilab and Eli Al'Halsimi, a professor teaching at CERN's graduate program. It seems implausible that they would discuss something like this if it was not actually happening."

"Okay, so let's assume it's real. How is he managing this *sort-of* perpetual motion?"

"Apparently he is utilizing a heretofore unknown property of element 126."

"Which is?"

"He claims Element 126 has enhanced gravity."

"You're shitting me."

"I am *shitting* nothing."

"But gravity? That just sounds impossible."

"*I* believe it is real."

"If it's really happening, why hasn't anyone figured this out before? The Censors' background notes say 126 was discovered 20 years ago."

"It was. But no one has been able to create more than a few atoms; little chemical or property analysis has been possible."

"It says something here about an 'island of stability' and that the element is stable and inert?"

"Element 126 has no discernable half-life. But not necessarily inert."

"Damn straight. Hard to call enhanced gravity inert."

"You could put it that way."

"And this son-of-a-bitch can synthesize it in measurable amounts. So what is he going to do with it? Create a black hole in the middle of Chicago?"

"Worse."

"Worse than a black hole?"

"He is using it to generate electricity."

"Shit. Smogging shit."

"Must you swear so much? It makes you sound like a moron. I can't abide employing morons."

"You pay me to shoot people in the head at 800 meters, not to hold my pinky out when I drink tea. So how is he making electricity with this shit?"

"It seems that was what the 'continuously falling' part was about. Our best guess is that the device uses the 126 to create a closed system. First water or some other medium falls through a turbine, then the 126 allows it to then *fall back up* through another turbine into the original container."

"A goddamn hydroelectric dam in his bathtub... does it work? I mean has he created a prototype?"

"Just listen."

The connection was so sharp the tap of the mouse was audible as it was clicked.

"Unbelievable! You are telling me that you have a device that will continually generate power with no other input? Does it really matter what it is called so long as it works? It does, in fact, work?"

"Just look at my electric bill! It has been powering my entire home for almost six months."

"Fantastic Luthor, simply fantastic. It is hard to believe that in my lifetime someone would discover how to control gravity."

"I think you give me too much credit."

"If anything, I am not giving you enough credit! When you told me you had something huge, I thought it was just something you were going to publish; I did not think it was going to be world-changing."

Click.

"This is a smogging disaster!"

"You see why this needs to be taken care of."

"This has the potential to destroy everything we have been working for."

"Everything we have already achieved."

"If this polluter can honestly create energy out of thin air it—"

"—would be the single most valuable discovery in the last one hundred years."

"That might actually be an understatement."

"Very possibly. Call up his utility bills. We can find out very quickly if this is real or not. I would very much prefer to forget about this."

"Six months he says he has been running this huh? Let me check."

"Check back to October 2047 as a reference. Look for a dramatic change in the bills."

"I know how to do my smogging job."

"Then do it."

"I am, these high-efficiency processors are slow as—damn!"

"What is it?"

"It says here that he went from paying his power bill every month, to suddenly having a *negative* balance in February. Six goddamn months ago."

"He is making enough energy to sell some off to the utilities?"

"Yeah. And it looks like he is making more every month than the month before."

"He is optimizing his device."

"We definitely need to kill him. Like yesterday. We need that tech before it spreads."

"My sentiments exactly. Fortunately, he took the liberty of telling us where he is going to be next week. Listen to this."

Click.

"It has already revolutionized my life. The energy savings alone are allowing me to afford to attend the International Energy Convention in Geneva next month. When I figured out I could sell off the excess power, I made enough to bring my girlfriend. She hasn't been to Europe since before the war. I'm even buying passage for my intern to attend the convention with us."

"Amazing."

"I know. If it could do this for me in a matter of months, think of what it could do for the world if implemented on a large scale. Not to mention the applications for this stuff that I haven't even imagined yet."

Click.

"So we nail his ass when he is over there at the IEC. Perfect."

"Convenient at least."

"We gotta take care of this intelligently. Quietly."

"I will make the necessary arrangements."

"What *arrangements* are you planning? Bringing in the Sabers on a respected scientist would be risky."

"We will wait until he arrives in Europe; it will be less suspicious."

"Good idea. What about Al'Halsimi? How much does he know?"

"That is still unclear. Our phone tap doesn't indicate that he has any specifics on synthesizing 126."

"Any ties with the Chinese? We could get the media to brand him as a spy and then 'arrest' him."

"There are not any obvious connections."

"Spies don't need obvious connections. That's why

they're called *spies.* You said he is teaching at CERN? Maybe he's selling tech secrets to the Chinese."

"Our Government is trying to open up talks with China. They are pushing the media to suppress any stories with anti-Chinese sentiment."

"Fine. Then we go back to our normal M.O. We kill him right after he spills his guts on everything he knows."

"That is why our normal M.O. involves the Sabers."

"What will you do with Tenrel once you have his gravity-perpetual-motion thing?"

"Kill him too. Along with his whole team."

"No loose ends huh?"

"Like you said, I pay you to kill people at 800 meters, not to second guess me. Do what you need to ensure there are no 'loose ends' on your end. No one else in Fermilab can see that technology."

"That could be a problem. How many people have his data? Shit like that spreads faster than the plague."

"It seems from the tape he hasn't told anyone. I think he wants to make a big splash at the IEC."

"Let me hear."

A short pause indicated that the file was loading a specific part of the conversation.

"...you understand. Everyone *needs to have this—even the Chinese, for it to work. Businesses too. Who knows what would happen if only a single government controlled the knowledge of 126 and it's production? World War III started because China tried to control all the energy sources. I can't let that happen with 126."*

"You are right, old friend. Of course. I was just thinking of the credits you could have earned."

"I will be fine. Once this gets out, nations and businesses will pay me handsomely for my expertise."

"Let us hope so, I would hate to see your altruism unre-

warded."

"I don't think it will be a problem. Like you said, no matter what, I have a guaranteed Nobel Prize and the money that comes with it, right?"

"Yes, and you'll never have an energy bill again."

"True. One other thing, while I want to share this with the world, I do also want credit for its discovery. I haven't even told anyone in the lab out of fear someone would steal the research. They don't even know I found a way to manufacture 126 out of our puny cyclotron. So please don't say anything before I present. I don't know what would happen if it got out early what we're really working on."

"You aren't going to try to publish anything in advance of the conference?"

"No. You know how the Censors are these days. If I send research like this to a journal, the censors would get at it first. America would never let me give it to China."

"I see. Now that you mention it, I imagine a monopoly on limitless, free energy would be a rather strong temptation for any government."

"That's it. I sure do miss the good old days when I could have put something online for everyone to see without a government Censor reading it and editing it first."

"You're sounding pretty old, Luthor. Just don't start talking about dollars and euros okay?"

"Very funny. Anyway, you can see why I want this kept quiet."

"I will not speak of it. However, I am going to push very hard for you to be a keynote presenter on Saturday night. This deserves some pomp and circumstance. I will tell the planning council that you have a very important surprise for them."

"That would be splendid."

"I am confident I will be able to reserve you a spot as speaker. If not Saturday, perhaps some other day, but you will need to bring a prototype for demonstration."

"I already packed it."

Click.

"So Tenrel hasn't spread it around because he wants credit for the discovery. How very smogging scientific of him."

"And very convenient for us."

"Yes. All you need to do is eliminate his ass and get that prototype. I will have a team here ready to raid his house and their lab. I think we should be able to get everything without too much trouble."

"Do wait for us to make our move before you strike. It would be a shame for you to tip our hand by acting prematurely. I don't want Tenrel getting any phone calls that is home has been broken into by a team of well-armed men."

"I will wait for your signal. Just take care of your shit. Then we will have the prototype, the synthesis method, and Tenrel's corpse."

PART I:

EUROPE

CHAPTER 1:

Marseille, France, European Union

Luthor found it hard to believe that a few common ropes could moor such a massive vessel to the dock. The nuclear-powered seabus had just made the weeklong transatlantic journey from New York to Marseille carrying almost 15,000 passengers, now it was held in place by braided twine. Of course, there had been plenty of time to consider the resistance and tensile strength of the rope as well as the mass of the ship because he had been standing on the exit gangway staring at it for an indeterminate time approaching eternity. Even his girlfriend, Tanya, normally entranced with boats and the sea, stared glassy-eyed somewhere at the sheer white side of the ship.

Luthor gripped the railing a little tighter as they shuffled a few more nanometers. He tried not to think about the twenty meter fall to the water below, but it was hard not to as the line snailed forward. Luthor was terrified of heights. He wanted off that walkway. To distract himself, he focused on Tanya's sandy hair fluttering in the breeze, her blue eyes locked on his and she gave him a smile. It helped, but his stomach was still performing summersaults.

In the distance, Luthor had a glimpse of the giant offshore wind farm off the coast of the iconic Île du Planier. It churned the air providing the majority of the power for the energy-starved city of Marseille ten kilometers to the Northeast. Surrounding the small island, thousands of stately white masts rose out of the sea in perfect rows. The three massive composite blades topping each windmill marched in the air together like something from the blackest nightmares of Don Quixote.

The second hand on his watch actually appeared to be slowing, each tick more reluctant than the last. Luthor cursed Einstein for teaching the world just how relative time really was. *But I've just proven that Einstein was wrong, haven't I?* Luthor thought. *He said that the closer you get to the speed of light the slower time passes, theoretically leading to time stopping completely at the speed of light. In actuality, he got it backward. I've just proven that time actually moves slower at slower speeds. It is physically impossible for this damn line to move any slower, and look! Time has stopped completely.*

According to his watch, it was another fifteen minutes before they made it into the warehouse-like port authority building and another thirty before they made it to the immigration security checkpoint. However, he was certain that due to the slowing of time, the rest of the earth had already passed well into the twenty-second century and his discovery of synthesizing element 126 was now hopelessly outdated. *Mental note: write satirical paper disproving relativity.* Luthor thought.

Inside the looming building, the snaking line was held in check with retractable barriers that sharply reminded Luthor of draft day at the beginning of the war. The waiting passengers were entertained with signs giving security instructions in different languages. "Remove any gloves or hand coverings." And "Remove shoes and coats." Luthor tried to read the signs in Spanish first to see if he could still read any. It didn't go well. His foreign language skills were an anemic husk of what they had been during the war. All around him people took off gloves and stuffed light coats into their bags.

Soldiers clad in strange-looking, bulbous body-armor prowled the periphery of the lines, a sober reminder to take the directions seriously. Tanya stared. "What are they wearing?" she asked. "They look ridiculous."

"Its cutting-edge body armor called *gelvar*," replied Michael Laramy, Fermilab's cyclotron intern. In gratitude for his long hours working in the lab in the previous months, Luthor had decided to pay his way to the IEC. He sincerely hoped that decision hadn't been a mistake.

"Why does it look like that? It's so round." Tanya asked.

Michael smiled. His bright teeth contrasted with his black skin in a way that most women found irresistible. "Gelvar is made of a special type of ballistics gel. It has the same resistance as several meters of water, but crammed into a vest only a few centimeters thick. When bullets hit it, the impact diffuses laterally around the surface of the gel."

"Like ripples on the water." Tanya summarized. Though not a scientist, she was anything but stupid. She was a History Professor at the community college in Aurora, Illinois and was fluent in French and Spanish.

"Exactly. It makes them almost impervious to conventional bullets."

Luthor would have given the rest of his seven toes to have had a Gelvar vest in Antarctica, better yet, one for everyone he knew. But they hadn't been invented until the last year of the war, and the United States of the West wouldn't have been willing to fork over 200,000 credits for a soldier's safety. Luthor had learned their priorities the hard way. He shuddered and shook his head, trying to clear it of the terrible memories trying to claw their way out of the cage he had made for them.

"All of it feels a little over the top for a security checkpoint, if you ask me," Tanya said. "It's not like we can fake these stupid ID's anyway, they're implanted." She gestured toward an angry white scar on the back of her right hand. She, like nearly everyone else this side of China, had an implanted Computerized Personal Identification chip on the back of her right hand. All the signs were abbreviated CPI for short.

They continued to shuffle forward. Ahead, in front of the x-ray scanner, a zealous security agent was meticulously ensuring everyone scanned their CPI chip properly. His drab, green carbon enforcement pants were tucked into high, black military-style boots. Every buckle gleamed as if he personally shined it every morning. He had the lopsided look of a man who spent every free moment in the gym but had very little idea of how to actually work out. He intensely scrutinized each person to an almost comical degree. Luthor fought back a laugh, but he couldn't help but be impressed by the diligence with which he worked at what was undoubtedly, a menial job. Of course, it was also probably his fault that this line was taking so long. If he weren't trying to win the Bronze Star, they would have been through an hour ago, and he wouldn't have disproved General Relativity.

Luthor noticed most of the heads in the crowd turning toward some sort of commotion coming from the front of the line. Luthor wished he were as tall as Michael, he would have been able to see more easily. The CPI agent had taken a timid Asian man out of the line quite a bit more forcefully than was strictly necessary. Another, far more portly security guard stood next to him with an open suitcase on a utility table. Their raised voices were audible over the startled queue.

"Customs found a hidden liner in your suitcases, Mr. Akobe," said the diligent guard in fluent English.

The other one sneered, "If that's your real name."

"I... I don't know what you're talking about."

"Its nice work, very professional. Most people wouldn't have noticed anything," the guard stuck out his chest as if trying to blind him with his buckles. "But I discovered a distortion of the X-ray and decided to investigate."

The Asian man's eyes darted about, as if he were looking for an exit.

"Do you know what I found? At least twenty-five hundred grams of powdered coal in each liner. Making sense yet?"

"Please sir, it's not what you think—"

"Here's what I think: We banned coal for a reason. I won't let you piss on our most important laws and dump carbon into the atmosphere because you think you're better than everyone else." He crossed his arms over his perfectly tucked-in shirt.

Luthor suddenly appreciated Soldier Boy's attention to detail. He felt his temper flare at the diminutive Asian. *Damned Chinese.* In Luthor's opinion, no punishment was too severe for the bastards who started World War III. Fighting the Chinese block in that war had been unequivocally the worst four years of his life. While he didn't hate every Asian, he found zero pity in his heart for a coal-smuggling polluter who happened to be one.

The small man looked around frantically. "I was just trying to keep my family warm this winter. My daughter died of hypothermia last year. Please, sir—"

"You are going to have to come with us, Mr. Akobe. It's a minimum 15 years in prison for burning coal in European Union. You can add another 10 if we found out you were planning to sell it here." The man pulled the set of handcuffs hanging from his belt.

Without warning, the Asian man kicked up violently, hitting the security guard in the groin. After the unmistakable sound of squishing man-parts, the guard's eyes rolled back and he collapsed. His handcuffs clattered away on the finished concrete floor. A leather-soled shoe stomped on his groin again. Hands proved to be a futile defense for the crushing blow, and he let out an anguished moan and curled into a fetal position. Spectators crowded the edges of the barrier to get a better view of the commotion.

"You don't know what it's like!" the Asian cried as he sprinted off around the line. Despite the demise of all future children, the crumpled guard managed to rip out his comm, he shouted angrily—if higher pitched than usual—into the device in French.

The real soldiers began converging on the fleeing Asian. One took out his rifle and fired a burst of rounds off into the air. Luthor shivered. It was an MX-5 assault rifle; the sound of its discharge had too many bad memories that went with it. The crowd flattened to the ground in fear, clearing the way to the fugitive. The soldiers leaped easily over temporary barriers in their pursuit; the bulk of their gelvar didn't seem to inhibit their movement.

"Stop!" one yelled.

The Asian didn't comply.

"Stop, or we will shoot!"

Luthor heard the solitary crack of a gunshot. It silenced the crowd as fully as if someone had hit the mute button. The soldiers stopped running. Some began waving instructions, telling everyone that all was clear. Luthor got to his knees immediately, instinctively looking for his rifle. It wasn't there. Through a small break in the line, he glimpsed a body sprawled in the gaping cargo entrance. A moment later soldiers surrounded the figure and Luthor lost sight of the dead Asian.

The crowd recovered from the traumatic scene remarkably quickly. They had survived much worse during war. No one had escaped unscathed from the economic collapse and chaos in those years.

"Did they just shoot him?" Tanya asked.

Luthor nodded soberly.

"If you ask me, he deserved it." Michael shook his head,

"trying to smuggle coal into the country."

"Seems like there should have been another way," Tanya said. "What if he really was trying to keep his family warm?"

"No," Luthor said. "He had four bags. That's 10 kilos of coal. The bastard was smuggling it in to sell it, probably hoping to pay for his passage on the seabus."

"He sounded pretty sincere."

"Nah, Luthor's right," Michael said. "Definitely a smuggler. But I bet they only checked so closely because he was Asian."

Luthor could've asked anyone in that building and they would have lost loved ones due to Chinese bombing raids, knew someone who froze to death in Antarctica, or more likely—they themselves had been on the brink of starvation during the war. Their prejudice against Asians had been earned.

"How much is coal worth anyway?" Tanya asked. "It must be valuable if he'd risk going through customs."

"It's still cheaper than gasoline, which explains why people will buy it," Michael said. "I heard the going rate is 2 kilos for the same price as one liter of gas, at least in the West."

"I couldn't afford five liters of gas if I saved for 2 months!"

"At least you get paid," Michael said.

Luthor interjected, "It's part of your education, besides you scored a free trip to Europe out of the deal."

"Yeah, but I can't enjoy it, I have to hang out with you two."

Tanya gave him a disparaging look, but he grinned, apparently achieving the result he wanted. "I guess you'll just have to settle for the honeys at the convention. I've heard pocket protectors are the new thong."

Michael was known to be a womanizer. Luthor had

been forced to endure months of daily drama stemming from his dozens of trysts and subsequent breakups. He did not relish the thought of Michael finding European women to seduce instead of helping him change the world with the miracle of Element 126.

A paramedic arrived on the scene and knelt next to the broken agent. Going through a checklist affixed to a clipboard, she checked his vitals. She helped him as he limped away to some unseen office to, no doubt, begin a long bureaucratic report on the situation.

The replacement carbon enforcement agents were more like guards ought to be: fat, balding, and preoccupied. They looked as though they knew something had gone wrong, but were still struggling to produce the additional requisite effort.

A few minutes later, Luthor slung his bag containing his computer and notepads onto a long conveyer belt that led to the X-ray machine. He had spread his supply of element 126 out throughout his bags, which muted the gravity difference significantly. To the untrained senses, being next to his bag would only make one feel *off* somehow, as the inner ear complained of being pulled in a subtly different direction. At worst it would be searched. In that case, all they would find were little plastic BBs, nothing to be suspicious of. They wouldn't know that each plastic sphere had several hundred thousand atoms of 126 contained inside.

Element 126 was Chemistry perfected. His isotope had 126 Protons 184 Neutrons making a flawlessly balanced element of supreme power. The fully closed proton, neutron, and electron shells stabilized the roiling atomic forces coursing through the enormous nucleus giving it an indeterminately long half-life. It fulfilled the predictions of a stable, super-heavy element existing in an "Island of Stability" originally hypothesized by Glen Seaborg 80 years ago. But 126 exceeded his most optimistic hopes. Seaborg had hoped for an element with a half-life measured in minutes. 126 was *stable*, or at least appeared to be. It was also the rarest substance on earth, with Luthor personally possessing all of it —minus a few stray atoms here and there in labs around the planet. He had been the only one to stumble upon a method of efficiently synthesizing the uncooperative element, which had allowed him to discover its gravitational properties.

He hated letting it out of his sight, but there was no way around it without explaining what he was doing. The dead Asian in the cargo bay reminded him what could happen if one messed around with customs. He took a deep breath, feeling his heart begin to race. *Nothing to be worried about here Luthor, you will be fine. No one is going to find anything.* He forced himself to grab a durable plastic bin off the stack and put his shoes and belt inside. Once the bin lay on the conveyor, he stepped up to the security guard.

"Right hand," the guard said. His predecessor had just been nut-stomped, but he already looked to be losing his focus. Luthor couldn't really blame him. His sole job was to make sure that no one subverted the most impervious security ever devised: the Computerized Personal Identification system. Luthor admired the simplicity of the solution CPI offered to the complicated problem of monitoring and curbing the carbon dioxide output of the earth. Nearly everyone outside of the Chinese block now had a CPI biochip, implanted in their right hand. It contained their ID, other personal information, and recorded their activity. Using the subject's own blood flow to generate electricity, it transmitted a short-range, unique, highly-encrypted signal that was impossible to fake. It also was impossible to steal, because as soon as a person's blood stopped flowing, the chip would immediately—and permanently— shut down. It could not be cut out or taken from a person in working order.

Luthor pulled back his sleeve slightly to fully expose his hand. He lowered it under a scanner that reminded him of an antique video camera with an opaque lens. Feeling a bit like produce at the supermarket, he waited for a mechanical beep. The hyper-efficient computer methodically crunched through his record; upon deciding he met the standard required by the EU, it beeped. It was a single, pleasant sounding computer tone. The good beep.

Luthor imagined all his personal information flying away, as it was sent to be stored on the massive servers located in the worldwide Carbon Enforcement Headquarters in the European Union, the organization that was synonymous with CPI. Every time a person scanned their hand, no matter where they were in the world, their information was sent to those databases. Their carbon output, purchases, immigration status, passports, and criminal record were all crosschecked, and their location recorded. Chip-scans were required to buy or sell anything because it was in the creation and use of goods that carbon dioxide was created. They were also used to withdraw or deposit carbon credits and as a universal ID. Luthor's information had already been updated twice since he woke up.

As long as this guard made sure that each passenger was, in fact, scanning their own CPI chip, the system did the rest. If it beeped in one way, then you were cleared and on to the metal detector; if it beeped the other way, incarceration. It took no thought, no insight. Just one functioning ear would suffice. Not only that, anyone branded as a fugitive or a terrorist wouldn't step within a hundred meters of a scanning station. It was suicide. In the fifteen years since he had been implanted, he hadn't ever heard a single bad beep.

Hard to imagine not having your brain turn to slush and run out of your nose on a job like that, Luthor thought. But then he preferred the challenge provided in science. Perhaps this job was the perfect match for this guard and his temperament. Either way, he didn't much care. If this guard lost focus, he would be less likely to notice anything abnormal in his carry-on. Luthor just hoped he still had enough agility to avoid any stagnant puddle of guard-brains.

"Step forward."

Luthor complied and stepped through the standard doorway-like scanners dedicated to finding any hidden items on his body and his luggage. After he'd ensured his 126 wouldn't be confiscated, he stepped to the side to wait for the others.

#

"I get so tired of these damn Marks." Tanya said, glaring distastefully at the scar on her right hand. "They are such a nuisance."

"You mean *CPI chips*." Michael said confrontationally. Tanya's insistence in using the Christian term for the chips bothered Michael to no end. Maybe that was why she kept doing it; as a professor, she thrived on debate and disagreement.

"I meant *Marks*."

"You can hate them if you want, but you have to admit it really was an elegant solution to enforce the carbon restriction laws," Michael said. "How else could they monitor everyone's carbon output when we were still using cash?"

"Elegant." Tanya said the word like it tasted rancid in her mouth.

They sat in a large, crowded terminal waiting for the next train to Geneva; it was due any minute. Luckily, Luthor had snagged an elusive bench. He stood, having offered his seat to Tanya. She gently leaned against him and hugged him in thanks. Luthor relished the feeling of her body next to his, it had been too long since they had been this happy.

Luthor hoped the trip would prove to be a breath of fresh air for their relationship. In the last year since the stumbling upon the gravitational properties of 126, he had become engrossed in his work to the exclusion of everything else—including her. He had spent days on end at Fermilab, sleeping on a couch rather than coming home. He hadn't been on a proper date with her in months. Of course, her stubborn refusal to move in with him didn't help. But bringing that up had perennially proved as dangerous as any battlefield, and Luthor had no desire to lose any more body parts now that the war was over. In the end, Luthor knew that she was a far better woman than a deeply broken man like him deserved. He desperately wanted to keep her around as long as she would have him, antiquated Christian notions of relationship propriety or not.

Tanya knew how important his discovery could be, but she had also informed him, in no uncertain terms, that his current pace was not going to be tolerated much longer.

Luthor thought he heard the squeal of a breaking train in the distance and began to move to get a better view. He threw his bag over his shoulder. The safest place for element 126 to be was on his person.

Winding his way through a milling crowd of people, he moved toward the train platform to get a better view. The terminal's high peaked ceiling seemed to make the space feel much roomier than it actually was. Clearly a relic of an older society, it had been built with concern for form rather than function. The vast volume above them sucked up all the ambient heat from the waiting passengers making the room still remarkably cool despite being so crowded. It would have cost a king's fortune if the port authority ever had to heat the space.

A dog started barking ferociously right next to him. Adrenaline flooded Luthor's veins; he turned sharply to face the new threat. His instincts, hardened from war, forced his fists into the air in preparation for a fight.

Instead of a threat, he found an overly done-up old woman with a dog in her purse. The barking turned out to be little more than yapping. A bow that gathered the dog's hair on the top of its head succeeded in eliminating even the faintest hint of ferocity. Luthor strained against his own killer instinct, willing his fists to lower and unclench. *It's just a little rat-dog, you have nothing to fight, nothing to worry about,* Luthor told himself. *Just breathe. Damn the war! Why can't it ever quit haunting me?*

He murmured an apology to the woman in what he hoped sounded something like French.

"That's okay dear," she said in a formal southern drawl, sounding like she might be from a plantation in Georgia. "I don't know what came over Mr. Snorkles here. He almost never barks." The miniature canine continued to yammer while its white paws bounced on the edge of the purse. Luthor's heart rate plummeted back to normal.

"Dogs and I have never really gotten along ma'am. I am sure there is nothing wrong with him." Maybe it was something to do with the fact that he was a scientist. Small animals must innately understand that rodents and scientists are arch nemeses. Scientists are always caging them and experimenting on them. The dog just kept barking, it was probably trying to avoid getting shoved in a cage with the other rats. But then again, it seemed not to mind the purse, so it probably wasn't afraid of cages, maybe it just didn't like needles. Luthor looked for an exit. He didn't want to be around the wretched thing any longer. Looking up he saw that the train was finally rolling into the station.

"Excuse me, ma'am. This is my train." Snorkles yapped his shot-glass sized lungs out until Luthor, Tanya, and Michael boarded the train.

#

Luthor had splurged on a private cabin for them on the train. It was wholly unnecessary, but he had wanted to make the trip in style. They were about to present the most earth-shattering discovery since the atomic bomb. The only difference is instead of threatening to destroy the world, 126 had the potential to save it. Luthor figured that justified a little splurging. And if Eli was right, then after the conference, he would never want for credits again. Like Garcia always said while they were deployed, *"Eat before the food freezes."* Antarctica—food was a premium in that frozen hell. Luthor shuddered as more bad memories clawed their cage.

The window was a moving postcard of the countryside. The land sped past at over 250 kilometers per hour. Alternating green and hazel fields undulated like an ocean of land. Giant modern wind turbines saluted from the top of every hill, the very symbol of the new, fossil fuel-free world. Blocky, oddly proportioned electric tractors were tethered to the windmills. Each plowed perfect concentric circles centered around the mast of each turbine; the power of the wind bringing in their crops.

Starkly juxtaposed with the wealth of the modern farms was a field with a man driving a donkey-pulled plow making erratic rows. This man had not made it into the new green world. An old diesel-powered combine rusted outside his barn. It was completely worthless now that a single tank of diesel for that tractor would cost more than Luthor made in a year. Now the harvester was nothing more than a rusted, forgotten symbol of an age when oil fed the world. Those people had possessed neither the foresight nor the means to avoid the Oil Crash or the consequences of a world war with China.

At least he hadn't starved with the two billion other people around the world during the *Culling*. Such an apt name for the mass starvation of the human race. Two billion people had died because war and scarce oil had destroyed the world's ability to feed itself. Without cheap oil, people couldn't run the tractors to plant and harvest their crops. Even the food that was harvested never got anywhere because there was no fuel for the boats, trains, and trucks to transport it to the population centers.

The man with the donkey had survived with the sweat of his brow, while the rest of the world had limped into a new equilibrium of green-energy food production and distribution. People didn't like to talk about it, but donkey driven plows were far more common than the idyllic, green wind-farmer politicians put on their re-election posters. Consequently, even though the *Culling* was officially over, the world was still ravenously short on food.

The door knocked to the cabin and a server brought in an expensive bottle of French champagne. People might not be able to eat, but there always seemed to be enough booze to go around. Luthor had remembered a previous mental note to not pass up the opportunity to taste real champagne if he ever made it to France. As such, he'd made sure to order a bottle. True champagne only came from the Champagne region of France, everything he had ever tried in the USW had been imitation "sparkling wine."

They laughed their way through the bottle. They recounted stories of their endless lab hours and unhealthy diets, and the time they accidentally imploded the detector with gravity because they accumulated too much 126. Tanya had been around the lab enough that she had no trouble laughing right along with them.

Laughter finally depleted, Tanya had flipped on the TV. It was a luxurious meter-sized screen mounted in the corner of the room. Luthor hadn't seen a personal TV anywhere near that size since he last visited Qwiz—Fermilab's head computer tech—and this was even larger than one of his unnecessarily wasteful monitors. Of course, Qwiz had six of them.

"You want to turn on the news? I haven't been keeping up on things since we left," Michael said.

Tanya smiled and raised her glistening glass to him and hit a button on the remote to change the station to the United States News Network, America's only official news station since the government took over the media for security reasons during the war.

The screen flickered, then displayed the familiar face of USNN's Anchorman Allen Wilcox. He was one of those men that everyone instinctively trusted, a touch of gray around the temples, a smattering of distinguished wrinkles issuing from his piercing blue eyes. His chin was strong yet didn't evoke a military stereotype, and he spoke in a deep comforting voice that was impossible not to believe. He was the quintessential news anchor.

"The climate change Progress Committee released their much anticipated fifteen-year report earlier today in a press conference in Philadelphia. We now go to Jaili Fendra for more."

"Today the CCP presented their historic fifteen-year study on climate change since 2033," said Fendra. She was an exotic beauty in USNN's attempt to represent the Central and South American States in the USW. Her tanned face was framed by perfectly manicured black hair that fell past her shoulders. Her full lips compelled viewers to concentrate on what she was saying, though many were successfully distracted by her proclivity for wearing revealing clothing. Luthor suspected she was the real reason Michael had asked to watch the news. "For the tenth straight year temperatures have fallen, though the decrease seems to be slowing based on the current figures."

The screen transitioned into a sound bite from what must have been a member of the committee. The nameless suit stood behind a wooden podium with a round government seal on the front. A large graphic to his left dominated the stage. The graphic showed a red temperature line that zigged in a distinctly downward motion with a blue icepack line that zagged slightly upward. "We are pleased that the worldwide effort to undo anthropogenic climate change is continuing to be successful. The Paris 2 protocols have cut carbon emissions by 90% since 2025 and there has been a correlating drop in world temperatures, as well as a slight increase in the polar icepack." The figure changed, zooming in on the red temperature line. "The temperature has dropped by 1.26 degrees Celsius since the end of World War III, but the change is slowing. So far in 2048 we have seen only a one hundredth degree of change and a small, unexpected decrease in the polar ice coverage–"

The screen faded back to the bosomy Fendra, who summarized. "The report indicates that the most dramatic drop in temperatures stems from the increased atmospheric debris caused by the massive bombing campaigns of World War III. The slowing rate of temperature decrease has been attributed to the normalization of postwar cloud cover combined with the increasing use of carbon producing fuel sources worldwide, particularly as increasing oil exports from the Antarctic are beginning to affect fuel prices. As expected, the Chinese block is by far the single largest contributor of carbon. But the report shows that rural areas in the western hemisphere are emitting greenhouse gases at increasing levels. Most are emanating from the Midwestern and Amazon States."

"How are we producing carbon?" Michael asked, "all coal power plants were banned over 20 years ago."

As if answering him, Fendra continued. "The committee speculates that there are two main carbon culprits in North America: The growing popularity of the 2180 movement centered in Colorado."

"Why would anyone support those goddamn terrorists?" Michael spat. "I swear the stupidity of people is so—"

"Quiet." Luthor hissed. "I want to hear this."

"...2180 advocates dangerous climate change practices by burning coal for electricity. They claim that the United States of West contains enough coal to power the western hemisphere until the year 2180. Their destructive ideals are gaining traction in isolated rural areas. Coal is easier to mine than natural gas since fracking was outlawed in the 20s. It is believed that coal is being mined and burned illegally in increasingly large quantities, accounting for the increase in the western states.

"However, the burgeoning Amish and Independent Christian communities across the heartland remain the main polluters. Citing their 1st Amendment rights for religious freedom, they are currently exempt from many carbon laws, and often use wood or coal for heating. Congressional leaders and climate scientists are calling for stricter regulation on the Amish and increased carbon-police presence in the rural communities of the West."

"Those selfish pricks," interjected Michael. "Don't they realize their beliefs are jeopardizing our chances of getting this planet back on course? I don't understand why the Amish aren't subject to the same carbon regulation as everyone else."

"It's a question of freedom of religion." Tanya said. "Their understanding of religion forbids them from using technology, without burning something in the winter they would freeze, particularly with these crazy winters we've been having."

Luthor gave Michael a fierce stare to try to dissuade him from taking the conversation further. Michael was unwittingly entering a deadly minefield. It had certainly singed Luthor enough times to know. Tanya had an odd, sometimes irrational sympathy for the Amish. It all started when her parents had joined an independent Christian community in Wisconsin after she started college. They believed, like the majority of fundamentalists, that the advent of CPI chips—what they called "the Mark of the Beast"—would usher in the end times. So they fled society with the rest of the religious radicals to isolated farming communes. Convinced her parents were paranoid, Tanya stayed behind, unwilling to sacrifice her education to go with them. Despite everything, she still deeply cared for her parents and always stuck up for their decision to leave. Luthor still had no idea whether she agreed with their choice or not, but then he was pretty sure that Tanya didn't know either. All he knew for sure is that it was dangerous as hell to state strong opinions either way about it. It was never safe to argue with Tanya when she was insecure about something. She was too smart and too emotional for it to end well for anyone.

Michael blundered on, unhindered by Luthor's unvoiced warning. "This is more than just a matter of religious conviction. If I were a religious fanatic who believed God told me to light people on fire, I would be arrested *today*."

"Your argument is fallacious. We both know that isn't the same thing, the Christian Communities aren't hurting anyone—"

"It's *exactly* the same. They might not be lighting people on fire, but they are definitely hurting people. In fact, they are hurting the entire human race with their reckless use of carbon. Can't you see what–"

"Michael, if you value your manhood, I would shut the hell up right about now." Luthor said.

Michael scowled, but didn't continue. Tanya glared at him, but her face softened somewhat as she looked at Luthor.

Flashing back to Allen Wilcox, the report continued. "President Jimenez who just began a three day visit to Chicago, also commented on the historic report."

The handsome Latino spoke to a crowd outside of the John Hancock building. "Our Coalition has been at the forefront of the battle for our planet, but we cannot grow weak in our resolve in light of our success. I am urging Congress to continue to take steps forward in regulating and eliminating the use of carbon. This war on warming will not be won until we see carbon dioxide emissions drop to pre-1850 levels. Only then can we ensure a safe, sustainable future for not only the Coalition, but the human race." The President's face faded from the screen.

"Jimenez will be doing a live interview from the Chicago USNN building tomorrow, after a tour of the CPI carbon monitoring system. For a complete coverage of the CCP report please log on to WWW dot USNN dot gov.

"After the break, tensions continue to increase between the Americas and Europe over the inclusion of China in the International Energy Convention. The story of the controversial decision by E.U.'s Prime Minister Pollock and his push to get the Chinese to accept the Paris 2 carbon regulations up next."

"You're still sure about wanting to present, even though the Chinese will be the unwitting beneficiaries?" Tanya asked, ignoring Michael for the moment.

"Yes, I am," said Luthor, infusing as much confidence as possible into his voice. As much as he tried not to let his hatred of the greedy Chinese influence his decisions, this one was tough.

"I suspect that after we are done, the Chinese presence at the conference isn't going to matter much. What is international intrigue compared to this?" Luthor indicated toward his bag, where they all knew the 126 for the demonstration was kept. The subtle gravity field it possessed gave him an uneasy feeling today, like he was being watched. His inner ear never quite figured out how to communicate its dislike for *down* being somewhere other than *down*. As a result, his mind interpreted that pull in unusual ways.

Throbbing, bass-heavy music exuded from the TV's speakers, compelling their attention. Luthor saw a montage of images portraying a stylish new phone that seemed to pulse with the beat of the song. He caught the tail end of a sales pitch, "smaller, smarter, more energy efficient. the new Lidius E9. Lidius, greener than any other brand. Period."

Lidius was a fantastically successful global corporation that made everything green tech, from batteries to screens to phones. Tanya had her own E8 and loved it. Luthor wondered what would happen to all the companies like Lidius who had made their billions by capitalizing on the scarcity of energy. Starting next week their energy-miser products would be obsolete.

CHAPTER 2:

Geneva, European Union

They exited the train with the rest of the throng, bags in hand. Most of the passengers were not continuing on, they were here to attend the International Energy Convention. The IEC had become something of a tourist attraction for the city in recent years. An energy thirsty world could not be sated by the trickle of power it was currently offered. They came here for hope. Hope that there would be enough energy to run their machines, appliances, business, heat their homes, and grow enough food so they wouldn't have to worry about starving again this winter.

It was this hope that Luthor planned to give them.

A traffic jam of rickshaws clogged the curbside, bicycles crudely attached to carriages, men pulling carts, all vying for attention and business. A violent smell of unwashed human accosted their senses, emanating from the vehicles' owners. A horse-drawn stagecoach and two electric taxies sidled in the wings. The average Joe walked rather than hire human beasts of burden, but dozens still climbed into the probably unsafe, and certainly unsanitary, vehicles. Only the fabulously wealthy could afford a ride in an electric taxi. It didn't matter where you were, electricity was ludicrously expensive. They'd made plans for Eli to pick them up blocks away from the train station, so his electric car would not be confused with transportation for hire.

They pushed past a burgeoning crowd of homeless begging for handouts from the rich travelers. It seemed there were as many poor bastards here as there were in the States.

Luthor ignored them. The Oil Crash had done its grisly work here too.

In the years leading up to the war, the world's rampant use of oil had continued to climb despite the precipitous decline of world oil production and widespread adoption of electric cars. The best attempts of China and the United States to control prices failed, and the simple laws of supply and demand caused the price of gas to skyrocket. It wasn't long before a liter of gas cost the same as a full barrel of crude had months before. The batteries to run electric cars ballooned in price even more. There simply wasn't enough Cobalt and other rare-earth minerals to make even a fraction of the batteries necessary to replace all gas-powered vehicles. People abandoned the Suburbs of the world in droves and flooded into the major cities simply because it didn't require a car to live there. The Suburbs became burned out third-world nations ruled by gang-tyrants; the cities became giant homeless shelters as only a small percentage of the millions of suburban refugees managed to find work. The Culling and the war had killed off huge swaths of homeless, but they were still everywhere and any that hesitated to beg didn't survive long.

Luthor waded through the last of the suburban refugees; he wanted to see Eli. He had not seen him in five years. Fermilab and CERN had exchanged professors for a semester in '42 as a publicity stunt. Eli had come to Chicago and had stayed with him for the duration of the exchange. They had become fast and enduring friends. Both had served in the war for the Coalition and afterward had both fled their dark memories for the intellectual safety of academia.

As they rounded the cinderblock edge of the station they saw Eli's car. It was cherry red, and resembled a 9 mm bullet with solar panels covering the top.

Eli waved and rushed toward them. A meek Arab with graying hair, Eli wore a pale blue shirt under a 30-year-old sweater-vest with khaki pants and sandals. "Greetings my friends!" he said, hugging Luthor. "My dear Tanya, you look ravishing." He grabbed her hand and kissed it.

"Easy buddy," cautioned Luthor. "You know she has a weakness for your French charms."

"I wouldn't dream of it. She is far too beautiful to ever fall for an old man such as myself." Tanya smiled and a hint of a blush touched her cheeks. "And you must be Michael." Michael received a warm handshake instead of a kiss. "Welcome friends. It is a pleasure. Please allow me to take your bags."

The idea of the small man carrying all their luggage was comical, but the genuine sincerity in his request kept anyone from laughing.

Not that there was any place to put it. Eli's car was larger than most, but even with 2 PhD's and Four Master's degrees between them, it would be impossible to cram all four of them inside with their luggage. "My friends, I am afraid that this is going to be a bit cramped," Eli said.

#

Geneva, European Union

Michael was happy to be out of the clown car. Eli's house itself was composed of a series of intersecting domes designed to minimize building material use and heating costs while maximizing living space. The domes themselves were covered in solar panels that powered most of the house. A bulky battery pack abutted one dome to keep the lights on after the sun went down.

Rubbing his hands together, Eli stood in his small, round study replete with only a sturdy metal desk and a folding chair. The walls were covered in typical academic paraphernalia, framed degrees and awards everywhere. A single LED bulb in the ceiling provided illumination.

"Show me this device of yours. I have been holding my

breath for two weeks waiting to see it," he said, shutting the door behind them. Tanya seemed content staying in the kitchen, not seeing the demonstration for the 100th time.

Michael watched as Luthor methodically took out the components for his demonstration generator. Eli stood completely transfixed, watching, staring at the monotonous construction of the device without saying a word. It was honestly pretty pathetic; he treated it like it was a holy relic of some forgotten god. But there was nothing to watch except Luthor bending over some black boxes.

The machine itself was deceptively simple, the only complexity lay in synthesizing Element 126. They had been doing that every day for the last year to accumulate enough to run the generator in Luthor's apartment and this one.

They had talked about putting a generator in Michael's apartment as well. But Michael lived with three other students, and Luthor thought the risk of someone discovering the 126 was too great. At the time, Michael had been pissed; it just didn't seem fair to have Luthor get all the financial benefit even if he had discovered the damn thing. But Luthor promised to split any profits with him down the middle. Michael had seen enough of the world to know that such a claim had a 99% chance to be total bullshit. But Luthor remained true to his word and had paid all the expenses for Michael's trip here, which probably cost more than he would have saved by having the generator power his apartment. And though he would never tell Luthor so, the act had earned Michael's respect and loyalty, something he had never given easily. Growing up on the streets during the Culling, Michael had learned the hard way that trust got you taken advantage of, if you were lucky.

Luthor grunted as he struggled to secure a small tank of water to the top of the device. The hard part was making sure it sealed properly so it didn't leak water where it connected to the rest of the generator via a circular channel. The channel fed into an empty tank at the bottom before arcing back up to rejoin a matching tank at the top. Small turbines intersected the circular tubing throughout the prototype. Wires ran from the turbines to a center console that displayed the electricity output. Those wires had a tendency to get upset when water dripped on them.

Finished with the water conduit, Luthor opened and tinkered inside bland black boxes that were affixed throughout the exterior.

"May I surmise that those boxes hold the element?" Eli asked.

"Yes they do. Care for a peek?"

Eli stepped forward, and Luthor pulled out a claw-like device. Michael always thought it resembled the arcade machine claws where you used a joystick to try to grab a prize, Luthor's just had more prongs. Ironically, as simple as they were, they were what allowed the machine to simulate perpetual motion. Eli beheld the strange machine with a quizzical look on his face.

Element 126 had the interesting property that the gravity effect increased significantly the closer the atoms were together. The more 126, the greater the effect. The claws allowed them to capitalize on that property. Inside each box, the claw held the 126 at the tips of its prongs. When the claw clenched its tips together—thereby concentrating the 126—the gravity increased around the box. When it opened, the 126 spread apart, and the enhanced gravity dissipated. The ability to turn the gravity on and off allowed the water to be circulated through the turbines and thus generate electricity.

Eli retuned the claw to Luthor who placed it back in the box. After a moment, Luthor stood up, hands on his back, looking like an 80-year-old man working out the kinks. "It's all hooked up," he said.

Eli walked up tentatively, "may I?"

"Of course. It isn't made of glass."

Eli flipped a switch on the top tank and water flowed down through the turbines, and lights flickered on around the machine. The black boxes clicked mechanically. Eli gasped. The water began flowing up the other side and back into the original tank. The little LEDs grew brighter and did not flicker any more as the water gained momentum and generated a more consistent electrical current.

"This is amazing. Genius."

"I wouldn't call it that."

Luthor and his damn humility. Michael thought, *this device is genius! And I am a part of that, thank you very much. That makes me a genius too.*

"Seriously Luthor. Most people would have tried to create something too fantastic to be practical. You know, a flying car or something." Eli paused dramatically. "You? You used it to solve the world's biggest problem. And instead of making something too high tech to be accessible, you made a cheap, simple device accomplishing the same thing. Simplicity, not complexity, it is said, is the hallmark of genius."

"Eli, will you do me a favor?" Luthor said. "Will you write that down, and read it at my funeral? That was beautiful."

Michael laughed unabashedly, but it didn't seem to deter Eli, he bent close to the black boxes. He traced the wires lacing up and down with a finger, "I love how you used the electricity you already generated to manipulate the 126. It's a perfect closed system."

"Well that's the real trick, isn't it?" Michael said. "It wouldn't do us much good if it didn't. That's how we can simulate perpetual motion. Good thing those claws don't take much juice."

Luthor nodded. "They only have to move 10 centimeters, so it doesn't consume much of the power we generate. The remainder is available for use elsewhere."

"You are going to be the talk of the world in a few days, my friend."

"I certainly hope so. Were you able to get me a presentation time?"

"Thursday night. I know it isn't one of the headliner spots, but it was the earliest time available. I figured it would be best to demonstrate this as early as possible so everyone has time to see it, and more importantly—"

"To talk about it." Luthor said. He turned back to Michael. "If we do these next few days right, you and are I going to be flying around giving lectures and demonstrations for the most powerful people in the world."

"Flying?" Michael questioned. For Luthor to say something as absurd as flying, he must have misspoken. *Flying would be unbelievably awesome.* Luthor was the only man Michael knew under 60 who remembered being in an airplane.

"Flying." Luthor said with certainty. "People are going to want this technology implemented immediately, they aren't going to wait weeks for us to get there by seabus."

"Hell yeah, that's what I'm talking about!"

"It isn't all its cracked up to be." Luthor said cryptically.

"Whatever, boss. You can tell me all you want about how flying at 10,000 meters traveling a thousand kilometers an hour is boring, but I am not going to buy it. Because its bullshit. Flying sounds like the most smoggingly awesome thing I will have ever done."

"Try flying at 20,000 meters. Then jumping out." Luthor closed his eyes. Luthor never talked much about his time as a paratrooper, but every time he did he got that same terrible expression. Whatever happened after jumping out of those planes was not a happy memory for him.

Must be something wrong with you if you don't think skydiving is fun, Michael thought. *At least the war ended before I got out of Boot Camp and I didn't have to find out.*

Eli's watch beeped an alarm. "It appears that dinner's ready," he said. "I do hope you like pheasant."

"Love it," Michael said, though he had never tasted it. He was at least reasonably sure it was a bird. The majority of the meat he had consumed in his life had been sewer rats he hunted during the *Culling* to survive. Any normal meat these days was a delicacy.

Eli opened the door for the two of them in a hospitable way, the delicious floral aroma of home cooking wafted in. "After you, gentlemen."

#

They walked back out into the small dining area. Eli was busy bringing the food to the table. He placed the small pheasant as the centerpiece. It was golden brown on the outside and looked like the most delicious thing Michael had eaten in weeks. Luthor hadn't told him that Eli was a chef as well as a professor.

Eli showed them their seats. "My apologies. I forgot to tell you we have one other person joining us for dinner. She is my secretary and long-time family friend. This is Vika."

Michael looked toward the door of the kitchen as Vika walked in. He felt his jaw open involuntarily, but simply didn't have the will to retract it. Vika was the single most beautiful woman Michael had ever seen.

She stood, tall and lean, her straight black hair framing a face that could have been carved by Michelangelo. Piercing green eyes stared out at him. She was boldly beautiful, painfully attractive. It was not a soft pretty that seemed to beg for love and affection, but a hard, sharp-edged gorgeous. She was a dangerous beauty of the type that constantly dared men to make a move so she could enjoy the sport of shooting them down.

He snapped back to awareness at the sound of derisive laughter. Both Tanya and Vika were laughing. At him.

"Your friend is drooling." Vika had an accent he couldn't place, but it made her even more mysterious and alluring. Nonetheless, the sheer quantity of embarrassment he was accruing forced his mouth shut and helped him regain control of his higher motor functions.

Well, you've really breathed in the smog this time Michael, he thought. *Nothing to do about it now but roll with the punches.*

Michael cleared his throat casually, "I suppose you have heard all about me by now. My name's Michael Laramy."

"Vika." She said curtly. She took his offered hand with the firmest grip of any woman he had ever shaken hands with. It was like she had nothing but coiled, knotted muscles under her long coat. *Enough smogging superlatives with this one. Jesus!* He thought. He made a conscious effort to not rub his hand.

"You'll have to forgive my reaction. I just wasn't expecting such a stunning woman to appear." He hoped the sweet talking would do some good. Maybe he could make up for being so pathetic. *Who knows? Maybe this could turn into— No. I promised Luthor no girl-drama this trip. Better to keep this professional... but damn!* Michael made another conscious effort not to drool.

"Since we just met, I will forgive you once. But, Laramy," Vika raised an eyebrow at him, "I have one rule. Learn it." As the pause lingered, Michael wondered if she was flirting or not. "If you hit on me, I ***hit*** you." By her expression he had no doubt that if he ever tried flirting again she would in fact, punch him, and it would in fact, hurt.

Luthor chuckled from the other side of the table. Tanya smiled and slowly shook her head.

"I thought you were still living alone," Luthor said.

"After my wife took the kids and left, I was alone." Eli said. "But Vika is an old friend of my children who came on hard times. She needed a job and a place to live. I needed the company. She stays in the spare bedroom."

"And works for you now."

"Yes, but let us eat while the bird is hot." Eli said jovially. "My lovely and talented secretary can finish introducing herself while we eat."

#

"Your invention sounds remarkable," Vika said during a lull in the conversation.

"Remarkable hardly does it justice, my dear." Eli said. "Earthshattering would be a more appropriate adjective."

"And your goal is to release the technology for free to everyone. Noble of you; it would be worth a lot if you sold it."

"I don't know how noble it is." Luthor said. "We just went through one war over energy, I'm not really interested in causing another one for the sake of my own profit."

"You still think war would be inevitable, Luthor?" Eli asked. It was a topic they had discussed at length on several occasions.

"Positively certain of it."

Tanya squeezed Luthor's hand affectionately. "It is far too dangerous to sell. And we certainly aren't in a position to try and defend ourselves if anyone powerful tried to take it from us. So it's a safe bet that if we advertised we were selling 126, the research would simply be stolen."

"And then they would kill you," Vika said.

Luthor felt the blood drain from his face at the cold declaration.

Vika continued. "It would be worth less if you were alive to sell it to others. They would want a monopoly."

"Exactly," Tanya said, ignoring the arctic chill from Vika. "There are really only two possibilities if only one major player has 126." Tanya began to enumerate the potentialities. "One, the country with the technology could simply use it to further their own economic goals."

"Is it so bad for a country to want a thriving economy?" Eli interjected. "We are talking about finally having enough energy to grow enough food again. Would it be so terrible to knock *starvation* off Europe's top killer list?"

"That is a wonderful goal. But what happens when one country has unlimited energy when the rest of the world is still ravenous for it?" She paused as if the conclusion were obvious. "That country dominates in *every area,* not just food production. Military, manufacturing, data processing, transportation: it would create a massive power imbalance. Every time there is a power imbalance in global politics, it inevitably leads to war. The other countries are either forced militarily into subservience where they continually rebel, or are pushed to a preemptive war to try to equalize the power."

Eli nodded, conceding the point. "What is the second possibility?"

"They could simply use their heavy advantage to strike first and gain total domination. The world powers have already shown they won't use nukes even in all-out war, there would be almost no risk to attacking first. The country with the most energy would win."

Eli crossed his arms. "So, in both your scenarios, war is the only possible outcome."

Tanya nodded. "That's the way I see it. There must be equality or there *will* be war. Imagine what would have happened if the soviets were the only ones who'd discovered atomic weapons, or the Nazis." She let the idea linger, it was not painting a pretty picture in Luthor's mind. "Even in World War III, parity was important. Both the Coalition and Chinese Block had nukes, so no one dared use them. We both had the capability to saturate each other's missile defense systems; the small percent that got through would have still destroyed the earth. So as bad as the war was, it would have been much worse if the powers hadn't been roughly equal."

Michael frowned. "It's hard to believe that anything could be worse than 2 and half billion people dead."

"How about 8 and half billion people dead?" Tanya said. "We would have nuked China to glass if they hadn't been able to do the same thing to us. Regardless of what *might* have happened, there needs to be equality with Luthor's invention, or it will lead to yet another war."

"Those arguments are irrelevant. Spies would likely steal the technology," Vika said. "It is impossible to hide something this important."

"And having spies steal your most valuable technology has always led to peace," Tanya replied sarcastically. "The Soviets stole much of the Manhattan project. That led to 50 years of tension and an arms race between the two powers. Vietnam and Korea both stemmed from that conflict.

"Regardless, all of those risks can be avoided if Luthor simply gives it all away in the first place. Then everyone will have the technology from the get-go. There will be no imbalance of power, and everyone receives the benefits without the chance of war. Imagine knocking starvation off the *world's* top killer list. Not just Europe's."

"And I honestly don't care about having a few extra credits," Luthor added. "Simply being the man who discovered this will be more than enough," Luthor grinned at Eli. "What was it you were saying a few weeks ago about Nobel Prize money?"

Eli smiled back, but Vika frowned. "What have you done to protect your research?" she asked.

"All of my research has been very secretive, there is only one person not in this very room who even knows what we have done. And I trust him with my life." Luthor thought fondly of his friend, Qwiz, back in Fermilab.

"Are you certain of that? This is not the sort of secret that is easy to keep."

"I haven't published anything because I was worried the government would just confiscate my work."

Nostalgia tinged Luthor's thoughts. It would have been so easy 30 years ago to post his findings online. Everything had been free and uncensored. But that was before the war changed all that. To protect against Chinese cyber-attacks in the war America rerouted all internet and communication lines through central, controlled locations. Now there were tens of thousands of sensors who did nothing but monitor emails and online activity.

Luthor sighed. "You know how they screen everything before it can be posted online. I think it's fair to say that if it popped up on a censor's computer, my government wouldn't just give 126 away. That's why I came here in the first place. The IEC is the only place I could publish my findings about 126 without fear they would be stolen first."

"What about your lab?"

Vika certainly was persistent in her questioning.

"They think that I have been running a bunch of unfruitful experiments for the last year. And I moved all relevant data to a more secure location."

Vika raised a skeptical eyebrow.

"Trust me, in the world of accelerators and superheavy elements, a year of trials to produce even a few atoms is considered impressive. They won't suspect that we have been mass producing element 126 with such a historically inefficient approach. They wouldn't even know why we'd want to."

Vika nodded. "What's to keep someone from just stealing your laptop here?"

"It's heavily encrypted. And only two people know the code."

"I will not ask who the other person is," Vika said, "for their safety."

"Besides, they would need to know what I am doing to even want to steal this old thing," Luthor gestured at the venerable laptop in his bag, "it's a powerhog." Behind his smile, Luthor felt doubt's creeping tendrils clawing their way into his mind. Had he thought of everything? And why was Vika so interested in their security? Her questions had been relentless, and suspicious. *Mental note: be careful what you say around Vika.*

"Let's make sure nothing happens to that computer," Eli said smiling. "Shall I show you to your rooms? I am afraid we don't have enough space to comfortably accommodate you here. But my office at CERN is more than ample. It also has the added benefit of 24-hour security. Unfortunately, we will have to walk there. The solar panels have not yet recharged my car."

#

It was cold that night. The homeless shivered in the shadows and looked hungrily at Luthor's suitcase. But the homeless inundated every city, it didn't matter the continent. Even after the Culling, there were still so many left. Vika walked silently, glaring at any of them brave enough to peer out of the shadows looking for a handout. They shrank back from her gaze.

After a short walk, they arrived at the CERN student lab where they could sleep in his office. Eli carried Tanya's bags for her. Vika slid her right hand so the scanner could read her CPI chip. The door to the lab opened.

As they began to enter the facility, the beam of a flashlight suddenly accosted them. "Halt," a female voice said from behind the bulb.

Eli said something in French, gesturing to rest of them.

The light lowered. The outline of a pistol shaded the

beam. “I’m sorry,” she said in slurred English.

“That is one of the security guards that monitor this place. You will be safe tonight.”

Inside was one of the many labs connected to the CERN complex. It was a basic lab for students to conduct general research on any number of subjects. Wide open spaces with tables scattered regularly end to end of the long room provided ample room for experiments. Eli pointed out projects in various stages marked by beakers, Petri dishes, and trays of pipettes. One end of the room held three large, industrial sinks and a laboratory quality dishwasher. Eli grumbled his displeasure when he noticed the far sink was full of soapy water soaking glassware students had been too lazy to scrub. Opposite the sinks was a bank of centrifuges, replicators and other equipment, and at the end, the most complete rack of pure elements Luthor had ever seen.

Luthor placed the pieces of his prototype under the rack of elements, it seemed an appropriate place to store it. Apart from highly radioactive elements, 126 was the only missing piece of the periodic table. There was even a tray for the absurdly reactive Cesium; it was likely stored in vacuum-sealed glass tubes to keep it from setting fire to the lab. He was careful not to disturb the 126 and accidentally pull everything off the shelf with its increased gravity. That many elements crashing together would undoubtedly make for some violent, if interesting, chemistry.

Eli and Vika led them to the back of the lab. There was a hall flanked by doors on either side. It led to another area of the complex they did not enter. The right door led to the lavatory, the left to Al’halsimi’s office. Eli discretely made a right turn, leaving his secretary, assistant, supermodel—whatever—to show them their room.

Once inside the office, it was obvious why he had brought them here. It was an expansive room almost as large as his entire house. It was clearly a relic of the pre-Oil Crash days. It probably cost a fortune to heat. The floor was richly carpeted in warm earth tones, darkly stained bookshelves lined the walls, and a matching desk stood alone as a centerpiece. There was an old leather couch and two over-stuffed high-back chairs that completed the décor.

"Tanya will sleep on the couch," Vika said. It was not a request. Michael affected a sullen expression, which didn't look like a joke. She didn't give much direction as to where Luthor or Michael were to sleep.

"Thanks," Michael mumbled. Luthor shared a knowing glance with Tanya. Despite his appeal with women, Michael wasn't exactly what one would call chivalrous. With a scowl for Michael, Vika left to sleep back at the house.

It didn't take long before Tanya and Michael were both twitching with the early signs of sleep. Luthor and Eli sat around one of the student tables in the lab quietly reviewing his presentation notes.

"You really need to find a way to make your speech memorable or it won't have the impact you want." Eli waved his hand in the air as if grasping for an elusive word. "How is it you say... you need to make a *splash*."

"I can't just come into a convention with the smartest people in the world and claim I can control gravity."

"You might very well be laughed off the stage."

"And my prototype isn't exactly flashy. It looks like a high school science project." Luthor pretended to look astonished. "Wow. A couple of LED's turn on!"

"Luthor...don't be so hard on yourself."

"I'm just being realistic. What was it you said earlier, that simplicity was the hallmark of genius? It's simple, not boring. I just won't be able to turn it on and have the audience gasp."

"Your other problem is that your audience won't instantly associate controlling gravity with generating electricity. They will think of space ships."

"And hover boards," Luthor agreed. "Well, it seems like we need to scrap what I have here and start with 126 itself and what enhanced gravity actually does." Luthor began scribbling notes on a new piece of paper.

"You have to include how the proximity of the element's atoms effect the strength of the gravitational pull. You were telling me that the closer the atoms are the greater gravity they have, correct?"

Luthor nodded. "Yes. That is the quirk that makes the generator work. The more densely packed the 126 is, the stronger its gravity gets, and the wider the gravitational field becomes."

"So you *can* control the gravity."

"All I can do is turn it on and off. I need to emphasize that I can't control its direction. Gravity— from 126 or not — pulls from *all directions*. When I spread the atoms out, their gravity all but disappears. When I smash them together, their gravity increases enough to pull the water up through the second set of turbines. On and off, that's it. I cycle them quickly enough that I can create circular motion."

"Like the cylinder of an internal combustion engine."

"That's a good comparison."

"Do you have measurements on that property exactly? What is the correlation between the amount of 126 and gravity?"

"I can't know for sure, but it increases dramatically. It's possible that the gravity even grows exponentially the more 126 is there. We have been afraid to test densities much higher than it takes to run a generator."

"You could destroy your lab if it's exponential!" Eli said in amazement.

"Or for all we know it could create a runaway black hole. That's why we haven't tested it. Actually, that's how we discovered we had been making 126 in the first place. It crumpled our detector and spilled our drinks."

Eli laughed and shook his head. "You made it on accident?"

"Yes. The element we were trying to make would have had 132 protons. But it wasn't stable. It kept crapping out helium atoms until it stopped decaying and stayed as 126. I don't know why it works, but it turns out it is a very efficient production method. We are able to create thousands of atoms per trial that way."

Eli laughed again. "I am not sure I have ever heard anyone refer to alpha decay as a nucleus 'crapping out helium atoms.'

"Truth be told, it was Michael's description. I just thought it was funny."

"You might want to stick with the technical terms at the conference."

"Agreed." Luthor scribbled more notes on his page. The new developing structure of his speech just *felt* right. There was still the matter of creating the right "splash."

Eli's eyes suddenly lit up, "Luthor, I know how we can finish your speech. You, my friend, are going to walk on the ceiling."

Luthor stroked his chin. "That's a great thought, but how am I supposed to get the 126 to stick up there? And even if we did get it up there, how do we keep it hidden until the end of the speech?"

Eli crossed the room to a locked supply cabinet. He opened the door with the turn of a key. Inside was a small safe.

"What on earth do you need a safe for?"

Eli began turning the dials. "Do you remember the post-doctoral research I began with one of my former students a few years ago?"

"Only vaguely. It was something about geckos, wasn't

it?"

"Yes. We were researching the microstructure of their skin that allows them to climb sheer glass walls." Eli excitedly removed a tray of a violently orange, gooey substance from the safe.

Eli continued. "This was our result. We were trying to improve on similar research that had been done thirty years ago. Perhaps get it to market applications."

Luthor tentatively poked the orange substance, it had the consistency of moist play dough.

Eli grinned excitedly. "This polymer has some remarkable properties. "It is essentially a strong, but removable adhesive, like a gecko's feet. A gecko doesn't get stuck on the glass, it can freely walk up and down. A palm-sized slice of this would be able to hold up a man of your weight on a sheer wall."

"You're kidding." Luthor said, poking the polymer again.

"No, and here is the best part. A gentle twist and pull, and it will release, and come free. It also does not stick to fingers or skin." Eli took a pair of scissors, and cut a square from the sheet. He folded it around the bottom of a beaker. Then, to Luthor's amazement, stood on top of the table, and stuck the beaker to the ceiling. It held.

"That's fantastic! Have you found any corporate buyers?"

"Unfortunately, I'm better at research than business. But there has to be some carbon credits in this thing somewhere," Eli paused dramatically, "particularly if you knew I could hang from that beaker, and it would still stick on the ceiling. The beaker would break before the adhesion would."

Eli reached up calmly and with a twist and a pull, the beaker came free. "Imagine for a moment, what you could do in your presentation with some of this."

Luthor found himself leaning forward.

"If you wrapped a few of your extra beads of 126 in this and then threw it at the ceiling, it would stick. You could have normal gravity for the entirety of your talk and then throw this up at the end and suddenly change the pull of gravity."

"Brilliant!" Luthor said. "Or I could stand on a wall, or simply suck some poor sap's science project to the ceiling."

"The applications would be limitless."

"Looks like maybe you have found a buyer after all," Luthor said.

"I look forward to doing business with you."

"Looks like I won't be needing this anymore." Luthor crumpled his previous speech and tossed it in the trash. It bounced on the rim and flipped onto the floor.

"You didn't miss your calling as a basketball player, did you?" Eli laughed.

"I'm better at throwing grenades. Harder to miss."

Eli nodded soberly. "Yes, but I much prefer paper to high explosive."

"Amen." Eli was one of the only people with whom Luthor had ever discussed the war. He had still never revealed the blackest memories he'd locked up tight inside, but Eli had been a part of the European infantry in Antarctica; he understood the need both to commiserate and compartmentalize.

"You still have dreams, don't you?" Eli asked, "about the war?"

"Every night," Luthor admitted. "They never get any better." Luthor flinched as the angry, scarred man he had imprisoned in the deepest part of his mind rattled his cage.

"Me too."

"I sleep as little as I can, I hate reliving that frozen hell. Nothing helps."

"Maybe you should try my trick. I keep a loaded gun in every room in my house."

"Isn't it illegal to own guns in Europe?"

"Every bit as illegal as in the States. But I swear on my honor it helps. I no longer feel helpless. I wake up, check the magazine, and know that I will be able to protect myself. That is enough."

Mental note: buy a gun. "I hope you never fall asleep at your desk," Luthor said.

Eli chuckled. "I keep one there too. Duct-taped under my desk." Luthor laughed too.

"Come now old friend, let's get some rest. I don't feel like walking home."

Minutes later Luthor lay on the plush floor feeling comfort in his camaraderie with Eli. He fell asleep with a contented smile on his face for the first time in years.

CHAPTER 3:

Eleven Years Ago: Titan Dome, Antarctica

"Don oxygen masks." The speakers crackled. "Nearing jump zone." The converted cargo plane rocked with the high-altitude turbulence common over Antarctica. They were flying fifty thousand feet above sea level and thirty seven thousand feet above the raised plateau of solid ice named Titan Dome. Luthor didn't know what the hell it was in metric, and didn't much care. He didn't appreciate the government suddenly deciding that the whole country had to convert to meters and kilometers just because they had annexed all of the Western Hemisphere and were allied with Europe. United states of America or "the West," miles or meters, Luthor just hoped they were far enough away from the Chinese surface to air missiles, guided artillery, and dragon gun installations they had been charged with destroying. With any luck there would be some cloud cover to hide their contrail, but there were no windows to be able to know for sure.

Hundreds of men stood around him, lashed to the utility mesh that honeycombed the innards of the flying warehouse. They shouted to each other in unheard conversations over the un-muffled roar of jet-engines. There were a lot of men, but their plane was only one of dozens of other aircraft similarly stuffed to capacity with specially trained, elite paratroopers. They were the first stage of the biggest allied offensive of the war to date. The men were calling it D-Day 2. And they, like their comrades 90 years before, hadn't known when they would leave until the day before.

Luthor played with his oxygen mask. He hated wearing it; it made him feel like he was suffocating, even though it was all that kept him from passing out from the extremes they endured. He had to use it long before the actual jump to help flush the nitrogen from his system, otherwise he could die from decompression sickness that soldiers called the *airbends*. His flight suit was shock-white, made of high-tech fibers that would repel water and reduce his drag in the air, while still keeping him alive when the temperatures dropped to 100 below zero Fahrenheit.

He took a deep breath from his tank and removed his mask to adjust it. It was so itchy. When he exhaled into the open air a thick puff of white steam reminded him how cold it would be out there. A single stitch of exposed skin could net someone frostbite in minutes. He quickly replaced his mask, retightening his straps.

"Won't be long now, Ten." Chaz had called Luthor *Ten* since they were kids. He thought it sounded better than Tenrel. The other men had picked it up too. "Jake, get your mask on!" Chaz shouted, his own oxygen muffling his voice.

Jake fumbled with his mask. "How many smoggers you gonna cap this time?" He fingered the scope of his MX-5 fondly, like he could barely contain himself from pulling the trigger inside the aircraft. The MX-5 Assault rifle was a variant of the HK-436, the new standard issue weapon for coalition infantry. "Me? I'm gonna kill so many greedy Chinese Rats that they're gonna start calling me the Orkin man."

Luthor grimaced. He had never relished combat, he just did what he had to do—what the commanders told him to do. Jake was one of those rare men, who made up only 2-5% of the military that were capable of killing without remorse or negative effects. At least that is what the military Psychologists said. The rest of them would likely suffer from PTSD, or at least need counseling, but not Jake. Jake would have made a great serial killer, if he hadn't been drafted to shoot Chinese for the Coalition.

"My goal is blow as many SAM sites up as possible and stay alive. Maybe help win this goddamn war."

"Ah, don't be so gloomy, Ten." Jake said. "It's not like we are doing a high-altitude jump, into an ice-covered shit storm in the middle of winter, behind enemy lines, without more than a dozen drones for support." Luthor looked at him sideways. That was exactly what they were doing. "Oh wait. We are!" He actually sounded excited about it. Luthor himself was scared shitless; he just wasn't telling anybody.

Jake was something of an enigma. 6'4'' and rail thin with a purported proclivity for thrift store cardigans, he looked like the last person one would ever expect to be a hard-ass soldier. In reality he was the best shot in their unit, flapless in battle, and tried to convince everyone he was raised from birth by an inner-city gang. Luthor was fairly certain that he was raised in a rich white suburb—not that those existed anymore. He surmised Jake's skill came from playing enough first-person shooter video games that he actually had been warped in the way the crazy whistleblowers were always warning about. Killing digital zombies was a lot different than shooting a real gun at real humans; maybe it hadn't been for Jake. Luthor had never been much for video games himself, he'd gained the reputation as the second-best shooter the old fashioned way: by shooting actual guns.

Most of the men seemed less excited about the prospect of being shot at than Jake and were relieving their tension in other ways. Chaz loaded his massive rocket launcher with an anti-drone rocket, checking it in preparation for the drop. Martinez was crossing himself and praying to saint somebody-or-other who was supposed to protect paratroops.

The plane rumbled again. They must be getting close. Luthor checked his gear one more time. His MX-5 was safely harnessed to the side of his chute, grenade launcher affixed to the barrel, more explosives were attached on the side of his pack. He wore a belt full of extra magazines he had loaded by hand. Special-issue retractable skis were clipped to the other side of his parachute. Heat batteries were tucked in every spare crevice to keep him warm and melt ice for water along with a week of frost resistant food rations. He still didn't know how they made food that didn't snap freeze like everything else, but he didn't care. Food was fuel in war, nothing more. It kept the human machines running the same as oil kept planes flying. The thin, high-tech fabric that formed the wings of his flight suit was intact. It terminated at his wrists and ankles and allowed the soldiers to travel much deeper into enemy territory than the planes could safely fly. Any rip in that, and he would have to pull his chute too soon and ski untold miles to meet up with the rest of his squad.

A few minutes later a crackling signaled the speaker system coming online. "We are approaching the drop zone. Make final preparations for jump." Men tried to raise a cheer, but the howling sub-zero wind swallowed it, giving it a lackluster pall.

"This is it baby!" It was Sean Marrison, or Marri as everyone called him. Marri was a hulking man that had probably played defensive end for the Bears before the war. He affectionately stroked their unit's only drone. It was folded up like a falcon on the side of his parachute. It had lasted through more battles than anyone had hoped, saving their asses on each of its multiple deployments in the North Sea. The men affectionately called her Claptrap. Supposedly, Claptrap had been derived from "the Fucking Clap of Doom." Luthor liked the name.

Luthor just wished he had a pallet full of Claptraps. They were becoming almost extinct in the Coalition military. The first year of the war had spawned the largest drone battles in history. Hulking bomber drones swarming with mini drone escorts crashed into battle with each other like angry hives of bees. The Chinese won most of the battles due to their heavy use of remotely controlled drones. They conscripted the best professional gamers in the world to control them. But as the world ground to a halt while it recklessly spent its resources on frivolous attempts to secure key oil assets, it had become prohibitively expensive to replace each destroyed drone. Now both sides leaned on infantry like a crutch. Men were cheap, and unlike drones, they didn't cost any oil to run or any steel to build.

Luthor patted the drone like a beloved dog. "Kick some ass for us today, Clap."

Marri pumped his fist. "Like the fucking clap of doom, brother. Oorah!" He still considered himself a Marine, despite his reassignment to the 501st.

Their Jump Master, Sergeant Garcia, raised his voice. His mask muted his voice enough that he must have been shouting at the top of lungs for them to hear him. "Listen up! Remember to fall in formation away from the mountains and toward our rendezvous zone." Naming directions had become incredibly difficult on Titan, which was the current magnetic South Pole. Literally every direction could be North around there. Traditional compasses were all but useless. They used the craggy Shackleton mountains as a reference point. "Wait as long as possible before you pop your chute. It'll be hard to see the ground coming up so keep track of your altimeter!

"Good luck men. Godspeed."

A row of yellow lights erupted on the ceiling. The men unhitched from the mesh and lined up to jump in three rows. The hydraulics opened the back door with a squeaking grind. Luthor waited, hardly daring to breathe. He'd made hundreds of jumps, but jumping out of an airplane always played havoc with his insides. This time was much worse.

Solid red lights splashed their vision. That meant that some of the planes had started unloading. They would be next. Everyone was quiet. Checking his claustrophobic oxygen mask and dawning his infrared goggles, he waited. This was not a routine jump and he wanted to be ready. They were coordinating a high altitude jump with thousands of other men. So many things could go wrong. The terminal velocity of a fully prone person with arms and legs outstretched was only about 125 miles per hour, and even slower in a wing suit. But a trooper in a full dive could reach speeds in excess of 300 mph. Diving with this many men was dangerous. In training, two men at dangerously different speeds had collided; they found pieces of them spread over a 3 square mile area. Luthor had no desire to be the human projectile that impaled one of his friends.

The plane hit another patch of turbulence. It was horrible timing, they were about to jump. Suddenly green lights replaced the red and the men started leaping out of the plane. No one hesitated; they had been too well trained for that. Luthor walked forward as the distance between him and the open end of the plane decreased. His heart raced furiously. He looked up and the last man in front was gone. All he saw were white clouds puffing by below and other cargo jets in formation behind them. He took a deep breath from his oxygen mask, and took a running jump out of the plane.

Wind crashed into his body, and the familiar disorientation came as freefall hit him. For an instant he could not tell up from down, images of planes seemed to come from every side of him. Forcing down the rising panic, he reoriented himself. Little red blips on his goggles showed him where the others were. Without infrared technology there would have been no way to see anyone. Their white camouflage was completely invisible on a backdrop of clouds and the endless white of Antarctica.

Luthor tucked his arms to his sides and fell into the aerial formation taking shape in the clouds below. He made slight adjustments in his position and direction by subtly tilting his hands. The tiny changes in aerodynamics allowed him to turn and stabilize his body. The airborne army flew in a loose configuration. They all gained similar altitude and then opened their wing suits and angled their descent toward the drop zone which appeared as a green flashing dot on their goggle displays.

Even inside his specialist gear, it was freezing. HA drops were always cold, but it just felt different when dropping over the coldest place on earth. Luthor felt like his very bones were frostbitten, cooling down the rest of his body from the inside out. He had strict orders not to activate any of his heating batteries yet, so he wouldn't show up on the enemy infrared. The insulation and his adrenaline would have to be enough to keep him warm. It wasn't working.

They passed through the high clouds and saw the endless ice field. It was barren, no hills, no plants, or even rocks to break up the inexorable whiteout. Over millennia of freezing temperatures, snowfall had accumulated on Antarctica in giant domes of ice that where miles thick. Titan Dome was one of the thickest at 13,000 feet above sea level. Maybe more. The weight of the massive glacier was so heavy it had actually depressed the land underneath it far below sea level. Before the war broke out over the resources, oil rigs around the ice plateau were drilling through three miles of solid ice before they even hit any land.

Tiny black specks were emerging in Luthor's vision. Enemy emplacements. Mobile Comm units, Tanks, Dragon guns, missile sites, anti-missile batteries, Artillery, and infantry spotted the ice. The Chinese had dug in deep on Titan, it was where the largest of all the newly discovered oil fields was located. It was easily four times bigger than any other field ever discovered on earth. The Allies believed if they could shove the Chinese off Titan then they could push them all the way into the Indian Ocean and end the war. The paratroops were supposed to soften up the defenses ahead of the main assault.

The commanders claimed that the enemy couldn't see them with their camo under cloud cover. Even if they did start shooting, their heat signatures were too minute to be tracked effectively by surface missiles, and they were too high to be hit by the Dragon guns. Luthor hoped it was true.

After a minute of gliding Luthor glanced up. They had traveled far enough laterally that the clouds were dissipating. It looked like they were going to disappear completely if they didn't change course. Other men around him were looking up too. *Damn it,* he thought, *this wasn't supposed to happen. I hope all that crap they told us about not getting shot wasn't complete bullshit. They are going to see us.* He thought about trying to signal to change direction and hike in farther on foot.

It was too late.

White-hot streams of bullet fire strafed up from the surface. Dozens of gun emplacements were pouring bullets into the sky. He couldn't hear them, but he imagined the ominous drum roll of the smaller guns, and the relentless waterfall of bullets spewed by the Dragons. *How the hell do they see us?* Luthor didn't have time to reflect, he joined in on the evasive maneuvers of the rest of the airborne column. Thankfully the guns were still out of range. But they wouldn't be for long.

There was a flash from the ground, followed by the telltale contrail of Indian-made Surface to Air Missiles. *Shit shit shit. They had better be right about this,* Luthor thought, following the column. He held his breath as the missile closed the distance at frightening speed.

It homed in on men half a kilometer in front of them. They dodged and the missile passed through them. Three more flashes issued from the ground. More missiles. One of them was aimed right at Luthor's position. He spun sideways and went into a full dive directly at the missile to minimize his cross section. In seconds the missile was in range. He leveled off, directing his body away from the projectile.

The missile missed wide, fizzling out harmlessly above him. No more flashes from the ground. *What a shame, waste enough on us, and maybe we wouldn't have to blow them up.*

Many other paratroopers had tried the same trick, diving straight at the missiles to avoid them. That put them in the extreme range of the Dragons. They were getting closer to the ground, but there was no way in hell he was going to pop a chute here. It would make him a stationary target. He followed the rest of the main force above him toward the landing site. The Dragons pissed bullets at them. Luthor tried to avoid the streams of ammunition lancing up between them, but mostly he trusted his luck. Mathematically, the odds were poor any of the bullets would find him; unfortunately, the Dragons fired enough ammo to negate his advantage. A few men, several hundred yards below him, were the main targets. A trooper underneath him twisted and turned trying to outsmart death. He failed; a shower of sparks poured up from below. The man had been hit. No longer in an aerodynamically optimized position, the body flew up through the formation. Luthor had no time to react, and only managed to tuck in his left arm. The change spun his body sideways, and the corpse missed him by inches. Any closer and he would have sprayed his own frozen body parts on the enemy position.

Two other sprays of sparks bloomed from other plummeting paratroopers. Bullets penetrated their thin armor and bounced off metal chute encasements, lighting them up like fireworks.

Luthor cursed Murphy and his law. Things had become much worse. A small swarm of mini drones began systematically slicing through their ranks. Their calculated shots fired the precise quantity of ordinance to knock a man from the sky, but no more, maximizing their killing potential. Dozens of men tumbled toward the earth like drunken gymnasts, their life stolen by the deadly machines. One drone streaked toward Luthor. He tucked in his limbs and dove frantically to avoid it. Jake tumbled next to him in free fall, looking as if he'd been hit. But a second later, Jake leveled out, rifle in hand. As the drone circled back for another pass, Jake ripped off a ferocious burst of fire. The drone sparked and died, a small explosion tearing off its dorsal stabilizer.

Men and drones fell from the sky. Too many men.

Luthor looked at his altimeter. He was quickly approaching the magic number where he could no longer safely deploy. He narrowed his eyes. Seeing a spot sufficiently far from the Anti-Air guns, he made for it, praying he would be able to make it to the rendezvous zone in time.

2000 meters.

1500 meters.

He was running out of time.

1000 meters.

If he opened the parachute too late then it wouldn't matter if he wasn't shot, he would have a broken leg, if not a worse injury, in the middle of Antarctica. That could be a death sentence. *I am not going to end up a human Popsicle in this God-forsaken continent.*

500 meters.

He pulled his chute. Straps dug into every limb as the parachute guzzled air and rapidly decelerated his fall. The ground rushed up frighteningly fast.

More bullets erupted from the ground directly underneath him.

CHAPTER 4:

CERN labs, Geneva, European Union

Luthor woke up in a sweat. He had been reliving his worst memories again. It happened frequently, it was supposedly a common occurrence for the surviving soldiers who fought in World War III. The overwhelming majority of returning men and women had been diagnosed with Post Traumatic Stress Disorder. He had worked long and hard to not be crippled by his own struggle with his broken mind. He attended years of counseling to help heal his mental wounds and had thrown himself into his studies to help distract from his dark thoughts. Luthor still never had been able to come to grips with why *he* had survived and so many of his brothers hadn't.

The only evidence of his continued battle were the occasional explosions from the angry, violent Luthor. Luthor kept that part of his psyche, his Antarctica-Luthor— "Anti-Luthor" as he thought of it— locked up tight. He gained better control over Anti-Luthor every year. The only other daily reminder of his PTSD was strange, but debilitating fear of heights that had not existed before the war either. He struggled to climb a flight of stairs at times.

He could never go back to sleep right away after a dream like that. The best way was to get up, move around, use the bathroom, and try to forget. He exited the office by the side door, leading into the hall. It creaked horribly, like most doors. Oil was too expensive to waste on something as frivolous as a noisy hinge. He hoped it didn't wake anyone up. He left it ajar to minimize the creaking when he came back in. He shuffled drearily into the dimly lit bathroom and sat down on the toilet, resting his face in his hands. He was glad that the solar relay lights were almost out of charge for the night. There was nothing worse than a bright LED after a bad dream to ruin any chance of rest. Maybe Eli was right; maybe a gun would help. *Mental note: thank Eli for the advice.*

Going through his routine he tried to think of other things. Put anything into his brain other than the freezing cold of war, the thrill and fear of jumps, his dead friends, the sound of gun shots. That was one of the worst. He still thought he heard them sometimes when doors would slam, or if he dropped something on the ground. The sound of them had never left. They were ominous. Hearing them meant you were still alive; but probably wouldn't be for very long. He could almost feel them in his chest, still ringing there, that one bullet waiting to find his willing flesh. The sound of a single bullet shot filled his mind, he failed to remove it no matter how hard he tried.

Wait! That wasn't my memories. That was real. Luthor realized. He *had* heard a gunshot. It sounded like it had come from inside the lab.

#

A door creaked. Cracking a sleep-crusted eye, Tanya saw Luthor leaving to use the bathroom. It was a common occurrence. She knew he had a legitimate reason for his sleeplessness, but the man acted like he was a geriatric with an overactive bladder. No matter, if the man ever got off his ass and proposed there would be vows to deal with that: "For better or for worse." 3 AM pee runs would definitely wind up in the "worse" category. *So what if he can't sleep through the night if his life depended on it, I love that boy anyway.*

She had always liked the way that *Tanya Tenrel* had sounded in her head. Alliterative names always had a ring to them, rhyming names, not so much. Marriage would be wonderful, she knew it would be.

But Luthor didn't make sense. It seemed to her that he should appreciate the security that came from marriage. Instead, he always said that it was an "antiquated notion of an exiled religion." She supposed to an extent, he was right. It was old fashioned, and pretty much nobody outside of the Christians out in the boonies got married anymore. That didn't mean marriage was a stupid idea. *Not everything that's old is bad Luthor, even if it has to do with God.*

She sighed and rolled over, wishing she slept on her bed in Aurora. The couch itself had seemed like a good idea, but in practice a half-meter wide bed just didn't satisfy.

The hinges of another door squeaked their protest in the lab. Tanya wished for the ten thousandth time that oil was cheap enough to properly lubricate them. Luthor must be having a rough night if he had decided to go out into the lab. *Oh no. I hope he isn't going to start playing with the chemistry set out there.* She rolled over again, putting her back to the lab door, hoping to shut out a little of the noise she feared was coming.

A rustling came from the floor where Michael was sleeping, accompanied by a muffled groan. She rolled over for a look. *If he is a sleep talker I swear I—*

A man in all black restrained Michael, and had a hand over his mouth. She jerked to attention.

"What—" A cold glove slapped over her own mouth. She tried to move, but she was being restrained against the back of the couch. In moments her face was mashed to the floor, hands duct taped together behind her back. Michael was next to her, struggling with all his might without success. Another length of duct tape adhered to her mouth. It all happened so fast. There was no time to think, to process or react. She wanted to scream just to vent the frustration and overwhelming fear boiling inside of her. She tried, but the men were thorough. All that came out was a muted gurgling behind the gag.

Her captor shoved her hard in the back with his boot and she flopped to the ground. Trying to ignore the pain of the kick she rolled over on her side, giving her a chance to survey the room. Michael was similarly bound but they had taped his legs too. His thrashing continued despite the restraints along with a constant stream of mumbling yells that refused to travel far past the tape.

A man wearing military-looking gear stood over Michael; his expression was immutable behind a black face-mask, but his shouldered machine gun spoke volumes. Tanya spotted another one, also clad all in black. He had a pistol hard against Eli's head. Eli remained frozen obediently, his terror more obvious than the beard on his face.

Tanya's insides boiled. She wanted to do something, *anything*. None of this made any sense, but she could not bear to see that wonderful man harmed. Her heart thumped, she strained against the tape, but was powerless to escape. All she could do was watch in utmost horror as the second man shoved Eli to his knees in the middle of the room. He never let the gun slip for an instant.

The other grabbed a fistful of Michael's curly black hair and yanked him to his knees. He was frighteningly strong, manhandling Michael easily with only one hand. He pulled a pistol out as well, cruelly cramming it against Michael's head. It was like something from one of Luthor's dreams. But this was real and happening in the present. She had to alert Luthor, he was the only one who had any chance of doing anything. But he just sat there on the crapper while they all were about to be executed. There were too many thick industrial walls, meant to contain a chemical fire, insulating him from the meager noises she was able to produce. Tanya knew she had to act now or it would be too late.

She jumped up and yelled against the tape, knowing she was being stupid, but it was all she could think of. Michael and Eli certainly couldn't do anything with gun barrels affixed to their heads. Now was the time to act. She charged the man holding Eli. He moved dizzyingly fast and kicked her hard in the side of the knee. She crumpled, and without her hands to catch herself, she fell ingloriously on her face.

Her knee hurt like hell. She hoped that he hadn't broken anything. *Who the hell cares?* Bitter thoughts and resignation flooded in. *We are all going to be shot in a minute and Luthor is going to die as soon as they find him!*

As if in answer to her screamed thought, the man next to Michael spoke. He had a French accent. "I am an impatient man. Do not play with me. Do not stall. Just tell me what I want to know." He ripped the tape off Michael's face drawing an expectedly painful yell from the bound man.

"Son of a bitch! What the f—" The man next to Eli fired his pistol into the floor and Michael shut up mid-word. The gunshot echoed in the silence.

With a wisp of smoke still issuing from the gun, he spoke. His English was clear but he slurred around words uncommon to his mouth, "Where is the device? We want it. Now."

"I think you are mis—"

"Shut up fool and answer the question." Eli was being pushed sideways with the force of the gun. "I will not ask again. The gravity machine. Where is it?"

Michael looked frantic. "Slow down. Please just don't shoot. I will—"

He pulled the trigger.

The opposite side of Eli's head exploded, tearing the air with the sound. Red chunks of flesh, brain, and skull splattered on the floor with the unmistakable exit wound of a close-range gunshot. His body slumped in the direction of the blast, falling into the pile of gore that was already soaking into the carpet.

Michael shouted in disbelief, his cries quickly turning to tears as he watched a new friend transformed into a corpse before his eyes. Tanya echoed him behind her tape.

"I told you I don't play games. Thanks to you, Tenrel is dead." The killer walked over to Tanya. She felt the hard barrel of imminent death pressed against her head. "If you delay again, I will kill his bitch next." The man jabbed his gun at Tanya. "Now, where is the device?" Michael's mouth opened and shut repeatedly. He couldn't make the words come out.

Even in the meager ambient light, she could see he was crying. "In the lab. It's in the lab!"

Something clicked in Tanya's head. *They thought Eli is Luthor! They don't know he isn't there. Maybe he will have a chance to escape*! Her hope quickly died as she remembered the sort of man Luthor was. He was not a man who would leave her to save himself. He would try to save them and would die trying.

They were all going to die, and there was nothing she could do about it.

#

Luthor sneaked out of the stall, peering around the empty bathroom. None of this made any sense. Why would there be a gunshot in the lab? Worst case scenarios flashed in his mind, overlapping each other into one horrible montage of gunfire and gore, mingled with memories of war. After a quick glance in the dimly lit laboratory, he concluded that it must have come from the office.

Another gunshot rang out, echoing off the steel and tile in the lab. He froze with fear, wondering if the shot was at Tanya. He could not let her die. *The gun! Eli taped one under his desk! I have to get it and save her.*

He sneaked along the wall leading to the side door into the office. Voices were coming from inside; two of them he didn't recognize, but one was clearly a very frightened

Michael.

"It's in the lab!"

Someone in there was dangerous enough to scare the smog out of Michael and probably was the source of the gunfire. He wanted Michael to give them something in the lab. *Shit. They want the 126! How does anyone know about it? Damn it, this is all my fault! I brought them here!*

Luthor remembered his breathing exercises, pounded into him for years by army therapists. *Breathe. Breathe.* It helped. As frustrating as it was years ago to have something so simple taught to him like he had a learning disability, Luthor was glad for it now. It helped the adrenaline flooding his veins to give him the focus to be able to act rather than drive him to panic.

He realized that this was his golden opportunity to get the gun. They would be entering the lab, thereby vacating the office and giving him one chance to get in through the side door undetected. He hadn't made up a place to sleep, he had just dozed off on the floor. It was possible in the dark that they didn't know he was here. Why would they expect another person sitting on the john? He might actually have the element of surprise so long as the door didn't give him away.

With his head next to the crack in the door he heard the rustling of people moving around and several ripping noises; it sounded like duct tape.

"Over here," Michael said. "By the far wall." More ripping.

"Walk," said a commanding, cruel voice.

Luthor mentally counted off a few seconds, knowing it would take a second to get all of them out of the office. The unnamed voice was probably not alone. *If there is one of them still in there...* He heard a boot on the cold floor and acted. He slipped inside the door, moving it as little as possible, and knelt behind the desk. The door obediently stayed silently in place.

He remained with the desk between him in the lab entrance for a few long moments as he gathered himself. Not hearing anyone, he chanced a look. His eyes instantly affixed to a corpse on the floor. The graying beard, tanned skin, and bloodied sweater-vest, could only have belonged to Eli. He had been the target of the gunshot. He almost threw up in spite of himself.

Why did it have to be Eli? Why him! Eli had been so alive just that night, hospitable, vivid, and creative, the best of humanity. Now, he was just an empty shell on the floor. Whatever had composed the person of Eli was gone as surely as the flesh above his right ear. He was dead. *To make it through Antarctica, only to be assassinated in his office. It isn't right.* He thought, trying not to recall the own times in his life where he had yearned for death to find him. Voices in the lab shocked him back to the cold, dark, awful place called reality.

"Here. It's under this table," said Michael.

"The files."

"On the computer. In the bag."

Luthor slipped under the desk to grab the gun. *Those sons of bitches are going to die.* He thought. Then he realized that it was duct-taped to the desk. *So much noise.* Why did everything have to make noise?

He heard a particularly loud creak from the side door as it settled back on its hinges and panicked. He knew they had heard that. He ripped off the tape, setting the sticky sidearm into his palm.

"What was that?" said the cruel voice. "Go check."

Luthor heard no footsteps this time. Not a good sign, this was a professional. Now aware that someone else might be in the building, this person's training had kicked in. *Why can't you just be a bumbling idiot?* Luthor thought.

"Is there anyone else in here?" said the voice again.

"I... I don't think so." Michael replied. Remarkable that he was able to keep his composure enough to lie in the face of murderers.

Luthor stayed under the desk. He flicked the safety off. He would have the advantage if the man checked under the desk. Soft muffled footfalls moved around the room as the man checked the dark office. Luthor's heart pumped angrily. He wanted to jump out, guns blazing and shoot the murderer in the face. But that would be suicide. If the man saw him first, he was dead. Even if he managed to drop this one, there was at least one other man still in the lab with Michael and Tanya as potential hostages. The only way to have a chance was to get the jump on them both. With luck he wouldn't be seen in the dim light.

The footsteps moved around the desk to the side door and stopped. He didn't move. Luthor didn't breathe. His heart thumped like a drum in his own ears. *That gun-toting bastard probably hears me already. He is just waiting for me to come out.* Luthor did not relish the idea of waiting for his quarry to fire a round or two into the desk—just to be sure. All that protected him was a single panel of wood. It might not even stop a hollow-point. Luthor knew he couldn't wait forever. Perhaps his best option was to shoot through the desk and hope to injure the man. If he aimed for the legs, he might be able to disable him. Luthor leveled his gun at the side of desk hoping he was aiming at the right place. He drew his breath, preparing to shoot three or four times to make sure one of them connected. He slowly began to pull back on the trigger.

Suddenly the door creaked again, then repeatedly. Luthor froze, releasing the trigger.

After a second he realized what the man was doing. *He's testing the hinges to see what made the noise.* Luthor lowered his gun.

"Goddamn hinges," he said through the door. "Piece of

shit." The door thumped with the frustrated kick of a boot. It stayed open. The man exited the side door walking back to his partner.

Luthor carefully climbed out from underneath the desk. He followed through the wide open entry, his socks making no noise on the floor. The man was short, muscular, wearing all black. He had the bulky torso of a man wearing a gelvar vest. Luthor cursed to himself as he realized he was going to need to put a round through the back of his balaclava to put this guy down. Any shots to the back would just make him angry. It was a tough shot, and he hadn't shot a pistol in years.

Both hands on the 9mm Walther, Luthor steadied his aim, and leaned into the shot. He breathed out. At the end of his breath he gently pulled the trigger.

The recoil shoved his arms back into his shoulders, the bullet casing dropped out the side, and the bullet zoomed at 400 meters per second into the back of the man's head. *Just like riding a bike.* He thought bitterly.

Blood splattered. Tanya's screams filled the lab. Luthor dashed next to the dead man crumpling to the laminate floor and flattened himself against the wall. He leaned around the corner and took aim again. Michael and Tanya were awkwardly sprawled on the ground in fear with their hands taped behind their backs. Michael had a thick strip of tape across his face and he thrashed silently against his bonds. Luthor didn't have time to line up his second shot. He had to act quickly if wanted to keep any scrap of surprise.

A black-clad man scanned the room for the shooter who had killed his partner. *I'm right here, you bastard. You're next.* Luthor exhaled and pulled the trigger again. The bullet slammed into the side of his chest. A visible ripple spread from the hit as the gelvar vest absorbed the impact, diffusing the force of the bullet over its entire surface. *Shit!*

The man fired back at once, taking cover behind a steel lab table on the side of the room. He was shooting something very automatic. Luthor compressed his body back behind the corner. Bits of wall exploded around him. He knew that he was in a compromised position. The second man now had cover and Luthor had lost the element of surprise.

He dove behind the nearest lab table, hoping it would protect him against whatever high tech rounds were likely to be fired. Luthor was too terrified to peek to get a fix on his foe. A moment later a torrent of bullets shattered the beakers above him, showering glass down on him like sadistic confetti.

The weapon's rapid shots reverberated in Luthor's sternum. The steel surfaces and flat walls acted like the sides of a drum, magnifying the ear-splitting discharges to a deafening volume.

Luthor cowered behind his cover. The odds of winning a gunfight with a guy with a sub-machine gun and gelvar were low. He had more firepower in one burst than Luthor did in his entire magazine. But if the soldier—or whatever the hell he was—killed Luthor, he would kill the others and steal his research. Images of Tanya lying next to Eli with a matching head wound filled Luthor's mind, giving him purpose. He had to save her, had to avenge Eli.

Tanya had contorted herself so her face was in the middle of Michael's back, wriggling back and forth as she bit through Michael's tape cuffs. After a moment, Michael silently brought both his hands free of the tape in triumph. He turned toward the containers of elements as if he were looking for something. *What is he up to?* Luthor wondered. He must have some sort of plan. Luthor needed to keep the other man occupied.

Luthor quickly looked up and fired. He ducked back down and moved away from his friends hoping to keep any stray bullets on the other side of the room.

The man in black suddenly popped up in front of the

sinks, flanking Luthor and releasing a hail of potential death. Luthor dove out of the way, ducking behind another table, just as the floor exploded where he had been crouching. Luthor fired back two rounds, just to keep him honest. He was running out of ammunition, and without knowing the precise size of the magazine, there was no way to tell how many he had left.

Michael gestured urgently, he had something in his hand. There was a stick of some element resting on a scrap of foil. Luthor still had no idea what Michael was trying to do. Michael bolted up and threw whatever it was in his hand across the room towards the gunman. He drew fire, but was back down safely before any projectiles found a home in his flesh. The element sailed across the room, bounced off the wall, and dropped into the sink where the glassware was soaking. *That was effective. Why don't you throw a paper airplane at him next time? Maybe you can –*

Then the sink exploded.

A plume of water arced up to the ceiling spraying the area with broken glass shards. The side of the sink exploded outward mingling fire and water, throwing the man from his cover. He landed in the center aisle.

It took Luthor a moment to notice that their assailant lay dazed on the ground not three meters from him.

"Shoot him!" Michael screamed.

Luthor obliged. He pulled the trigger on the semi-automatic weapon until the firing pin clicked on the empty barrel. He didn't hold back, this was the best chance to kill the man. He hoped at least one of the bullets missed the body armor. The body didn't move. It stayed in the same contorted position as when it landed. A pool of red began growing underneath.

Luthor cautiously approached the dead man. At least he *looked* dead. He feared the thunderous beating of his own heart might wake the guy back up. Luthor took off the gunman's ski mask to reveal curly African hair and a hole right in the middle of his skull. He was very dead.

Thankfully hair and blood covered most of the grisly details.

In an odd, painful way, it was relieving to see the lifeless corpse. Luthor had never relished death in the way Jake had, counting kills as points in a grand, fatalistic game. This was different, these men had a malicious, personal intent. War always felt evil and gruesome with no purpose; nameless soldiers shot at other nameless soldiers because they were ordered to do so by more important people. Lives were spent and taken like currency and every death in war felt like a sin. Killing this man felt like justice. At the same time, it was surreal, two dead assassins in as many minutes. Both of them by his hand. Luthor didn't even know what to feel. He hadn't seen anyone killed since the war, let alone taken a life.

Tanya, now free of tape, tackled Luthor in a hug.

"I love you," she said repeatedly into the crook of his neck through sobs. Her body heaved as she struggled to breathe over her tears. By the time she broke contact her eyes were red and her cheeks were stained.

"I can't believe how well that worked," Michael said. He stared disbelievingly at his open hands.

"What did you throw?"

"The entire tray of potassium. Since it reacts with water, I thought I could distract him with an impromptu grenade."

"Quick thinking."

"I only hoped to distract him, I didn't think the reaction would be powerful enough to knock him down!"

Tanya clenched her fists. "Will you two stop being such *goddamn scientists* and figure out what the hell just happened!" As soon as the words had flowed out she clapped a hand over her mouth, eyes wide. "I… I didn't mean to say that."

"If ever it is okay, it is now." Luthor said, holding her close. Tanya had a strange peculiarity with cursing. She prided herself on never saying 'God' as a curse. It was in the Ten Commandments or something. For her to curse in such a manner indicated that she was well beyond the breaking point. But death and murder could do that to people.

Michael seemed to be losing his body's steadying epinephrine surge and had started crying. They were big, pitiful man-sobs, the kind of lament Luthor wished he still had inside him. Crying got the pain out. Now the only kind of catharsis available was a heart rate that was three times higher than usual and a mind full of terrible memories. Michael's eyes leaked tears and his voice quavered. "Eli…he's dead. It's all my fault."

Eli was dead. Luthor had killed two others. Everything had changed.

#

They had arranged Eli's body as peacefully as possible on the office floor. His hands were folded across his chest and his legs straight. A blanket covered him and pillows braced his head, failing to fully hide the gruesome exit-wound. It just didn't seem real. He had been so alive, so passionate; he cared about everyone in his life. As Tanya cried, she found herself wishing she had known him better.

Tanya longed for answers, but none appeared. The two dead men didn't provide any clues either. The one in the hallway had held nothing of note to identify him or indicate his true purpose. All they knew was that he was a young, muscular, south Asian man with a smog-load of firepower on him. Apart from his high-tech bullet proof vest—'Gelvar' Michael had said— he had a pistol and a fancy-looking machine gun strapped to his back, not to mention a dozen clips of bullets—or were they called magazines? She couldn't remember. And two grenades.

The other body looked like something from a bad vampire movie. Water from the destroyed sink had mixed with the man's blood, greatly exaggerating its quantity. The red water spread from the body in a giant swath. He was similarly equipped with gelvar and a miniature armory.

"No! Not this!" Michael yelled. He picked up the brown satchel soaking in blood water. It was the bag that held their presentation computer. "Why did he have to grab the goddamn laptop?"

They had elected to not copy the research before the presentation to any other devices as a security precaution. The only other copy was back in Illinois. Luthor always said the reactions and cyclotron data were too hopelessly complicated to remember, they needed that data.

Slowly, Michael lifted the gray computer out of the blood-soaked bag. "Damn it Luthor, I told you it was stupid not to have a back-up with us!"

Luthor's head drooped visibly. "How bad is it?"

"I can't tell." Michael turned the computer over in his hands. "Looks like the bag kept most of the water out. Qwiz could probably fix it."

"We don't have Qwiz."

"Then we wait until it dries out and hope it turns on."

"That is our only copy of the research. How are we going to present our findings if it's ruined?"

Michael put the computer down on the table, his eyes red and puffy. "Not that it even matters. Eli is dead!" His pain and guilt were as evident as the blood on the floor.

But it wasn't Michael's fault. Tanya mentally listed half a dozen things that could have changed the outcome. For that matter, if they hadn't come in the first place, he would be alive too. But, ultimately, he should never blame himself for the actions done in cold blood by another person. Michael hadn't pulled that trigger, how could it be his fault? Tanya tried to concoct the best possible arrangement of words to help Michael, but Luthor interrupted. His own demons seemed to blind him to the fact that his intern was drowning in grief.

"We came half-way around the world to present," he said. "We have been working years for this opportunity. And if men are willing to kill to steal 126, it shows us just how important our presentation is!"

"I just never imagined a situation where we would be fighting for our lives, Luthor," Michael said. "I haven't had to see that since the Culling..." he trailed off, apparently not wanting them to hear his voice crack again. Tanya couldn't blame him.

"Then imagine this: finally we would live in a world where another Culling is impossible. 126 can ensure there'd never be another food shortage and people won't freeze to death in the winter because they can't heat their homes. We'd be able to make enough medicine to stop plagues; kids wouldn't have to hunt rats on the street to survive. Think of a world where we don't have to go to war and kill each other over resources. If we can get that computer to work, all of that becomes a reality in a matter of years!"

Luthor picked up the soggy laptop. "It's long past time that we called carbon police. While we wait for them to arrive, maybe we can dry this thing out."

"The carps aren't going to like this." Michael said. "Three dead bodies. This isn't going to look good for us."

"We will explain what happened. Forensics will clearly show their bullets killed Eli. We just have to pray they will let us present in the meantime."

"I think we might need to revise our expectations," Tanya said quietly.

"What do you mean?" Luthor asked.

"I mean, maybe we should forget about presenting. At this point, our goal should be to stay alive." Tanya felt a hole open up inside her, all her hopes sinking into its blackness.

She couldn't believe this was happening, yet she understood where it led. Neither Luthor nor Michael seemed to have put the pieces together, so she continued. "Don't you see? Two men with grenades and Uzis came in here willing to kill in order to get your research. These aren't scientists trying to steal fame. This is much bigger and more dangerous. Whoever is behind this, is well-funded, well equipped, and ruthless."

"They each had a Gelvar vest, " Michael added. "I've only heard of Special Forces having those."

Luthor swore.

"Whoever wants this is powerful enough to afford their own armed forces," Tanya continued.

"Then why did they only send two?" Luthor asked confrontationally.

"Maybe that's all they could afford at the time, or maybe they didn't expect a couple of scientists to be able to kill two men armed to the teeth. I don't know and won't speculate. But it would be foolish to assume they won't send more once they find out these two failed. carps aren't going to help us much. We need to get out and we need to do it now. Before somebody else comes in here and kills us."

"Before they kill *us*?" Michael said. "Luthor, we have to call *Qwiz*!" Michael frantically pulled out his cell phone. "They thought Eli was you, Luthor! They *knew your name*. They probably know everything about you by now. Like where you *live.* What if they send people to your house while Qwiz is there? We can't let him die too!"

CHAPTER 5:

Aurora, Illinois, United States of the West

An ominous red LED glowed on Qwiz's canvas sandals. It beamed out of a transparent panel on his towering computer. The machine was unseemly in size, unwieldy in its sheer computing capability, and a glutton for power. Just the way he liked it. Thanks to his speedy solid-state drives—four 2-terabyte units linked in RAID 0 to be precise— it booted in seconds, and Qwiz had yet to ever see a loading screen on any game. The muted whine of the various fans that helped cool the electronics spun together like an orchestra. Another red LED, visible through the clear side panel of the tower, illuminated the rectangular, nickel-coated copper heatsink sitting on top of twin 16-core Intel processors. He had overclocked them to 5.1 ghz, possible thanks to an aggressive water-cooling array that siphoned off the excess heat. He had named the ultra-powerful machine, *Norquist,* after a legendary sword he'd read in a story as a kid.

He harmonized with the fans with rapid clicking of his mouse and long strings of crisp clacking from the mechanical keyboard. The keyboard was another old piece of technology, like all the components of his machine, but he preferred the high raised buttons with their responsive mechanical switches to the modern slim-line or touch screen counterparts used everywhere else.

Qwiz was old school and not ashamed to admit it.

Three blazing screens, arranged in a semicircle, cast

dancing shadows in the dark room. Each screen's 30-inch surface was crammed with four times the pixels of modern displays its size. Society had quickly abandoned the ESHD format as energy prices soared in the '20s. It was simply too energy intensive for processors and video cards to render images that detailed. As a result, the monitors were something of an antique, but still provided unparalleled resolution, so Qwiz had kept them. He had always preferred monitors to VR; they didn't give him vertigo. At his house he had three other identical screens, doubling the size of his display. It took four of the most powerful video cards ever created all working in tandem to power his full set up. Today he only had two of them activated to save money. Admittedly, he wasted all of his spare income to power this beast, but that didn't mean he had to be wasteful and use all four cards when it wasn't strictly necessary.

But this time he wasn't spending his own money on energy. Luthor had *asked* him to watch his house and had *given him permission* to bring over his computer and use his power. All that free electricity, just bubbling up from that machine in the basement, just waiting to be used. It couldn't hurt to turn the other GPU's on too, right? *No, I promised Luthor I would watch his house. I will not ferret away extra power for a few extra frames per second. He's selling it to make money. It would be the same as stealing.* Temptation overcome, he clicked his mouse rapidly and watched the head of another monster explode.

Qwiz was on the front-end of a late-night video game marathon that could easily stretch all the way to the morning. The game of choice tonight was *Devolution*. Qwiz had not played the game before, but was intrigued by the concept. An unknown source was causing people's DNA to *devolve*, reverting normal humans into base, mindless, half-animal monsters. His character led a team whose job it was to find the source of the devolution and stop it.

"Oh Shit. Qwency, help me!" cried Bill, his video-game

buddy and long-time friend. They lived next to each other in a large apartment building outside of Chicago. Bill provided the Mountain Dew and Qwency paid for the power to play the games. They made a good team. Even though Bill was almost three times the age of Qwiz, they had become good friends. Bill was one of the few who had been willing to look beyond Qwiz's Korean heritage to see the man underneath. Most everyone else just saw a racist caricature: another greedy member of the Chinese block who had incited World War III over Antarctican oil. Qwiz hated the racism. He had nothing to do with the war. He had been 14 when it had started. Bill had never cared that he was Asian. Qwiz never cared that Bill was old.

Bill looked over to Qwiz in a panic. "Hurry, the Rhino-var's eating my face!"

Qwiz ignored the unholy predators slashing away at his own life and sprinted to save Bill.

"It's too late," Bill said. "Just save yourself!"

"I never leave a man behind!" Qwiz shouted. Real heroes gladly sacrificed their lives to save their friends. Qwiz had never had the opportunity to be an actual hero, but he had no intention of letting his friend die in a video game if he could help it. He digitally pulled out a very large gun and wailed away at the Man-Rhino on top of Digital-Bill. The beast shuddered and collapsed; Bill limped away with less than 10% health. Qwiz turned and fired at his own assailants. They clawed him viciously, but with his last bullet, Qwiz managed to put them down. His character too limped away, with barely 2 hit-points to rub together. The icon indicating that they had just reached a check-point flashed on the screen. They had made it.

The gray-maned man heaved a sigh of relief and paused the game. "Sorry, I need a breather after that one. That son-of-a-goat almost had me."

"I thought you said it would take more than a mere

monster to take down the mighty Stone," Qwiz said. Bill insisted that everyone call him Stone. Apparently, it had been a nickname he had received in Iraq after he had charged alone into a building occupied by terrorists. According to Bill, after he was done there were four dead terrorists. His commanding officer gave him the name *Stone* at that point, referring to the quality of his man-parts.

"That was no mere Monster." Bill said, "that thing was at least half Rhino." Unexpectedly, he wrapped the younger man in a bear hug. It hurt.

"What was that for?" Qwiz asked.

"You risked your life to save my ass back there."

"It's just a game."

"It's the point of the thing. If we were ever in a war together, I know you'd do the same thing."

Qwiz blushed slightly at the compliment. "I don't know about that—"

Bill cut him off. "But I do. I've been there. I've been shot at; I've shot at people. I can tell when a guy is going to lay it on the line for me or not. You would. No matter what it cost you."

"You think so?"

"Does shit stink? Hell yes, I think so. Qwence, you got more character in the tip of your dick than most men have in their entire selves."

Qwiz didn't know how to respond to that one. "Thank you?"

Bill threw back his grey head and laughed. Raspy laughter filled the small apartment. His voice was ragged from a lifetime of sucking on every form of rolled up tobacco that was legal. And probably more than a few other things that weren't. Its jagged tone had a certain endearing appeal for Qwiz.

"I miss having you next door. How long are you going to be over here house-sitting for your co-worker anyway?"

"Luthor is away overseas for another few weeks. And I'm not really house-sitting for him. He just said I could use his house for power while he is gone; so, I moved my computer over here."

"Generous man, that Luthor, with the way you run electronics."

Qwiz felt the urge to tell his old friend about the new power source Luthor had devised. It was just sitting there wasting current while no one was living there. It wasn't actually so generous to give Qwiz something that was free anyhow. He suspected that the real reason for asking him to watch the house was to ensure that no one would discover his invention before the International Energy Conference and steal his credit. Regardless, Qwiz had sworn never to tell anyone about the new element or the generator. Qwiz prided himself on always keeping his promises—that's what it meant to live by honor.

"Yes, very generous." It would also easily save him a week's salary to not power his own computer for the next month. He had a number of things he planned to purchase with his burgeoning financial margin, including *Devolution 2*.

Luthor had been saving a tank-full of carbon credits himself. By selling off some of the energy he was able to take both his girlfriend and his intern to the IEC. He had used the 126 at home instead of work, out of concern for its security. Luthor had been completely paranoid about that. Qwiz could only imagine the bureaucratic paperwork and documents required if he had built his generator at Fermilab; then he would have shown his hand too soon. There would have been no way to give it away for free once the politicians got a hold of it. Qwiz respected Luthor's selfless decision, if he succeeded, Qwiz might be able to actually speak with his Father again. Unexpectedly, Luthor's phone buzzed on the counter.

"Pretty damn late for a phone call." Bill said. "Do I need to make myself scarce? Is it a booty call?"

Qwiz gave his old friend a withering look, and Bill laughed again. Both of them knew very well that Qwiz wasn't the sort of man to play fast and free with women. It wasn't an honorable way to treat them.

He pulled the still-buzzing phone off the countertop. The meager power-saving display read "International call." It had to be Luthor—or his father, but there was no chance of that… he had been stuck in oil-greedy China since before the war. They were father-greedy too, never letting Qwiz speak with his own dad without rampant censorship. He remembered it was Luthor's phone anyway—definitely not his father. Luthor had left the phone so Qwiz wouldn't have to pay international phone rates. Qwiz did some quick mental math and realized it was barely 5:00 am over there. He quickly answered the call to find out what had caused them to call so early.

"Hello L—"

"Quiet!" Luthor snapped. Something was clearly wrong.

"Sorry—"

"I don't have long so please just listen. We're in trouble. Deep trouble. Somebody broke into the lab early this morning and tried to steal our 126."

Qwiz was stunned, Luthor had taken extreme measures to ensure the intellectual security of his research. He had personally asked Qwiz to encrypt his computer data so it would be impossible for *anyone* to hack into it. Qwiz had done an excellent job of that. "How did they even know about it?"

"I have no idea. And that's what scares me." Luthor stopped talking. Qwiz waited for him to continue. "They murdered Eli."

Qwiz had never met the professor from CERN but

knew they were close. “Are you all okay?”

“We’re alive. There was only two; we stopped them. The problem isn’t our safety. It’s yours.”

“But I haven’t told anyone!”

“I know. But I didn’t either, that’s the thing. They still knew about my research. If they know that much, they must also know where I live too.”

“What can I do?”

“Get out now! Grab the element and the research if you can.”

“I will.”

“Don’t let them get it. Please. And hurry!”

Qwiz tried to assure him he would, but the line was already dead. Qwiz’s mind raced, trying to figure out what could have possibly occurred.

“What’s going on? Somebody die?” Bill asked.

“Yes.”

Bill suddenly focused with a hardness Qwiz had never seen on him before. “It was Luthor, he says he’s in trouble. He’s says we’re in trouble too.”

Clearly, there was an imminent threat to both Qwiz and the 126 in the generator downstairs. A twinge in his gut told him to check the window. He had occasionally glimpsed someone in the shadows following him, perhaps there was someone there now. Heroes always trusted their instincts, so Qwiz decided to trust his. He slowly pulled the curtains back just enough to peer out.

Three jet black SUVs were parked along the street. Qwiz had been at the apartment for a week and had only seen two small electric cars parked there in all that time. Everyone else rode a bike, like Qwiz himself did, or walked. Cars just cost too much carbon to buy and use for normal people to have access to them. And these were *SUVs*. Charging batteries that large enough for them spewed more carbon than Bill on a tirade.

Qwiz realized that there were people walking—rather, prowling— next to the intimidating vehicles. He hadn't seen them at first because they too were wearing black. Qwiz jerked back from the window.

"Stone, come look at this," Qwiz said, noticing the fear in his own voice.

Bill squinted to get a better look. "Son, those bastards are packing some heat. MX-5's and some other big shit I've never seen. Those men are black ops or my balls ain't hairy."

Qwiz had no desire to be on the other end of a black ops raid outside of a video game.

"Luthor was right. We are in trouble. Why haven't they come in?"

"They have probably been here for a while and are just waiting for their signal to strike."

"Crap."

"What has Luthor gotten himself into that makes him call you for help and has three goddamn trucks full of soldiers at his door?"

Qwiz hesitated, he had promised. He'd given his sacred *word* as a man to Luthor that he wouldn't tell anyone about the 126. But now he had a dozen men apparently ready to charge into the apartment. "I'm sorry. I swore I wouldn't tell anyone. Not even you."

Bill's expression softened. "I know you would never betray your word, but those guys aren't messing around. Let me help before they bust in here."

Bill was right. Honor now dictated that his duty to help Luthor trumped anything else, even his promise of secrecy. Maybe Bill could help him. "Dr. Tenrel's team discovered… something. This is going to sound crazy, but they found a way to generate unlimited power."

Bill stood there for a moment, considering. "Qwency my boy, I have never known you to lie. If you say it, I'll believe it."

"Luthor said people are trying to steal it. We have to get it out."

Qwiz led Bill downstairs to a small storage room connected to the apartment. He unlocked the door and illuminated the dark room.

"What in the name of shit, is that?" he asked, gaping at Luthor's generator. A muted whirring came from a tangle of tubes and wires as water whooshed unnaturally through the lattice. Small turbines were placed throughout, harvesting the movement of the water at peak efficiency.

"That's his generator. Think of it as a hydroelectric dam you can fit in your garage."

"That's one hell of thing," Bill said in wonder.

Qwiz quickly summarized the gravitational properties of the element Luthor had used in the generator. Bill listened quietly without a shred of disbelief.

As they approached the device, gravity fluctuations became overwhelming. Qwiz's stomach desperately needed a reboot.

"I feel like shit," Bill said. 126 seemed to do that to everyone. Altering gravity, even subtly, after a lifetime of it being constant, wreaked havoc on the inner ear. This was no subtle change. Massive gravity oscillations several times per second made the generator a veritable vertigo repository.

A rapid clicking noise became audible as Qwiz staggered toward the machine. It came from little black boxes.

Qwiz's stomach finally stopped churning when he flipped the master switch. The clicking stopped and the water in the tubes drained into irregular nooks and crannies before it settled in the larger tanks sprinkled around the generator.

Qwiz pointed at the boxes. "These power the whole thing. We have to remove them." He didn't want to try to explain the science to Stone; about how the black boxes constantly altered the density factor of the 126 thereby adjusting the overall gravity and making the water move. Science took time to explain, something they didn't have in abundance. Four screws anchored each box containing the invaluable element. With two screwdrivers, they made quick work of them.

"There's big money in this. No doubt."

"The money isn't in the generator though. It's the research. Luthor wants to give the knowledge of how to create Element 126 away to the whole world. If he succeeds, then everyone could have one of these in their basement. It would end the energy shortage forever without fear of carbon pollution."

"Unlimited energy's great, but I couldn't care less if it spews carbon or not. If I've told you once, I've told you a thousand times, global warming is faker than a prom queen's ID. Carbon dioxide is plant food, damn it! It is not, and has never been, a pollutant. It sure as hell isn't warming the world."

Qwiz didn't have time to debate Stone's delusions by informing him of the scientific consensus now four decades old. There were men outside. Men with guns. Plus, it was always dangerous to disagree with one of Bill's conspiracy theories and global warming denial was his favorite, probably because it was the only one that was a felony to state in public. "You have to understand what something like that would be worth to a world that doesn't believe what you do about carbon."

"Damn straight. It'll tangle up the panties of the solar and windmill companies."

Qwiz hadn't thought of that. The biggest companies in the world are getting rich from selling solar panels and windmills—not to mention the lucrative battery packs to store the energy for peak use—Luthor's invention would supersede their technology and market share.

"Do you think they are the ones outside?" he asked as he shoved the last black box into a suitcase.

A burst of light flashed from the outside window. Bill cursed. "Move it Quency. That was a gunshot."

Bill zipped the suitcase while Qwiz stuffed Luthor's laptop and his three redundant hard drives into a duffle. They worked quickly, but it was too late.

A deafening thud blasted from upstairs. The footsteps of many men reverberated through the floor joists.

Qwiz whispered frantically, "out through the back door."

Each hauling a bag, they quickly and quietly exited through the back door into a long apartment hallway. Luthor had the luxury of living in one of the nicest apartments in the area. All of the units were two stories and had their own exterior front door. But they each also had a back door into a standard apartment hallway leading to the garbage and laundry facilities. Qwiz couldn't be more thankful for that second door; it might have just saved his life. Not only was he still breathing, he had a chance to complete his mission and keep evil men from stealing Luthor's research.

They hurried down the hallway, careful not to trip on the rips in the ancient industrial carpet.

A steel breakaway door, designed to keep out even the most determined suburban refugee, led out into the back alley. Qwiz cracked the door. The alley was vacant save for a solitary Markless huddled in bundled rags.

Qwiz felt even worse for Markless than for the Suburbians. They were the ones who hadn't managed to get CPI chips implanted before the final deadline or whose parents had chosen, for religious reasons, not to have them implanted at birth. They legally had no identity, and without a Chip, could not get one. Markless could neither buy or sell anything, nor legally hold jobs. They would forever be homeless until they starved. Qwiz spared the poor man a glance, but knew he didn't have time help him. He sat against the piles of trash mounded up against the green dumpsters looking hungry and cold. Qwiz struggled to suppress his conscience and turned away. It was a short sprint to the vestigial parking lot behind the building where Bill had stashed his truck. They could make it. The SUVs were parked on the opposite side and would never see them in the dark.

Qwiz pushed the door open and sprinted toward the truck.

Only a few steps into his run, Qwiz heard a voice from behind him. "Target moving South of the building. In pursuit."

The Markless held a walkie-talkie and dashed after him. He was no Markless. Qwiz only made it halfway to the car before the man tackled him.

Though not a file in his memory, Qwiz instinctively recognized that the firm, metallic object shoved into the side of his head was a pistol. He shivered unconsciously in fear as the face of a man that could never have belonged to a Markless stared fiercely at him.

"Give me the 126 and the research. Now."

"Okay, okay!" Qwiz began to hand him the bag when a massive suitcase slammed into the side of the man's face. He lurched sideways and his gun skittered to the ground.

Bill dropped the luggage and jumped on top of the fallen man. He began punching him in the face with the fury of a Velociraptor. He didn't land many before the much younger, more athletic man had flipped him on his back and took his turn dishing out punches to the face.

"The gun!" Bill blurted between blows.

Qwiz snapped to and picked up the unfamiliar weapon. With unsteady hands, he raised it.

"Let him go." Qwiz said as dangerously as he could manage. He was no Batman, but the man put his hands up anyway. Bill stood and promptly reached back and slugged the man with all his might. He spun, crumpling to the ground.

Bill grabbed the weapon from Qwiz, flicking something with his thumb on the side. "Stay down, you son of a bitch." The man obeyed, putting both arms out in front of him. Bill pointed the gun at the man.

"Stone, please don't kill him."

"I'll do what I want." Bill leveled the gun at the prone man. He approached the fallen soldier and cracked him hard over the head with the butt of the pistol. He went limp. Bill turned and handed the pistol back to Qwiz with a smile. "I wasn't gonna shoot him. I put the safety on. *He* just couldn't know that. Let's go."

Qwiz heaved a sigh of relief as they hurriedly chucked their bags in the bed of the truck. Bill's face was puffy and bleeding freely from several cuts.

"Stone, are you okay?"

"I'm fine," he said. "I coulda taken him."

"Uh huh," Qwiz said.

"Really, I would've had his balls ... in a minute or two. I ah...Um.... Let's get outta here!"

Bill put his foot down and the ancient batteries struggled to accelerate the vehicle away from Luthor's apartment. He pulled out onto the street directly away from the SUVs. The three lanes were originally designed to move thousands more vehicles than now occupied its space. It was nearly empty of any non-human powered vehicles, those clogged the side lanes. A bus idled on the opposite side of the street, spewing passengers wealthy enough to afford its services. A small, green, bullet-looking electric car coasted by in the opposite direction. Bill stopped diligently at an intersection. Red LEDs glared from the stoplight as bicycles and pedestrians finished their long commutes from work.

"Don't stop. Floor it!" Qwiz said.

Bill did not floor it. He waited patiently for the light to change. "We can't look too obvious. They'll be looking for one guy on foot, not two in a truck. If we take off like a bat outta hell we'll stick out like a sore thumb. And this old piece of electric shit can't outrun a bicycle. We'll make it. Just don't panic."

Bill knew he was lucky to own any vehicle at all, but truthfully, his truck was a direct descendent of a junkyard. Its ubiquitous dents and rusted paint resembled hopelessly moldy Swiss cheese. The batteries were very overdue for a change; it could only drive 40 kilometers before they needed to recharge. The old-style cab was so far forward that it felt like driving a miniature school bus. But Bill didn't care, he didn't drive much and he certainly didn't have the credits to upgrade. Qwiz never cared much about the fashion of cars either; right then he wanted desperately to leave, and Bill's jalopy was sufficient for the task.

When the light turned green, they slowly rolled down the strip. Densely populated multistory apartments in various stages of disrepair rose up on either side. Street level stores lined the sidewalks hawking wares whose prices had inflated due to scarcity. The ubiquitous Markless held signs with nearly infinite iterations of "will work for food." Qwiz always tried to save slices of bread to give them, because without CPI chips they were unable to legally buy food.

Bicycles and rickshaws whizzed by the dozens of homeless on each corner, ignoring them. They clogged the side lanes of the street leaving the center lanes—reserved for cars— deserted.

"Damn it!" Bill bellowed. He beckoned his unwilling vehicle forward.

Qwiz looked back and instantly saw the SUV's in pursuit. They closed the distance frighteningly quickly. They accelerated faster than anything Qwiz had ever seen. In seconds the three vehicles overtook them. Two flanked them and one pulled directly in front. The SUV's roared a loud, pulsing noise. At first Qwiz thought it might be bass-heavy music. But it became clear when he saw the twin exhaust pipes spewing fumes at the rear of each vehicle that it was not music.

"Bill, those things are burning gasoline."

Bill began a string of curses so long and so vulgar, Qwiz thought the windows might crack.

Qwiz had never seen a car that used an internal combustion engine in his adult memory. Whoever was chasing them must be fabulously wealthy. The cost to fill one of those gas tanks would be stratospheric. And there were *three* of them.

Bill slammed the brakes; the heavier SUVs with their greater inertia continued forward. He yanked the steering wheel to the left before they could react and squealed toward a side street. Their pursuers skidded wildly but were quickly back on their tail. Bill laid relentlessly on his horn and the heavy pedestrian traffic made a small hole for them to pass through. The hole was barely large enough for the small truck; the SUVs would have to wait for a larger opening.

They didn't wait. They blitzed through the intersection like Hitler through Poland. They mowed down any poor person who wasn't able to get out of their way in time. A bicycle and rider sailed next to their truck, inches from Qwiz's window. The woman seemed frozen in time as he passed. Her face was bloody and her mangled limbs twisted at unnatural angles.

Qwiz wanted to throw up. The side-mirror revealed a war zone where the crosswalk had been. Broken, bloodied bodies were strewn about like confetti, bikes lay in twisted ruins. A man sat on his haunches staring disbelievingly at a pile of splinters. It had been a rickshaw, crushed in the speeding cars' wake. It had probably been his only source of income.

Qwiz's heart broke for the poor people. The urge to bring those drivers to justice surged in his chest. They had ruined a crowd of people's lives just because they were in the way! A real hero would have punished them for all the pain they had caused and foiled whatever evil plot they were concocting. A real hero would avenge them. He pictured himself breaking arms and flipping their bodies while being impervious to their bullets like a caped crusader. But he didn't know martial arts and suspected that his body would have a magnetic effect on bullets. *Maybe that is why they all wear capes. I bet a swirling cape makes it harder to see where you're supposed to shoot. I need a cape, maybe then I could punish those men for their deeds.*

He still had the pistol. He could at least do something. He remembered to flick the safety off and started to open the door. A strong, weathered palm restrained him. Qwiz struggled against Bill's firm hand. "We have to go help those people!"

"Get your head on straight!" Bill shouted. "You can't do anything. We don't even have_" The truck lurched as they were rammed sideways by an SUV.

The driver rolled down the midnight windows and pointed an Uzi at them. "Pull over," he said, smiling cruelly.

Bill saluted him with his middle finger and continued to charge forward. He whipped his unwilling vehicle around another corner dodging more Markless holding signs. The SUVs paid no attention to them, forcing them to dive out of the way. Several didn't make it in time.

"We can't out run these smoggers much longer!" Bill yelled, frantically swerving.

"What are we supposed to do? You saw what they did to those pedestrians back there, you think they are going to let us live?"

Bill shouted something unintelligible as he weaved around a bus. The truck tipped precariously on its two side wheels but didn't flip. "Try and shoot their tires out!"

"I've never shot a gun before!" Qwiz said.

"Do your best son," said Bill, strangely quiet. "We're probably dead anyway."

Qwiz rolled the window down and leaned out.

"Line up the sight in the front with the rear sight."

Qwiz did his best. He hoped whatever happened, his father would be proud of him. That he would think he acted in honor.

"Keep your arms straight. Use both hands!"

The weaving truck made lining up anything on the pistol almost impossible. Qwiz pointed the gun and tentatively pulled the trigger. The blast reverberated through his hands up into his shoulder. The sound was deafening. He missed.

"Try again!"

Qwiz fired more. After a few shots he saw the headlight wink out of one of the SUVs. He didn't hit the tire.

He pulled the trigger back again. Nothing happened. "I'm out!"

The nearest SUV revved its massive engine and rammed the back corner of the truck, sending it careening sideways. Qwiz was thrown forward into his seatbelt as the increased G-forces tested its tensile strength. They slammed to a stop against the brick side of an old building.

Pedestrians screamed, running away from the accident.

Six men jumped out of the SUVs, all holding weapons. They surrounded the truck, their faces inscrutable in the dark.

"Quency, it's been an honor to fight by your side," Bill said.

Qwiz smiled weakly. He shut his eyes as the men leveled their weapons at the windows. He couldn't believe all of this had happened so fast. He expected to feel the sharp pain of bullets lance through his flesh any second.

They didn't come.

He didn't hear any gun shots at all.

He chanced a look. Men held hands to their ear-pieces, cursing. One by one, the men lowered their weapons and got back in their cars. Then, inexplicably, they drove away.

"What? Why are they leaving?" Qwiz asked.

Bill frowned as he watched them leave. "I don't know. I don't like it when my enemy doesn't do what I expect them to."

"But we're alive!" Qwiz said.

"For now." Bill squinted into the distance. "Let's get out of here before they change their minds."

They drove a circuitous path back to Bill's apartment. Bill killed the lights on the truck and circled around the block once in the dark to see if anyone was following them. He then whipped into the secure parking structure underneath. Bill normally parked on the street to let the solar array on his truck charge the batteries, but Qwiz doubted they would risk driving it any time soon.

Neither of them saw a black-clad man on a moped that had followed them.

CHAPTER 6:

CERN labs, Geneva, European Union

"Tell me you weren't calling the police," said an ice-cold voice from the door.

Luthor whipped around and in an instant had Eli's gun zeroed on the person in the doorway. It was Vika. Luthor took a deep breath and lowered the sidearm; he hadn't heard her enter. Her hair was up and a long black trench coat concealed her body. It was the middle of the night and she still looked as if she belonged on the home page of Cosmo. Luthor suspected the only thing keeping throngs of photographers from capturing her every movement was her expression, which would have frozen their lenses off.

"No, I called a friend to warn him." Luthor said.

"Did you use his name?"

Luthor thought for a moment and then shook his head. "No, I don't think so."

"Did you call a traceable number that could be linked to him?"

"No, I left my phone there, and called it, so he wouldn't have to pay international phone rates."

"Good. You might have just saved his life."

Luthor was getting tired of the inquisition. "Vika, why are you here? What made you just walk over here at the crack of dawn?'

"I saw gunfire. Tell me what happened." The sheer force of her tone and expectation of being obeyed disconcerted Luthor. It was just too incongruous for Eli's beautiful —if terse—secretary to have a voice like that.

Michael obeyed before he could. "Come see." Michael had not yet mastered his voice, it still quavered as he spoke.

Vika followed Michael to the office, scanning the room like a hawk as she did so. Her eyes lingered longer on the broken sink than the dead bodies, which strangely, didn't seem to faze her. *Who is she? Whatever she is, she's no secretary.*

Eli's corpse was a different story. She sagged against the doorframe as she viewed it. Eli had been dear to her, that much was certain.

"This is what happened." Michael's voice cracked. "They put him on his knees and shot him. They shot him because.... All because I *hesitated* in answering their questions."

Tanya put her hand on Michael's shoulder and whispered something in his ear. His red-rimmed eyes looked grateful for the comment.

Vika remained frozen in the doorway as she absorbed the scene. Abruptly, she turned to address them, as if turning away blotted the grisly event from her memory. "We have one hour, then we must leave."

Luthor ground his teeth. "I understand the danger. But I still think we should call the carbon police and get protection. They just broke about fifteen laws and then murdered Eli on top of it. Why should we run?"

"For the same reasons I've been suggesting all along," Tanya said. "More people will probably come to kill us. If they know these have failed.

"You are right." Vika produced something from her coat pocket, it resembled a watch battery with a tiny wire protruding from the center of the cylinder. "I found this in Eli's office."

Michael leaned in to get a better look. "What is—"

"A bug. It is like the transmitter in your CPI chip,

but more powerful. It could have transmitted several kilometers. I disabled it."

"Wait. Really? What does that mean?" Luthor asked, simultaneously wondering why Vika would even think to look for a listening device.

"It means that they—whoever *they* are— know everything. They will have heard our dinner conversation."

"All the more reason to call the carps."

"If they have the resources to bug Eli, then there is a good chance they have infiltrated the carbon police, or worse."

Luthor felt his face getting flushed and his anger rising. Not good. He took a deep breath, but it didn't help. "What, precisely, is worse than my friend getting murdered, and my life's work almost stolen?"

"They could *be* the carbon police. They could have agents in any part of the EU. Better to not take chances. We have to assume that the EU itself is behind this."

Luthor began to pace in frustration. "This is crazy! If we run we will look like the guilty ones."

"You stay here, you die. Your choice."

Luthor felt his anger unhinge. The broken, dangerous Luthor who had been born in the frozen death of Antarctica broke out of his cage and took control of his body. "How do we know that *you* aren't behind this?" he yelled. "*You* were asking all those questions at dinner. *You somehow* found the bug. *You* were conveniently *not* here when Eli died. And now you want us to run so you can kill us and steal my research for yourself!" Luthor stabbed a finger at Vika. "I'm not listening to one more piece of bullshit that comes out of your mouth. Michael, call the carps."

Luthor stepped closer to Vika. He had no control of his body. He never did when the war-torn part of his mind took control. Antarctica-Luthor— Anti-Luthor— simply wanted to hurt that murdering bitch, make her pay for Eli's death.

Luthor yelled unintelligibly and hurled a coiled fist directly at her face.

In one instant Luthor registered a slight shift in her posture, the next instant his nervous system began transmitting pain signals up his spinal cord. Luthor found himself face-down on the vinyl, his arm cranked behind him at an awkward angle. The pain shocked Luthor back into control, and he wrangled his broken self back into its cage at the center of his mind. He added an extra lock. Trying to hit a woman was a new low, even for him.

Control back firmly in hand, Luthor then began to try to make sense of what had just happened. His neurons struggled to make the connection that Vika had just flung him on the ground like a rag doll and now had him in a hammer lock. Luthor scribbled in his memory, *Mental note: don't get beat up by secretaries.*

She gave his arm another jerk, leaned in and whispered so only he could hear, "If I had wanted to kill you, I would have done it already."

She glared at him for a moment longer, then, seeming satisfied, she released his arm. It slithered back into place slower than it ought to, like an overstretched spring.

"I cared about him too," she said. "He stood up for me when I had nothing, and gave me a job to keep me off the streets. Insult my honor again and it will be the last thing you ever do."

Luthor regretted the whole event. But then again, he always regretted every action he took when he lost control. Tanya glared at him, her arms crossed. In the whole of their relationship, he had never lost control around her so completely. "I'm sorry. I shouldn't—"

Vika cut him off. "You just killed two people and you have PTSD. We have more pressing issues."

Luthor blinked at the declaration.

Tanya glared at Luthor, but addressed Vika. "I still

don't understand why you're so sure some aspect of the government is behind this."

"Because that bug," Vika held it up for all to see, "is *Saber* tech."

Her words echoed in the stunned silence. The Sabers were the EU's most Elite special-forces unit. Their very name struck fear or awe into anyone who heard it. Luthor had interacted briefly with them during the war, they had stopped by the Shackleton base in the foothills of the Trans-Antarctic mountains for supplies for a mission to destroy a Chinese recharging depot. The depot had been destroyed and they made it look like an ice cave-in. Over the course of the entire war they gained a reputation as the most deadly warriors from the entire continent. And whoever was chasing them was using their technology.

"Well that narrows it down," Michael said. "There can't be many people with access to something like that."

"Very few."

"And how do you know what a Saber bug looks like? That's a pretty specific—"

Vika cut him off. "Unimportant. What matters is who is behind this attack."

"Why would anyone go to those lengths to eavesdrop on a physics professor?" Tanya asked.

"It's clear they *already* knew of Luthor's device and only then planted the bug."

"But the only people who knew of my discovery are standing in this room," Luthor said.

"And anyone working for European Intelligence or the Censorship Bureau," Vika said. "Since the beginning of the war, Europe has been recording every phone call, censoring every email. Luthor, you talked with Eli about this over the phone, didn't you?"

Luthor cursed. Everything was spinning so wildly out of control. It felt like jumping out of an airplane.

Vika continued. "They must have intercepted your call, then bugged Eli."

Vika moved to the dead man by the sink. She gestured for Michael to assist her in moving it. The two of them lifted the corpse onto the table.

"Look for identifying markers," Vika instructed.

Luthor was glad for the excuse to focus on something other than his lack of control. He found nothing on the body apart from a stray 6mm casing.

Tanya pointedly moved to the opposite side of the body from where Luthor searched.

"What about this?" she indicated to a large insignia tattooed onto the back of the man's calf.

Vika nodded approvingly.

The faded green ink bore the unmistakable symbol of the Sabers. These men didn't just have Saber-tech, they had actually been *Sabers.*

"Damn!" Michael said. "You're saying we just killed two of them? Badass."

It certainly explained where they got the Gelvar vests and sub-machine guns.

"Definitely bad…ass," Vika said, as if unfamiliar with the way the phrase felt on her tongue. "But if these were two Black Sabers, you would all be dead, and I would not have seen gunshots through the windows."

The Black Sabers were composed of only the top Sabers, and supposedly the most elite force in the world—though Luthor suspected Delta Force might have something to say about that.

"Damn." Michael whistled. "Still, we are alive and they aren't. It means we're pretty good, right?"

"Yes. And it also means I was right. The Sabers implies a connection to the European Government."

Silence sliced the air as the truth sunk in. It was as clear as the amputated toes on Luthor's feet. Someone with enough influence or money to send Sabers after them wanted his research. Someone ruthless enough to kill innocent professors to get what he wanted. A knot coiled up in his throat making it impossible to swallow. Luthor had no idea what to do.

"We must move quickly. We need to get out of Europe. Today."

"What do you mean *we?*" Michael asked.

"I am coming with you." Vika said, as if it were the most obvious thing in the world.

"Why?"

"The closest thing I have ever had to a father was just murdered. You want to end energy scarcity. How many reasons do you want?" She raised an eyebrow at Michael. "You can die, or I can help you and you can live."

Luthor looked hesitantly at Tanya, but she was still too angry with him to offer worthwhile advice. Michael was in no condition to help either. Luthor had to act, so he listened to his gut; it was the only member of their party who seemed to want to offer any assistance. He didn't trust Vika, but a voice deep inside told him that they needed her help. She might be lying, might betray them, but she also seemed to offer the only shred of hope at the moment. Going to the police felt safer on the surface, but would risk exposing themselves to whoever had just tried to kill them.

If Europe alone gained control of 126 it was as good as starting another war. Perhaps it would be one of conquest, once Europe had all the power. Perhaps it would be one initiated by China or the USW over the scarcity of resources. *It would be World War III all over again, people fighting and dying for energy. I can't let that happen again.*

A razor blade stretched before him in his mind. On both sides were death, failure and war. They were all but inevitable if power-grubbing men ended up with his technology. The edge between them held a foggy chance to change the world. It was clear that his forthcoming decision could determine where on the razor they would end up. The only problem was that he had no idea which choice gave him a chance, and which would doom them all. For all he knew both choices were hopeless. Perhaps Vika would stab them in the back, perhaps the carbon police or Sabers would steal his research; maybe it was just a matter of time before he lost this game of Russian roulette crafted by circumstances.

After a moment, he made up his mind. He turned to Vika. "What do we do?" With Sabers after them, they would never make it without help and Vika was the only source of any at the moment.

"Go find me some plastic bags and any small batteries you can find."

#

Unknown location

A man with a southern accent waited impatiently for his phone to establish a secure line to Europe. The Asian and the old man had gotten away, right when they were in his grasp. Not because of any cleverness they possessed, but because he had been fucking called to stand down immediately; they weren't even allowed to follow them! Goddamn orders! There had better be a good reason for that Omega Abort. And now, their trail was completely cold. Chicago didn't spend the smogging credits to run the video cameras on the streets, so there was no way for him to even know the direction they went.

The phone finally routed through the complicated matrix of wires, towers, and satellites required to communicate securely between continents. A cold voice answered. His boss.

He had never been one for subtlety, and didn't bother with small talk. "What the hell were you thinking?"

"You need to be more specific." His boss's normally icy voice was accompanied by annoyance today. Too bad; he had some answering to do.

"I had two men, the research, and all the goddamn 126 within arm's length when you sent me the *Omega Abort* code!"

"What?" his boss seemed to be speechless, rare for him.

"That's what *I* want to know. I'm telling you, I had *everything.* Then I get the code that informs me that my whole goddamn team is supposed to leave immediately and not pursue."

"I never sent any abort code, Omega or otherwise."

Now it was his turn to be speechless. "What?...But it came with your clearance code! How is that possible?"

"I don't know."

"You were the only one who authorized the mission. As far as I know you are the only one outside of my team who even knew it was taking place."

"I had to report to the USW that I was conducting an operation in the Chicago metro area because the President was in town."

"Did they send the code?"

"Impossible. They had no specifics. They don't even know you exist."

"Then it doesn't make any smogging sense! Even if they did know about the operation, you are the only one who knows the codes."

"Then there is only one possibility."

"What?"

"There is a mole on the inside, helping Tenrel."

"A mole?"

"It gets worse. My agents never reported back this morning. The most probable outcome is that Tenrel got away in Geneva."

The Texan cursed violently. “I told you to send more than two men! Shit, now we don’t have anything!”

“As I told you before, my hands were tied. I can’t authorize more than two Sabers *and* keep the mission a secret. Europe is much less lenient with us than America, they would have wanted *details*. I never would have been approved for a hit on a professor.”

“So we’re back to square one. No research, no 126. And now we don’t have the element of surprise either; they know we’re after them!”

“I wouldn’t say that. They still have no idea who we are. And we have taken away the televised stage of the IEC for Tenrel. He won’t have any way to publish his research away before we can stop him. All we need is a new strategy.”

“Okay,” the Texan said, “we have to assume that Tenrel isn’t going to be stupid enough to try to go to the European media with this.”

“We could only be so lucky.”

“If he does go to the media or the carps, we’ll have him. But we have to assume he won’t. Which means he is going to try to get back to the USW. How soon can you get agents to the seabus terminals?”

“A matter of hours. But he has a head start.”

“What if we don’t catch him?”

“That is where the new strategy comes in,” his boss said. “We need to make it impossible for him to sneeze without us knowing about it. Then we track and capture him.”

“How?”

“I will spin the story with the media here, it won’t be too hard to blame all the deaths at CERN on him. What we need is a reason for him to have killed two *carbon cops*.”

“But they weren’t carps– ah I see. You are going to say that our Sabers were regular carps trying to bust a criminal.”

“Sabers are close enough to carbon police anyway. But we will make Tenrel more than a criminal. After the news today he will be a *terrorist;* one who's goal was to bomb the IEC."

"Nobody is going to believe it, the guy is a respected scientist."

"They will if his apartment inexplicably explodes."

He blinked, absorbing the statement. "You want me to blow up his apartment?"

"Search it first of course—in case your two fugitives missed something before they escaped—then blow it up. Make sure it is as destructive as possible, lots of collateral damage."

The Texan smiled. Blowing things up was one of his favorite past-times. "Boom. Instant terrorist. With his face plastered on all the feeds, every smogger from here to China will be looking for him."

"Precisely."

"What about that mole? I don't want Tenrel getting any more *help.*"

"You let me worry about that. For now, just ignore any more codes unless you hear my personal voice telling you to stand down."

"Understood."

"And for carbon's sake, find those two men and recover the research."

#

CERN student labs, Geneva

The four of them began scouring the lab for bags and watch batteries. It hadn't occurred to Tanya, until she brought Vika a few sandwich bags she discovered in Eli's desk, why she would want them. She asked the question.

"It is simple." Vika replied. "We use the batteries to power the CPI chips from the dead.

Use their identities to buy seabus tickets, and sneak

out of the country disguised as them."

"Oh, is that all?" Michael said, "what are we going to do after breakfast?"

Strangely, Vika laughed. Short staccato bursts of mirth.

Michael was right, Vika's plan had no chance of working. The damn Marks were just too brilliantly designed. There was the small problem of them permanently ceasing to function in the event of any interruption in blood-flow. It was a safety feature built into the hemo-kinetic batteries that powered the implanted devices. If the bloodflow stopped at any point, such as might happen in a heart attack, the chip would power down forcing the person to go into a CPI clinic to get their heart checked and replace their mark. It also made it impossible for anyone to steal someone's identity. As soon as it was removed, the mark would stop operating. Naturally, it would also immediately shut down on the event of someone's death. Tanya had often seen it publicized on billboards. It helped deter attempted thefts and increased health awareness.

"So, tell me Vika, how do we manage this?" Michael questioned. "Everyone knows CPI chips are designed to shut down when you die. They have been dead over an hour."

"Look who knows so much." Vika shot back. "The chips themselves are not hemo-kinetic, they are electric. The only thing that shuts down on death is the current that recharges the batteries. If the chips are stored in the subject's own blood and fed the same electrical current as the batteries, they can still operate for 24 hours. We will not have the exact voltage, but we only need them to last six. Just long enough to get on a seabus."

Michael shook his head. "I have never heard of this."

"This is not widely known."

"Not *widely known?* Vika, what you are talking about is supposed to be impossible. How do you know it?"

She merely raised an eyebrow. Those damn eyebrows were perfectly manicured and frustrating as hell. And those eyes, they were gorgeous and piercing. Michael shrunk before her gaze and didn't question her any further. Vika flipped open some sort of utility knife and she deftly sliced away the layer of flesh containing the black man's CPI chip like she was filleting a fish. She plopped the slice in a slim plastic bag and then smothered it in the thick, purpling blood drawn from the man. She worked with a medical precision, removing air from the bag and then tossing it to Michael. He cried out in shock and revulsion, dropping it back on the table before Vika.

"This will be you," Vika said. "Go find another battery."

She continued barking orders to the rest of them while Michael kept rooting around, looking for batteries. The man followed orders like a golden retriever when Vika gave them.

Vika then began to tinker with the battery and the CPI chip. She tangled strands of wire with a fine screwdriver. Tanya didn't know enough about electricity to guess what she was doing, other than that her hands were covered in coagulating blood. Finally, she sealed up the bag with the chip and battery both inside.

"Is this really going to work?" Tanya asked. She had no interest in digging through the flesh of dead bodies for marks.

Vika didn't respond. Instead she placed the bloody bag on the table between them and began taking out gloves. They appeared to be SeeBees, a brand of gloves designed to block the signals produced by a person's CPI chip.

"I gathered these from Eli's home."

Tanya owned her own pair or two of Seebee gloves at home. Almost everyone did, they were the original—and in her opinion—the best looking brand of signal-blocking gloves. After the Paris 2 carbon restriction protocols were enacted in 2027, it became illegal to buy or sell anything without a mark scan. The government then began to place scanning stations everywhere, constantly monitoring and recording everyone's location in real-time. The idea of having the government knowing that much bothered almost everyone. Already forced to scan their marks every time they bought a coke, people hated being scanned every time they entered a building or rode mass transit.

A company quickly found a way to capitalize on people's fear, and developed a glove— the SeeBee—that would block a person's signal, making them invisible to any scanner when they had the gloves on. Consequently, the gloves exploded in popularity. Almost overnight, a billion pairs were sold. Tanya didn't know anyone who didn't own a pair, or a knock-off imitation.

Unfortunately, their popularity became their downfall. Hiding from the new elaborate carbon monitoring system didn't sit well with those in power and it was quickly made illegal to wear any Signal-Blocking glove in public.

Tanya had quit wearing hers altogether after her second ticket for wearing them –she hadn't even seen the stupid carp before he'd appeared and asked to scan her gloved hand. A third ticket meant she would have to take one of those insufferable climate change classes where they would try to scare people into compliance with the carbon laws. Not that she saw much connection between wearing gloves and contributing to global warming; it smelled more like a government power-trip.

Vika made a careful cut on the top of the left glove. She sliced open the top layer of fabric without damaging the delicate mesh underneath that actually blocked the signal, then inserted the new chip right on top of the mesh.

"The glove will block your own signal, allowing the new chip to be the only one detected by the scanner."

Tanya couldn't help but be impressed. If it worked, it was an ingenious plan.

"I will prepare more of these. Sew them shut."

Tanya fished her needle and thread out from her suitcase. They were a necessity for travel. It wasn't like she could just afford to buy new clothes if her pants ripped. You had to be prepared. She grabbed some black thread and got to work. She hoped she did her job correctly. If she did, the glove would block their own signal, conceal the counterfeit mark while still transmitting its signal.

Just as she finished her first glove, she heard yelling. It came from the office.

#

"No!" Luthor shouted. "Absolutely not." He would not abide desecrating Eli just so he could have a disguise. They wanted to burn the bodies so it would take longer for the authorities to identify them. *Not again, I can't handle this again.* Images flashed in his mind. *Dismembered corpses, frozen blood, skeletons in a corner...*

"Don't be stupid. If you don't have— "

"I said no! I will not chop up my friend for my own benefit! He is dead and I will not let you desecrate his body! *Men screaming, dying. Garcia's leg in his hands...*

Vika crossed her arms. "It would be one cut Tenrel. He has a hole blown out of the side of his head."

"No! He was a part of my team." *Fear, Jake's dog tags, hunger.*

"Tenrel, this is not the war any more. You have no team."

"He died. I didn't. Sounds like *war* to me."

"Stop being irrational. He is dead. He does not care."

"But I care!" Luthor shouted. "I will not stand by and let you mutilate his body!" *A burned Chinese man, Chaz's —*

Someone gently touched Luthor's shoulder. He flinched. It was Tanya, he had not seen her enter the office. Her intention was obvious and he shoved her hand away. He did not want to be comforted. He wanted to forget.

"Honey, please listen. I know this is hard, but I think Vika's right." She looked at Vika who squatted next to the body, knife in hand. "There is nothing we can do for him now. If you want to get out of here alive, then we need his Mark."

"Don't cut him. Not that…" Luthor mumbled. "Never again." Another frozen memory tried to resurface. He forced it down.

"That's not Eli. That's just a husk where he used to live. Now he's in a better place."

"I don't want to be preached at right now, Tanya. He's dead, and neither you nor anybody else in this damn world has a clue about what happens after death." Tanya sighed, her sometimes-faith wavering.

Luthor set his jaw, "use the Asian instead. Not Eli. I don't care if you hack that bastard up."

Michael, already wearing a counterfeit CPI chip, shook his head. "Luthor, you aren't Asian. If they check the screen, you won't look anything like him."

"I'm not Middle Eastern either."

"But you have a beard and gray hair, just like Eli, you two are close enough that the Sabers confused him for you."

"Tenrel," Vika said, "you said you wanted my help, so take it. We need three chips; he is the best match for you. Deal with that or turn yourself in now."

Luthor turned and met her stare. She had no idea what she was asking, or of whom she was asking it. His eyes bored into hers. Neither wavered. Like two giants arm wrestling, they stood locked for a long moment. Then Vika blinked. Luthor had won. For the first time since he had met her the night before, his will eclipsed her own. "Sometimes what's best isn't what's right. I will take the risk with the Asian's chip."

He shoved open the doors and walked outside into the brisk, predawn air. None of them understood. None of them could.

CHAPTER 7:

Eleven years ago: Titan Dome, Antarctica

Luthor's parachute guzzled air as it strained to stop him from impaling the ice. He grunted into his mask as the straps that held his chute cut off the circulation to his legs. The Chinese dragon guns lived up to their name; their sprays of bullets were so dense it looked like a solid column of flame. The bullets were gigantic and had such a high velocity they sawed through light armor like an arc-welder through tissue paper. Luthor didn't want to think about what they would do to his body.

His altimeter cranked toward zero, and so did the probability that computer assisted targeting systems would continue to miss him. He floated directly overhead one dragon gun, it was only a matter of time before it locked on to him.

At 100 meters Luthor reached to his waistline and popped the pins of his two grenades.

No sense in saving ordinance if he wasn't alive to use it. He dropped them on top of the massive gun, praying they hit. The seconds ticked away, Luthor continued to descend. At five seconds, two blossoms of fire blasted either side of the massive machine. The gunners in charge of its operation were tossed away like burning voodoo dolls. Heat and shrapnel flew up toward him. His parachute ripped.

He was coming in too fast. He pulled up hard, turning downward momentum into lateral momentum. He bent his knees to cushion his fall as he'd been trained. He hit hard on the ice, rolled and crumpled. Hours of repetition helped him unhitch his straps and draw his MX-5 in one fluid motion. One of the gunners crawled away from the smoldering dragon, clothes burning off his body, while his exposed flesh simultaneously froze in the horrific cold. Luthor rattled off a burst and he slumped to the ground. *Maybe I did him a favor, freezing to death is a shitty way to go.* Luthor crouched low and scanned for other movement. He found none in the immediate vicinity and so he took cover behind the hulk of the Chinese war machine. It looked relatively unharmed. The grenades had impacted on either side of it, licking its carapace with flames without doing much structural damage. He suddenly had an idea.

He climbed the short ladder leading to the gunner's seat. A contorted Chinese corpse greeted him. His lifeless eyes were wide with fear. His frozen arms clutched at his burned body. He had suffered. Luthor shoved the man off the other side with both feet, trying not to dwell on the fact that he had been the one to cause the poor bastard's suffering. *No, this goddamned world caused this man's suffering. Not me. If not for his greedy government making war with my greedy government, no one would have died here today. I didn't kill this man, oil did.*

Sickening syllogism played out before him in a macabre flow chart. *If we don't have enough energy, then we mine Antarctica. If we mine Antarctica then we go to war over the oil. If we go to war over oil, then Luthor Fucking Tenrel kills these poor bastards. Therefore, if we don't have enough energy, I kill. Not my fault. Just deductive, predetermined, irrefutable logic.*

Luthor had no idea how to use a Dragon, but at the end of the day a gun was a gun. Aim and pull the trigger. A large U-shaped control stick dominated the controls, and clear screens overlaid his reticule with real-time targeting data. He tried moving the stick to the right. The hydraulic gears twisted the massive device in that direction. He then shoved it forward. The business end of the weapon moved parallel with the ice. *Time for some more of you to die,* Luthor thought. He aimed it at the nearest enemy gun emplacement. A red light popped up on the screen, indicating a lock.

Luthor took a deep breath. He depressed both triggers and the dragon came to life, roaring with unimaginable ferocity, breathing liquid bullets at his target. With an earth-rattling rumble Luthor felt in his chest as much as he heard, hundreds of bullets lanced out from the beast before the first one found its target. An explosion ripped through the unsuspecting enemy gun as the cold-resistant hydraulic fluid ignited. Moments later the gun smoked, now lifeless, and incapable of taking any more of his people's lives.

It only took seconds to find another target, press the trigger and end more lives. *I'm saving my people,* Luthor thought. It was true. Each gun he downed saved dozens of paratroopers. A deployed parachute was an easy target for the nimble dragons. Luthor destroyed two more. The enemy didn't seem to notice that their own gun was the one blowing them up. Each gunner had tunnel vision, intent on racking up the highest score to report to his Chinese masters.

Soon the entire field smoldered with dead dragons. Luthor and coalition anti-armor ordinance had wiped them out. He climbed out of the seat, accidentally stepping on the dead gunner. The man's exposed fingers cracked like ceramic pottery. No blood spilled, it had already frozen solid in his veins. Luthor carefully avoided the jagged pieces, but couldn't take his eyes off them.

Jake walked up to him. "Nice work Ten! You made a *corpse*sickle!" It wasn't funny. It was another dead man swallowed in Antarctica's insatiable appetite for flesh. Luthor shivered, and for once it wasn't from the cold.

#

CERN student labs, Geneva

They found a dead female guard just outside the door for Tanya. Elizabeth. The Sabers had forced her to open the door with her CPI Chip, then executed her. It wasn't a perfect match, but it would do. Vika had deftly removed the CPI chips and attached them to the batteries with the skill of a surgeon and electrician.

Michael kept trying not to stare. It was hard. Not only was she the most beautiful woman he had ever seen—and that was saying something, he had seen *a lot* of women—but she was intelligent enough to make him feel insecure. That was saying something too. She knew *things*, things that nobody knew. Running a CPI chip without the host was supposed to be impossible. Even the technicians in the CPI clinics just chucked them in the recycle bin when carbon enforcement released upgraded models. No one ever worried about them being stolen. They couldn't be. Or so he thought.

After hooking them up, Vika checked their functionality on the exterior door to the lab. If they were working, the door would register the attempt. Michael was prepared to offer a polite "I told you so" to Vika when they didn't work. They would have to be transmitting a proper signal to work, which –of course—was impossible because the owners of each chip were dead. Vika slid Tanya's glove under the scanner. The door opened. The door beeped and denied entrance for the Sabers' gloves. All three worked.

They drug the three bodies outside and at Vika's instruction lit them on fire. Luthor, after his giant fit about taking Eli's chip, didn't seem to have a problem immolating the others. Smogging strange. Vika had told them that burning the bodies would buy them valuable time.

Apparently, Vika—along with all the other impossible things she knew—understood the inner workings of the Sabers and European Carbon Police. She claimed if the bodies were burned then the local carbon police wouldn't notice the missing CPI chips, nor would they be able to quickly identify the bodies. They would then be forced to do a full autopsy to find their identities and the missing chips. Vika explained that it would be a bad thing if they were caught boarding a seabus with someone else's identity. Her logic made sense. She, on the other hand, didn't.

With the bodies smoldering in the distance, they left the lab with Eli's car. Vika drove.

"Where are we going?" Luthor asked, still terse from his tantrum earlier. Michael had never seen him that angry before. When he left the room, he had looked *powerful.* Like someone important. But there were a lot of things he was learning about his boss, he had never seen him kill anyone before either. Or try to punch a woman.

"The train station. To lose them."

"How do we do that?" Michael asked, trying not to sound as awkward as he felt talking to her.

"That is easy, now that we have their CPI chips."

Unfortunately, she didn't explain how exactly, it would be easy. She just drove in awkward silence the short trip to the train station. Michael shot a questioning look to Luthor, who returned it. She might be hotter than burning magnesium, but Michael felt some serious trust issues developing with Vika.

They parked and walked up to the automated ticket station.

"Each of you buy a ticket with your own chips headed to Paris."

Luthor hissed his disapproval so the queue couldn't hear. "What the hell was the point of carving up three people, if we aren't even going to use their chips! They will know we have been here."

"They already know we are here." Vika said. "Let them think we are going somewhere else. We will actually be headed to Marseille."

Michael realized what she was planning. "This is going to work." Michael stepped forward and slid his hand under the ticket scanner. The faint, overly efficient screen, displayed payment options. He could use his CPI Chip as cash and have it directly withdraw from his bank account or select his credit card. He pushed the Visa icon; it gave him points he could put toward his energy bill. If he was going to die, at least he could afford to have the lights on at his funeral. A train squealed into the station just as they finished purchasing their tickets.

"As soon as you get on, put a regular Seebee glove on and walk back off the train."

Luthor nodded, the old codger seemed to be finally catching on. "The system will have recorded us as traveling to Paris, but we won't be on the train. Smart."

"Will this work?" Tanya asked. "They are going to expect us to have SeeBees. You could do that trick without a CPI forgery."

"They might suspect we did not stay on the train, but they will *know* that we haven't boarded another one," Vika said.

Michael continued. "The train scanners don't check for much except that the ticket and CPI scans match. If our scans don't show up as purchasing another ticket, we can't have gotten on another train."

"So they will have to check here, and they will have to check Paris. But no one will think we have made it back to Marseille," Tanya said.

"And no one will expect us to go there anyway." Luthor said, "that's where we entered the EU in the first place. Good thinking, Vika."

Two minutes later they stepped back on the train, put their gloves on, and stepped back off. For anyone who looked at the data on the massive CPI servers, Luthor Tenrel, Michael Laramy, and Tanya Hazelwood, were all headed north.

#

Luthor wondered again if his phone conversation had been explicit enough. He hoped he hadn't said too much. Vika had been clear that any international calls would be overheard, taped, and scrutinized to the smallest detail by the EU's censors. Whoever had heard Luthor's original phone call was probably listening to it right now. Luthor had not used Qwiz's name or any of his alias's –not that there were many outside of that Vanguard character of his— but who knew what other context clues they would be able to sift out of the conversation. Luthor hoped Qwiz was not yet known to be an accomplice and he yearned to keep it that way. Eli had been shot just for knowing about his discovery.

Besides, what was the 126 after all if not a dead, lifeless thing? It might be important, even a historic fulcrum, but if Luthor had learned anything after fighting and killing people in Antarctica it was that human life had more value than any mere substance. Oil in Antarctica, 126 in a lab, Uranium, hydrogen, natural gas. Whatever. All of it was worthless without human beings to use it and give it worth.

Here he was again, killing people for a substance. *Two men dead by my hand already, two other innocent bystanders too, just from their proximity to my invention.* How many lay frozen in Antarctica, put there by his bullets, for an archeologist in the future to dig up? *Enough that I deserve to die.* Luthor thought, but he was still kicking, and people were dying for it.

Luthor stood by himself in the back of their car, looking out the window. Rolling hills, pock-marked by massive windmills, rumbled by displaying man's vain attempt to feed and power itself within the vacuum of fossil fuels. The entire train ride to Marseille had been eerily silent, each of them alternately staring at their elicit seabus tickets or out the window. No one dared to question if they had done the right thing or not. None of it made any sense. It felt like a dream. A nightmare.

Michael appeared at his shoulder. He had wanted to talk with Luthor. "Do you think we can trust Vika?"

"I don't know. Eli trusted her, and I trust him."

Michael looked behind him furtively. "I don't care, she's hiding something."

"I think she's hiding a lot of things," Luthor replied. "I wouldn't have pegged you to be questioning her after the way you were ogling her last night."

"She might be fine, but she isn't *right*. The shit she knows Luthor… damn. Where the hell does somebody learn how to fake CPI chips?" Michael leaned in and whispered in his ear. "She flipped you like a rag doll and you killed two Sabers!"

"I got lucky…" *But Eli didn't. Because he just happened to be my friend.*

Michael shook his head. "Whatever. The point is…this is crazy. We are running for our lives, four people are dead, and now she just happens to come in and have all the answers. Doesn't that feel a little *convenient* to you? Why is she helping us, really?"

Luthor frowned. It *did* feel like more than coincidence. He had tried to suppress the feeling. "Smog it." He paused, looking the younger man in the eye. "Do we have a choice? We can't very well stay here. And she has helped us this far."

"She might even help us get out of the country, but I don't want to end up floating face down in the middle of the Atlantic."

"Me neither, but we need her right now. Maybe her motives are pure."

"And maybe I'm a virgin."

"Right… regardless, I'm not convinced she is out to

kill us. I feel like if she wanted to do that, she would have already."

"Sure, but there could be something deeper going on here. What if she's working for someone outside the EU and just needs to get us out of the country?"

"Good thought. Just keep your eyes open, okay?"

"I don't mind watching her—already made a fool of myself doing that—but if she's as good as she seems I don't think it will matter."

CHAPTER 8:

Aurora, Illinois, United States of the West

Qwiz had planned to be up all night, but he didn't need the Mountain Dew coursing through his digestive system to keep him awake. He doubted he'd be able to sleep for days. They had split everything related to the 126 between Bill's tiny flat and Qwiz's own apartment down the hall. He hoped his mom wouldn't mind him having world-altering contraband in his room. He hadn't planned to tell her anyway, for her own safety. The idea was to have it in multiple places, in case one of them was caught. That way they wouldn't lose everything. They spread the black boxes around, to diminish the gravity. The hard drives, they hid in Bill's gun safe—after Qwiz copied them to his own backup drive, of course. Qwiz was careful to leave them unplugged so no one could hack in and access them remotely.

Now that they were done hiding the contraband, they walked back through the parking garage entrance into the apartment. There was a suspicious moped Qwiz didn't recognize parked next to the truck. Vehicles were rare enough that Quiz knew all of the normal ones in the garage by sight. He hoped it didn't belong to someone tailing him.

Bill shoved his hands into his armpits as he walked through the CPI scanner imbedded in the entry-way. He looked positively ridiculous.

"Why do you keep doing that?"

"Don't need to give any bureaucrats my location if I can avoid it," Bill replied. "Did you know that armpits can block mark-scans? If you walk through like this, your signal won't get to the receiver."

Qwiz overcame the temptation to roll his eyes. This was a new one for Bill and one of his less-believable ones. The truth was the mini-RFID chips imbedded in their hands had no trouble getting through armpits. They were short-range and omni-directional. Short of an absurdly thick wall or a Faraday Cage, it took a dedicated signal blocker, like a SeeBee glove, to stop a CPI scanner. "You have to know that doesn't work."

"How do you know?" Bill asked. "I didn't realize you'd moved to Europe to work in the CPI databases."

Qwiz sighed, he didn't have the energy to disprove Bill *and* climb the ten flights of stairs to his apartment.

He plopped on Bill's sagging, mite-ridden couch, breathing hard. "How did you do it? I mean, in the war." Qwiz asked. "How can you function after getting shot at?"

Bill took a deep breath. For some reason he had always been very forthcoming about his experiences from his time in Iraq and Afghanistan; most other people who had fought in World War III never said a word about it. Luthor snapped up tighter than 4096-bit encryption if anyone brought it up.

"It's not easy," he scratched his beard, "but the first time is the hardest. Your body just doesn't know how to react when faced with its own death."

"How do you move on? My heart is still thumping in my chest and it's been hours."

"It'll do that. I'm sorry you had to experience it; it ain't fun." Bill put a fatherly hand on his shoulder. "It'll pass."

Qwiz took another deep breath. It helped a little. Maybe.

"But as for me, well… you sort of get used to it." Bill shook his head. "No, that isn't the right way to put it. It's more like you get familiar with it. You learn what it's like to get shot at, to feel the adrenaline pumping, to see your life flash before your eyes. And when you know what to expect, it's easier to handle. You can even use it to do stuff you never thought possible."

"Like when you charged that house full of terrorists?"

Bill huffed. "Yeah. Killed every bastard in that place. They sniped one of my friends and I lost it. That's even worse than getting shot at, seeing your friend die. I hope you never experience that either."

"Me too."

"That life-or-death feeling made me start drinking. It took the edge off a little, but don't. Don't drink your problems away. It's just makes more of them."

Bill didn't drink any more, but had become a violent alcoholic after he returned from Afghanistan. He lost his wife and his son and just about everything else due to the stuff. Qwiz himself didn't drink; Bill was a shining example of why.

Qwiz's father would never approve of trying to escape his problems. Qwiz hadn't seen him in 20 years, but had tried to live out what he had taught him about being a man. He had been called home to serve in the Chinese block before the war started and Qwiz missed him. Even as a child he'd taught Qwiz about honor, honesty, respect, and keeping your word, no matter what. Qwiz thought his dad would be proud of what he had done to honor his word to Luthor. His father had always said, *Courage isn't defined by your deeds, but by what you are willing to lose.*

Qwiz had risked his life.

"Hey, Quency. Wake up." Bill said. Qwiz's head jerked backward as he realized he'd dozed off. The sun lay low on the horizon, its rays streaking through Bill's solitary eastward window. It was beautiful. But that wasn't what Bill had drawn his attention to. It was the small, energy-saving TV.

"They're talking about your boss, Luthor."

Qwiz shook himself to wakefulness and focused on what the USNN anchor was saying. "The blast killed at least

32 people in the apartment, with 17 still missing. We now go live to the scene of the devastation with William Benyard."

Bill's breath caught in his throat as a young, good looking, reporter held the mic in front of the smoldering ruins of an apartment building. At least that's what it had probably been. Smoke drifted up between hunks of brick wall and personal detritus. It looked like the entire right side of the structure had been completely demolished. Rescue workers swarmed over the wreckage like maggots on a dead bird.

Benyard's flowing blond hair ruffled in the breeze as he began to describe the shocking scene. "According to witnesses, the blast ripped through the Rockton apartments in Aurora a few minutes before 5:00 am this morning."

"Bill, that was Luthor's apartment!"

"I know. That's why I woke you up."

Benyard continued. "The explosion was felt by residents over a mile away. It destroyed half of the building, instantly killing 32 innocent people who hadn't yet risen for their morning commute."

The screen panned to a line of white body bags, as the rescue workers pulled another limp body from the rubble.

"There are still at least 17 people unaccounted for, as firemen and other first responders search tirelessly for survivors. But even in the midst of this terrible tragedy, there are signs of hope."

The screen flashed to a gray-haired woman in a soot-stained night gown. "It was like someone picked up my bed and shook it around. I fell and then the whole wall crashed right down on top of my bed. But my neighbor heard me screaming and managed to get me out."

"Its stories like these that keep the brave men and women searching, hoping against all odds to rescue someone who is still trapped," the reporter said. He walked toward the mobile command center the carps had set up. The camera followed smoothly, allowing him to stare into the camera with his piercing blue eyes—eyes that reminded Qwiz of Bill—and continue talking.

"While rescuers work to save residents, the carbon police have been working on another problem: the source of this explosion. What they are finding points to a conspiracy that spans two continents, with possible ties to a notorious terrorist organization."

"That's the sedatives talking, the bastards don't even know they're taking them," Bill said.

"Sedatives?"

"You know the ones they put in the water to keep everyone from rebelling against the government? It's working well if you don't know you're taking them either." Qwiz ignored him.

The camera focused on a balding man wearing the same black and green uniform of the other carbon officers. He stood behind a podium in what looked to be a makeshift press conference area. A subtitle informed Qwiz that it was the Chief of the Aurora Carbon Police.

"Our team of investigators has confirmed that the explosion originated on the second floor of apartment 231, belonging to Fermilab Scientist, Luthor Tenrel."

"We barely escaped in time." Qwiz said. "We would have been vaporized."

"I think they blew it up *because* we escaped," Bill said darkly. "Listen."

"...residue analysis confirms the presence of large quantities of highly volatile materials used in bomb-making."

"What a pile of burning hogshit! Are they are going to frame him for this?" Bill asked.

"We are using every resource available. We are working closely with the Federal Carbon Enforcement Agency. They have revealed that Tenrel was last seen in Geneva, and had planned to attend the International Energy Conference.

Their sources have found a strong connection between Tenrel and the 2180 terrorists."

Bill slammed his fist against the couch. "Those goddamned bastards!"

The stern face of the Chief grew even more serious. "They believe this explosion is part of a larger terrorist plot by 2180 to bomb the IEC itself. It is also suspected that Tenrel was involved in the murders of two carbon police officers in Geneva earlier today."

"That must have been what Luthor was talking about on the phone," Qwiz said.

Bill shushed him as the screen showed an image of Tenrel. It looked like it had been taken from his Fermilab ID badge.

The Chief continued. "We won't know any more until we can bring him into custody. Please inform your local carbon enforcement office if you have seen Tenrel or have any information leading to his capture. Thank you."

A small crowd of reporters blurted questions, but the police chief raised his hands. "No questions at this time."

Qwiz stared at the screen, disbelieving the words popping out of it. "I can't believe this is happening. Luthor would never bomb innocent people."

"He wouldn't." Bill replied matter-of-factly. "I saw his house, there wasn't so much as a firecracker, let alone a lab that could make a bomb that size. Trust me, I've seen bomb making labs. That ain't one of him."

"How can they do this?"

"My best guess—and this is just an old codger throwing crap against the wall to see what sticks—is that he pissed off somebody big enough to publicly frame him on two continents."

"Big enough that they can just murder dozens of people?"

"Big enough that they *don't even care* about murdering

dozens of people."

Qwiz took a deep breath. "He's in deep, Stone."

"*We're* in deep, boy. Like you said, never leave a man behind."

Qwiz breathed a shallow laugh. "I guess you're right."

Bill shrugged. "So Luthor has been framed by some polluted ass-hats as a terrorist. We almost got dead last night and are now his accomplices. But we need to look at the bright side of this whole damned shit-storm."

"What's that?"

"William finally got his big exclusive! He's been waiting to do a report like that for years. Did a good job too."

"You know the reporter?"

"Course I do," Bill said. "He's my son."

#

Marseille, European Union

Usually one seabus left every day, carrying masses of people. Most were old luxury cruise-liners converted to nuclear propulsion and retrofitted to accommodate as many passengers as possible. The one in the dock looked to be a midsize seabus, probably capable of holding 10,000 passengers, not including the crew. While not as large as the behemoth that brought them to Europe, it still towered over them, sitting easily 20 stories out of the water. Luthor felt queasy just seeing something that tall. Smogging heights. Thankfully their economy tickets would place them in dormitories located toward the bottom of the vessel, but they would still have to cross that cursed walkway to enter the ship.

They stood in line, waiting for the inevitable test of Vika's CPI hacking skills. Michael voiced what everyone was thinking. "Vika, is this going to work?"

"We got on the trains, didn't we? This will be similar,

except with an x-ray."

"What if they have ID screens? If Luthor's scan shows up as a smogging Chinese body builder we're going to be boned."

Luthor had opted not to voice the concern because he didn't want to believe it was possible. Somehow hearing something aloud always made it more frightening.

"Europe doesn't spend the credits to power screens for people leaving the country. Only for those entering."

"Easy to get out, hard to get in?"

She didn't respond, apparently it was too obvious a question to warrant a response.

"Just act normal," Tanya said. "If we don't draw attention to ourselves, we should be fine."

Suddenly Tanya pursed her lips: her thinking face. Luthor had seen that face before, and knew enough to get out of the way. Tanya turned to Vika. "You need to unbutton your shirt a bit."

Vika's expression would have killed a puppy. "I will not."

Tanya smiled mischievously. "You said you wanted to help us. Here's your chance. If you make yourself look as sexy as possible, and then go first, security won't be thinking about us. They'll be thinking about you. You are the only one of us who doesn't need a fake Mark, so if they search you, it won't matter."

"I will not be an object for them to lust after."

"Too late for that. Your parents made sure you didn't have a choice. We just need to spice you up a bit."

"What if there are female carps?" Michael asked.

Tanya shook her head. "If you are worried about that, then you clearly don't know the first thing about how women think. They will be even more distracted than the men. They will hate her because she's beautiful, be jealous of the attention she's getting, and thinking up enough synonyms for *whore* to fill a thesaurus. They will think about her for rest of the day if we do this right.

"Now Vika, give me your trench coat, and for God's sake, let down your hair."

Luthor had to hand it to Tanya, she did great work. Vika's dark hair was down and flowing, Tanya had done something with makeup around her eyes to emphasize them alluringly, and she was definitely showing more skin. Luthor had trouble not staring, though had enough self-control to not do so in Tanya's presence. Vika would certainly be an excellent distraction.

By the time they reached the front of the line, both guards in their line were openly gaping at Vika every chance they got. Hopeful smiles plastered their faces as she placed her hand under the scanner. She scowled so fiercely at them, Luthor half-expected to see laser beams lance out of her eyes and burn theirs out.

"Thank you, miss," one of them offered.

"Have a good day," said the other.

Vika grunted something and frowned forward in the line.

Tanya's tactic worked, the rest of them waltzed through the checkpoint, their CPI chips beeping pleasantly under the scanners as they matched with their tickets.

Several long minutes later as they regrouped with their luggage, Vika snatched her coat back from Tanya.

"See, I told you that would work! They never even glanced twice at our gloves."

Vika arched an eyebrow, it loomed like a big sister about to strike a younger sibling. "If you ever ask me to do that again, I will tear your throat out."

Tanya winced.

Luthor put his arm around his frightened girlfriend and smiled, "Look on the bright side, at least you don't have to worry about drama with her. You always know *exactly* how she feels."

Despite their worries, they made it through the rest of security with surprising ease.

They stashed their meager luggage in a locker between four bunks in dorm 5E. It held 46 other bunks. They could have chosen to get a private room, but opted instead for the anonymity of the economy dormitories.

The CPI chips still had a few hours of life in them—or so Vika had told them—and now Luthor didn't see any reason to doubt that. It occurred to Luthor for the first time that he had access to all the Asian's accounts. He had access to his digital wallet, ID, credit cards, all through a scan of his hand. They had all purchased expensive trans-Atlantic seabus tickets with no problem. Why shouldn't he spend a bit more? Two small meals a day were included on the voyage, but the drinks, not so much. Besides, it was always easier to tolerate the heights of a seabus with some libations. Everyone agreed that a drink would help take the edge off the worst day of their lives.

The drinks were outrageously expensive, but Luthor couldn't care less. He was spending a murderer's money and only had an hour to do it. It didn't take long before two rounds of shots went burning down their throats and a pitcher of a beautiful brown ale from Germany graced their glasses.

As Luthor raised the ale to his lips he noticed a horrified expression on Tanya's face. "What is it?"

"Look at the screen," she said, pointing toward the TV. A USNN broadcast panned over the ruins of a bombed-out building. A handsome young reporter with luscious blond hair and piercing blue eyes named William Benyard began to tell the story of an explosion that had rocked Aurora, Illinois early that morning.

#

Somewhere in the mid-Atlantic

Seeing Luthor's face on the news with the word *terrorist* underneath had terrified Tanya, she had hardly spoken with anyone outside of their group for fear of being found by someone in carbon enforcement. Each had done what they could to modify their appearances. Michael shaved his head, Luthor scraped off his beard and dyed his graying brown hair black. Tanya herself had cut 8 inches from her auburn locks and gave herself bangs. She hated bangs, she hated them a lot. Leaving them long made them impossible to keep out of her eyes, but cutting them short looked positively revolting. She just hoped her forehead didn't break out in acne like it had when she was a teenager and first developed her hatred for them.

There was no way to explain away Eli's death, but time, even a few days, had taken the sharpest edges off the gash that his murder had made on her psyche. Crying no longer ambushed her without warning, it came on slowly, predictably, and she had been able to confine it to her solitary bathroom breaks.

Mostly.

Instead of crying all the time, a question had nestled down deep in her mind; it plagued her unoccupied thoughts. Who were they, these people who can summon Sabers and manipulate the news? She didn't even know what to fear—who to fear. They had tried to steal the 126 and were influential enough to corrupt the media's portrayal of the battle in the CERN lab. They were powerful. They could be anywhere. Literally, anything she did could be the thing that gave them all away.

Fortunately, despite their best efforts to the contrary, the men who had killed Eli had failed to steal Luthor's laptop. All of Luthor's research was safe—assuming they could ever get the water-logged device to boot up. That meant all they had to do was to get back to the states and they would hopefully be home free—so to speak. In the USW they had the benefit of being citizens, so even if they were arrested for their supposed crimes, they would have the chance to present their case in court. A big-time trial would work just as well as anything to publish the research, and potentially clear their names.

Tanya was delighted to discover a distraction that helped take her mind off the minor problem of being an international fugitive: the 126 itself. It was bizarre. It had caused her to be more interested in an inanimate object than on people for the first time in her life. Which she figured was okay so long as she didn't actually turn into a scientist like Luthor. *God, don't let me become a scientist.*

As crazy as the enhanced gravity was, he had repeatedly emphasized that the synthesis of 126 – not its properties—was the truly remarkable discovery. Before, scientists had only been able to produce single atoms at a time. Luthor was pumping out thousands, if not tens of thousands, in a single reaction. He had told her about it several times. It had to do with specific voltages and frequencies in the cyclotron. It was all very technical. All she knew for certain was that he had gotten lucky in finding two cheap elements that combined to form element 126, he got them both as byproducts from a nearby Nuclear power plant, depleted Uranium and a fancy isotope of Krypton. They sped up the Krypton in the accelerator and shot it at the Uranium. Luthor often said that the two elements "really liked to fuse together." Apparently, they combined, ejected a few protons and neutrons and settled into the stable form of element 126. Or at least she thought that was how it worked after Luthor's continual explaining; he wasn't a very good teacher. After a year of production, they had a measurable amount of the new element. In larger quantities, it did some unbelievable things.

Right now she was witnessing one such phenomena. She sat in one of the game rooms, transfixed on Michael. He stood calmly in the center of the room.

Upside down.

On the ceiling.

Good thing they had shut the blinds and jammed the door. He might give an innocent old checker-player a heart attack. He turned toward her, his normally winning smile now felt very wrong. But then, someone standing upside down was always wrong. He smiled and Tanya noticed a fresh cut about two centimeters long over his left eye. "What do you think Tanya? Want to give it a try?"

"I'll pass." She had a short list of adrenaline-filled activities that she had permanently banned from her life. Defying gravity edged dangerously close to all of them.

"Your loss." Michael pointed toward a small tape measure on the ground. "Will you do me a favor and measure this for me? I'm doing a little experiment."

"Measure what?"

"From this point here," He pointed to a small strip of tape on the ceiling where he was standing, "to where I fall off. I'm testing the effective range of the 126 in different concentrations."

Michael shuffled forward on the ceiling. After he had progressed half a meter, he slowly began floating away from the ceiling like a balloon without enough helium. "This is so cool!" he exclaimed. Michael imitated an astronaut as he reoriented himself to earth's gravity. He gradually gained speed until he thumped, butt-first, on a table. He grinned ear to ear. "I am telling you, I have never felt anything like this! So, how far did I make it?" She held the tape measure up, "about 50 centimeters."

"Wonderful," he said, jotting a note on a hand-written chart on the table. He placed a strange orange ball of goo on the table next to him. An extra pen that had been perfectly content, suddenly rolled toward it.

The violently orange polymer was Eli's artificial Gecko's feet. The bottom of a gecko's paws had a unique structure allowing them to walk up even something as smooth as glass like Spiderman. Now they had incased the beads of 126 from Luthor's generator to small lumps of Eli's polymer and were having a little too much fun playing with them.

Michael hefted the orange substance in his hand, admiring it. "I wish we had had a handful of this stuff six months ago. Who knows when we will need to be able climb walls?"

"Or hide on the ceiling?" said Luthor.

Tanya tried to suppress her gag reflex as the nerdiness quotient in the room approached toxic levels. She moved closer to Vika, hoping for some semi-normal company. Vika wasn't exactly typical, but she was far better than the alternative which was currently as testosterone flooded as a sperm bank.

Now that they were safely on the boat Tanya had gotten to know the enigmatic woman a little better. Vika had settled into the routine of being ridiculously good looking. Her other hobbies appeared to be scowling and brooding, both of which were better than masturbating to science.

Michael stood on the table, braced a hand against the ceiling and removed the little putty ball. He handed it to Luthor, "your turn," he looked the older man in the eyes, "remember, this thing is constantly pulling things toward it no matter where it is. Be careful."

"I know. I discovered the property!"

"It's different when you experience it, old man."

Luthor took the ball of goo and tossed it against the varnished wall next to him. It stuck perfectly, about 10 cm from the ceiling. As soon as the 126 left his hand, Luthor's feet started sliding along the ground toward the wall. He slipped and fell as he slid into the new gravity well. He started wailing pathetically as he was pulled off his back and bounced up against the wooden panels. "Oh crap, crap.

Help!" he cried.

Tanya and Michael burst out laughing. It was one of the most ridiculous things she had ever seen, she just wished she'd had a video of it. She would've watched it every day. Luthor eventually managed to remove the 126 from the wall, allowing earth's gravity to regain superiority over him and the 126. He fell foolishly to the floor.

Luthor breathed heavily, but didn't seem to notice everyone laughing at him. "That concentration has an effective radius of about two meters laterally, while only half a meter vertically."

"That must be because when you are upside down you are fighting directly against earth's gravity. When it's next to you it doesn't have to be able to counteract your whole weight to move you. It just has to slide you a little bit until you get into the effective radius of the gravity dimple." Michael said, jotting another note on his lengthening chart.

"Gravity dimple?" Tanya said incredulously, "you don't have a better term than that? Sounds like you are describing an elementary school kid. Oh, look at your cute little gravity dimples!"

Vika smiled, which Tanya had discovered was equivalent to another person snorting with uncontrolled laughter.

"But that's what it is!" Michael said, looking genuinely offended. He must have come up with the term. "Earth's gravity bends spacetime over a gigantic volume. We're talking a radius measured in millions of kilometers. 126 just *dimples it* a little over a very small space. Like one of those little holes on a golf ball. A couple of meters wide, that's it. Come on, stop laughing, it's the perfect descriptor for the phenomenon." Tanya laughed harder as Michael struggled to make "dimple" sound cool. It felt really good to laugh again.

Michael pointedly turned toward Luthor, ignoring her. "Why don't we see what happens with double that concentration?" he suggested.

"Good idea," Vika said. "Give it to me."

Michael looked troubled. He consistently appeared to be afraid of Vika. Tanya didn't fully trust her either, but she suspected Michael feared her due to the fact that she was completely immune to his charms—probably a new experience for him. He didn't know how to react around a woman he couldn't seduce. But he couldn't leave her alone either; she was just too gorgeous. He was too terrified to make a move, but too dumbstruck to have the good sense to give up.

Luckily, Luthor came to his rescue. He mashed two of the balls of 126 together like silly putty and handed them to Vika. Tanya felt her stomach churn as the gravity altered around her. Gravity was one of those things one takes for granted. It had always pulled her down her whole life and she wanted to keep it that way. She leaned slightly against the new center of gravity to keep her balance. She adjusted instinctually, avoiding looking as spectacularly stupid as Luthor.

Vika didn't seemed perturbed at all by the change caused by the *gravity dimple.* She rolled it around in her hand, testing its weight. Both beads wrapped together with the polymer weren't the size of a ping-pong ball. A nearby chair shifted ominously, sliding toward Vika. Without warning, Vika started sprinting across the room. Vaulting up on the table, she took a flying leap at the far wall. She threw the 126 against the wallboards and spun mid-air to land feet first against the wall. She crouched, unnaturally parallel to the floor, bracing herself with her hand to balance against earth's gravity.

Michael stared open mouthed at the feat of balance and athleticism. Tanya herself didn't really know what the appropriate response was, so she started clapping. It made sense. Luthor and Michael joined in.

"I like this," Vika said, looking up at them. She removed it from the wall, landed on the floor adroitly. She put a hand on the table and tossed the little ball back to

Luthor. As the ball passed Michael, he lurched, almost face-planting, Luthor fell toward it tripping and crumpling again. The chair slid and fell on top of him. He grunted in surprise. Tanya stifled another laugh.

"Brace yourself when it is in motion," she said, slapping her hand on the table in emphasis, "or you will look like a fool."

"Not that he needs much help with that," Tanya said under her breath.

"Like Laramy said, 'they are always pulling.'"

"Yes, and with a lot more smogging force that time," Michael said, "that had to be almost double the power of our first concentration."

"How did you do that?" Luthor asked, hoisting himself up from the ground, "I can't even keep my feet."

"Remember where gravity is pulling you," she said, as if flipping halfway across the room was the simplest thing in the world. Those two had been playing with 126 for almost a year—albeit without Eli's goo—she had seen it for less than a week and made them look like they were still potty-training. "Know where down is going to be."

"You have a point." Michael said, seemingly reluctant to admit she could teach them something about their own element. It was a rare effort at humility from him. "We have to be proactive and always think of wherever the 126 is as *down*. Like this," he threw a third lump of 126 up which promptly stuck to the ceiling. His body began rising off the floor; Michael struggled to swing his feet above him. He tucked at the last second and managed a kind of roll that left him standing, upside down, at the end of it. He seemed very pleased at himself for not falling again. "I need to think of the ceiling as the floor, and you guys are all upside down."

Tanya didn't want to egg them on, but she couldn't help it. The stuff was fascinating; particularly when paired with Eli's adhesive polymer. It was also a safe bet that no one, at any other time in history had ever played with altered gravity before. There was an irresistible appeal to be the first. So—knowing very well the risk she was taking—she asked her question. "If that stuff counteracts Earth's gravity, why doesn't it float?"

Michael smiled. "It doesn't really counteract earth's gravity. It has its own miniature gravity field. A *gravity dimple*, remember? If you are between the fields then you will fall toward the one with the greater relative gravity."

Luthor chimed in, evidently happy to have the attention away from his balancing failures. "It's still affected by Earth's gravity even though it has its own," Luthor said, "like the Moon and the Earth. The Earth's gravity affects the Moon enough to keep it in orbit around us, but if you get close enough to the moon, it will still pull you in. That's why men can walk on the moon without floating into space toward earth. 126 behaves like a very, very small moon."

"It's also why we can walk around on earth without getting sucked into the sun," Michael added.

Tanya thought she was catching on. "So normally it would still fall to the ground, but when it's stuck to a wall or ceiling it pulls you toward it."

"You got it, girl." Michael said hefting a ball of 126, "this little guy doesn't weigh very much, so the polymer only has to counteract a couple grams of weight."

"Why doesn't it get pulled off when you are standing on the ceiling? You weigh more than that."

"Because the earth pulls on each different object independently," Luthor said.

"Don't you mean that the Earth bends spacetime and each individual object traverses that field independently?" Michael asked.

"Yes, but I am trying not to confuse her."

"The polymer doesn't have to hold up my weight," Michael said, "it only has to hold up itself and this little bead of 126."

"Even if I am standing in its gravity dimple, the whole bead of 126 still only weighs a gram or two with respect to the earth." Luthor indicated to the small plastic bearing, where they encased several hundred thousand atoms of element 126.

"I don't add any weight to it at all by standing next to it. It still weighs the same.

"What happens if you pick it up while you're upside down?" Tanya asked.

"This happens." Michael pointed to the wound over his eye. "It dropped me right on my face. When I picked it up, it was no longer being held to the wall so it got pulled back down with me."

"I guess that makes sense. That's why we can hold it and not float away."

"Exactly," Michael said. "You know Luthor, she's pretty smart. You're the big boy scientist, and you don't seem to have figured it out yet." Tanya smiled. *Brownie points for you Michael.*

Luthor made a face, but ignored him.

The concept of bending space was just weird. She had seen it demonstrated in college. The professor used a suspended bed sheet with a ball sinking down in the middle. Stuff rolling toward the ball was supposed to help them visualize how gravity worked with planets. The sheet bent around the heavy ball and the lighter stuff rolled in toward it. It painted a nice mental picture, but it never really satisfied. Bed sheets were 2D bending in a third dimension. Space was already 3D, so how could it be bent in a fourth dimension? Weird. It was the kind of thing that only made sense in math, not reality. As a result, it didn't make sense to her. 126 only altered gravity locally, so it was like a mini divot in the vast curve of space caused by Earth. Or something like that. She preferred the complexities of human history over the unfathomable mysteries of physics. She was out of her element here.

Vika shook her head. "Don't be such a man. This is how 126 works." She threw some 126 at the ceiling above Tanya. It stuck there.

Tanya froze. The sensation she experienced was immediate and unforgettable. She felt like someone had taken 50 kilograms off her shoulders; she realized she was totally weightless. Her feet drifted off the ground and she floated toward the ceiling. Her instincts did not fail her. She rotated around to have her feet facing the ceiling which had instantly become down. As she gravitated up, she felt the weight flow back into her limbs. It was like getting the sensation back after her leg had fallen asleep. It started with her feet and progressed up toward the extremities closer to the floor. She hit the ceiling standing and though she was upside down she still felt strangely normal. It was everyone else who was upside down, not her. Apart from being a little light headed, but that was understandable, she was defying gravity.

A thrill rushed through her as she realized what she had just done. She looked around seeing everyone upside down. "Okay first, Vika, you're dead. Second, thank you!"

For some reason Vika seemed to think Tanya threatening her life was hilarious. Tanya tried to laugh with her, but her head still felt very wrong, like it was being pulled in the wrong direction. She took small steps away from the 126 just like she had seen Michael do. In seconds she was back on the floor, head feeling normal. Tanya massaged her temples.

"Your head hurt too?" Michael asked.

Tanya nodded.

"I finally figured out why we've been getting headaches since trying this. The outside edge of the 126's influence is weaker, so the farther you are away the less it pulls on you. Your head was probably being pulled more by the earth than by this thing. While you were standing there, you were actually being yanked in opposite directions," he said as he jumped up to retrieve the 126.

It made sense to Tanya, and somehow helped, knowing she wasn't crazy. It was also a little unnerving to think about being pulled by two opposite gravitational fields at once.

The speakers crackled, a voice boomed in French, "Your attention please. We are requesting everyone move to their respective sleeping quarters for a mandatory CPI inspection. You have 15 minutes to be in your dormitories or rooms."

The message then began to repeat in other languages. The English translation would come soon.

Tanya looked at Vika, she was the only other one who had understood the message.

"They know we're here."

CHAPTER 9:

Aurora, Illinois, United States of the West

Qwiz flopped into his computer chair, and flipped open his laptop—while still very capable, it barely held a candle to the power of his old rig. The jerks had blown it up while it sat in Luthor's apartment. Qwiz missed the venerable *Norquist*, but was thankful to have a powerful laptop in reserve.

Today was his day to receive emails from his father. His father had been an ambassador for the Chinese before the conflicts leading up to World War III. He'd been called home as tensions escalated. He was forced to leave his wife and only child. China wouldn't accept them because they were American citizens. Qwiz had managed to keep in touch with his father all that time through heavily-censored, weekly emails. The Chinese Block didn't allow communications from their officials to the West any more frequently than that.

Qwiz clacked another password, unlocking his email. He never saved any passwords; it seemed to defeated the purpose. Sure enough, there was a new message from his father in his inbox. In the post-war years since communication lines were reopened, he had never missed a week. Qwiz depressed his index finger on his 12,000 DPI laser mouse, opening the message. A bitter laugh forced its way out of his mouth as he saw the extent of the unapologetic censorship. Unnatural spaces perforated the entirety of the message making it a challenge, as usual, to read.

He had learned over the years about the multiple

layers of censorship that were involved with even casual communication with China. When his father sent a message it was first screened by whatever agency he now worked for —in years of reading messages, the specific level of government and father's current role was still a mystery. After his agency approved the message, it was screened again by the Chinese censorship bureau. Then the message was sent from behind the Great Firewall of China, through a network of communication satellites and entered the USW intelligence bureau pipeline. There it underwent yet more scrutiny until, after being read by untold American censors, it ended up in his mailbox.

Qwiz began his ritual of reading any message from his father. First, he ran the message through the browser's grammar check. Small green underlines popped up everywhere, marking additional spaces where words had been deleted. The governments never seemed to bother rewriting the message, they simply deleted any perceived national security threats leaving a single extra space to mark their ingress. Unfortunately, he never had any idea how many words had been deleted, it could have been entire paragraphs or a single word. All he was able to see were those annoying green lines. After the grammar check he then skimmed the message inserting underscores to emphasize where words had been removed. Then began the tedious job of trying to decipher what his father had been trying to say to him. His current message was worse than most:

Dear Quency,

I am ______ today. I hope this email finds ______ health. Remember how I told you about the ________? The ______ was very impressed with my work on ________ and has decided to_______. At the end________ will result in a net____for me. I doubt that _______ will reach you____ uncensored ________ try. This _________ 40th anniversary for

_________ and ________. I miss______.

I am delighted _______ Chinese ________ conference. I earnestly ________ better relations between _________ future. Perhaps that means ________. I look forward to that day.

Thank you for always replying. I know _________ difficult. _______. proud of you. _________.

Blessings _______ .

Courage_________,

Your father,

____

Qwiz let his breath out again in another bitter laugh. *They even sensor the name of my own father. What could someone possibly gain through knowing a name?* It was clear from the slash and burn editing process used by the censors that they didn't care if any actual content managed to squeeze through so long as no unintended messages did. Qwiz had wondered often during his disjointed conversations with his father if their respective countries had a censorship quota when reading emails. They probably didn't care which words they removed so long as they removed a certain number of words per page. That way they could destroy any secret code imbedded in the message.

His eyes lingered on the last lines of the message: "proud of you." Bill had said the same thing to him during their escape. He sincerely hoped his father knew how hard he worked to be worthy of those words.

Thanks to the zealous censorship he probably had no idea about the sort of man Qwiz had truly become. He always tried to live by his Father's motto, which he always used as his salutation. Today it had been censored, it should have read, "Courage isn't defined by what you do, but by what you are willing to lose." Father had always tried to instill the importance of living with honor and the use of strength and honor to accomplish good deeds. He had been successful in that task. At least Qwiz earnestly hoped he had been.

#

Obscured by an empty two liter bottle of soda, Qwiz noticed the clock on his monitor read 1:30 am. His computer science degree and extensive video game collection had conditioned him for this sort of marathon. But he wasn't frantically troubleshooting code or head-shotting aliens. Now that he was back safely in his mother's apartment, he pursued a different task: research. It had consumed every spare moment of his time since the incident, and every spare thought.

It haunted him that he'd been forced to flee like a coward as he watched SUVs run over innocent poor people. Heroes didn't do that. Heroes stopped the bad guys before they killed people. *I guess I'm not a hero,* Qwiz thought bitterly. He hoped to redeem himself by finding out who was responsible. Inevitably, Luthor knew more about what was going on and Qwiz needed to catch up in order to help him.

Despite Qwiz's failure to be a hero, his sidekick had never faltered. Stone sat with him in his cramped room and they had read and reread every document, periodical, and commentary they could find on Luthor's supposed terrorism in Geneva. It was clearer than ever that the whole thing had been fabricated.

The rampant inconsistencies they'd uncovered would never have occurred in a true terrorist plot. Most of the papers claimed Luthor's team was affiliated with 2180, but a major paper from Italy claimed that Luthor was with Chinese agents trying to kill important allied scientists. That particular irregularity had been fixed hours after it had been posted, but Qwiz had been lucky enough to catch it before it had been retconned. Others disagreed on the number of members of his team. In some Luthor was a lone wolf, others said he had as many as four collaborators. In fact, the only elements of the story devoid of discrepancies were Luthor Tenrel's name and his intent to set off a bomb at the International Energy Conference as an act of environmental terrorism.

None of that helped him figure out who was masterminding—or bankrolling—the propaganda against Luthor. Their initial guess had been a multinational green energy corporation. They seemed to have the most to lose if Luthor managed to publicize their research on element 126. All of their current infrastructures and products would be made completely obsolete overnight. Wind generators, effective but expensive, and the ubiquitous photovoltaic cells would be a thing of the past. With 126 there would truly be no need for alternative energy.

Why make an alternative to unlimited, perfectly clean, and free?

The only problem with his hypothesis was that there was not one shred of evidence substantiating it. Qwiz had checked out SOLmax photovoltaics, the massive company located in Phoenix that kept the city from sinking into the desert. He had hacked into the intranets of Thanex Energy and Lidius and unearthed nothing. It was infuriating, but Qwiz felt he had no choice but to move on and search for something else, or somewhere else.

The problem had been finding entities powerful enough to make people disappear, fund personal armies to blow up apartments, and have the influence to counterfeit international news. Bill supplied a constant stream of new conspiracy theories to track down. The old man lay on the floor with his tablet braced against his knees like a teenager messaging a crush. It was almost two in the morning, but he needed some new leads and the old man hardly ever slept. He said he hated dreaming. Qwiz himself loved dreams, he got to have grand adventures every night.

"Stop trolling the forums, Stone. We still have more

work to do."

"Did you finally crack into Thanex? They're one of the largest green companies in the world."

"I finished it an hour ago. I haven't found anything that could explain how Luthor's been framed so completely."

"The media sure is smoking something good. Or else they have an imagination bigger than my—"

"I'm sure it's a big imagination, Stone," Qwiz finished hurriedly. Bill laughed. He had heard enough such comparisons to infer where it had been going.

"I guess it's time for plan B then, huh?"

Qwiz was not excited about Plan B. Plan B was trying to hack into the EU network to see if they were behind it. "It is going to be a challenge without my desktop."

"You're a goddamned genius, Quency. You can do it."

Bill didn't understand. Hacking was a not a secret magic button that only IT professionals could press. It involved decryption programs and algorithms, luck, and an intimate knowledge of the systems and subsystems he was trying to bust into. Much of that would be much more difficult—if not impossible—without the massive processing power of *Norquist*.

"I might be able to do it, but I am worried."

"About what?"

"About somebody in the censorship department getting suspicious of our browsing history. I've been spoofing our IP addresses and running some other counter-measure programs, but you can't truly hide anything. If someone really wanted to find out what we're doing they could. Hacking into federal-anything is a criminal act. And I'm not sure if I could even do it."

Bill scratched his beard thoughtfully. He was a much smarter man than he liked to let on, hiding it with his *Stone* persona. Apart from his rampant conspiracy theories, Qwiz appreciated his insights.

"So you think hacking in to the EU is too dangerous," Bill said. "But is there a way that you can get access legally? I mean, without hacking?"

Qwiz thought for a moment. "Well, yes actually. It's a lot harder than breaking in, but if I could get my hands on a user-name and password of a sufficiently high-ranking official, I could have access to the whole network—or at least most of it."

"Let's get on it then," Bill said, "what can I do?"

"Start searching the feeds for EU officials who have current scandals, they would be most vulnerable. We'll get a list together and start searching."

Bill began clacking away. And Qwiz went back to his own computer. He checked his email briefly and found a strange new message with an unknown attachment. The sender had clearly used a throwaway email address, judging by the spam-tastic characters it contained. The title was equal parts intriguing and frightening. It simply read: **Help.**

Qwiz quickly opened the message. There was no greeting or salutation.

If you are reading this, I am glad you are still alive. I hope this helps in your search.

Username: pjrangpart.eu.bc

Password: 435Sabemas534

Input the password into the attached program. I trust you will know what to do with it. Good luck. I will continue to send help when I can.

Qwiz stared at the email. He read it repeatedly, still not quite believing what he saw. Bill came over and read the message over his shoulder.

"Son-of-a-bitch," Bill said, "I told you they bugged every apartment in the States. We were just talking about passwords."

"I don't think they were listening, this was sent over an hour ago."

Bill humphed. "Then what the shit is going on?"

"I see only two possibilities," Qwiz said. "This could be a trap from the same people who tried to kill us. They found out who we were and are trying to locate us. If I open up that attachment, it will tell them where we are."

"And the second possibility?"

"Someone is legitimately trying to help us, and just gave us the key to unlock the EU government network. That would also mean that Europe is definitely behind everything."

Bill scratched his beard, saying nothing for some time. Finally, he said, "I don't think that first possibility makes sense."

"Why not?"

"Cause if they knew enough to send you an email, then they could have found out where we lived. They wouldn't need a tracking program. They would have already stormed the apartment, killed us, and grabbed everything. Why send an email? They gotta know you would see it as a trap, it would just warn you to get out of here." Bill shook his head, "nah, this is something else; it ain't a trap."

"Then who is helping us? And why?"

"Smog-it if I know. But this ain't the first time someone has helped us. Remember when they had us pinned against the wall, but just left? That's been chafing my balls since it happened; it didn't make sense. But if there is someone on the inside who wants to see Luthor succeed, then maybe this is from them. Maybe they were the ones who called off those SUVs."

"You think I should open the attachment."

"I think it isn't a virus. Doesn't mean you should open it."

"If this really is from a good guy, then this might be

a scrambling program. Basically, it takes an approved password and username combo and mixes it all up and changes it to make it unhackable. It's an extra layer of security to their network. Even if I got a username and password, they wouldn't do any good without this program."

"I think you should open it."

Qwiz was inclined to agree. He downloaded the program, disconnected the internet, unplugged the router, and pulled out the wireless card from the laptop's motherboard. If the thing was a virus, at least it wouldn't be able to broadcast their location. He scanned the program's code, but didn't see any hallmarks of a virus.

He executed the file and held his breath.

A simple input screen appeared. Qwiz input the information provided in the email and hesitantly hit *enter*. The program worked for a second and then provided a re-arranged password and login. Underneath, a red timer clicked down from five minutes.

"The program encrypts the password with a timestamp," Qwiz said. "It will expire in five minutes."

Bill slapped his calloused hands together. "Hot damn. Thank you—whoever-the-hell you are."

Qwiz quickly began plugging things back in. It was time to get to work.

#

Somewhere in the Mid Atlantic

"Took them longer than I expected," Vika said, as the panicked faces of the men absorbed the message.

Tanya shook her head "You knew they would discover us eventually? And you didn't tell us?"

"Of course they would find out. There are guaranteed to be at least a couple of carbon agents on every seabus."

"Damn it Vika, how were we supposed to know that?"

Luthor said.

"What did you think was going to happen when they identified the bodies?"

Tanya frowned. Vika was right. Again. She should have known a dead person buying a seabus ticket would raise some eyebrows in any homicide investigation. They might not have enough electricity to waste on security cameras any more, but they could still afford a phone call to catch an escaping fugitive.

"We should have been planning something at least." Michael said. "Now they've got us with our pants down."

"It would not have mattered," Vika said.

Michael looked frantic. "Why not? We have been here for days, we could have found a place to hide. Something!"

"We are on a boat," she said simply. The implication was obvious. *No place to hide.*

Michael turned to Luthor. "I told you she was going to stab us in the back once we got out of Europe. And now look at us. There is no way they will let us off into American territory. We will get shipped off and tried as terrorists." Michael glowered, "that is if *she* doesn't kill us first."

Vika had confounded Tanya's best attempts at empathy and this bombshell sounded every trust alarm in Tanya's mind. Michael had been expecting an imminent double-cross, now that they were in international waters. Michael also expected her to build a submarine from spare parts around the ship, and use the 126 to power her escape. But Vika had *risked her life* to help them. For all her quirks and severe manner, Vika *had* gotten them on the boat, and out of the EU. That was certainly worth a measure of good faith.

Tanya didn't understand it, but she didn't always need to. Sometimes she just *felt* something. She'd always supposed it was God speaking to her in that "quiet whisper" her parents were always preaching about. Despite her parents' warnings, the feeling didn't leave when she got her Mark even though getting one was supposed to have damned her to hell. Now that voice said to trust Vika. "Why don't you boys shut up and see if she can help us, instead of blaming her. Maybe she already has a plan."

Vika nodded appreciatively. "I *did* have a plan." She produced a utility knife with a dangerous flourish. "But you have given me a better one." She paused, with a better sense of drama than Tanya supposed her capable of. "Exactly how much of that 126 do you have?"

#

The bow of the seabus bore a vestigial helipad; though Luthor doubted any of the others would have recognized it as such. Anymore, helicopters were about as useful as an appendix. Perhaps at one time in the past they too had served a purpose—Luthor had even ridden in a helicopter early in the war—but now they remained the single least fuel-efficient mode of transportation humans had ever devised. They used twice the fuel of a fixed wing aircraft, to go half as far, a quarter as fast. Even for the fabulously wealthy, using a helicopter was akin to flushing solid gold down the toilet.

Luthor's mental clock told him that they were out of time to be in their dorm. Vika pointed over the guard rail. "We'll hide there."

Michael's eyes brightened. "We'll use the 126 to counteract the earth's gravity and cling to the side of the seabus!"

Vika nodded. Luthor shivered involuntarily.

Heights. And they were easily thirty meters above the water. It was too high. He couldn't speak, his mouth had suddenly locked up.

"Hurry! They are already searching the ship." Michael mashed two bundles of 126 together with the polymer. The feeling of altered gravity instantly rushed over Luthor and managed to heighten his terror even more. And they wanted him to just hang that high above the surface of the water. The only thing holding them there would be a strange property of a strange element that he only faintly understood. What if it failed? What if the element wasn't actually stable and began to fission? What if they didn't use enough and they just fell into the water?

"If we can hide here long enough, will they conclude we aren't on the boat?" Tanya asked.

"That's what I would say, if it were me looking for you," Vika said, "I would assume you bought the ticket to throw me off your scent." Tanya nodded and swung her leg out over the side. She didn't look afraid, just wondrous. She deftly stuck her 126 below her and then disappeared. Vika followed.

Michael looked back as he climbed over the edge. "Come on, Luthor!" he hissed. "What are you doing?" Luthor hadn't even noticed he was backing away from the edge. He felt like he was on top of a ball, like a move in any direction would cause him to fall over the side.

"I... I can't," Luthor said.

"Yes, you *can*. Now move." Michael spoke with such urgency that Luthor began walking toward him. Michael held out his hand, "come on, I will help you."

Luthor grasped his hand and looked out over the edge. The frothing sea looked up and licked its lips, hungry for Luthor's flesh. The waves reached up for him, trying to pull him down to the unfathomable depths below the Atlantic.

It called out to him, *you're going to fall. Just fall. You can't control gravity. You* will fall!

The world spun, he couldn't focus. Luthor screamed and fell on his back and began scooting away. "I can't. I can't." Luthor kept repeating as he pushed himself farther from the edge.

Michael looked down at the women below him. "Stay

here. I'll go with Luthor." He climbed up and grabbed Luthor's hand and hustled him away from the deck. Luthor's vision still swam in front of him. Michael was muttering something that had a lot of four-letter words.

Luthor could barely walk, his encounter with the edge of the boat had left him broken. Michael was shouting something. Luthor didn't understand him.

Michael slapped him full-on across the face. "Wake up, you smogging pansy! Get in here and pray they don't find you."

Luthor walked into an open door on the side of the ship. It was filled with ropes, netting and life-preservers. There was only room for one person, barely. "Damn you Luthor, stay here until we come back." He shoved the door shut leaving Luthor in total blackness.

Luthor hated himself. His stupid fear had compromised everything. If only he had been able to do what all the rest had found easy. Michael had been forced to risk his life to find him a hiding spot. Now an unknown number of carbon agents patrolled the ship, scanning everyone's CPI chip and looking for any irregularities. Eventually, they would cross off every paid-for ticket except for Vika's and their three forgeries. It was only a matter of time.

Visions of the sheer height of the ship above the water replayed in his mind. He grabbed the netting on the wall to secure himself. It was like the netting on the inside of a plane before he jumped out. He hoped his unconquered fear hadn't doomed them all.

#

They had lined the 126 up on the side of the seabus in regular spaces, which they had taken to calling BOGs—Michael's idea— meaning Ball of Gravity. Tanya didn't much care what they called it, but BOG was easier to say than "several beads of 126 wrapped in Eli's polymer." The regular spacing of the BOGs allowed them to move around in almost normal gravity despite being angled upside down toward the water.

It felt strangely normal to Tanya. It was just natural to see the side of the ship as down. Her body told her it was down and she simply chose to believe it. The giant wall of water rising up next to her was merely a fascinating curiosity, but ultimately unalarming. They watched the sun set sideways into the vertical ocean; it made it more beautiful somehow.

Tanya worried about Luthor. They had left him in the storage closet for hours now, it had to be past midnight. Vika wanted to stay until they heard an all-clear announcement from the bridge. Tanya did not. She wanted to know the man she loved was alive and not incarcerated for international terrorism. She had become familiar with his debilitating fear of heights when he had refused to climb a spiral staircase during one of their first dates. He had shut down so completely they'd been forced to change plans. Something absolutely awful had changed him during the war. Unfortunately, asking about it clammed him up as quickly as heights did. All she knew for sure was that it had something to do with the battle of Titan Dome. It had been so traumatizing that it had changed him from a fearless paratrooper to the broken, PTSD-ridden man she knew today.

Abruptly, a horrible alarm rocked through the hull of ship, buffeting them.

"Is it too much to ask that they wouldn't find Luthor?" Michael said.

"We have to do something!" Tanya cried.

They began replacing the BOGs in a new trail back up the side of the ship. In a minute they were all back aboard, each with a few wads of 126 tucked safely around their waists.

“This way,” Michael beckoned, leading them around the opposite side of ship where he had secreted Luthor.

Luthor stood flattened against the wall with a man pointing a gun at his chest. With his free hand the man shouted into some sort of walkie-talkie.

“I’ll distract him. You two save Luthor.”

“Are you sure you know what you’re doing?” Tanya asked.

“Nope.” Michael said with a grin and he ran toward the man with the gun. He pulled up short of the carbon cop in an exaggerated way. “Oh shit!” he yelled. “They found me!” He turned and bolted down a side corridor.

The man immediately yelled something into the walkie-talkie, left Luthor, and sprinted after him.

CHAPTER 10:

Somewhere in the Mid-Atlantic

Michael sprinted around the deserted jogging track of the seabus. No one was out enjoying the chilly North Atlantic air. The shrill alarm continued wailing banefully throughout the ship, which tended to mean it wasn't a good time for a stroll. Michael didn't much care at the moment, which sometimes happens when being chased by a dude with a gun.

Michael hoped the others were still alive. *Why am I worried about the others right now? I am the one who just risked his life. What is happening to me? Am I in danger of becoming a gentleman?*

He rounded the bow of the ship and realized he was screwed. He looked ahead at almost 300 meters of straight, unobstructed track. There wouldn't be much cover for its entire length. Even at this time in the night any carp worth his weight in carbon would take that shot, probably several.

Michael darted into the basketball courts. Nets designed to catch wayward balls before they went overboard stretched up into the darkness. He doubted they would be very good at catching bullets. Various poles, balls, and other sports paraphernalia lay packaged for the night. Michael wound his way through the courts, putting as many things between him and the Euro-carp as possible.

The plink of bullets came from a pole next to him. He ran behind a cart full of sporting equipment and heard the loud pop of a basketball being blown up like a balloon with a needle. There was no sound from the gunshot, the suppressor combined with the ambient noise of the Atlantic effectively masked the sound of the explosion in the chamber.

He turned back on to the jogging track and cursed at himself again. More straight-aways. It seemed like the carp was gaining on him. His adrenaline continued to flow, giving him speed.

Life boats, hanging well off the side of the seabus, whizzed by, but the stern of the seabus wasn't approaching fast enough. He had to get off the track. Maybe if he was fast enough, he could use the 126 to hide on the side of the ship like before. He ducked into a shallow doorway and yanked on the handle. It was locked. *Smogging alarms!* He slammed the door with his open palm. The lights through the little porthole remained dark. He wanted to run for it. *Too late now,* he thought. *You get out of this doorway and you are going to find out what it feels like to be shot.*

His mind raced. There were only seconds to spare. He thought of the element 126 around his belt; he had four BOGs. Maybe if he cracked the glass and threw them inside, it would be enough weight to break the door in. He punched the little porthole as hard as he could. He winced at the pain, as a trickle of blood began flowing from his middle knuckle. He hadn't even cracked the damn thing.

He started to panic. Chancing a look, he saw that the agent was running by the same life boats Michael had passed only moments before. An idea bloomed in his mind. Quickly taking all four BOGs from his belt, he mashed them together. He couldn't make them open the smogging door, but they might still be able to save his life.

Michael's panic grew as the gravity clenched around him like a fist. He held twice as much 126 as they'd tried in the game-room at his waist. His feet were being pulled up and his head was being pulled down. He was being crushed.

Grabbing the chrome door handle behind him, Michael lobbed the ball at the nearest life boat, 3 meters off the side of the ship. Gravity nearly tore him free as space warped around the powerful element as it moved through the air. He held on to the door, managing to avoid getting ripped off by the moving gravity dimple. The polymer adhered to the side of the lifeboat, holding the 126 soundly in place. He felt the pull ease, but even meters away, the gravity distortion was still detectable, churning his stomach. Michael sagged against the door.

The agent's pace never slowed, his gun out, ready to arrest or shoot Michael. As he approached the boat, he abruptly lurched sideways, pulled in by Michael's trap. He screamed in fear. His legs smashed into the low glass wall on the side of the track, flipping him violently toward the lifeboat. He shrieked louder. The terrified man struck the side of boat with a sickening thud. He stopped screaming. He careened down off the hull toward the water, flipping in the opposite direction. His descent slowed as his momentum and Earth's gravity fought against the 126 for dominance. The agent almost completely stopped 2 meters underneath the life boat, floating like some ghostly apparition. A second later, Earth broke the deadlock and he slowly began accelerating toward the water. Michael watched as the man dropped out of sight, eerily silent.

He couldn't believe how well his plan with the 126 had worked. Not only that, he wasn't seen. He doubted anyone even on the lower decks could have seen the splash in the dark. So long as no one saw the unearthly battle with gravity, then Michael was in the clear. He waited to hear any type of man-overboard call, but none came. He wanted to whoop for joy. He settled for a silent fist pump.

Michael went to retrieve his precious supply of 126. If it possessed enough gravity to yank someone completely off their feet, it was sure to draw attention. He couldn't just leave it on the hull of the lifeboat. Gingerly letting go of the door, Michael slowly slid toward the 126. It felt like a pair of hands pulling him from his groin inescapably to the lifeboat.

Might feel a little better if it was Vika pulling on—No! Shut up you idiot! He told himself. *She would rather castrate me than do that.*

He jumped over the glass barrier and instantly felt his orientation change. The life boat was now down. Which was a nice feeling as he knelt parallel to the frothing Atlantic thirty meters away. He did not want to think that he was looking down. The ocean had just gone sideways for a bit. That was all. *Perfectly normal. Sure, it happens all the time.*

The white hull of the lifeboat was marred with red streaks. They splattered out from a small circle, dripping down in sickly rivulets. The agent must have hit his head, and hit it hard. It explained why he had stopped screaming. *Shit. I just killed a man.* The realization hit him like a punch to the face. He struggled to rationalize the simple fact that if not for his actions the agent would still be alive. Michael hoped that the man was single, that way he wouldn't have ruined any poor soul's life back in Europe too.

The heavy gravity weighed him down in equal parts with his conscience while he wiped the blood away with his shirt. It wouldn't do to have a bloody lifeboat for cleaning crews to find in the morning. It was hard work. His arms weighed far more than they did normally. A few minutes just wiping felt like half an hour in the gym.

Satisfied, he split up the 126 lump in two. One chunk he threw at the glass wall, the other he held. He jumped off from the lifeboat, falling into the new gravity well against the seabus. He clambered over the short wall and replaced the strange, but increasingly useful element around his belt in its four constituent pieces.

Michael sighed in relief as he tried to walk away nonchalantly. He just hoped the others were okay. They didn't have guns either.

#

It hadn't taken long for another officer to pick up on Luthor's trail. And the son-of-a-bitch carp was gaining. Luthor wasn't in the shape he'd used to be in. He was flabbier —and older—than he had ever been in his life. Compounding his fitness deficiencies, he had fewer toes than he used to have. Smogging frostbite. Rehabilitation had helped him relearn to walk, but he no longer had the same top speed. Tanya and Vika ran ahead of him, dodging lawn chairs and towel carts by the pool.

Vika threw 126 against the wood-paneled wall above the outdoor music stage. She leaped up and started scrambling for the roof. Tanya was right behind her, she had caught on unnaturally quick too. Maybe it was a woman thing.

Luthor, only steps behind, took out two balls of 126. He pressed them together. He tried to will himself to throw it against the wall exactly like the women, but the newly increased gravity began churning his stomach, amplifying his already significant fear. His hand shook, the thought of climbing up that sheer wall paralyzed his muscles. He couldn't move. *Damn it Luthor, not now!*

"He's almost here!" Tanya shouted.

Luthor tried. But his body wouldn't work. It was bad enough just being this high on the seabus without having to climb five meters on the side of a wall. It was just too high.

"Smog-it, Luthor. Move!" Tanya screamed. It was too late.

Veneered wood splintered inches from his head. Ducking in panic, he froze, arms up in surrender. The 126 slipped from his hand and fell innocently in front of him. It tugged, willing Luthor to bend over and put his arms down, but he didn't dare. The carbon agent approached from the other side of the pool, pistol in both hands aiming carefully at Luthor. He wore plainclothes, indistinguishable from other passengers. Luthor wondered how many carbon enforcement agents were assigned to each boat. Would he have backup? Not that it mattered at this point, Luthor was already a dead man. Stupid heights. But maybe if he could distract this guy long enough, Tanya and Vika would be able to get away.

The irony of his looming death or incarceration didn't escape Luthor. I survived a war that claimed over 300 million soldiers, and 2 billion civilians. I lived when two thirds of the 501st are still frozen in Anti. But now I am going to die because I am too much of a pussy to climb a goddamn wall!

Longing to glance up to see if Vika and Tanya were safe, he focused straight ahead. Even if his damn fear of heights was going to get him killed, Luthor refused to give away their position in the off chance the agent hadn't heard them. Maybe he could buy them enough time to escape. The agent had his gun out and jogged forward. "Don't move." Choosing to lead with English indicated the agent knew his target.

The agent slowed his jog and then unexpectedly pitched forward, hands extending to catch his fall. He fell humiliatingly right in front of Luthor's feet. Bewildered, it took Luthor a moment to realize it had been the 126 that made him trip. It made sense, Luthor himself probably would have tripped too if he suddenly weighed three times normal.

Luthor seized his chance, immediately stomping down on the agent's gun hand. With a cry he released it, and Luthor kicked it away.

Before he had a chance to think about what to do next, Vika landed with a crash right on top of the fallen carp. He grunted in pain. Grabbing a fistful of his hair she jerked his head back, pulling a knife deep across his trachea. Red blood oozed out of the cut like pus, pulsing with the beat of the dying man's heart. "What the hell are you doing?" Luthor yelled.

"What needs to be done," she said, her voice was liquid nitrogen.

Tanya landed next to him after hearing his yell. She looked sick, either from the 126 or the dying man in front of her. He gurgled as the blood pumped out of his arteries, Vika placed a white pool-towel under his head that caught most of it. In moments the noises stopped, his arteries no longer shot as much blood, and Vika dropped his head on the towel.

It was hard to believe it but the man was dead, and he —Luthor was not. *I should be the dead one on the deck here. Smogging heights. If I hadn't gotten lucky with him falling, I would be dead and this would all be over. I escaped again.* Luthor felt resolve harden in his belly. Never again would he be controlled by fear. *Never again!*

She dropped the body on top of the towels with finality. It didn't feel right. This wasn't like the black ops in Geneva. This man had just been trying to uphold the law.

Luthor glared at Vika. "I do not see why this man needed to die. He was –"

"You are more of a fool than I thought Tenrel, if you think we could escape with this man alive."

"I don't know, we are only on this boat three more days. We could have eluded them and then been safely on American soil."

She raised her eyebrow, "Right now we only know of two men who know our identity here, it won't stay that way for long. You think we could hide from them *and* the entire boat security for three days? Were you planning to eat Tenrel? What about sleep?" Luthor had gone without eating for far longer than that, but that had been in Antarctica. He shuddered; thinking about the experience made him want to retch.

"It doesn't mean he deserved to die," Tanya whispered.

"Neither did Eli and you did not deserve to become fugitives," Vika replied, "this is not simple. You need to be willing to fight—and kill—other men who also do not deserve to die if you want to succeed."

"How many..." Tanya's voice caught. "How many more people are going to have to die for us to do this?"

"I don't know. But if you think this will stop once you get on American soil, then you are badly mistaken."

Tanya opened her mouth several times before actually managing to speak. "I am starting to think that it might not be worth it. Maybe we should just give up and turn ourselves in."

"You can't be serious," Luthor exclaimed. "This could prevent future wars, provide enough food for everyone again; your parents could move back to the world!"

"How many deaths can you justify with that reasoning? Ten? A hundred? Maybe a couple thousand? What about a million or two? All to *maybe* prevent a war? So my parents can *perhaps* live in civilization again?"

Luthor wanted to argue back, but found himself agreeing with her. Death was horrible. He could feed hungry people, heat cold people, but no one could fix death. "What about all the food shortages? This could provide the power to mass produce crops again like during the oil era. It would be like having diesel powered tractors again."

"I wish you could have given your invention away before the Oil Crash and the war, but you didn't have it then and now the damage has been done. Two billion people *already starved* Luthor, you know that. This won't change their fate, any more than it can change Eli's. We have reached a new equilibrium between population and food production without 126.

"Even if you do get your research out to the world, who's to say that the new food supply will go to those who need it most? It won't, it will go only to those who can pay for it, or to anyone who's marked. You know I'm right."

She was right. Of course she was. He longed to believe

that if there was enough food for everyone that they would all be fed. But it was a lie. He remembered enough history to know differently. At the turn of the 21st century, the world grew more than enough food to feed everyone, but almost a billion people were still malnourished or outright starving. It was hard to wrap his mind around the idea that there could be that many people suffering when there had been more than enough food to feed them. How had people lived with themselves, particularly when food was so cheap?

But Tanya was also wrong. She knew more history than he, but he had *lived* more history than her. The war was beyond horrible. Even those that survived had scars that would never heal. He had to live with his own irreparable wounds every day. There were still millions of unrecovered bodies freezing in Antarctica for archeologists to discover in the future. Who knew how many of those Oil Crash starvation deaths could have been prevented if not for the bombing of the world's strategic oil reserves? The war had pitted the world against itself in a struggle not for dominance, but for survival. Nations destroyed each other for rights to the last of the world's scarce resources, but pissed their existing resources away in order to do it. It was total war in the truest sense. If Luthor could prevent another war over energy he would. If properly distributed, his technology could create a world without scarcity. *I will kill again if I have to. If whoever is chasing us wants to take this for themselves and eliminate a chance for peace, then maybe they deserve to die. Hopefully, they don't have too many pawns.*

Vika tucked the man's pistol in her belt then wrapped the body in more white pool towels. She ripped off the agent's comm mic and handed it to Luthor. "Tell whoever is listening that it's over."

Luthor scowled at the bloodstained mic, but he clicked a button on the earpiece and spoke clearly into the receiver. "Targets eliminated. They jumped overboard. Do not rescue."

The top of the ship hung over the lower decks maximizing sun bathing space, and it also made a convenient gangplank from which to drop dead bodies. Tanya stood at the side and watched them heave the body into the darkness. Her face clouded with revulsion and anger. Luthor hoped he could make her understand.

With everyone still confined to their quarters, there was no one to hear the splash of a dead body twenty decks below

CHAPTER 11:

Fermilab, Batavia, Illinois, United States of the West

Qwiz slapped a steel lock around the frame of his bike, securing it next to the endless line of other bikes. Four solitary government cars and a strangely familiar moped were parked in the empty lot. All that pavement looked naked with nothing on it. Qwiz holstered his backpack and strode down the long concrete sidewalk toward the front door of Fermilab. He was vaguely aware of exhaustion eating up RAM in the background of his mental desktop—too many late nights trying to save Luthor and Michael from the clutches of the villains in Europe. Fortunately, the only thing better than a liter of Mountain Dew for a sluggish brain, was a twenty-kilometer bike ride at dawn. It was impossible to feel tired with the brisk autumn air slapping his face. The tired would come later, after an hour or so in his chair with no urgent computer problems to fix.

Qwiz whistled tuneless notes as he approached the front of the old Tevatron labs. Its elegant sloping sides no longer felt like an optimistic portrayal of human potential; they felt more like a mausoleum. It was a monument to a better time when energy was as unlimited as the human imagination. The Tevatron itself had been a multi-kilometer long particle accelerator capable of achieving impact energies in excess of one trillion electron volts. Which was to say, it was the second most powerful subatomic microscope ever built. In the quantum world, things were too small to look at directly. Instead the Tevatron—like other syncotrons—blew them up and examined the explosions. They did this by accelerating particles to near the speed of light and then smashing them together. The faster they went, the bigger the explosion, and the more data they could examine. It was a little like learning about how a watch worked by smashing it with a big mallet to see how the pieces flew apart. But it cost far too much energy to run any more. The massive Tevatron had been scrapped, the rare elements sold, and the rest melted down to build a denser, more efficient Chicago, leaving only the building as a testament to the triumph of science that the Tevatron had been.

The labs themselves remained relatively unaltered, apart from a drastically reduced staff. At one point they housed almost 2000 employees, now they were down to 320. They only utilized a tenth of the available space to save energy. The remaining scientists now focused on more practical projects than mining the quantum lattice that made up the universe. The only particle accelerator remaining was a puny cyclotron that fit in an average room. It had been appropriated from a much smaller facility in the late ‘20s. That cyclotron had been Luthor’s focus. He and a small team had been assigned the dead-end job of trying to create new super-heavy elements. It was the equivalent of a 4th grade science project for the government and everyone knew it; the only things missing were the gushing parents and blue ribbons pinned to tri-folded posters.

Qwiz thought he saw a dark figure out of the corner of his eye, but upon second glance, saw nothing, so he ignored it and pushed open the formerly automatic doors. Hard to believe the world used to be so lazy that they couldn’t even open a door without electricity. Even more frightening was that the electricity had come from coal-fired power plants. All that carbon in the atmosphere just so people didn’t have to open their own doors. Qwiz had never been through an automatic door and burning coal had been made illegal when he was a child. Now electricity was far too expensive to waste on such frivolities. Qwiz could open his own doors, thank you very much, and help save the planet from the greenhouse effect.

As soon as he crossed the threshold into the lab it became clear something was drastically out of place. Men in official black suits flashed badges, talked to employees, and scribbled on note pads. Several sat behind computer screens reading through documents. *They're here for Luthor.* Without a word to anyone, Qwiz slunk back to his small office next to the computer mainframes.

He slumped down in a chair that might have been comfortable 30 years ago. Leaning back, he laced his fingers behind his head trying to get his mind around all the nameless agents swarming the bottom floor lab. He quickly concluded that they were not the same men he had narrowly avoided days before. They weren't driving SUVs—presuming the electric cars in front were theirs—and they had badges. Whoever had destroyed the apartment would have been working for Europe and wouldn't be sanctioned by the USW. These men would be investigating Luthor's "terrorist" activities.

Qwiz's nerves bubbled uncomfortably under his skin. He had been house-sitting for Luthor; Luthor had spoken with him on the phone. He'd been his friend and confidant. It was conceivable that he could be detained for questioning or even suspected of committing terrorist actions of his own. Qwiz was also Asian. He wasn't Fermilab's only one, but there weren't many and he was the only one who knew Luthor. World War III was still too fresh for people to forget their prejudices. The temptation to escape cut through his other emotions like Superman's heat vision through a locked door.

A movement out of the corner of his eye caught Qwiz's attention. Outside his office door a lab technician talked to a suit, pointing his finger at Qwiz's office. His eyes darted around the utilitarian office looking for a place to hide. Every spare nook and cranny was crammed with steel shelves overflowing with computers, components, wires, and cables. There was no space next to his faux wood desk either; it was occupied by a bookcase of old software disks.

Qwiz had almost decided to duck under his desk when his eyes fell on an old picture he had taped to the white matte wall in front of him. A pencil sketch of a chiseled man in superhero spandex stared out of the picture. His fists defiantly placed on his hips emphasized the stylized V on his chest. A compartmentalized belt girded his waist while a black cape flapped in an unseen breeze. On the top of the picture was written *The Vanguard.* Qwiz had drawn the picture as a teenager. The Vanguard never graced the covers of any comic or the screen of any movie because Qwiz had invented him. He represented everything Qwiz wished he could become. In his mind The Vanguard was a citadel of justice in a crumbling world, clinging to honor and truth even as the world unequivocally embraced evil. His only superpower was his will, his only asset, courage. As Qwiz stared at The Vanguard, his own personal superhero, he found the strength to not hide. True heroes still felt genuine fear—and his was quite pronounced at the moment—what made a hero was not letting that fear control them.

The suit approached and flashed a carbon enforcement badge. The agency was global, having originally descended from the UN. carbon enforcement had supplanted it in wake of the world adopting the stringent Paris 2 protocols in an effort to fight global warming. They controlled the CPI system, and regulated the world's carbon output. The carbon police, or carps as everyone else called them, were the police force they used to enforce the carbon laws. As such they had authority over pretty much any legal dispute, so most governments simply contracted them to handle all police work, not just carbon. Qwiz felt his nerves clench; carbon enforcement also handled matters of terrorism and major crime since they had unrestricted access to the CPI databases. They had ultimate jurisdiction wherever they went, much like the FBI, though carbon enforcement had absorbed almost all of the duties of that atrophied organization.

The suit looked like he had absorbed the muscles of a few FBI agents himself. His bulk towered over Qwiz, with close cropped, graying black hair, and a face that could have been stolen from The Vanguard. Qwiz swallowed hard and stood up to meet him, trying as hard as he could to disguise the tempest of fear in his stomach.

"Can I help you?" Qwiz asked.

"Agent Glover," the suit said, as if trying to find the tersest possible introduction. "I have some questions."

Qwiz tried to look like an open book. If he was lucky, he would be able to hide the incriminating pages by appearing to disclose them all.

"You are the lead computer technician here?" Agent Glover scanned a clipboard, "Quency Park?"

"Yes sir," he said, feeling a bead of sweat forming near his hairline.

"When was the last time you saw a physicist named Luthor Tenrel?"

Qwiz was no actor, but he scratched his head as if struggling to come up with the day. "I think it has been at least two weeks. The last I saw him he was preparing to leave for Geneva."

"You knew he was leaving?"

Qwiz mentally winced. He had already said too much. No going back now. *Don't give them any information that isn't publicly available.*

"A lot of us did. He and one of the interns from here went to attend the International Energy Convention."

"Do you know who the intern was?"

Qwiz hesitated. Lying was wrong. Betraying your innocent friends was worse. Even honor dictated lying sometimes, in this case it would have the fringe benefit of keeping him out of jail. “I’m pretty sure it was the black guy that works with him.”

The agent peered down at Qwiz. He could have been three meters tall. “Why were they attending?”

“I don’t know,” Qwiz said. “Maybe to find a more efficient way of powering the cyclotron. It’s an energy hog.”

The agent jotted a note on his clipboard, his bulging forearm managing to make it look menacing. Qwiz resisted the urge to wipe his brow. He thought he was doing okay so far and didn’t want to botch his performance to remove a little sweat.

“What do you know of their experiments?”

“Not much.” Qwiz said, the lie tasting sour in his mouth, “they were in charge of the cyclotron. Basically, they smash atoms together and hope they stick.”

The agent frowned deeper, if possible, indicating he was impatient and wanted more detail.

“They were trying to discover new super-heavy elements. And study their properties if they made anything.”

“Were they successful?”

“They never discovered any new elements,” Qwiz said, relieved at being able to finally tell the truth. “The biggest one is still element 126.”

His pen scratched like a medieval torture device. He turned to exit. Qwiz felt his abdomen release some of its pent-up tension.

He turned around in the doorway. Qwiz glimpsed the words *investigate phone call* scrawled at the bottom of his paper.

“Have you had any contact with Tenrel since he left?”

Qwiz felt his intestines tie themselves in knots. “No sir,” his voice felt weak.

“You haven’t had a phone call with him?”

“I haven’t spoken to him since he left.”

More scribbling. “You are aware that Tenrel is the prime suspect in the Aurora bombing. If it is discovered you are intentionally withholding information, you would be considered an accomplice and prosecuted along with Tenrel as a terrorist.” He loomed, staring down into Qwiz’s Asian eyes. “Helping him would be dangerous particularly for someone with your— background.” They both knew he meant *race.*

Qwiz felt his resolve solidify. “I would never help anyone who would blow up innocent people.”

“Good. Just hope the voice-detection program doesn’t determine it was your voice on the phone with Tenrel last week.” The man walked out and began to question other people. Qwiz decided to move everything related to 126 to Bill’s apartment as soon as he got home.

#

Somewhere in the mid-Atlantic

Michael found them an hour before dawn in the same secluded game room where they had first tested the 126 with Eli’s polymer. Luthor wasted no time and gave him a full -n man-hug.

“I don’t know what to say,” Luthor began, “thank you. You saved my life. I’m sorry, I never should have put you in that position.”

“Damn straight.” Michael said, “just don’t be such a polluted pussy next time and maybe I won’t have to save you.”

“I won’t... I hope.”

“And Luthor?”

“Yes?”

“You can let go now.”

Luthor released his embrace and Michael informed them of his own narrow escape. He was particularly interested in Michael’s impromptu use of 126. It seemed that the gravity of the element did scale exponentially with its density, which was a frightening, if interesting, discovery.

"Luthor, why didn't we ever put this much of it together until now? It would be damn helpful to have more info on what it does in larger densities than we use in the generator."

Luthor nodded his assent. They had been so consumed with making a functioning generator that they had never studied higher concentrations. There had been the fear that if the concentrations became too extreme, they wouldn't be able to separate the 126 again. They really only knew that it changed gravity a lot more when it was condensed than when it was spread out, but apart from their time on the ship they'd never dared measure specifics.

"This shit is really starting to scare me. I just killed a man with it."

"We just need to be careful," Luthor said.

"Careful? What happens if we accidentally clump it together?" Michael asked. "I'm serious, could we make a black hole? I really don't want to be swallowed into a singularity along with the rest of this smogging planet."

It was a frightening idea.

"I honestly don't know what would happen."

The others silence indicated that they didn't much care for Luthor's response. The problem was, it was the truth.

"Take a guess, Tenrel. You discovered it," Vika said.

"I think there are some problems with that line of thinking," Luthor began. "We don't have nearly enough 126 to approach those kind of extremes, so I wouldn't worry too much about it."

"You don't know that," Michael said, "we have no idea how quickly the gravity increases. For all we know, I was only one more bead away from sinking the entire ship!"

"I don't think that math makes sense, Michael. Even if

it grows exponentially, you were a long way from destroying anything that size. And regardless, I don't think the physics works either."

"Why not? We have no reason to assume the gravity-increase ever levels off."

"You're right. And we can't test it. But, think about it, where does the enhanced gravity come from?"

Michael looked frustrated. "How the hell am I supposed to know? We haven't exactly had access to Fermilab's old Tevatron. Do you have any idea what it would cost just to get it running again? So, we can't exactly look for some mythical graviton or something subatomic. All we know is that the gravity is some property of the element itself."

"Exactly, so let's start there." Luthor waved his arm in the air, looking for an example. "Some elements are reactive, some aren't. Some conduct electricity, some don't. Why? *Because they do.* It's just an innate property of the element. It has to do with the nucleus and electron shells.

"All we can ascertain is that 126 *conducts* gravity somehow. Why? Who the hell knows? But we do know that the nucleus is absolutely gigantic. It's got 126 protons, 184 neutrons. It's bigger than any other atom with a half-life longer than a microsecond. Who knows what happens when you have that much of the strong and weak nuclear forces boiling around in there? Maybe it spills out into the macro world as gravity. Whatever is going on, it has to do with the *nucleus*."

Michael's eyes widened. "But in a hyper-gravity situation, the nucleus would be destroyed, like in a neutron star."

"Precisely."

"Sorry, will someone please translate that into English?" Tanya said.

"Basically, I am pretty sure we can't create a black hole. If we ever had enough 126 to create super extreme gravity, like in a black hole, the gravity itself would destroy the 126 first. But enhanced gravity is itself a property of 126, so once the atoms were destroyed, the gravity they created would disappear."

"Then if it gets too powerful, it destroys itself. That's comforting."

"Wait a minute, so could we create a gravity bomb then?" Michael asked.

"Maybe," Luthor said.

"I think we could. If we made enough of it and had a device to condense it like in your generators, it would create a reverse explosion. An *implosion!*" Michael became more animated, "Instead of blowing stuff up, it would suck everything in. Then the 126 would destroy itself and the bomb would stop imploding."

"Intriguing. I wonder if under those situations, the 126 would spontaneously fission? Would it blow back up again?"

Michael snapped his fingers, "I'm sure it would. You can't just collapse a nucleus without the release of energy. We might even see—"

Tanya interrupted him. "I am certain I didn't just hear you devising *military* applications for 126. I know the man who is willing to kill innocent people to prevent war would *never* create a new weapon to use in one."

Luthor looked at his toes. The ones he had left wiggled self-consciously in his shoes. Those were not the words and thoughts of the man who claimed to want to save the world from future war and poverty. They were the words of a borderline mad-scientist, a liar, and a hypocrite.

"So maybe we should try to figure out what we are going to do in New York when we get there, instead of figuring out how to kill more people, hmmm?"

Luthor hated that tone. All women were endowed with it from birth for the sole purpose of tormenting others when they screwed up. The fact that every woman in history possessed such a voice could be used as evidence for God's existence—and that God was actually a sadistic woman.

Fortunately, Tanya stopped using it. Unfortunately, half an hour later, they still were arguing. Vika continued to adamantly insist that they try to sneak past customs. Remaining a fugitive was not an appealing option to Luthor.

"They will not be looking for us. We aren't technically on board," she said.

"She has been right so far, we should take her advice," Michael added.

"She also murdered a man in cold blood last night!" Tanya snapped.

"So did I, if you want to call it that," replied Michael.

"That was different. Vika slit a helpless man's throat!"

Vika shrugged. "And now I have a silenced pistol. I can do it from a distance."

"No more killing!"

"We aren't having this discussion again!" Luthor yelled. "I don't see what else we could have done in the situation."

Tanya crossed her arms. "You have done nothing but preach about wanting to give away your research," she said. "Everyone besides me has killed someone by now to accomplish it. So, what better way to get out your discovery than a trial?"

"That *could* work."

"But what if we don't get a public trial?" Michael asked.

Tanya shook her head. "A scientist escapes Europe after being accused of drummed up terrorist charges and turns himself in? It would be huge news. Even if it isn't, we just have to stand on a few ceilings and we're guaranteed to get some cameras to appear."

"It would work even without the computer working!"

Michael said. "We could make a big show of it right as we get into port; show everyone what we have developed."

Vika clenched her fists, "it is not that simple. Your problems will not go away when you arrive in your precious America."

"What are you talking about? We're citizens, we have rights. Even if they catch us, we'll get a trial and be acquitted."

"Incorrect. You are not citizens."

"Like hell we aren't!" Tanya shouted back.

"You are not citizens," she repeated, "you are terrorists."

Luthor shivered at the sound of that. The newscast still haunted him. The explosion. All those body bags, all blamed on him and his supposed ties with 2180. They would not be safe anywhere. It didn't matter if he was a citizen with no criminal history and no ties to terrorists, he'd now been branded as one.

The only way to exonerate himself was to release his discovery worldwide, proving his innocence, or at least his good intentions. If only the governments hadn't completely rebuilt all communications networks leading up to the war. Supposedly, twenty years ago he would have been able to post something online without any censorship first. That would have been nice. Now all communication lines routed through central intelligence stations where calls, emails, and web activity were monitored. Long before video of them defying gravity ever hit the internet it would be read by multiple bureaucrats and undoubtedly confiscated. Illegal websites that circumnavigated the structural security still existed. They cropped up like weeds, but they were shut down long before any significant web traffic graced their URLs.

"I don't care what you say. I can't believe that our country wouldn't be willing to at least give us a fair trial. It dates back to the original Constitution."

Luthor was inclined to agree with Tanya. Maybe because he didn't like the alternative.

"That Constitution doesn't exactly influence policy much anymore," Michael said, "Not since we annexed the rest of the Western Hemisphere during the war."

Pre-crash America barely resembled the USW of the present. The Bill of Rights was a great idea for its time, but curbing the world's carbon output had necessitated sacrificing some civil liberties—rather, most of them. Luthor itched the scar of his CPI chip on his right hand. Thomas Jefferson could never have foreseen a problem like climate change. It was a different world now; it needed different rules. Even Tanya would admit that much.

"I don't see much choice in the matter," Luthor said. "If we can't get the computer to turn on, we don't have any evidence to acquit ourselves with. Going through customs should only be a last resort."

Tanya, crossed her arms. "Okay, I can go along with that. But on one condition: no matter what, we don't kill anyone else."

Michael began to protest, but Tanya cut him off. "I'm serious. If you start shooting, I won't be coming with you. I will turn myself in and you can fend for yourselves."

CHAPTER 12:

Twelve years ago: Somewhere in Northern Alaska

It was so cold. The cold leaked through every fiber in his high-tech clothes, through every pore in his skin, until it froze his very blood and gave his bones frostbite. His unit had been out on the Alaskan tundra for three days out in the dead of winter. One more day to go. It was supposed to prepare them for the extremes of the war in Antarctica and the North Sea. What haunted Luthor was that it was even colder in those places. Sometimes a lot colder.

The wind was the worst part. It transformed the plummeting thermostat into relentless knives stabbing him everywhere. It howled in his ears, a thousand wolves in concert. It whipped across the barren rock and permafrost, slapping their completely covered faces like an offended lover. Luthor only wished he could apologize to Alaska and make amends for whatever he did to deserve this type of torture.

They had been cross country skiing, but the current terrain made that impossible. They had strapped their skis to their backs. Marching in snow was awful.

Garcia knelt and put up a fist. Everyone crouched. Doyle bumped into Luthor from behind, he hadn't seen Garcia's order. Chaz swore as he bumped into Doyle.

Luthor shook himself to alertness, he hadn't slept since they'd parachuted in; they weren't allowed to on this exercise. Yesterday, Garcia had thrown a grenade when a man fell asleep. Luthor's initial hypothesis was that sleep deprivation would have a negative effect on focus; so far, he was right. Some of the men had started *droning*—marching with eyes open, but dead asleep. Others had begun hallucinating: seeing dead relatives, fire-breathing monsters, and enemy tanks. None of them actually existed, but many rounds had been wasted making sure. Everyone arrived there eventually; the "exercise" taught them how long it would take and how to push through it. Luthor wasn't at that point yet, but he suspected he was close. His eyes quivered from time to time, and there were stretches of time he simply didn't remember. He held his MX-5 at the ready and flicked off the safety just in case. He didn't know what Garcia had seen and wanted to be prepared.

The comms embedded into their helmets popped to life, "Pipeline ahead." They had finally reached their target, an aging Surface to Air Missile installation—or SAM site—protecting the trickling Alaskan oil pipeline. Its production was pathetic, but it still provided some meager oil, which had become more valuable than gold since the war began. The army had every intention of wringing out every last drop of oil from the earth like a ratty sponge. Their unit's goal had been to simulate an enemy pipeline to ambush.

Newer, completely automated surface to air missiles batteries, which the men affectionately called "Uncle SAM," were positioned periodically along the massive pipeline to prevent China from interrupting its production with a bombing raid. A single hole could take days to fix even during wartime, meaning thousands of barrels of oil lost—depending on the location of the hole. Oil meant human lives saved or taken, the more oil they had, the more lives they took from China, and the more lives they saved from their own ranks. Their practice assault targeted a much older, manned-SAM site that was being decommissioned.

A light snow fell. Luthor could barely see the men in his own unit. They wore shock white flight suits that blended in seamlessly with the rest of the landscape. Originally designed for the Green Berets and the Seals, the 501st had appropriated the specialized cold gear when they began intensive training. The suit itself was lined with heating coils, allowing it to be thinner and more mobile than standard Arctic clothing. The added mobility allowed them to carry more material and food and move quicker in the difficult terrain. The solid-state battery packs that heated them were designed to be recharged almost instantly at any command cube that dropped in with them.

They stayed well away from the pipe, even in the dead of winter above the arctic circle, stealth was pivotal. Standard procedure was to turn off the heating coils two hours prior to the assault to minimize the heat signature. An active heating coil was a death sentence with the accurate Chinese infrared targeting systems. More than a few were not following protocol since this was only an exercise. Luthor himself feared punishment more than the cold and had turned his off an hour ago.

Chaz joined Luthor and Doyle and dropped his comm. He yelled through his mask into the wind, "so what's your take on all this bullshit?" He was referring to their training. It had been the main topic of conversation. Talking helped keep them awake and so long as they weren't using electronic transmissions the wind kept their stealth.

"I don't know, man. I just want hot shower and a cup of coffee," said Doyle.

"That's what I'm talking about. Ten, wanna rig one of these batteries to make us a few cups?" Chaz patted the batteries that flanked the large Rocket Launcher on his back.

Luthor shook his head. "It would take too much energy. I would rather be heated for a day than boil water."

"You're a smart son of a bitch, you know that?"

"That's what they tell me."

"With all those brains, have you figured out where we're going yet? We hitting the North Sea? Siberian oil fields?"

"My guess is Antarctica."

"Anti's a bitch. I don't want to die there," Doyle said bitterly.

"Me neither," Chaz replied, "but I don't see why they would be training this many of us if we weren't hitting Anti."

"I think you're right. From the look of it, it's going to be a big fucking operation."

"What have you heard?"

"Even Sarge doesn't know much, but I have been hearing talk of a lot of shit getting shipped south. They are massing troops near Cape Horn."

"Are you thinking we're going to be a part of a D-Day style invasion?" asked Doyle.

Chaz slapped the insignia on his shoulder. "Just look at the name of our unit. The 501st is hardly a random designation. I bet we're gonna be dropped in to hit priority targets ahead of some big ol' main invasion."

"And you call me the smart one, Chaz. That's the best theory I've heard yet."

"I ain't as smart as you, but I also ain't afraid to kiss some old-fashioned ass."

Luthor laughed, but it was swallowed by the wind. Rapid beeping chirped in his comm.

"Damn I hate these fucking emergency drills. Why don't they just grenade us again to wake us up?" Chaz said. "I gotta get back in formation." He jogged away.

A voice popped into Luthor's ear. It was startlingly clear, despite the wind. "This is General Stutsman. Enemy fighters inbound. This is not a drill. I repeat, this is not a drill. Do not let them hit the pipeline. Beware pilot ejections and possible ground troops."

Pilots, that meant they were sending MiGs. Slower and dumber than long-range drones, but packing a lot more firepower. The Chinese had refitted the venerable fighters with a short-range drone package. Luthor had read that each fighter could mount up to six drones depending on their loadout and range. The drone swarm turned the old rigs into a formidable enemy. Still, the MiGs handled like a model T compared to the Ferrari of modern drone fighters; they had the severe limitation of keeping G forces low enough for their pilots to remain conscious in flight. The Chinese only sent them on the lower priority targets; soft targets where they could lose men and equipment but still inflict damage. They had sent MiGs to raid the Texas oil reserves early in the war. If the Chinese had anything to waste, it was pilots and rusty Russian fighters. Losses were irrelevant if they could destroy oil production and hamper the Western war machine.

The comm crackled again. “Defensive positions!” Garcia shouted. “Focus those drones, let Uncle SAM handle the fighters.”

Sean Marrison dropped to the ground and began prepping their drone, Claptrap to meet the intruders. Luthor started running with the rest of his unit toward the pipeline. It would be the target of the MiGs. Luthor was glad he hadn’t cheated with his heat pack, the drones wouldn’t see him.

Luthor seized his GI ice pick and started banging at the frozen ground, tearing a deep, narrow hole. He pulled the pin on a grenade and shoved it deep inside. The permafrost made it almost impossible to dig a fox hole in any other way. He flattened himself on the ice as the grenade exploded, leaving a crater with a half meter radius. It wasn’t optimal, but it served as a passable cover in short notice.

Fireballs lanced up in the distance as missiles automatically targeted the enemy planes and drones that had failed to transmit any proper digital clearance code. Most of the pipeline’s defenses had already been refitted with the Coalition’s most agile missiles, improving their odds of eliminating even the nimblest drones; the ancient cold war fighters would be easy targets.

Missiles fired from more distant stations as the enemy approached; Uncle SAM released his hot fury. Luthor quickly checked his magazine, wondering what good it and his compliment of C-4 would do against Asian air power.

As soon as the last of the missiles departed into the grey sky, others started coming back. The closest SAM site exploded in a spectacular fireball that billowed up above the ice. The heat from the fireball momentarily warmed Luthor's face. More missiles impacted around the charred remains, accurate only in their redundancy.

In front of him, a jet of smoke shot up from another impromptu fox-hole as Chaz fired a micro-missile. Its compact propellant rapidly accelerated it toward a nearby MiG. The howling fighter swerved and spewed its countermeasures to no avail. The American-made missile ignored the tempting bait and soared straight into the rear stabilizer. A spectacular ball of light splashed the overcast sky, the ruined fuselage expelled from the inferno. Doyle whooped from a nearby crater at the destroyed aircraft. They were flying lower than Luthor expected, evidently within range of Chaz's rockets. They'd sacrificed the safety of height to stay under coalition radar.

More MiGs began exploding as Uncle SAM defended his homeland. Fighters thumped in the sky like fireworks. Smaller sparks appeared around them as their drone escorts failed to escape.

One drone came in low and hot. Luther leaned against the lip of his crater and depressed the trigger. He knew it was improbable that any rounds would hit the computerized bastard, but he shot at it anyway. Tiny rockets sprayed out from its wings in retaliation. Luthor ducked as explosive death raced his way, trying to maximize his limited cover. Doyle valiantly kept firing as the drone approached. The unmanned craft burst into flame and crashed only meters from Luthor, crushing his ears with the thunderous noise. Dust, dirt, and melting ice were ejected into the sky. Still ducking in his meager fox hole, debris rained down on him. The melted ice felt thick and sticky as it splattered his back, instantly refreezing.

Luthor's ears rang horribly. Fires raged all around him. It looked like the airstrike was over. The fires gave his cover a red glow. Except it wasn't a glow. Somebody's blood had splattered everywhere. Luthor wiped the disgusting gore coating his hands on the ground and reloaded.

Luthor gingerly scanned the air again. The only fires were coming from the ground. He crawled out onto the snow-covered tundra, following the trail of blood splatter to a nearby crater. A burned body lay contorted just outside. One of the rockets had found it's mark. Nothing was left except for the charred boots. The crusted remains resembled the leftovers of a campfire. A glint of steel drew his eye. Dog-tags. They belonged to Doyle. Doyle had been one of his best friends.

Luthor stood up and screamed at the sky in anger.

As if in answer, another strike fighter's twin jet engines drowned out his cry. Luthor stood his ground as it came into view. Tearing his trachea with his screams he poured bullets towards the horrible machine. Luthor wanted the pilot and the plane to both spontaneously combust with the force of his fury. The MiG opened up its 30 mm cannon, and Luthor realized how stupid it was to take on a fighter with an assault rifle. The impacts of bullets raced inexorably toward Luthor in a line from the MiG's machine gun. A pair of hands grabbed him and pulled him out of the path of the strafing aircraft. Luthor fell on his back into another foxhole.

"Shit Ten, you got a death wish? Get down!" said the occupant of the foxhole. It was Martinez.

"Doyle's dead!" Luthor shouted.

The fighter shot two more missiles and pulled up hard, going vertical just beyond their fox hole.

"Don't get stupid and follow him, loco. Let Tio SAM do the work."

The missiles engulfed the SAM in fire, but not before

it had retaliated with a missile of its own. A contrail followed the deadly warhead as it hunted the fleeing MiG. After two tense seconds, the aircraft exploded with the thunder of a thousand fireworks.

Martinez exulted over the pyrotechnics, clapping Luthor hard on the back. “I told you SAM would take care of him. Too bad he had to take one for the team.” The twisted wreckage of the surface to air missile site smoldered in the cold.

Chunks of busted MiG rained down around them. Blackened metal shards impaled the ground like confetti. Luthor no longer heard the roar of jets, just the howl of the wind. It seemed the battle was over.

This was supposed to be a training exercise. Luthor left the hole, an emptiness in the pit of his stomach. It felt like the world was going to end and there was absolutely nothing he could do to change it.

His comm buzzed with an incoming message. “This is General Stutzman. Excellent work men! I am receiving data from the pipeline that it was not damaged, while Uncle SAM is reporting twelve downed fighters and their compliment of drones. Helluva job. You should be proud of yourselves in your resounding victory. Scout for any ejections and report to the rendezvous for immediate pick up. Consider your training exercise complete.”

Resounding victory? Luthor thought. *We did nothing except try not to die—and not very successfully. The auto SAMs did all the work.*

The comm crackled again but this time with Garcia’s voice. “Report in. Casualty report.” It was obvious, even through the mic, that he was furious. They each sounded off in turn, Luthor reporting that Doyle had died. In total they had 8 dead and 6 others wounded in the skirmish. They clustered back together, the wounded being treated by Martinez, the unit’s medic.

“This is bullshit,” Garcia said, “we lose eight men,

for what? So our Auto-targeting missiles can shoot those fuckers? We didn't need to be here at all, but he calls it a victory."

Chaz, normally genial, fumed. "This 'victory' isn't about the lives of men, Sarge. It never was." It was rarely spoken, but everyone knew what the war was really about; it was about trying to secure more oil than the Chinese and spend less. Simple as that.

"They don't give a shit about our lives." Marri threw two dog tags on the ice in front of him. "You know what these men's lives are worth? About half a fucking barrel of oil."

Luthor dropped his head. The stark truth was that the army measured lives in terms of oil. A single barrel of it held the equivalent energy of the combined labor of 8 men working for an entire year. That meant if hundreds of men died but they managed to blow up a couple planes, then it was an even trade. Oil flew planes, drove supply lines, and powered tanks; men ate food, required shelter, and protected the oil. Men were replaceable, oil increasingly, was not. Doyle and the others in all their humor, friendship, and life had been distilled to about twenty pathetic gallons of crude each.

"I bet the General's poopin' his pants over this one." Jake said bitterly. "They lose twelve planes and an assload of drones, and we lose a few expendable paratroopers? It's a great trade for him."

"It's a pretty shitty trade for Doyle." Luthor said, charred boots filling his mind's eye. His very thoughts seemed to be soaked in Doyle's blood. Nobody responded.

#

Aurora, Illinois, United States of the West

Qwiz cracked another two-liter of Dew from the refrigerator. It was an expensive way to keep hydrated, but Mountain Dew was an absolute necessity for good coding and, Qwiz hoped, good research. He rebelled against his mother's Asian sensibilities and drank it straight from the bottle. The Vanguard would not be shackled by convention in pursuit of justice, and neither would Qwiz.

The mysterious email had been the key to entering Europe's network. Whoever **pjrangpart** was had a high level of access, giving him a good chance to find something important. Over the last week he had begun following up on some excellent leads. There were isolated cases of disappearances over the last few years, all attributed to kidnappings. These particular cases had popped up on Qwiz's depth search because they had been high profile individuals whose cases still had not been solved. Perhaps this same person had attempted to make Luthor disappear, but failed. Qwiz had named this mysterious person or group, the *Stalker*. It seemed a fitting name for an invisible European villain who made people disappear. But there was no way to get much further than that. The government of the European Union was just so frustratingly enormous. There were bureaucrats just to keep track of the number of bureaucrats. There were the executives in the military, officials to oversee the carbon police, the Carbon Enforcement Agency itself, and European Intelligence; not to mention the thousands of delegates, congressmen, officials, and employees of more sub-agencies than Norquist could have counted in a year. All of them probably had the clout to arrange a hit on Luthor and each of them could have different motives for trying to steal his research.

Qwiz struggled to narrow down the vast possibilities for the identity of the *Stalker*. He found very quickly that posting anything required a CPI scan, so did editing anything. All Qwiz could do was read what had already been posted. Qwiz was not all-powerful with code, he still couldn't fake or hack a CPI chip. Chip scans added security without destroying the functionality of the network for traveling officials. So Qwiz began reading all the emails he could find and with enough computer wizardry to make Bill proud, even gained access to live conversations.

Qwiz clacked out some code to flag the most highly encrypted messages. It seemed logical that whoever was chasing Luthor couldn't be working alone and would try to avoid attention. Selfishly stealing a world-saving invention didn't make many friends. That meant a high level of security. The one benefit to living in a society more concerned with energy efficiency than performance was the level of encryption used. Encryption powerful enough to deter his efforts would have completely bogged down most modern computers focused on unadulterated efficiency. That encryption would make it impossible to communicate in real time, so it was almost never used. But Qwiz's laptop, while not as powerful as his desktop, was old, fast, and therefore an energy-hog. It boasted enough power to decrypt most systems in real time. As such, with a few skillfully applied algorithms he would be able to tap into any conversations that people didn't want to be overheard.

Thankfully, there were fewer high priority messages than he might have imagined with all the traffic the network received. There just weren't many powerful computers left in the world that could decrypt them; they were too expensive to run. Now everyone had the hyper-efficient sub-1 watt processors that couldn't decode a word search. The limited number of truly secret messages allowed him to follow up on the ones that were the most promising.

While he waited for flagged correspondence, Qwiz turned to one of his external monitors and read another account of the apartment explosion.

> ...identifying the likely culprit as one Luthor Tenrel, a tenant of the building. Recently indicted on charges of terrorism in Europe after trying to bomb the IEC, Tenrel escaped capture in Geneva.

> His current whereabouts are unknown, though it is believed he is attempting to return to the USW. The explosion originated in his apartment, leading investigators to conclude that some of Tenrel's bomb making materials destabilized, igniting the inferno that rocked Aurora last week.

Qwiz quit reading. He couldn't believe the house of cards that was being constructed. Luthor was no terrorist. The man hated war with a passion. He even refused to play video games with Qwiz, saying too many of them reminded him of the worst times of his life. Such a man was no bomb maker.

The laptop screen beeped. A new conversation had popped up. It was international and terminated in the States. Qwiz flipped on his speakers, it was an audio message. His fingers whizzed over the keyboard, tapping his way in like a digital locksmith. After a few tense minutes—with the help of some software of questionable legality— he successfully cracked in.

His laptop emitted a high-pitched whine as it worked.

The signal cracked and fuzzed. A moment later the decryption caught up to the audio.

"…escaped again?" an angry male voice said in a southern drawl.

This is promising, Qwiz thought. He began recording the audio to a MPEG file.

Another man responded who sounded decidedly European. German perhaps. "There was a transmission that indicated they jumped overboard."

"And it took you this long to know it had been faked?"

"The carbon enforcement agent failed to check in for two days, we can safely assume he is dead or compromised."

The southern accent made an angry noise that Qwiz

wasn't able to make out.

"Calm down. He has merely shown us that he is a formidable quarry." The voice was cold, calculating, and dangerous. Qwiz shivered as he heard it.

"He's a goddamn scientist. The only thing 'formidable' here is the incompetence of your people. He's killed four of them now."

Qwiz found himself leaning in toward the screen in anticipation. What other scientist could they be talking about but Luthor?

"It only serves to help us. Tenrel is stuck on a seabus and now we won't underestimate him when he arrives."

Qwiz couldn't believe his luck. After searching for only a week, he had found the *Stalker.* At least, Qwiz assumed the icy voice was the *Stalker.* He sounded like he was in charge.

"I don't see the smogging sense of letting him arrive. Like you said, he's stuck on a boat. If we inform the crew that Tenrel is there, you'd have 12,000 people looking for him. He'd never escape."

"And if our special agents are repeatedly failing, you expect untrained civilians to be able to bring him in?"

"Sure, he might kill some of them, but who cares? He's got nowhere to hide. What's the worst-case scenario here? The bastard kills the whole damn crew and holds the passengers hostage? Then we just arrest him wherever he's forced to dock."

"You are a fool," said *Stalker.*

"It's a good plan."

"There are too many variables that we can't control. Why wouldn't he just take a lifeboat and disappear? Even worse, he *could* take over the ship. What do you suppose would happen if someone took 12,000 hostages? Do you think the media might cover that?"

"Sure, so?"

"You heard his audio with Al'Halsimi. He wants an open mic. He intends to give the synthesis method to everyone *for free*. Even China. A massive hostage situation would give him that opportunity. And there is no way we could suppress that in real-time if he takes control of that ship."

The Texan let loose a string of curses that even Bill might have blushed at. "How the hell can we stop him from doing that?"

"He has been laying low, so long as we do not push him, I doubt he would try something so extreme. We let him think he is safe and play his hand."

"So, we let him arrive safely, then strike?"

"I am authorizing the entire New York Saber unit for your use in this operation. I want you to lead them personally."

"About time we allocated enough damn people."

Qwiz's eyes nearly popped out of his head as he stared at the screen. Sabers! Luthor, Michael and Tanya were walking—sailing—into a trap. He had to warn them. But how?

"Do not squander this opportunity."

"Just watch and learn. You don't send two amateurs, you send overwhelming force, crush him under your heel, and then piss on his corpse."

"By all means, teach me. Just get them in custody." *Stalker* said. "What progress have you made on Tenrel's hard-drives from the lab?"

"We got every last stick of data Tenrel ever touched at that lab. But we are having a hell of time recovering anything. The encryption is a bitch. We still don't even know if he stored anything there."

So the men who searched our lab were working for Stalker? Qwiz thought. *But he's working in the EU, those men were American. Why are they helping him?*

"I don't like having that technology in multiple places. There are too many chances for something to happen."

"I won't let it out of my sight. Got a lead on the Mole?"

"Whoever did this hid their tracks well. There is no trace of that omega abort code. I could not have done a more complete job myself."

"Does that mean it's someone inside the Sabers?"

"Possibly."

"Who else has enough clearance for a complete wipe?"

"It could be someone high up in the government. It wouldn't be the first time the Jimenez administration has interfered, but I have no way of knowing if it's him."

"If we can't find the mole, we'll have to satisfy ourselves by finding those two bastards he helped escape."

"It appears Tenrel made a phone call to one of them right before you went in. I have people analyzing the audio, but there isn't enough data to work with. We needed one more sentence for a voice ID from the CPI database. If he so much as says '126' online, we'll find him. Call me when you have Tenrel in custody."

Qwiz gulped. They had been talking about him. He needed to make sure CPI didn't get any more voice data to work with.

The little light flickered out indicating that the connection had been terminated. Qwiz racked his brain to find a way to alert Luthor before the *Stalker's* accomplice captured him. It didn't matter if they had his voice recording. Luthor was going to need a miracle to merely survive disembarkation, let alone have a chance to publish their findings.

But then again, how were they supposed to do that, exactly? To get anything posted on the internet required going through government censorship. Qwiz could hack into systems and networks, but anything uploaded was still routed through the censors. Qwiz had plenty of experience with screened emails, albeit in a much more extreme way. He simply couldn't imagine how on earth they would ever accomplish their goal without someone in the government stealing it first.

Qwiz decided not to worry about the research, saving their lives took priority. He quickly found a voice modulator program in his audio driver. After changing his voice, he looked up a phone number from the internet and dialed it from his computer.

CHAPTER 13:

New York Harbor, United States of the West

Tanya felt she had won a decisive victory in their argument. It was one thing to battle nameless rogues surprising them in the night, it was another entirely to shoot at Americans.

Tanya watched through a porthole as the Seabus passed through the wall of endless windmills that guarded the East Coast. The turning blades marched in unison to an unseen conductor in an endless coastal procession. The USW had been building them and installing them constantly for the last twenty years. The result was the most massive, continuous wind-farm in the world. It stretched from Boston—farther north than that and sea ice became an increasing problem—to Florida. The only breaks were shipping lanes that allowed boats in and out. Floating on top of the sea itself bobbed countless tidal generators. They harnessed the up and down motion of the waves to generate electricity. Around New York the ocean was literally blanketed with them.

Tanya picked at her bulky uniform. It was uncomfortable and yellow. Tanya hated yellow. Somehow Vika had acquired employee uniforms for them; how exactly she procured them from the ship's laundromat without a pass was anyone's guess. *She probably had to snap a few more necks, just in case.* Tanya thought bitterly. *I wish she'd just sleep around to get what she wants instead.*

With their uniforms, they left via the crew exit without notice and slipped away into the loading dock. It was easy. Tanya had not expected easy, she might have been more amenable to this course of action otherwise. The primary security was for passengers leaving or entering the ship. The dock seemed devoid of checkpoints except for the exit leading into the port proper.

That was closed up as tight as a submarine's hull—or so Vika had said. They had no intention of going through that way, they intended to access the roof and exit down the sheer walls behind the guard station. Such a feat was nearly impossible without defying gravity. Fortunately for them, that was not a problem anymore.

Vika scrambled up the side of a pile of stacked steel containers. Deftly grabbing one BOG while throwing another higher up, she jumped and jogged all the way up the side without stopping. She acted as though she had walked up walls her whole life.

She lay prone on the top of the rusty containers, scanning for any guards, ensuring they were safe before they began their own, albeit slower, ascent. At least slower for the boys. Tanya was certain she could have made it up almost as fast as Vika. Vika would knock on the containers repeatedly if she saw anyone coming, carp or not.

A knocking came from up above. It didn't stop. Tanya tried to duck behind a container.

"You there! Stop!" Too late.

Tanya froze. A carp held his gun out, pointed at them.

#

Luthor stared at the barrel of the gun, completely unable to think or move. This was exactly what Tanya had warned against. He wasn't sure they would be able to escape the docks even with the 126 if the other guards were alerted. There were just too many carps roaming around when a seabus arrived. Michael also seemed to be frozen in place, as if his neural synapses had turned to stone.

Tanya strode forward confidently as if she didn't even see the gun.

She affected the single least intelligent voice Luthor had ever heard from her. It was almost comical – if not for the gun. "Oh officer, we were just looking for you!"

The officer looked confused, but lowered his sidearm. "You… you were?"

"Oh yes! Thank you for finding us."

"Do you realize this is a restricted area?"

"My goodness, it is? I am afraid we took a wrong turn when we were getting off the seabus. We ended up out here." Tanya slumped her shoulders. "I thought I knew a way past the crowds, but I just got us lost!"

The officer didn't seem to register their uniforms. "Ma'am, you are required to enter the country through customs."

Tanya turned and shouted back at them. "I told you it wasn't pronounced costumes." Luthor actually had to fight back a smirk. *Laying it on a little thick, aren't we? This guy must be a total moron if he is buying even a second of your charade.*

Tanya turned back to the officer. "Would you please point us in the right direction?"

"Ma'am I will have to escort you back myself."

"You don't need to do that, sir. Just point us in the right direction and we won't bother you anymore."

"I'm afraid that's not possible, miss. In a restricted area, you need a police escort or you will be arrested." The carp softened enough to look sympathetic, like he didn't want the poor simpletons to get into any more trouble.

"I promise, we won't be a problem sir."

"No, I insist. This is what they pay me for." He flashed her a smile. "This way, miss. I will lead you to the short line." He gently guided her toward the customs station in the next building with a hand on her back. Michael and Luthor followed. Vika stayed hidden on top of the container stacks. At least with her BOGs she would be able to escape. Luthor patted his own 126 for comfort. It was nice knowing they were there.

Luthor shot a glance at Michael. *Are you ready? We are about to be arrested.* Michael just shrugged, but made no attempt to escape. At least Tanya had given them a fighting chance to look innocent. It would have been much worse to be caught standing horizontally instead of vertically while they climbed the containers. Luthor took a deep breath, hoping Tanya was right about the trial. If she were wrong, these could be the last free steps he ever took.

They walked through a massive warehouse where full containers of food were being guarded by heavily armed men as they were loaded by crane onto the seabus. The empties were stacked next to them in multicolored pyramids of storage.

The adjoining building overflowed with a mass of humanity as the ship disgorged its passengers. People clumped up in giant queues that snaked for hundreds of meters to wait to gain entrance to the United States of the West. It was very reminiscent of their exodus in Europe. Even if they were arrested, the one bright spot was that he wouldn't have to endure the incarceration of that damn line again.

With a carp for a guide they made their way to the rear of the building. It seemed to be a separate scanning station for VIPs. Only three people stood in front of them.

Luthor and Tanya locked eyes silently. *The moment of truth.* It was clear that there was no way that they were going to be able to slip though the security sieve by anonymity or by managing to don their Seebee gloves. There was the infinitesimally small chance that the CPI databases had not yet been updated with the terrorist label tagged on each of them. But that hope felt hollow, like rolling dice, but needing 13 to win.

Tanya went first, exposing the back of her hand to the scanner. It beeped angrily, a machine gun rattling off digital decibels instead of bullets. Luthor had never heard the bad-beep before, but it was a befitting noise to announce a criminal. Tanya made an effort to look surprised. But it didn't matter; they all knew this was going to happen. She was handcuffed immediately.

"I wonder if you are going to flag in the system too?" the carp said. His kindly countenance when talking with valley-girl-Tanya transformed into a sneer. He took out his gun; he didn't exactly point it at him, but made Luthor very aware of its presence. It was a not-so-subtle order to undergo a CPI scan.

The shrill squawking poured out of the speakers again as Luthor scanned his CPI chip. The people in the massive queue to their left stared openly; they had probably never heard the bad-beep either. Rough hands forced him into a pair of handcuffs, shoving him next to Tanya. Michael likewise failed and was cuffed. Anger fizzled under a mask of defeat on his face.

They were pushed and prodded into a low room resembling a small post office, but with prisoners instead of parcels. They were frisked and searched thoroughly. No one noticed the small lumps of putty on the backside of Luthor's belt.

Still in cuffs, they were split up. Luther expected to be taken to an interrogation room with a one-way window. He suspected the next move in their playbook would be to try to catch the three of them in a lie. They would ask each of them the same questions one by one, and search for any inconsistencies. Given that this was their contingency plan, they had already agreed to tell the truth. Conveniently, the truth was they were innocent—which didn't hurt his chances.

The room did indeed have a one-way mirror. Luthor's face looked back timidly in its metallic sheen. He imagined the sneering carp behind it, making jokes about Luthor's ineptitude. *Costumes? Really Tanya? Is that the best you can come up with?* His feet were shackled to a solid steel chair with circular holes in the back. Sturdy bolts fastened it to the floor.

Half an hour later the door opened. A man in an official government green and black coat limped in. He had a military air, despite the obvious prosthetic taking the place of his entire right leg. He was Mexican—or tan enough to resemble it—with graying black hair combed as if to emphasize the early stages of male pattern baldness. A prominent scar stretched from his nose to his left ear. Luthor could scarcely believe it, but it was Garcia. His old sergeant from his frostbitten years in the 501st.

"Smog-it, but it's good to see you Tenrel." Garcia said. "It's been years." He slapped a manila envelope on the glossy table. "What are the odds that we would meet up again here? I would have a preferred a bar, maybe a double of whiskey."

"That's the truth," Luthor said, not having a clue how to act. Luthor hadn't seen him since he went to grad school, and now they were reunited with him in chains, accused of terrorism. Fun. "You look good. How'd you end up here?"

Garcia had aged, but so had everyone after Titan. He still appeared sharp and fit, just like the old Garcia, and still in charge. There had been jokes that he could have ordered Anti's ice to melt and it would have obeyed. Luthor was not looking forward to being on the receiving end of his interrogation.

He sat down opposite Luthor. "I decided since I gave the military all my innocence, most of my sanity and a leg, they owed me a decent job. I got placed in border patrol, so here I am.

"Unfortunately, with the seabus unloading, we won't have time to catch up. Oh, and don't worry," he said glancing at the one-way mirror, "I told big brother to sit this one out."

Luthor put his hands on the table in what he hoped was an innocent way. "If it's just you and me, then just tell me what it is they think I have done, and we can get down to business."

"You were never one to sit on your thumb and spin, were you?"

"When you've been put in the situation I have, you don't have a lot of options, so we might as well cut to the chase."

"Sounds good to me." Garcia shook his head, "I never thought I would be here with one of my own men. Damn it Ten, why'd it have to be you?" His eyes glassed over, he was thinking of Titan. It was one of the reasons Luthor hadn't kept in touch, seeing Garcia—particularly his missing leg—reminded him of the worst of it.

Garcia looked up, his eyes lanced into Luthor's as one accustomed to detecting lies. Luthor met his gaze; after what they'd been through together, he wouldn't have lied to Garcia even if he *had* tried to blow up the IEC.

Garcia began reading off Luthor's charges like a grocery list. "The Coalition has placed you on the known terrorist list, believed to be in league with 2180. They say you were building a bomb intended for the IEC. They report that you murdered two carbon police who discovered your intention and then you illegally fled the country. Your apartment also inexplicably exploded killing 41 people. From the bomb residue, they say you had another bomb there that destabilized." He folded his hands on the table with finality.

Mental note: don't build bombs. "You can't honestly believe that I was trying to blow up the IEC."

Garcia raised his brows, it was his job to determine the truth of immigrants and criminals entering the country. "Convince me."

"This is bullshit and you know it, Garcia. You know me! This is not me!" Luthor stopped shouting with effort. If Anti-Luthor got out it would not help his cause. He had to remain in control. "Do you really believe *I* would support 2180? I'm a smogging scientist for God's sake! You think I want to destroy the world with carbon?"

"You wouldn't be the first pissed off soldier to find solace in banned energy. The group was founded by ex-soldiers, you know. They thought if we would have just used our coal, we wouldn't have needed to fight the war in the first place."

Luthor looked at his hands. Everyone saw 2180 followers as stone-age, blind radicals who didn't care if the world burned around them so long as those fires warmed their houses. And in truth, that's probably what they were —ex-soldiers or not. Coal was the bane of the carbon-free world, and its supporters were rightly considered to be equivalent with Satan himself. Now Luthor had been attached to those same devils that hated everything the IEC stood for. They believed the world already had all the energy it needed until the year 2180 solely in coal and natural gas. They preached its affordability to mine and ease to convert to electricity, they denied anthropogenic global warming, and were probably the craziest, least educated smoggers in the hemisphere. And now thanks to propaganda and lies, Luthor had unwittingly become their herald.

"Please," Luthor said, "you have to see past this crap."

"Luthor, I want to help you. But this has the potential to be a major international incident." He stared more intently at Luthor. "Enough incidents can lead to war."

"You would throw me under the bus just so the world governments can roll on without any bumps in the road?"

"I am not going to abandon you here. I'm just suggesting if we don't go through the proper channels this could threaten peace. You know how tenuous our relations with the EU are lately. I *will not* be a party to anything that leads to another war. Even if that means abandoning one of my men. Even you."

"Right," Luthor said bitterly, "what was that line you always told us? *Don't be a hero?* Looks like you've got that part down."

Garcia looked hurt. "You would really say that after Titan?"

"I'm sorry. You didn't deserve that."

"Damn right I didn't. I want to help, but you are going to need give me something bombproof."

There was a long silence. Garcia appeared to take this job every bit as seriously as he took the military. He would never compromise. Right now Luthor sat chained to the floor, stuck between two very powerful governments, and Garcia had no intention of saving him before he was smashed between them.

Luthor had hoped that Garcia would just believe him out of loyalty. Luthor sighed. He reached into his belt and grabbed one of his three BOGs. He slapped the little orange lump of putty-like polymer on the table. The only indication that it had the potential to radically change the world was the small bump in the middle which held the plastic beads encasing element 126.

"What the hell is that?" Garcia snapped. Luthor realized that it had a striking resemblance to the plastic explosives they had been trained with for the campaign in Antarctica. Yet more "proof" that he had been building a bomb.

"This," Luthor said, "is the reason why the EU wants me at any cost."

#

Luthor was relieved that his former CO still trusted him enough to listen to his story. He folded his hands on the table, not interrupting once until he had finished. At the end he remained quiet for another few minutes, considering.

"Ten, I know you're an accomplished scientist now, but gravity?" His expression was the epitome of incredulity.

"Can't you feel it?" Luthor said.

"Feel what?

Mental note: not everyone is as accustomed to the small gravity changes I am.

Luthor grabbed another BOG from his belt. He mashed them together and Luthor felt the gravity clench. He tossed them casually to Garcia. Luthor's innards lurched as the gravity dimple moved across the table. His shackles kept him from being yanked toward the BOG's but Garcia slid toward the table. As he caught it, his eyes grew wider. With the power physically moving his body, Garcia had definitely noticed the feeling. He held the 126 in his hands as one might hold a stick of enriched Uranium.

"This is going to be the single strangest thing that has ever happened to you, but throw it at the ceiling. It will stick."

Garcia, who Luthor had always known to be fearless, now hesitated. The gravity distortion had clearly unnerved him. Finally, with a swift, decisive motion he stuck the 126 to the ceiling. He began floating up, out of his chair which was bolted to the ground.

"Holy shit!" he yelled, drifting up toward the ceiling. Rotating in the air while flailing his arms wildly, he cried out.

After an awkward bump—which helped Luthor feel slightly less pathetic for his own disastrous first attempt—Garcia managed to kneel upside down on the ceiling, his eyelids peeling back into his skull. Then he started laughing.

"Thank God we don't pay to run the cameras in this place anymore."

Luthor laughed, it was a good sign to have him veering from the topic of Luthor's incarceration. "Walk away from it when you want to come down." Luthor said.

Knowing what to expect this time, Garcia floated down without swearing. Carefully standing on the chair and bracing himself against the ceiling, he retrieved the bizarre little ball, placing it back on the table. Luthor immediately separated the two BOGs and felt a marked dissipation of altered gravity.

"You really can control gravity."

"With this powering my generator, I can create limitless, carbon-free energy. Can't you see how Europe might be willing to lie, murder, and steal to get their hands on my research? This element, if mass produced, could completely revolutionize the world, or if someone gains a monopoly, could be used to control it. I, for one, want to keep it out of the wrong hands."

"Ten, right now all I have is your word that you're innocent and this smogging ridiculous gravity trick. For me, that's good enough—I'm sorry I ever doubted you. But if you want me to have your back, I am going to need more evidence."

Luthor held up one of the BOGs, "how is this not enough?"

"It certainly provides you with credibility, but just because you have something that can control gravity doesn't necessarily mean people will believe you weren't intending it for the purposes of terrorism."

Luthor swore. "They murdered my friend and threatened to do the same to us! It was self-defense damn it! What did you want me to do?"

"Calm down. Look, I am on your side here and that is a big start. I am going to make sure this gets to trial and that it gets publicity."

"What if they try us as terrorists? That would mean a closed military tribunal. No publicity at all."

"Trust me, it *will be* a civilian trial."

"What about extradition? How are you going to stop them from shipping me back to Europe? That's where the goddamn Sabers tried to kill me. What can you do to stop forces that powerful?"

"Shut up, Tenrel. Please. This is what I do now. When

have you ever known me not to do what I said I would do?"

Luthor didn't respond. The man held to his word like the strong nuclear force. "It isn't going to take too many people floating up to the ceiling, before people start believing you. You're going to be okay."

The door cracked open and a man in a faded leather jacket popped his head in, motioning for Garcia. Garcia stood and walked out, leaving Luthor alone with his thoughts and the blasted one-way mirror.

Luthor crossed his arms, trying his best not to look guilty. His left leg was cramping. He strained against the ankle cuffs, wishing he could relieve the tension. A fair trial in the States wasn't ideal, but it polluted a lot less than a lifetime of incarceration in Europe. And with Garcia on his side, he might actually have a chance of winning.

Garcia walked back in, "I just spoke with someone using a voice modulator calling himself the Vanguard. Do you have any idea who that is?"

Relief flowed over him in a cresting wave. Qwiz was alive. He had escaped and was aware enough to figure out that they were trying to get home. It was almost too good to be true. It was the first good news he had heard since that fateful morning that had transformed them into fugitives. The emotion got the better of him and Luthor laughed despite himself. "Yes! He is a coworker," said Luthor.

"Well he just told me that there was a terrorist getting off a seabus from France today. Said his name was Luthor Tenrel."

"What?" *This doesn't make any sense, why would Qwiz call to tell them something like that? Is he trying to get us arrested? I guess he didn't understand my message after all.*

"He said he believed that man—you—to be *extremely dangerous.* He said that if we get him into custody we should hold him in the highest possible security until 'justice is done.' What is he talking about?"

"I don't have a clue." Luthor said. "He must have read the stories about me and believed them."

"He was adamant that I have 'lots of extra men guarding you at all times' because you were so dangerous."

Luthor shrugged. It didn't add up. Qwiz called himself the Vanguard, so no one would be able to find his identity —except Luthor. Not the action of a person trying to turn someone in. Not at all. If Qwiz really believed they were all dangerous terrorists then he would have wanted to give his real name to distance himself as far as possible from Luthor. Could it be Qwiz was trying to send him a message? If so, he was doing it in the least helpful way possible.

Garcia shrugged too. "I guess that is to be expected, if the media has been spun as much as you say. Regardless, I am still going to send two extra vehicles to escort you to the station. My ass is grass if the higher-ups find out I didn't listen to a tip like this and something happens on the way. We will talk more later tonight when I meet you there."

He left the room, leaving the door open behind him, a good sign. Luthor sat alone with thoughts spinning in his mind. He just couldn't figure out what Qwiz's call had been about. Why use the Vanguard? That was the most confusing part. He could have used a complete pseudonym to remain anonymous if he thought they were guilty. But the Vanguard meant he was trying to communicate with Luthor personally. *Maybe that is all.* Luthor wondered. *He just needed an excuse to call immigration so made up that bit about me being extremely dangerous. If they already think I am a terrorist, a phone call isn't going to change much is it?* Luthor unclenched, forcing himself not to dwell on the other possibilities.

#

Tanya wished she could put her face in her hands so she could weep, this was all her fault. If only she had listened to Vika and not been so quick to give themselves up. It had made so much more sense in her mind, it wasn't supposed to have happened like this. *They were supposed to realize this was all just a big misunderstanding. Do we really look like terrorists?*

The carps threw their belongings, including Luthor's laptop with all his research, into the trunk of the lead car. Luthor stared at it as the trunk was closed, he wouldn't like having it in someone else's control—even if it was still broken. A hand on the top of Tanya's head shoved her into the back of the small car. Michael grunted as he was jammed into the seat next to her. They crammed Luthor in last. The vehicle had never been designed to accommodate this many prisoners, of that she was certain.

The door shut with an ominous thump. Luthor leaned over and smiled at her. Smiled, at a time like this. "Everything is going to be okay," he said. Something about the way he said combined with his familiar voice, really did make it better. She knew it was irrational, but didn't much care at the moment. It was Luthor's job to be rational as a scientist anyway.

"What's going on?" Michael said.

"I met my old CO, Garcia. He was in charge in there. He believes us."

"That's fantastic!" Tanya replied. "Is he going to help?"

"How does a *public civilian* trial sound? He said he's going to take care of everything."

"How'd you convince him?" Michael said. "Mine outright laughed in my face!"

"It is hard not to believe someone when they can stick you to the ceiling," Luthor said.

"Wait, you showed him 126?" Michael said. "Ah, come on man!"

"Look, it's going to be just fine. He let me keep the 126 and we aren't going to get extradited."

"That's fantastic news," Tanya said, her head now spinning with possibilities. They had clawed their way out of Europe with the goal of being able to release Luthor's research to the world. What better place to do that than a high-profile court case? She had been suggesting all along that they turn themselves in so that this might actually happen. Not only that, but they were going to be able to do it all without fulfilling the morbid predictions of more killing from Vika.

They glided down a claustrophobic street, presumably toward the nearest police station.

Two carp cars sandwiched them in front and behind as an escort.

Buildings rose up to stratospheric heights all around, several of them still under construction. New York had grown exponentially since the Oil Crash. All major cities with effective mass transit had burgeoned, and pretty much any other place where a gas-burning car wasn't required to get around. Once gas became prohibitively expensive, the only choice for most people in the Suburbs was to sell everything they had and move someplace where they didn't need a car.

It was still hard to believe how poorly many cities had been designed in those days. Suburban sprawl was such an inefficient and expensive design. The majority of the population of America had lived in places so spread out that it was impossible to get anywhere without a car. *No wonder the world ran out of crude so quickly.* Tanya thought. *People had used gasoline just to pick up groceries. So unnecessary. Why hadn't the world been able to see where they were headed?* Now all but a few suburban cities were veritable ghost towns, inhabited only by scavengers, criminals, and Markless. Even the carps had given up patrolling their naked, burned-out, and picked-over streets. Once they left, even those with electric cars followed suit and fled for the cities. The only regular travel to the sprawl was by the wildly successful— and well-armed— scavenger companies. They picked over the abandoned suburbs and sold the scrap and useful items back to the big cities.

The surroundings darkened as they passed under a massive solar farm. Increasingly, they were being built over the roadways, the only place in the city left to build. Not much more than a concrete overpass completely covering the road, the solar farms often stretched for blocks. The tops were used to house solar panels, windmills, and grow food.

They drove on in the gloom under the solar farm. Fading, blue-hued LEDs imbedded in the concrete sides managed to push away total darkness. Rotting garbage piled high in the corners hid the equally unsanitary population of homeless. They crowded the sides of the street like ants. The storefronts had long since abandoned the stretch of road, bricking over their doors and moving their wares to the new prime real-estate on the platform above.

As they exited the tunnel, skyscrapers again shot up on either side. As they passed a small alley a large gas-burning SUV pulled out in front of them. It was amazing to see all that power contained in such a small place. All that waste. Whoever was driving could have paid someone to pull them around in a rickshaw for months instead of driving that machine for a single hour. She tried not to pay attention to the exhaust emitting from underneath the bumper or think about its effect on the climate.

After a minute of following the SUV through the man-made canyon of buildings they passed under another solar farm, this one much longer. Stairs ran up the sidewalk leading to a safer walking path above the farm. The tunnel was so massive the light from the other side failed to illuminate the dark center. The homeless congregation stayed at the periphery.

At the very center of the solar farm angry red lights popped up on the SUV in front of the lead carp car forcing it to skid to a halt. The carp driving their car swore and slammed on the brakes to avoid an accident. The seatbelt dug into her bra uncomfortably as she was jerked forward. Brake lights stained the inside of the car like blood.

"Who the hell does this guy think he is?" the driver yelled. He picked up a comm and shouted into it, "Go put the fear of carbon in that smogger!" Tanya couldn't hear the reply.

"I don't care if he is driving the goddamn presidential limo, he can't block traffic at the center of a farm! Get out there now, I'll call it in."

Then, without warning, the car in front of them exploded.

Blinded by the flash and deafened by the shock wave, Tanya couldn't think. The fire ball blasted out the glass windows and lifted the lightweight electric car into the air. It crunched back on the pavement, a flaming husk of a vehicle.

"Get out!" the driver screamed, unlocking the security doors from the front. He sounded like he was shouting at them through a pillow. Her ears hadn't recovered from the assault. In seconds, the carp had his gun out and had bolted outside.

They hastily unbuckled, but froze as gunshots rent the air. They cut clearly through her foggy ears. The carp collapsed back into his seat, forehead covered in blood.

Seconds later, both side doors were pulled open and Tanya found herself being yanked outside. Men in black gelvar and balaclavas held her fast while they hand-cuffed her. *Not again! How can this be happening again?*

Michael thrashed, straining to free himself against his captors. There had to be a dozen of them. One man hit him across the back of his knees with the butt of an assault rifle. He dropped to the ground. Another wrenched his arms cruelly behind his back and cuffed him. Luthor was also on his knees, head down in defeat, cuffed as well.

It was too similar to the events that had unfolded in Eli's office just days before. They had burned themselves forever into the living pages of her personal history. There was no alternative, they were just there, ferocious images slapping her in the face every time she gave them an inch. Flashbacks were bad enough, but now she was literally reliving them again.

Another SUV appeared behind them. It completely blocked the right side of the tunnel. Cars driving by in the other lanes braked, gawking out their open windows. The ubiquitous suburban refugees slunk against the walls, unwilling bystanders, witnesses with no credibility.

One man approached Tanya with something that looked suspiciously like a blindfold. She tossed her head like a little girl throwing a tantrum, she wanted to see what was going on as long as possible. Michael and Luthor were next to her, blindfolds already on. Michael still fought with all his might, Luthor was resigned and docile. She noticed in the background another gelvar-clad man toting some sort of long cylinder over his shoulder. It had the look of a weapon. Then everything went dark as the blindfold was successfully secured over her face.

As she was shoved into the back of the SUV another explosion reverberated off the walls of the makeshift tunnel. They'd blown up another police car.

CHAPTER 14:

New York City, United States of the West

Dark thoughts filled Luthor's mind, matching his blackened vision. His arms ached after being stuck behind his back. His only comfort was the familiar feel of Tanya's shoulder at his side. None of them had dared to speak; they were in the custody of enough men to take over a small country.

At least Vika had managed to escape, he hoped she might be able to eventually get the word out about their imprisonment and maybe the power of 126. Or maybe Vika had planned to betray them from the start and she had been setting this ambush up for weeks. Luthor didn't know and felt despair creeping into the edges of his mind trying to make him not care either.

Curiosity kept him from giving in. Who were these men? Who did they work for? Luthor had assumed he would be relatively safe in the States—at least from the Sabers. The Sabers were a European special forces unit, there was no way the Feds would have let this much foreign ordnance into the country. Did that mean there was another well-armed group trying to steal his synthesis method? Not a comforting thought, but there didn't seem to be any other logical destinations for his current set of initial conditions.

They continued driving in silence. It was impossible to tell where they were going or how far. The only obvious fact Luthor could discern was that they were moving fast. *How have they managed to avoid any other carps in pursuit? For once I would love to hear those damnable sirens! I suppose an*

RPG would effectively dissuade anyone from following you. Mental note: never chase someone who has a rocket launcher. Luthor abruptly lurched forward as they slammed on the brakes.

"Get out," a gravelly voice said in a southern accent.

He filed the accent to the back of his mind. *Definitely not European.*

Rough hands shoved Luthor out of the vehicle and tore the blindfold from his face. He found himself in an ancient, dimly lit parking garage, strangely devoid of any suburban refugee camps he had seen in other parking garages. He concluded they must be in a basement parking structure that was possible to secure from the displaced masses.

"Go," said the same gruff voice. Luthor debated about refusing to move just to see what they would do. Luthor's only copy of the research had been engulfed in the fireball that destroyed the lead car, if they shot him now, they would never be able to duplicate it. Unless they had recovered a hard drive from his house. That was a sobering possibility. But then again, there was that phone call from Qwiz. He was indeed alive, Luthor could only hope he had been able to grab the research and that his phone call had not been a betrayal. Hope glimmered weakly below the blanket of despair. They probably didn't have anything, besides him in chains, of course. That meant they couldn't shoot him if they wanted to get his technology. He could just refuse to move and see what happened; it would be a good litmus test to see how much they knew. Luthor weighed it in his mind, deciding that death was not a good consolation prize if he were wrong. He stumbled forward in the direction they indicated. The tingle of 126 at his belt heightened his fear.

The man took off his mask. He was easily 10 centimeters taller than Luthor, and wore all black. His chest bulged with the telltale profile of a gelvar vest. He held a pistol at his side that looked like it could stop a tank.

"Luthor Tenrel." It was an accusation.

Luthor felt his rage bubble up. No more calculating. It

was time to roll the dice and see what happened. He didn't want to give these bastards anything more than he had to. If they were going to shoot him anyway, what better time than now?

"Who the fuck are you?" Luthor spat.

A fist crushed the side of his face like a wrecking ball. Luthor spun sideways. Unable to catch himself with his hands still bound, he landed hard. Pain throbbed with every beat of his heart. Blood dripped into his left eye. Tanya babbled unintelligibly in the distance.

The big man leaned down, pressing his face inches from Luthor's. His breath stank.

"All you need to know about me, Tenrel, is that if you want to live, do what I say," he stood, then turned back and kicked Luthor hard in the ribs. "If you don't, you will know me only as Pain."

Luthor coughed against the cold concrete. His boot was inches from Luthor's head.

It had a Saber's emblem hand-stitched into the tongue.

Luthor might have a broken zygomatic process and some bruised ribs, but he had learned that there wasn't a new force chasing them. The Sabers had chased them in force all the way to America.

#

After the man calling himself Pain reentered the SUV and made a phone call, they picked up Luthor and shoved him toward the side of the parking garage. They walked through an open, solid steel door into a disgusting alley. Garbage was piled a meter high against the walls. It smelled strongly of rotting eggs. The occupants of this quarter of the sky-high metropolis appeared to be less diligent about moving their trash to the local transfer stations. Luthor stepped over a pile of refuse blackened with mold and swarming with flies.

They prodded him along a winding trail through the garbage. Men in front and behind him all held sub-machine guns, a good choice for close-quarters, urban warfare. They stopped at a narrow ladder running up the side of the building. It looked to be about 10 stories high. Given the choice between the ladder and being stabbed by a rusty knife, Luthor would take the knife every time.

With a jiggle and a click they unlocked his cuffs. "Climb," someone said with another jab of a gun. The standard fire escape had been cannibalized for scrap, replaced with this torturous, utilitarian monstrosity of a ladder. Pain and several others went first, climbing the sheer wall to the summit.

Just looking up made Luthor want to vomit.

He continued to stare up at the terrifying thing without moving. The temptation to stop and see if their pokes with guns changed to anything more serious multiplied exponentially. *A little death can't be all that bad, right? At least if I'm dead I won't have to worry about 126 anymore. As a significant fringe benefit, I won't have to climb this smogging ladder!*

The prodding became a stabbing. "Move. Now!"

"Give the man a minute!" Tanya snapped. Luthor almost started climbing just from her tone—the one that commands male obedience. "He is terrified of heights."

Luthor winced for more retaliation of some sort, but no gun shots came, no cries of pain. Nothing. Apparently, her voice worked on anyone. Tanya walked up to him and put a hand on his shoulder and another on his waist. "You will be fine," she said, "just don't look *down*." She squeezed gently and returned to her captors. There was something about the way she said down...

Luthor took a deep breath and put his hand on the bar, then placed his foot on another. Hand over hand he began the slow terrifying ascent up the side of the old building. His aches faded as fear overwhelmed them. Four steps up, it felt like the ground opened up into a bottomless chasm, trying to suck him in.

A tingling sensation swept through his shaking knees up through the crown of his skull as he climbed. It was like he was being pulled through his fear, inexorably to the top of the sheer ladder. He couldn't stop. Luthor didn't know if it was the fear of death, heights, Pain, or Tanya's voice that compelled him to climb. But step after step he mounted ever higher. The butterflies in his stomach became a flock of seagulls. Still, he didn't look down. *How the hell did I ever jump out of airplanes?* Luthor thought.

As if summoned from the past, his government sponsored therapist began speaking in his head in his soothing, if irritating, voice. "*You needn't be frustrated over your fear of heights, Luthor. It is a symptom of your PTSD. You have associated high places with parachuting, which in turn you associate with pain. It will probably take a long time, but you can conquer this too.*" Luthor never had managed to kick his fear of heights or his flashbacks. But the association psycho-babble at least made sense. Every scarring, bloody memory from his past had come as a direct result of jumping out of an airplane. So naturally, he now hated and feared heights.

Minutes passed, but Luthor made the impossible climb to the top of the building. He didn't know what the subtle pull had been to help him continue, but he was thankful for it. Maybe it was God, now feeling sorry for screwing him over in the first place. Luthor quickly rejected that idea, deciding it was the great flying spaghetti monster helping him instead.

He reached over the top rung of the building and stared straight down the barrel of another sub-machine gun. Three meters away from the edge, a black clad man in gelvar stood, indicating with his weapon, that Luthor should move toward the other soldiers. They stood in one corner of the roof. Pain walked around, talking on a phone, seemingly looking for something.

The roof itself was very strange. Not a single plant or fruit tree grew on the roof, nor were there any wind turbines mounted to harvest the high city winds. It was totally flat, paved only with the sturdy new solar panels that they had begun to slap on sidewalks. But that was the least efficient thing to do with a rooftop. All of those photovoltaic panels together wouldn't approach the energy output of a single windmill, and a typical rooftop could support four. Not only that, wind turbines generated power day and night, while still allowing for space to grow food. Solar panels needed be equipped with expensive battery packs to last the night. The rest of the rooftops in the city were green with gardens and buzzing with the blades of windmills. It just didn't make any sense why this building didn't have either. It was so inefficient.

Luthor walked with his captors and noticed he still felt the strange pull upward hadn't gone away. He put a hand on his shoulder where Tanya had touched him and felt the mushy stick of chewed gum. He pulled it from his shoulder and saw that it was actually two BOGs. She had put them there, altering gravity enough to help him climb more easily. His lower body had literally been pulled up the ladder. He replaced it on his belt with his others. There was another of Tanya's BOGs on his waist where she had squeezed him. She had only carried three of them to start with. *Why did she give all of her 126? If she was just trying to help me climb, she wouldn't have needed to give me all three. Now I have seven.*

Several neurons in Luthor's brain grew a new connection. *She thinks if I have more 126 then I can help us escape. Three or four might not do the trick, but if one of us had all of the 126 then maybe they could do something.* Luthor didn't have a clue what to do with it yet, but felt a determination swell that he couldn't let her down.

The man Luthor thought of as Pain put down his phone and forced Luthor farther away from the ladder.

"You'll never get away with this," Luthor said, "I know you're with the Sabers. Bringing foreign troops onto American soil is an act of war!"

He laughed, "you really don't know the first smogging thing about the Sabers do you? These *are* American troops."

Luthor had no idea what to make of that. The Sabers were European, but Pain was clearly American. It didn't make any sense.

Michael finished his climb and was followed by three more guards. There were now nine on the roof. Luthor wanted to find a way to save them, but still didn't know how on earth he was going to be able to dodge that many different guns. He looked around at different buildings near them, hoping for some escape idea to pop into his brain. The only thing of note was a larger building, opposite the ladder, that loomed another five stories above them. Yellowing corn and windmills covered its roof. Perhaps they could use the 126 to jump to it. He just needed to find an opening.

As Luthor studied the corn-stalks, a red flash hit his eye. He blinked, trying to get rid of it. A moment later another searing red flash blinded him. It took a moment before he found the light's genesis; it came from the rooftop cornfield. Up there, hidden among the stalks, lay Vika.

She held a laser scope on a long rifle she used to flash him in the eye. The gun was mounted on the edge of the building pointing down at them. Luthor wanted to jump for joy, she hadn't abandoned them! He shook his head slightly, telling her to wait. It wasn't time yet. He still needed a plan once the bullets started flying. There were too many of them for her to kill before they were able to shoot back. The other guards had not put handcuffs back on them, but still had guns leveled. They appeared to be waiting for something.

A low, rhythmic thumping grew in the distance. The sound was familiar, but Luthor couldn't place it. It gradually grew louder like an approaching machine gun, until it deafened them. Then he saw it.

A helicopter.

That was why there was nothing on the roof, this damn thing is a helipad. The helicopter flew in from across the street, blades rending the air. Its large black, military-style body looked like a bloated dragonfly, its stunted wings fitted with missiles and advanced auto-targeting MX-234 mini-guns.

If the Sabers really were chasing them, Europe was sparing no expense. First, they were stopped by gasoline-burning SUVs and now a helicopter. *No one* flew helicopters. Luthor couldn't imagine what it would cost to fuel and operate one for a trip, but it was easily more money than he made in a decade.

The helicopter slowed as it prepared to land on the empty roof and Luthor suddenly knew what he needed to do. He had to act fast or it would be too late.

Grabbing all seven BOGs from his belt Luthor mashed them together in his hands. Instantly, the gravity around him increased exponentially. The forces compressed around him in a vice grip more powerful than he ever imagined. Holding the 126 at his waist, his legs buckled, tucking into his torso and he strained with every muscle to keep his head from crunching into his belt. The periphery of his vision blotched into blackness as the prelude to passing out. He struggled to even think. *Mental note... seven is. Too many...* Luthor palmed the bundle in one hand and chucked it toward the corner of the roof in the direction of the helicopter.

As soon as the 126 left his hand Luthor's body followed it; the gravity field was so strong that even as it departed, it still had the strength to drag him. He lurched sideways along the ground for 5 meters before it was far enough away that friction with the roof was able to stop him. Everyone else on the roof fell to the ground as the 126 passed them, pulled toward its massive gravity dimple.

The helicopter cleared the edge of the roof and started dropping, hard. The pilot revved the massive motors, pushing them to their limit. But the helicopter couldn't escape, it was tethered to the 126 as surely as if it were chained down by a steel cable. It tilted, tangent to the sphere of altered gravity. But all its straining and smoking couldn't keep it aloft. It smashed against the corner of the roof, tail first. The stabilizer crumpled, hydraulic fluid sparking and bursting into flame. The body hit next, impaling the side of the building. Its massive gas tank exploded violently. The rotors kept spinning, ripping up solar panels and splintering them into the air.

Several of the soldiers were caught between the altered gravity and the explosion, they weren't getting back up. Others still lay dazed on the ground, the combination of changing elemental forces and their exploding ride, freezing them in place. One got up, swearing and swinging his gun around as if looking for a target. As he rose, a bullet tore through his head, splattering blood everywhere. His body crumpled, lifeless. As he hit the ground, his gelvar vest rippled outward, uselessly absorbing the impact of the fall. Seconds later, another soldier dropped, another round making a gruesome exit wound through the back of his skull.

The men realized they were getting picked off by a sniper and started shooting toward Vika's roof, suppressing her enough that she couldn't shoot back. Luthor realized this was his best chance. He dashed toward the burning helicopter, hoping to retrieve the invaluable element that had caused it to crash. Once inside the massive artificial gravity well, he started sliding toward it. It felt like slipping down a steep slide made of solar panels. The gravity was intense. He accelerated with frightening speed. With his hand outstretched he grabbed the 126, which sat innocently in front of the helicopter husk on a mangled solar panel. Doing his best to emulate Vika's maneuver on the boat, Luthor turned his body as his momentum carried him into the side of the blasted-out cockpit. He managed to absorb the landing with his feet, somewhat surprised he hadn't broken anything. Luthor's dimming vision reminded him he still had the enormous wad of 126 in his hand. He managed to peel it apart before he passed out and returned the individual BOGs to their home around his belt. Gravity instantly returned to normal.

With a lurch, the helicopter shifted. No longer held securely to the side of the building by artificial gravity, the Earth resumed its dominance over all matter. With the crunching and squealing of steel on concrete, what was left of the helicopter slid off the crushed corner of the roof to the street below. Luthor imagined screaming pedestrians on the street as their pyrotechnics show turned into a plummeting knot of steel falling on them. He hoped no one was caught in it. Another explosion rattled the building as the helicopter impaled the sidewalk.

The soldiers had taken cover behind the lip of the roof and were periodically firing off bursts at Vika, but she was doing an admirable job of keeping them pinned down. As he watched, Michael and Tanya flew across the void between the buildings and landed sideways on the edge of an adjacent building. Michael stood up against the wall, parallel to the street, and kicked out a window. He and Tanya ducked inside just as bullets started pinging around them. Vika shot back, taking down another soldier before they resumed their suppressing fire at the roof. Michael poked his head out and motioned for Luthor to follow.

The thought of jumping between buildings terrified Luthor. They were ten stories high!

But he knew if he could crash a helicopter then the 126 would protect him from falling too. The guards had completely ignored him while Vika made their lives difficult. He probably had time to make the jump before they could react.

Luthor's heart thumped against his ribcage like helicopter rotors as he ran toward the edge of the roof. *Damn damn damn! This better work!* Timing his steps to leap he prepared to throw element 126, he got to the edge.

And hesitated.

His muscles seized up. He stopped running. He didn't jump. It was just too high; it was just too far.

"No Luthor!" Michael screamed.

Luthor grabbed the top rail of the ladder to keep from falling the 10 stories to his death. Then he noticed that he was in the sights of two soldiers who had taken cover behind a large battery array. They stared at him, disbelieving looks obvious even through their masks. Luthor swore again and swung out onto the ladder to avoid their gunfire. Heart fluttering, he finally looked down. It felt like his stomach actually fell all the way to the trash-lined alley below. With shaking limbs, he quickly stepped down the rungs. He was never going to make it to the bottom without being shot. He pressed his body against the ladder to limit the size of his human target.

He looked to the side and noticed an apartment window ajar. Still shaking, he grabbed two BOGs and in desperation, threw them against the window. He let go of the ladder and rolled awkwardly toward it. The 126 kept him firmly mounted to the wall. Even though he was on the side of building, 9 stories up, the artificial sensation of down still felt good. He pulled the window the rest of the way open, retrieved his 126, and climbed in.

The apartment was filled with dirty, dusty, floral print furniture like some geriatric horror show. Two mite-ridden mattresses squatted in the middle of the floor. It looked like ten suburbians lived there, though no one seemed to be home. Luthor ran toward the door at the other end of the room. A rusty deadbolt held it securely closed. He glanced back and saw a rope hanging down outside the window and two booted feet dangling beside it. Luthor struggled frantically with the lock, but got it open and ran out into the hallway, slamming the door behind him. It splintered with 6mm rounds as he shut it.

#

"What the hell does he think he's doing?" Michael shouted. They hid behind the concrete wall as bullets popped in. Slugs smashed through desks and paper flew into the air. Office employees screamed, ducking under their desks or running for the exit.

"You know exactly what it was." Tanya said. "He did the same thing on the boat! Now it's finally going to get him killed."

"He was more scared of jumping than getting a bullet hole in his chest?" Michael pounded a fist on the floor. "I risked my life for that polluted son-of-a-bitch."

Luthor had no chance, he had half a dozen trained killers chasing him through an apartment. His cursed PTSD was going to accomplish what years of Chinese bullets and bombs had failed to do. It was going to kill Luthor Tenrel.

"We have to help him."

"How exactly are we supposed to do that? I know you love him, but I sure as hell am not going to run back in there and get shot."

Tanya clenched her fists. She was not going to let him kill himself while she had the will to stop it. "Vika." She said.

#

Luthor sprinted out into an empty hallway of closed doors, trying to ignore the pain in his ribs. He tried one. It was locked. No one would dare leave their apartment unlocked with all the suburban refugees looting everything that wasn't bolted down.

He cursed himself for being so stupid. What kind of moron would be more afraid of jumping than bullets? He had no chance now. Who knew how many of those damn bastards were chasing him? They had guns, what did he have, 126? That, and his oh-so-wonderful fear of heights. First, he'd exposed his friends on the seabus, and now this. His inability to master his fear had endangered all their lives and now he would die for it. If only he could do it all over again, he would suck it up. He would swallow his fear and jump.

But Luthor wasn't ready to succumb to the inevitable. Not yet. He took the stairs at the end of the hall quickly, leaping down the last three of every flight. Some of the men had come in from the roof entrance and were only two stories above him. He ran faster; his ribs ached.

Luthor had an idea. He ducked on the bottom stair of one of the levels and threw two bundles of 126 up, sticking them to the stairs above him. The wad held fast, looking like orange chewing gum. *It's going to be a little harder to run down the stairs when you suddenly weigh twice as much.* He thought. *Good luck!* Moments later the rhythmic thud of descending footfalls became a cacophony of noise and cursing. Luthor couldn't help but grin as he imagined trained soldiers falling down stairs on top of each other. It didn't matter how well trained they might be, if they came across a change in gravity, they would fall. Luthor knew he was going to lose the two BOGs, but if it bought him enough extra seconds to save his life then it was worth it.

At the bottom of the stairs there was another locked door. Luthor jerked the handle, but it would not budge. He didn't see a locking mechanism anywhere. The men above him had started running again. He hadn't slowed them as much as he hoped. Luthor sat on the bottom step with his feet facing the door. He threw a triple dose of 126 at the door. It instantly became down, and he plummeted toward it. His feet slammed the door with the force of a giant. His knees buckled, but so did the hinges. The door blasted outward with Luthor on top of it like a surf board. It landed on a slender patch of ground devoid of trash. A gaunt homeless woman with an even gaunter dog looked up at him in surprise.

Luthor picked up the 126 and sprinted toward the street opposite the helicopter. Three soldiers exited moments later. Reaching the street, Luthor turned toward Vika's apartment building. The door was locked. Frantic, he ran to the next building. It was locked too. He ducked into an alley as he heard more gun shots. Not looking to see how close they were, he hurdled trash piles and shoved vagrants out of the way.

"Smog you, moron! Look where you're going!" One grizzled old man shouted after him. Luthor had evidently smashed a whole village of suburban box-houses in his hurry.

Luthor had been paying so much attention to not falling in the trash he hadn't noticed a fence looming up ahead blocking his way. Its top was wrapped in barbwire. Luthor thought he would have to scale it with more 126, but decided to try the door next to the fence first. The door was open.

He ran inside. Homeless crowded a small entryway; it was a rare opportunity for indoor shelter for them. An antiquated elevator stood at one end of the room with a highly graffitied sign that read "Out of Order."

"Cheapskates," Luthor muttered. He knew as well as everyone else that it wasn't broken, it was just disconnected from the power because the landlords didn't want to pay the electricity bill to run a carbon-hog like an elevator. Next to the elevator was a sturdy metal fire-escape door. It was locked, though probably could be opened from the opposite side.

"Back away everyone!" Luthor shouted in a commanding voice, waving his arms away from the door. The smelly suburbians obediently skittered away to the corners of the room like cockroaches. Luthor knew he had only seconds. It was a sturdier door than the last one, and he wanted to make sure he could knock it over. He threw all five of his remaining BOGs at the door, and instantly started falling toward it, feet first. Everyone in the room fell and slid toward the door. As Luthor braced for the impact he wondered what the poor people must think when sideways suddenly became down. The door blasted open, Luthor hitting it much harder than he expected. The shock jerked tendons in his ankles and knees. He crumpled against the open door without falling to the ground. He had ripped the deadbolt completely out of the frame as the door swung inward.

"Stupid idea, Luthor," he said to himself.

"Mental note: you can't support ten times your weight!" He separated the BOGs.

He moved his legs around. While they were painful, it didn't feel as if he'd splintered bone. Of course, it could just be the adrenaline, that's what the smogging substance was for.

The angry homeless shouted obscenities to each other, wondering loudly what Luthor had done to cause the strange phenomenon. Luthor began limping up the stairs. His painful knees and badly rolled ankles screamed protest at his demand that they support him. Looking up he saw an unending staircase stretching up. There was no way he could climb that many steps fast enough to avoid being shot with messed up legs. And it was unlikely that any of the doors to the apartment floors would be unlocked.

Luthor split his remaining 126 into 2 bundles. He threw one ahead of him, and started a pathetically slow jog toward it. His legs shot angry pains at him, but the gravity did most of the work for him as he climbed the next flight. It was more like running slightly down-hill than climbing steps. He reached his first BOG, grabbed it, and threw the other one ahead of him pulling him higher. It was a game of gravity leapfrog. He stumbled up the stairs, half falling, half jogging to each new gravity dimple.

His relentless pursuers had entered the stairwell too.

They were 4 floors below Luthor and his staggering gait. He ran much more slowly than they, but also did not tire thanks to 126. While they laboriously climbed flight after flight, Luthor ran down hill. He managed to keep the minimum safe distance to avoid getting shot. At the top he pushed open the door into another rooftop field of corn.

He limped diagonally through the tall rows, hoping to stay out of sight. He quickly reached the edge of the rectangular roof and looked down onto a busy street. He was running out of options. His ankles and knees badly needed a rest and he didn't have a gun. Jumping to another building would only buy time. *That is if I can manage to actually make the jump this time.* Luthor thought bitterly. In his condition they would inevitably catch him. Climbing down would be a death sentence. *If only I hadn't blown up the damn helicopter, maybe I could have tried to steal it.*

The helicopter.

The crushing force of that much 126 still echoed in his memory. A force so intense and the gravitational field so wide, it had sucked in everyone on the roof and destroyed a 4000-horsepower helicopter. The very act of throwing it had sucked him toward it.

He knew what he had to do, and it terrified him, almost as much as bullet holes in his sternum did. The odds of his crazy plan working were slim, since he had ditched two BOGs in the stairwell. He would probably end up splattered on the pavement. But then, he was guaranteed to be splattered with lead if he stayed. At least a crazy plan offered him a chance. He hoped Tanya and Michael would make it out safely. If he died, they could finish what he'd started.

He heard the door open; men were breathing hard. Summoning all of his courage and delusion, Luthor smashed all his 126 together. He looked out at the four-lane street a dozen stories below. Hundreds of people gawked at the downed helicopter, blocking any semblance of traffic. Rescue teams had not yet arrived, but carps were swarming.

Luthor knew he only had seconds. Sweat dripped from his face. *Come on Luthor, this is your chance,* he told himself. *You wanted to conquer your fear. If you are too much of a pansy to try, then you will die.*

He took a deep breath, trying his best to imagine flat ground, and did the most petrifying thing he could think of: he jumped off the building, out into the street.

He threw the 126 as far as he could at the same instant he jumped. The little orange ball sailed away from him, but he was caught in its gravity dimple. No longer restrained by the ground's friction, nothing stopped the influence of the element's gravity this time. Luthor was pulled in a great sailing arc across the street trailing the 126. He was sixty meters above the ground. It felt like flying. Luthor screamed in fear. His inner ear told him that down was in the direction of the 126, but he knew that the real down was asphalt. Asphalt was not soft. Luthor kept screaming. People looked up, pointing and shouting at the man flying across the street. Flying men were perhaps the only thing that could be more perplexing than a crashed, diesel-powered helicopter on the sidewalk. The 126, still itself subject to earth's gravity, reached the top of its parabolic arc and turned down toward a rooftop filled with wheat. Luthor trailed behind it like the tail of a kite. The BOGs plopped in the middle of the small wheat field. So did Luthor, narrowly missing the twisting blades of a rooftop windmill. The plants and topsoil cushioned his fall, but he still hit hard. He rolled to a stop, and felt an ear of corn hit him in the back. It had been yanked off the other rooftop and followed him over. Every bone in his body ached. He had blood everywhere. He grabbed a patch of earth and kissed it, he had never been happier to not be falling.

With his adrenaline rush fading, he pulled apart the 126, painfully crawled to the edge of the roof, and peered out of the wheat. Across the street he saw three figures in black pop out of the corn field. They looked down on the side of the building and then moved to search the adjacent structures. They were looking in the wrong places! The corn stalks had been tall enough to block his flight. None of them so much as glanced across the street where he hid. Who would imagine a man jumping thirty meters across the road? They evidently did not.

Luthor struggled back to the crushed patch of wheat where he had landed. He lay down and passed out.

END OF PART I

PART II:

NEW YORK

CHAPTER 15:

Sixteen Years Ago

Luthor scratched the back of his hand. A pink scar stared back at him. A small bead of blood bloomed up from the middle of it. *Mental note: quit scratching it or it'll never heal.* It was still odd knowing that there was a miniature transmitter in there, constantly broadcasting his presence and just waiting to be scanned. It had been almost two years since the Paris 2 protocols had gone into effect. Since that time no one had been able to buy or sell anything without a CPI scan, and paper money had been completely abolished in the developed world.

Though to be fair, paper money had gone the way of the dinosaurs well before Paris 2. It had done so when the UN rebranded itself as the Carbon Enforcement Coalition and established the new currency of carbon credits. The goal of the policy had been to curb carbon emissions by directly influencing the market. Everything bought or sold was required to have Dollar value and a carbon credit value. If the Coalition wanted to lower emissions, it could simply lower the number of carbon credits in Circulation.

What few people predicted was the effect of a second required currency on world markets. There were far fewer carbon credits flowing around the economy than dollars and euros. People could have millions in the bank, but without carbon credits to go with those dollars, they couldn't buy bread. It hadn't taken long before the value of carbon credits dwarfed every other currency. Regular currencies tanked in value and people began exchanging dollars for credits at exorbitant rates. Lucrative crypto-currencies virtually disappeared overnight. Inflation exponentially climbed as people emptied their savings and retirements to buy the elusive credits. Luthor didn't know what the exchange rate finally reached, but had seen people taking briefcases of cash to banks to exchange them. The Credit had long since become the only currency that mattered, which worked well now that everyone had a CPI chip. Perhaps that was their plan all along.

Luthor looked across campus to see yet another raucous protest. He wondered which extremist group had commandeered the Loop this time. Yesterday the 2180ers had whipped a crowd into a frenzy and stormed downtown. The demagogues had been warning about the looming Oil Crash and that coal could save us. The morons had tried to light city hall on fire with flaming flags. Sure, banning coal had been a difficult decision to make, particularly in the USA. They were too coal-dependent for it to be an easy transition. Energy prices ballooned, which exacerbated the problem of the exponentially rising price of gasoline.

Just because it was hard, didn't mean it wasn't necessary. CO_2 emissions had to be lowered if the planet was going to survive. The Paris 2 computer models were unequivocal in the amount of time left to change course. If mankind didn't slash emissions in five years it would be too late to be able to turn the climate around in time. It meant that everyone was going to have to make sacrifices—big ones—not light the world on fire. Banning coal was just one such sacrifice. Why couldn't they understand that? Besides, they still had oil if they really wanted to burn something. Oil was too hard-wired into the infrastructure for the government to ban it too.

Chaz walked with Luthor to their next class. They were close enough to hear the bullhorn wielding man doing his best to incite another riot. He was spouting wild rhetoric about how CPI chips and carbon regulations were ushering in the "End Times". Not another 2180 rally then. The burgeoning crowd held the same signs Luthor had been seeing for the last few years in similar gatherings. "The End is Here," was raised on posters next to "CPI = 666" and "Revelation 13:16-17."

"These goddamn Christians are coming out of the woodwork lately, Ten. Where are they all coming from?"

"I heard that a lot of them have been traveling in from the country to try to get new converts."

"When all those churches went crazy and sold everything to buy those communes I thought we'd seen the last of them. Becoming Amish just to avoid getting a little computer chip in your hand?" Chaz shook his head. "It just doesn't make sense."

"Alfonzo and Marina thought it made sense. They had their chips removed and they shipped out to some big church-commune on Saturday."

"Really? Damn that was fast. I had no idea they actually took it that seriously."

"Everybody needs a cause to believe in."

"They believe in it enough to completely leave society?" Chaz asked.

"I can sort of see where they are coming from. There actually is something to the Christians' argument."

"You're shitting me."

Luthor raised his hands, "I'm not saying I buy it; still sounds like coincidence to me. Marina tried to get me to go with them. She showed me that Bible passage, you know the one they are always quoting? It talks about how in the end times everyone will be forced to get 'the mark of the beast' on their hand or forehead if they want to buy or sell anything."

Chaz grunted, "not bad I guess, considering its a couple thousand years old. Isn't the Beast supposed to be Satan or something?"

"Yeah. They think that if you get a CPI chip you are getting 'marked.' They think you are giving up your soul to the devil if you get one."

"Well, I guess I'm screwed," Chaz said showing his scar, "looks like I'm going to hell." Luthor laughed, "me too."

They entered the large lecture hall and found it buzzing with much more activity than Luthor typically saw for a political history class. Students milled around talking and looking at phones. Very few were in their seats.

"What's going on, Ten?"

"They're probably talking about the protest," Luthor said.

Professor Barlow's comforting voice boomed over the loud speaker. "Please take a seat, we are continuing our lecture on social media and its effect on presidential elections."

The class took their seats, but did not stop talking. Chaz took out his tablet to begin taking notes.

Barlow leaned next to the podium, his usual posture. He rarely looked at his notes. He flicked his presentation tablet and a large graph appeared on the projector screen.

"For those of you who actually read last night," the class offered a polite laugh, "your textbook told you that the 2016 election was the first election to be decided by social media, but it is wrong. It was a major factor, but not decisive. Please examine the graph." He indicated the screen, Chaz had it pulled up on his tablet and showed Luthor. "You will see that it wasn't until the 2024 election that social media became *the* decisive factor. Notice the jump in the polls here when Google, Facebook, and Twitter began suppressing differing opinions and officially endorsed a candidate for the first—" Barlow cut off mid-sentence as a lone student stood up and raised his hand. "Yes?"

The student cleared his throat, "Dr. Barlow, this is interesting and all, but a lot of us are wondering what is happening in Antarctica. There is stuff all over the web about China and the oil down there."

"Do you know what he is talking about?" Luthor asked. Chaz began flicking through web pages.

Students all over the auditorium began shouting similar questions to him. The only words Luthor picked out consistently were *oil* and *attack*. Barlow raised his hands again. "Quiet, please. Perhaps my lecture will have to take a back seat today." He called up a new page, the screen reflected his rapid-fire commands.

A new chart appeared which monitored the occurrence of certain words across the major social media sites. Fully 50% of them had both the words *war* and *China* in them.

Barlow struggled to keep the class in check. "The centrifuge of society has yet to completely separate truth from speculation, so do not believe everything you read on a Twitter feed." He cleared his throat. "However, judging from the traffic, there is one thing about which we can be certain. It appears that talks of sharing the Titan Dome oil field in Antarctica have broken down."

The students erupted, as if by shouting they could become the centrifuge the professor had mentioned. Luthor just wanted them to shut up, he wanted to hear more.

"As we discussed when the field was discovered earlier this year, Antarctica is strictly neutral territory; by international law no single country has a claim to any part of it. As a result, the talks of sharing its resources for the common good have been tenuous from the beginning. To any true student of history, whatever is transpiring should not come as a surprise. The combination of neutral territory and the most valuable commodity on the planet is nothing short of a powder keg waiting to explode."

Luthor had to hand it to the guy, he was still managing to squeeze in a lecture despite the bedlam. The students for their part were more engaged than they had been all semester. Dr. Barlow continued, "it is lamentable that the oil was discovered on the continent in the first place. Exploration of oil, or the mining any other natural resource in Antarctica, was completely illegal until 2021. The fools who we elect should have seen the inevitability of conflict if oil was ever discovered there. It seems their proclivity for lining their pockets with lobbying money has led us all to ruin."

Get to the point already. If— Luthor's thought was interrupted as an announcement began to broadcast over the classroom speakers.

"Please tune into channel 7 for an important broadcast."

Barlow flicked his tablet toward the screen which popped to life with the NBC logo. The classroom fell silent as a podium with the United States seal appeared. A caption informed the viewers that this was Secretary of State, Manuel Jimenez.

The class murmured, like water waiting to boil, as Jimenez walked to the podium. His eyes bored into the camera fiercely, anger and resolve painted on his face. "Several years ago, the largest oil field on the planet was discovered underneath the Antarctican Ice Sheet. It is estimated to be four to ten times larger than the Ghawar field in Saudi Arabia. Since, four other large fields have been discovered throughout the continent. The world leaders believed that Antarctica held enough oil to stall the oil crisis and be the bridge we needed to enter into a new sustainable future, free of the world-destroying effects of carbon dioxide. In short, we thought it would save the world from total economic collapse. With the *Titan Bore Resolution*, 156 countries agreed to equitable sharing and distribution of Antarctica's bounty."

Jimenez gripped the podium like a machine gun. "Two hours ago, the treaty was shattered. A combined force of Chinese and Indian forces attacked the oil drilling forces on Titan Dome. During the surprise assault over one thousand innocent oil workers were killed or captured along with twenty-five hundred Carbon Coalition peace-keepers. The remaining American and European forces have retreated to protect the Shackleton oil field and the civilians working there. It is clear that the Chinese-Indian Alliance intends to take the oil entirely for themselves and condemn the rest of the world to economic ruin."

The auditorium became deathly silent as they waited for the secretary to continue. "At the same time, they initiated a massive invasion of the middle east and have already secured 75% of the oil producing fields from that region. Our allies were helpless and unprepared to resist the ruthless, unprovoked aggression from the East.

"The President and Vice President are safe and en route to secure locations. They will address you within the hour. But I can assure you of this: The United States of America will not allow such heinous acts to stand. Our Allies in Europe and South America have already assured us they are standing together with us against this threat to world peace and stability."

"We will stand firm. We will not back down. And may God bless the United States of America."

Chaz turned to Luthor, "you've got to be kidding me! This is crazy! You know what this means, don't you?" Luthor never much cared for political science; it didn't deserve the title of science. It was the bastard child of history, law, sociology, superstition, and voodoo magic. But even with all its flaws, it pointed to one inescapable conclusion, and everyone knew it. War.

The ticker at the bottom of the screen displayed more disasters as if they were scores of college football games. *North Sea Oil Platforms Under Attack…Missiles Blow Holes into Alaskan Oil Pipeline, Hundreds Dead...Communication Satellite Destroyed, Spreading Space Debris Threatens Geo-Stationary Orbits…*

As the students screamed their protest at the news,

Luthor lowered his head in silence. Fighting reality was an exercise in futility. The future opened up before him in his mind. This would not be like the other wars of the 21st century. America hadn't even lost 5,000 soldiers in both Iraq wars, and not much more than that during the entirety of the subsequent occupations and the ongoing conflict with terrorist factions in the Middle East. But a war with China... something like that could claim the lives of tens of millions. If either country decided to employ their nuclear arsenals, then the earth would cease to support any life at all. Or equally frightening, it would be a drawn-out conflict spanning all the major oil producing sites of the world. The world would piss away its resources until one power dominated the scraps that were left.

#

New York City, United States of the West

"Get off my wheat, you filthy Markless!"

Luthor's eyes refused to open, blood and sweat had crusted over them. *How long have I been here?*

"I mean it! If you aren't moving in 2 seconds, I will shoot."

Luthor rubbed his eyes. His muscles ached from the meager effort. The sun sat below the artificial horizon of the skyscrapers. A portly old woman stood on the edge of the wheat field, three meters from him wearing a lavender floral-print dress. She held a pistol and a large trowel. He wasn't particularly excited about having either used on him. He rolled over and pushed himself to his knees.

"Go on. Shoo!" she said, swatting with the trowel as if gesturing to a stray dog.

"I'm going, I'm sorry." Luthor stood, his legs shot searing protests up through his nervous system. "How do I get down?"

"You managed to find a way up, didn't you?"

"I… I jumped from the next building."

The old lady's face crinkled up into an even bigger frown. "Stupid suburbians," she said under her breath. Without taking her eyes off of him, she walked to the edge of the roof. She removed a padlock holding a sturdy metal cage shut. It presumably sealed off the fire ladder from having roof access.

"Here. Now leave."

"Thank you. And… I'm sorry." Luthor limped to the ladder, trying to ignore the trowel trained on his chest.

Fear reared its ugly head again, but Luthor viciously shoved it down. *Fear is meant to be fought and conquered. I sure as smog am not letting it control me again. Never again!* Luthor grabbed the top rung and ignored the jarring tumult of fear as he descended. No sooner had he dropped below the roofline as the woman relocked the cage.

"Look at this mess. Stupid Markless." Luthor ignored her muttering, but legitimately hoped he had not financially impoverished her by using her crop as a landing strip. His legs and side did not stop their disapproval of his movement. But he had to move, he had to find the others, he had to find some smogging help.

The bottom of the alley flipped a switch, his fear unclenched, and Luthor's other senses regained consciousness. The foul stench of rotting garbage accosted his nose. The alley was as rife with refuse as others he'd seen. The omnipresent homeless sat or stood in small groups. They were dirty, disgusting, and gaunt; the forgotten trash of the new green society.

An emaciated woman in ripped rags sat next to the base of the ladder. Her hair was knotted and natty and might have been the same color as Tanya's if it hadn't been caked in dust and dirt. Dark smudges on her cheekbones highlighted her severely sunken cheeks. She might have been pretty if she hadn't been on the brink of starvation. She reached out and grabbed his leg with a grip that was stronger than it should have been.

"How did you get up there?" she said. Her voice fit her face. It was just as worn out. "Did you get any food? I heard there is wheat up there." She looked up at him with hungry eyes full of desperation.

"I don't have any food."

"But you got up there, didn't you? Why didn't you get food?"

"I... I wasn't hungry," Luthor said.

"You look like you eat often," she said, the hunger in her eyes deepening with a feral quality. "Tell me your secret." He had seen eyes like those before. They had belonged to broken men. Starving, freezing men in Antarctica. Luthor shuddered as he tried to push the memories away. He didn't even deserve to be alive to have those memories.

"I'm sorry, but I have to go," Luthor said. He shrugged her off.

She grabbed his ankles with both hands. He drug her a short distance, she weighed almost nothing. "No. Don't go! I'll suck your dick! Just tell me how to get up to the roof. Please!"

The thought repulsed him. "I can't help you." He gave his leg a violent yank. It drug her half a meter before she let go. The sound of weeping followed him as he exited the alley.

Luthor melted into the throngs of people walking the streets of New York. He was probably safer from prying eyes in the crowds than just about any other place in the USW. There were just so many people. Homeless bums, business women, and hardworking Joes blended together in a great melting pot of economic diversity.

Luthor limped by a window and saw a reflection of

himself. The spitting image of a Suburban refugee stared back. A purpling bruise from Pain's punch bloomed on his face; it was partially hidden by a layer of dirt from the wheat field. His clothes would not have been out of place in a dumpster. A bloodied knee poked out of a jagged hole in his jeans and his coat appeared to have taken a bath in dust. *No wonder that woman grabbed me, I look just like her.*

Luthor bobbed like a tidal generator in a sea of people, his mind buzzing with the day's events. With only the energy it took to throw a baseball from shortstop to first base, he had vaulted across an entire city street. He had also wrecked a helicopter and smashed doors. Never before had the raw power of gravity been more apparent. Gravity was a well of potential energy just waiting to be unleashed, yearning to be harnessed. It couldn't be more obvious that this was a world-changing discovery. If everyone had access to the energy contained in 126, the food shortage could be ended in a matter of years and he wouldn't have poor broken women offering to trade sexual favors for food—or *mere information* leading to food.

Unfortunately, others had different plans. The man who called himself Pain seemed bent on stealing the technology for whoever had hired the Sabers.

It makes sense that they would want to capture me or steal my technology, but why were they trying to shoot me as I escaped? Does that mean they already have the research, making us expendable? Maybe Qwiz isn't as safe as I thought. It's possible he lost the research but is still alive.

There were too many questions to answer. None of it made any sense. The only thing Luthor knew for sure was that he desperately needed to meet up with the others—if they were even still alive—and he needed to call Qwiz to find out what the hell was going on. And he had to do all of it without getting his CPI chip scanned or being seen by the Sabers. No easy task.

Luthor looked up at a billboard plastered to the side of a building. It proudly boasted that due to the current mayor's intervention there were now only four million homeless in New York city, down 23%. What the billboard didn't say was that almost all of the decrease came from starvation deaths. *The four million that are left ought to be enough to hide me,* Luthor thought as he melded back into the crowds.

#

I thought the son of bitch was afraid of heights. Michael squinted against the sun as he watched Luthor fly across the street in a great arc, doing an excellent impersonation of Spiderman. Ears of corn and dirt followed him, also pulled by the gravity. He landed in a puff of wheat and dust on the roof of the far building. Seconds later, the gelvar-bastards emerged from the corn looking in all the wrong places. They peeked down each side of the building and searched the adjacent structures. Not one of them even glanced across the busy street.

"I can't believe it," Tanya said, "he got away. Thank you, Vika. Thank you so much."

"I said I would help you."

"Yeah, but you came back to help. I didn't think you, uh...would."

"I meant what I said. Why are we still talking about this?"

"You had some impressive shooting back there," Michael said awkwardly, trying to change the subject, "but where the hell did you find a gun? We weren't gone for more than a couple of hours."

"A carbon cop on the roof of immigration."

"He just gave it to you?"

"Sure."

Somehow Michael doubted that is was that simple, but he knew better than to pry further.

"You must have hit five or six of those guys."

"Seven."

"You were awesome."

"My performance was unacceptable. I missed my fifth shot."

How could she possibly be upset about missing only one? "Vika, you single-handedly held off all of them. You allowed us to escape. How can you be upset about a single shot?"

"I *don't* miss." Vika glared at him like she was aiming down the sight of her rifle. She did not elaborate.

Michael had thought for a brief moment that everything had straightened out. With Luthor's carp friend on their side, they had a chance to release the data on that laptop during a trial and clear their names. Now, not so much.

His moment of hope vanished when the lead carp car made friends with an RPG. The explosion had flambéed all their belongings—including the smogging laptop. Actually, *smogging* wasn't a bad term for the smoldering, worthless mess now farting toxic, computer-fumes into the air. With that laptop had gone any chance of shedding the label of terrorist Luthor had acquired—and Michael by association.

The news had quickly picked up the story and blamed Luthor for the rampant destruction across the city. At least Jaili Fendra had made it look sexy when she described how Luthor had allegedly bombed the carbon police in protest of the twenty-year-old ban on coal. The story had centered on Luthor's supposed involvement in 2180. When homeland security had come to arrest him, he'd blown up their helicopter too. It didn't matter that there wasn't a molecule of proof to substantiate their tale. The result was they couldn't set foot in any police station with any hope of getting justice.

Now they didn't have a pot to piss in—literally and figuratively. But they did have Vika, and hell, maybe that would smogging be enough.

"Why don't we see if we can go find Luthor before they do?" Tanya asked pleasantly.

#

"And you're sure that this guy Pain was with the Sabers?" Michael asked after hearing Luthor's story.

Luthor had been limping along the street aimlessly when they found him, trying to seem like just another refugee from the suburbs.

"I'm sure," Luthor said, "he had their emblem hand stitched into his boot. Let's just say I got a pretty good look at it."

"How'd they get that many Sabers here? It doesn't make sense."

"Pain said that they were *American* troops, like they were already here." It was then that Luthor recalled his mental note. "Vika, do you know what he was talking about? You seem to know *everything*," Luthor paused then added, "oh, and thank you for saving our lives back there. That was smogging awesome!"

Vika pursed her lips. "You are welcome. But that is troubling news. I thought I would know about an American division of the Sabers."

"How would you have known?" Luthor asked. "They're secretive as hell."

"Because I used to be one," she said.

Luthor blinked. "Wait. What?"

Michael seemed to completely lose control of his higher motor functions. "*You* were a Saber?"

It was as if Michael's hot air blew away the vaporous mystery that had enveloped Vika. It all fit. Of course she would know the things she knew and do the things she did. She probably hadn't ever been a secretary. She was a member of the most elite force in the world. Or at least had once been. Luthor nodded to her in understanding.

"More specifically," she added, "I was a Black Saber."

"Holy smogging shit!" Michael raked his hands through his stubbly hair. "Why didn't you tell us?"

"After the Sabers killed Eli and tried to kill you, I didn't think it was the best time to mention it."

She was right. Luthor wouldn't have gone one step with her if he'd known she was a Saber. If she hadn't just saved all their lives by killing Sabers, he probably wouldn't trust her even now.

"So that's why you are… the way you are." Michael said.

Tanya slapped him on the shoulder. It didn't seem to faze him.

"Yes, it is."

"What…err… did you do with them?"

"I was a sniper."

"Oh! You really don't miss."

"No, I don't. I had a perfect record in covert ops for two straight years."

While the enigma of Vika and her peculiar proclivities for combat now made sense, much about her story still didn't. "Then why leave all of that to work for Eli?" Luthor asked.

Vika frowned, "I do not like to talk about it."

Tanya gave her a sympathetic look. Luthor had withheld his own war-torn past from Tanya for long enough that she knew when it was a good time not to press the issue. "How did you know Eli?" she asked.

"I grew up in the same apartment he lived in. I watched his kids for him. He is like the father I never had."

"Now he's dead too," Luthor said, "that's why you are

helping us."

"Yes. And I believe in your cause. The world needs your research, Tenrel. Badly. And... I have no problem fighting against the Sabers' aims."

"What can you tell us about them?" Luthor prodded. Maybe she could give them a better idea as to what they were up against.

"They are a covert branch of the European Special forces. I was recruited at fifteen to undergo training and in all the years since then I have never heard of an American branch of the Sabers."

"What was the training like?" Tanya asked.

"Unpleasant... I was one of only three females in history to graduate."

"Wow," Michael said, "and you were still good enough to make it into the Black Sabers. You're badass, Vika."

Vika still didn't seem to know what to do with that phrase, so Luthor asked another question. "So, you never went on missions to the States?"

"No. We did travel internationally, but rarely to the western hemisphere."

"What were your objectives?"

"The same thing we did in Antarctica. The same thing every military does. We bombed energy sources, we secured energy sources. What else is there to do?"

"Stealing research from scientists and killing civilians apparently," Luthor said bitterly. "Oh, and robbing the world of free energy and descending it into war all for the sake of a profit also seems to be on that list too."

"Tenrel, I do not know why we were sent on our missions. They did not tell us. We just did our jobs. Who knows who is giving the orders to the Sabers we have faced, or why they want your research?"

"Who gave your orders?"

"A Colonel named Franco Dimarin. He directed them

to Captain Jacques, my direct superior. We planned how to execute the ops as a team, but Jacques never told us why. We didn't ask."

"Why not?"

"Soldiers do not ask why, Tenrel."

"Garcia did." Luthor didn't say any more. The conversation where Garcia had confronted General Stutzman with that question was one of his worst memories. Anti-Luthor rattled his mental cage. Luthor held the door shut.

Once the shock of Vika being a member of the Sabers had begun to wear off, Luthor felt hopelessness creep back into the periphery of his mind. He sagged against a grimy wall in a suburban-infested alley. "I don't see how we are getting past this." The traffic rumbled as if emphasizing his words. "The laptop is a complete loss. Now we're fugitives on this continent too, and we might as well be Markless because none of us can so much as walk into a store without the whole damn Carbon Coalition coming down on us."

"What about Garcia?" asked Tanya. "I thought he was on our side."

"I'm sure he still is, but at this point I doubt it's safe to contact him. He could end up as collateral damage."

"I think it would be foolish to trust him," Vika said. "Perhaps he's the one who told them exactly where you would be?"

"I trust him with my life!" Luthor yelled.

"And yet he didn't personally escort you? And you were kidnapped minutes after leaving his company. That is dangerously suspicious."

"That's bullshit." Luthor felt the fury begin to boil up in him. He strained to keep Anti-Luthor contained, but it was hard. He had shared more with Garcia than they would ever understand. He would not stand for an insult to his honor.

"Bullshit or not. It is not safe."

Michael interrupted, "you guys are forgetting one important thing."

"What?"

"Pain—or whatever his name is—*is still alive.* Do you think he would hesitate, even for a moment, to blow up the whole police station to get to us if we went there?"

"How would he know?" Luthor asked.

"Think about it; he knew just which carp car to blow up, to trap us. Maybe Vika's right and it was Garcia, maybe not. But it sure looks like someone tipped him off."

"Garcia wasn't helping *them!*" Luthor shouted.

Michael shook his head. "Even if we could trust Garcia, we wouldn't be able to use a trial to release the 126 method anymore. Because we don't have it! That laptop is toast. Without any research we are up shit's creek without a paddle."

"What about Qwiz?" asked Tanya. "What if he was able to save everything from your apartment?"

"All we know is he's alive," said Luthor, "but I don't know if he was able to save anything."

"Then that is our objective," Vika said, "contact this Qwiz."

"How are we going to get our hands on a phone?"

Vika raised her eyebrow and smiled. She looked like a viper ready to strike. "I can take care of that." Michael watched her muscular body for a little too long as she left.

Luthor was no weather-man, but rain seemed to be inevitable so the three of them began to look for shelter. Luthor didn't want to be both cold and hungry. Fortunately, his angry joints were beginning to feel better; walking had loosened them up.

"Look at all this trash, Luthor. Entropy at work." Michael folded his arms and smiled, as if impressed with his handiwork. "It's a perfect illustration of the 2nd law of thermodynamics."

Luthor hadn't been contemplating thermodynamics. He had been thinking about the sheer volume of trash piled up against every wall, and the vast number of vagrants clustering in every nook and cranny around them. But Michael's sentiment certainly made sense. The second law of thermodynamics stated that the entropy of a system tended to increase. He had explained it to Tanya by saying that the *disorder* of a system tended to increase over time.

It was a simple enough concept, but had far-reaching consequences. If someone discharged a bunch of helium in one corner of a room where Luthor stood, his voice would resemble a chipmunk's. But over time the entropy would increase, and the helium gas would distribute itself evenly throughout the room making the helium undetectable. It wouldn't clump up in the opposite corner, or spontaneously inflate a balloon. Maintaining order required energy, something this city was ravenously short of.

When left alone everything degenerated to a less orderly state, even the universe. Most experts in theoretical physics expected the universe would – trillions of years into the future—eventually die a heat death, as the aggregate entropy increased to such a degree that suns and galaxies no longer shone. When no external energy was applied to maintain the system, entropy—thus the second law of thermodynamics—reigned supreme. The city, unable to afford to power mechanized garbage trucks, was a victim and unwilling example of this universal law.

Any useful garbage was scavenged immediately leaving constantly growing piles of entropy in the form of dirt, refuse, plastic, and paper. In more civilized quarters of the city, people applied the external energy to keep things orderly by hauling their trash to local transfer stations where it would be converted to Biofuel or paying Markless with slices of bread to do it for them. Trash duty was the only dependable source of food for the poor bastards who didn't have CPI chips. It was the government's token attempt to keep people alive that weren't legally allowed to buy food or have a job.

"It's still hard to believe that they used to have giant, carbon-spewing trucks whose sole purpose was to pick up trash. Such a waste."

"They didn't have four million people on the street to pick it up for them," Luthor said.

CHAPTER 16:

New York City, United States of the West

Tanya shivered in the rain. Their meager cover helped some, so long as the wind didn't blow at all. Naturally, it hadn't stopped blowing all evening.

She stared across the street at what had once been a public park. Now it had a four-meter fence with barbed wire at the top and armed guards patrolling its periphery. They guarded the posh garden plots owned by the ultra-wealthy. Even in the dark, Tanya could see succulent tomatoes and laden fruit trees just waiting to be plucked. Her stomach grumbled.

Luthor would probably say that being homeless was "suboptimal," but she just thought it outright sucked. Now that Michael had finally quit complaining, all she had to deal with was the dark, the cold, the wet, the hunger, and the very noticeable lack of a bed. She had dealt with some severe hunger during the war, same as everyone else, but she had grown soft in recent years as the world struggled to return to normalcy. It had only been a day since she'd eaten and there was a terrible crick in her neck from sleeping in the dirt. She didn't even want to think about what was happening to her hair and her complexion. *Vika doesn't seem to be having any smogging problems.* But Vika hadn't yet returned to show off her perfect skin. Tanya hadn't extracted a promise from her not to kill anyone to procure a phone. Hopefully, their quest to contact Qwiz wouldn't leave any bodies.

The worst part was when she had to pee. She couldn't

go into any store to use the restroom because she would be scanned and they would be discovered; even if she could get in, no store manager in their right mind would let someone as dirty and disgusting as her use the facilities. She had never before wished she were a man. Until now. They could just whip it out and pee any old place. She had to find a secluded corner and squat. But the homeless and Markless were everywhere, it was almost impossible to go without someone watching, or worse, commenting. Her bladder became bashful with an audience. The boys never could understand that it is really quite difficult to pee with someone watching. They could carry on a conversation midstream—so to speak.

She was not about to pee in front of Michael, so she walked out into the rain. She was already soaked, who cared if she got a little wetter? A row of bushes marched behind a bench in front of the barbed wire fence. She crouched down between them to relieve herself.

Undoubtedly, she was being watched by not only her cohorts, but an indeterminate number of fellow homeless. But she couldn't see them and that made all the difference. As she finished, she saw Vika return to their nonexistent cover and begin talking with the boys.

Through the haze in the distance a solitary black figure with an umbrella walked in her direction. She had no interest in being caught with her pants down, figuratively or otherwise. Wishing for toilet paper, or even a half-clean cloth, she zipped her pants. She breathed faster. She could think of better things than being raped in the rain.

She approached the others and Michael smiled broadly. "She did it! We got a phone! She even got the code to unlock it!"

"Wonderful," Tanya said, "but I think we have company." She pointed to the person still approaching. The shuffling step of the silhouette had the look of an older man. Vika had raised her rifle, laser sight unabashedly targeting the stranger. The man stepped under their meager cover and Tanya got her first look at him. He wore a tattered black suit that had been repeatedly patched. It had a familiar look to it Tanya couldn't place. He had wispy white hair without a bald spot that connected to a full, but groomed beard. His straight back implied he didn't need the gnarled wooden cane he carried. He smiled and politely shook out his umbrella as if he were entering their home.

"Close enough," Vika said. "What do you want?"

The man didn't seem to be disturbed at her threatening posture and continued forward. Smile still on his face, he spread his hands wide in greeting.

"Peace friends. I mean you no harm."

"Not a step closer until you tell us who you are," Vika gestured at Luthor, "search him for weapons."

"Luthor always gets to do the cool stuff," Michael said.

"Don't be pathetic," she replied, "we both know you are too incompetent to do it properly."

Luthor frisked the old man thoroughly, rubbing his hands down the inside of his coat and down each pant leg. Both acted like being frisked was normal, natural, and expected. In fact, nothing seemed to bother the guy at all, not the gun, the frisking, not even Vika's tone.

"He's clean," said Luthor.

Vika lowered her gun. "Speak."

The man bowed politely. "Thank you. I apologize for my intrusion, but I couldn't help but notice that you look a little out of place around here. I, for one, don't recognize you, and nobody who has any experience on the streets would try to weather a storm under this quality of shelter." As he spoke, a big raindrop fell from one of the apartment balconies, splashed on his head, and dribbled down the front of his nose. He wiped it away casually. "Is this by chance, your first time being homeless here?"

Are we that obvious? I suppose taking a pee out in the rain doesn't help our cause any.

"Yes, this is our first time, well mine, anyway," Tanya said.

Michael said nothing. Tanya didn't know much about his past, but he hadn't fared as well as she had during the Culling, that much was obvious.

"I assumed as much," the old man offered an empathetic smile, "allow me to introduce myself. My name is Rocky Farrano. But most everyone just calls me Father Roc."

"Father?" Michael said, "you're a priest?"

That was why the suit looked familiar, it had probably been the same suit he wore when he was a cleric. The collar had become too tattered to be recognizable.

"I used to be. I formally forsook that title when the Catholic Church officially condoned being implanted with CPI chips. But I didn't come here to tell you my life story. If you are interested, I can share more later. My true purpose is to offer you real shelter from the rain as well as a morsel of food."

Tanya frowned. Food was too scarce a commodity to offer, unless of course one's motives weren't entirely pure. Otherwise, the wealthy wouldn't hire men with assault rifles to patrol their gardens. But the man's kindly smile and twinkling eyes made it hard to believe that he would try to rob or rape them.

"How can we trust that you don't have people waiting to jump us and take our possessions?" Luthor asked.

"Why haven't you jumped me and taken my possessions, friend?" the priest asked.

The man had a point. He walked into a group of strangers and never worried about getting mugged. Luthor didn't respond.

"You see," Roc continued, "I like to believe that people have generally good intentions. I don't expect you to hurt me, and there should be no reason you expect me to hurt you. You are welcome to accept my offer or reject it. Nevertheless, I freely offer my services. You may even bring your weapons, now that I am confident you will not use them wantonly." He patiently waited for a response while more big drops of rain crapped on his head.

Tanya wanted to go with him. There was something that was instinctively trustworthy about the man. His calm demeanor and kindly countenance bespoke a good soul. She believed that he truly had no intention of harming them.

"I have just one question then," Luthor said, "if you have food and shelter to spare, why give them to strangers?"

"You ask a theological question, friend. Suffice it to say that my Lord once fed the poor and needy and I now seek to follow in His footsteps. I will not deceive you, we don't have much, but perhaps even a little will feel better than a completely empty stomach. And a warm dry fire might be preferable to a cold wet sidewalk."

"We do need someplace dry to make the phone call," Michael said.

Luthor ignored him, addressing the priest, "you haven't even asked us who we are, why we are homeless, or why we are armed."

"I don't care. All are sinners in the eyes of God, yet He loves us all the same. It is not mine to judge. Perhaps you fell on hard times, perhaps you are criminals on the run, or perhaps you are fellow Christians seeking asylum. It doesn't matter."

The decision made, the four got up and began trekking through the sodden, trash-lined street. The rain obscured the buildings ringing the garden. Tanya could make out a glow in the distance. Perhaps that was where their fire was. She quickly saw that they were approaching the telltale overhang of a solar farm covering the slim alley between buildings. It stretched out over the larger road that bordered the park. Vegetables drooped over the edges. The pillars supporting the farm were unfortunately as wrapped in razor wire as the garden was. She wouldn't be able to climb up and get any of the food. A windmill loomed amid the plants, blades slowly turning in the dripping wind of the storm.

Next to the solar farm, emblazoned with red LED running lights was *Tony's Italian Restaurant.* Just seeing a food establishment made her stomach clench with hunger pains. It probably owned the solar farm and used the fresh vegetables to supplement its stores.

It felt wonderful to finally be out of the rain. Tanya took a moment to ring out her hair, hoping that the rain had pushed her amber locks toward something that approached clean. Father Roc led them toward a small group of men and women gathered near the side of Tony's. The glow was coming from a rusted steel garbage can with bullet holes perforating the sides.

The group saw them coming and parted to allow them room around the garbage can. Strangers smiled at them with gaunt, but kind faces. Smoke from the garbage can obscured some of them. Tanya silently prayed that this had been a good idea.

#

"What are you doing?" Michael blurted, "you didn't tell me that you had *real fire* going!"

"Is there another kind?" asked Roc.

"Yes! Damn it, there is the *legal* kind. You know, an *electric* fire?" Michael frantically searched around for support, finding none. Tanya couldn't blame him, she hadn't been near a real fire since she'd been a child. It was too dangerous for the environment to burn things.

Too much carbon. Whatever burned in there certainly wasn't wood.

A very tall man with wild red hair who looked like he could have been a body-builder at an earlier time in his life, burst out laughing. He had a deep, brawny voice.

"What's so funny?" Michael said. "What if the carbon police catch you?"

"What are the carps gonna do to us?" the tall man said, "arrest us? That would really suck. Getting two square meals a day and shelter all year long? Sounds like a really shitty deal to me." He laughed again. An equally massive black man standing next to him joined in.

"You have to pardon Thaddeus and DeShawn," Roc said, "they don't mean any harm. It's just that we don't worry about the carbon police around here. We have an *understanding* with them."

"We're already screwed for life," said a woman with the voice of a life-long smoker. Her dreadlocks suggested she had been on the street with no respite for quite a while. "We can't never buy or sell nothing legally no more. We can't get no jobs, can't own property. Not since they took our Marks."

"They *took your marks*?" Tanya said, not quite believing what she was hearing.

"The jails get full pretty quick these days, just about everyone and their mom would rather go there than starve to death on the streets. So, if you get arrested more than once then they just take your Mark. It's cheaper than prison and pretty damn effective at discouraging repeat offenders."

Tanya began to see why the priest wasn't too concerned if they were criminals or not, he already lived with an entire group of them.

"And you can't ever get another one?" Tanya asked.

"Nope. If you don't have one, you can't get one. They only replace broken ones. They won't issue new ones to people that don't have nothing implanted. They say it's a *security issue*. We're stuck on the streets till we die."

"That's not fair."

"You got that smogging right," said the red-haired man Roc had called Thaddeus.

The black guy next to him punched him hard in the arm. "Come on Thadd! You told Father Roc you were gonna watch your mouth."

"Sorry man. I mean sorry, Father. Shit. I'm supposed to apologize to God." He looked up and folded his hands like a child first learning to say his prayers, "sorry Jesus."

Tanya fought back laughter. The priest was more than just a member of the group, it seemed he was the spiritual leader as well.

"You *all* lost your CPI chips?" Luthor asked.

"Everybody but Father Roc," said Thaddeus. "Never got one in the first place."

DeShawn grinned. "Getting arrested would be about the best thing that could happen to us. We can't even buy drugs without a Mark. So, I say burn as much trash as we can!"

Michael turned green. "You're burning trash? What about the pollution? All those greenhouse gases!"

"When you cold and tired, it's easy not to care," said DeShawn. "Global warming sounds amazing when you freezing to death in the winter and can't make no fire."

"Who's gonna get screwed by the warming anyway?" Thaddeus pointed up at the buildings, "all those bastards up there, they put us on the streets in the first place with their smogging carbon regulations and Marks!" DeShawn hit him hard in the arm again. "Damn it. Sorry Jesus."

Tanya found the conversation stimulating. Besides her parents who had fled society altogether, she had never been given the opportunity to hear the perspective of a Markless stuck in an urban setting. Tanya never imagined that anyone would become a Markless except by choice. The idea of someone's Mark being taken against their will horrified her. With the way the world now existed, it was basically a death sentence—albeit a long, drawn-out one by starvation or disease. A lucky Markless would get shot stealing food, they wouldn't have to starve. It made this group's generosity and openness that much more remarkable. They truly had nothing, yet offered it to strangers without the hint of complaint. Tanya wondered how much of that could be attributed to the priest's influence.

"Father Roc, why are you here?" Tanya asked. "Every other priest I've heard of is either still in the church, or retreated to the country."

Rocky stroked his beard thoughtfully. "We all had a choice to make after Paris 2 and the CPI regulation. The alarming similarities between the CPI chip and the Mark of the Beast described in the book of Revelation made it a difficult one for me. The new mandates seemed to be too much of a coincidence to be anything other than a stepping-stone to the end times. The Catholic Church didn't share my fear, claiming they could not identify a specific Beast. Therefore, without a Beast, how could a CPI chip be his Mark? They claimed any similarity was mere coincidence and not the fulfillment of prophesy.

"I didn't know if I should I follow my conscience and refuse the Mark. It would be tantamount to officially rejecting the Church's decree and thus my own priesthood. In the end, I lost trust in the Church when they violently disagreed with my beliefs. So, I left it and my priesthood behind. The Lord has written His law on our hearts in the form of a conscience and I followed mine. If there was even a chance that CPI was the Mark of the Beast, I was not willing to take it."

"So now that you've been a Markless for twenty years, who do you think this *Beast* is anyway?" asked Michael.

"Another time," he replied. "Now is not the time for sermons." The priest's soothing voice was easy to listen to and comforting. In the tumultuous situation they had found themselves in, it refreshed her. He never showed a hint of judgment that they had not made the same choice. He simply described his own life and his own decisions. Her parents had come to a similar conclusion, except they fled to a farm their church had purchased in Iowa. The priest had chosen to stay. Why? Tanya asked the question.

"I don't want to belittle your parents' decision by any means. But I don't believe Jesus would have retreated to the industrial farms of the Midwest like most of his followers. He would be here, in the mix of things, serving the poor and loving sinners. So that is where I have been. What you see here represents the small flock that has decided to follow my lead. We are all dedicated to the same purpose, serving the poor and outcast."

Over the next half hour Father Roc introduced the rest of their little band. They were quite an eclectic group. Thaddeus had been a farmer in Pennsylvania, forced out because of skyrocketing oil prices in the twenties. He had moved to New York City but never found work. DeShawn played D1 football in college as a linebacker but never made it to the NFL. He had lost everything due to a gambling addiction and ended up on the streets.

A cadre of women accompanied the two burly men. Serenity became a prostitute when she was sixteen. After the carbon regulation, carps arrested her five times for drug possession and solicitation. They removed her mark after the fifth one and she wound up here.

Abigail, a blond haired, single mother had been an executive at a safe manufacturing company. The plummeting demand for safes and vaults after the CPI regulation bankrupted her. People just didn't need as many safes when paper currency, paper identification, and pretty much everything else that came in a hard-copy had been abolished. She explained how her situation had grown dire with the introduction of the carbon credit. Her large savings accounts quickly became worthless as the value of the Dollar plunged. Her millions became pocket change that couldn't buy anything without a Credit to accompany them. She lost her house and fled to the city in hopes of finding food. After stealing a second time to feed her starving children, the carbon police removed her Mark. Then the state took her children. Tanya fought back tears when she told them she hadn't seen them since.

"I think it is about grub time, Father," said DeShawn. "Would you bless the meal?" *What meal?* Tanya didn't see any food.

A side door opened on Tony's restaurant and flooded the area with artificial light. A man handed a large plastic garbage bag to Thaddeus who set it next to the fire with reverence. "Ladies, gentlemen, dinner is served."

Roc prayed—a sincere, but thankfully brief prayer. Abigail produced a stack of multicolored, plastic plates. Everyone eagerly lined up around the garbage can in what was clearly a nightly tradition. Trepidation and bile rose in her throat as Tanya realized that the contents of the garbage bag *was* dinner.

"Are you barbarians? What are you thinking?" yelled Thaddeus. "We serve the guests first!" Sufficiently cowed, those in the front of the line moved away, making room for Tanya, Luthor, Michael, and Vika. "Don't you morons remember what the Lord said? The *First* shall be *Last.* And I sure as hell don't want to be last at *His* feast."

Tanya would have much preferred to have Luthor go in front, but Thadd insisted "ladies go first". There was just no messing with him, he had to be 220 centimeters tall, and had an over developed sense of male courtesy. *Are we really eating garbage? I appreciate it and everything, but gross!*

Abigail smiled warmly and handed her an orange dish and an overlarge wooden spoon. She then placed a slice of bread on her plate. Thaddeus loomed in front of the garbage bag and smiled at her with a gap-toothed grin. He reached in with a gnarled gardening trowel and shoveled a scoop of mush on her plate. A mixture of indistinguishable noodles, tomato and potato peels, crusts of bread, scraps of vegetables, and tiny morsels of meat and trimmed fat globbed in an ungodly marriage of sauces and seasonings. She left the line to stand awkwardly by the fire, waiting desperately for someone else to try the food first.

Abigail smiled encouragingly. "It's okay Tanya, you can start without us. The food has already been blessed."

She hesitated as Vika received her own plop of refuse. She sat next to Tanya and began eating with what looked like a chipped plastic spork. Looking at her own wooden spoon, Tanya realized that she had been given the finest utensil they had to offer.

"This is good!" Vika said in a rare moment of genuine excitement. She shoveled the food in as if she hadn't eaten in days. *Can't really blame her.* Tanya thought. *She hasn't.*

Michael and Luthor took their seats next to her and dug in as well. They hadn't been given any utensils at all; they used their bread as a spoon and ate with their hands like cavemen. Luthor hummed softly to himself. The food looked so gross! But she was so hungry. *Maybe just a bite.*

She ladled a bite onto the spoon and gingerly put it in her lips. It was cold, almost clammy; the slimy consistency was odd—at best—but it tasted… amazing. The spices and flavors mixed in a way that was utterly surprising and supremely satisfying.

Moments later her plate was clean, and she longed for more. Everyone else sat in silence as they munched the dregs of Tony's restaurant. She got up and walked over to father Roc with her empty plate tentatively in her hands.

"Is there enough for seconds?" she whispered.

DeShawn, who sat next to Roc, burst out laughing. She had whispered too loud. "We don't have much, but I've always got some to spare for a hottie like you," the large man picked up the whole garbage bag and emptied it onto her dish. Stray noodles, peels, and sauce speckled her plate. It might have been enough for a couple more spoonfuls.

"I'm sorry, but we're out of bread," Abigail said. "We weren't able to earn any more today."

In moments Tanya had cleaned her plate again. Michael and Luthor looked longingly at their own equally empty plates. Luthor wiped around the edge of the plate with his bread and proceeded to lick each individual finger. The others ate unhurriedly, methodically chewing and savoring each bite. Tanya envied their restraint. Their ability to not give into the hunger and wolf down the food as fast as possible allowed them to feel fuller, as well as enjoy the flavors. Each of them had their eyes closed, blissful expressions plastered to their faces. The light from the garbage fire highlighted their emaciated bodies and sunken cheeks.

Tanya's jealousy quickly faded as she realized how they had acquired the virtue of restraint. Each of them had been on the verge of starvation for the last ten years.

It fascinated her how they could remain so positive and generous in the light of such a difficult existence. Their faith went far deeper than a set a theological precepts they accepted. It led to action, to conviction, and a purposeful life despite their surroundings. Every single one of them believed in God like He was right there eating out of the garbage with them. And *that* was something to be jealous of. That sort of belief was something she had never experienced herself, but had secretly longed for. She wanted a faith of the same type her parents held; the type of faith with enough weight to give them the courage to flee society.

Michael licked his lips longingly at the now empty garbage can. "So how did you guys score this kind of food here in the city? Why hasn't anyone come in to try to take it?"

Thaddeus laughed. "Let them try." His smile suddenly appeared feral in the firelight.

"It wouldn't go well for them," said DeShawn, cracking his knuckles.

The priest interrupted, "we have entered into a covenant with the restaurant."

"As you might imagine, security for a food establishment is both difficult and important," Abigail added, "but typical security detail drastically inflates the cost of an industry with an already vanishingly small profit margin. So, the restaurant is forced to choose between prohibitively high prices or risk vagrants living nearby which scare away their wealthy clientele. Not to mention nearly guaranteed robbery in a place that stores food.

"We provide an excellent alternative. We provide around the clock security and keep the exterior of the building free of garbage and suburban panhandlers."

"Why do that for them?" Michael asked. "It's not like they can pay you. You are Markless."

Roc nodded. "True. But they do give us exclusive rights to their garbage."

"You're telling me you work all day long, just to get their garbage?" Tanya asked.

Abigail frowned, "we take what we can get. And every one of us is grateful for it. You actually seemed quite fond of that *garbage* on your plate."

Tanya flushed in embarrassment.

Roc smiled kindly. "Tony's is a restaurant. There are certain things they aren't allowed to sell by law. Uneaten food, scraps, leftovers, and the like. Anything the employees don't want goes into the trashcan for us. Without this food every night, each of us would starve."

"Or we'd have to do some illegal… crap, just to make ends meet," said Thaddeus.

"I *will not* go back to turning tricks," said Serenity.

"I ain't even gonna say what I used to do," said DeShawn. Thaddeus punched him in the arm. "Fine, no secrets. I know. They're the devil's tool to separate us."

"It's okay, you can tell us," Michael said, "we're sort of

fugitives ourselves."

He lowered his head in shame. "I used to be a hit man. I killed people, sometimes in robberies, other times I just got a name or a picture, and I put a bullet in 'em. You're looking at one hell of a sinner."

"Why did you do it?" asked Michael.

"I ain't got the best of reasons, but times were tough and I needed to eat. They paid me in food. Each kill fed me for about ten days; two weeks if I really skimped."

"You killed for food?"

"Shut up!" Luthor snapped. "Hunger can make you do some crazy things. Trust me." Luthor's eyes seemed to sink into his skull as he remembered some dark, unnamed memory. Something about Antarctica, he only got that look when he thought about that horrible place. Luthor recovered quickly however, and continued to defend the larger black man. "Besides, who are we to judge him? We've killed people in the last week."

DeShawn nodded. "Thank you, Luthor."

"For what?"

"For not judging me. It was the darkest part of my life, I ain't proud of it. It still haunts me."

DeShawn lifted up his baggy shirt and pulled out a very large hand gun that had been tucked into the back of his pants. Vika flinched visibly as she saw the weapon, but DeShawn held it open in the palm of his hand.

"This used to be my life," he said somberly. "I keep it around to remind me of who I don't want to be no more." He popped open the magazine with an experienced hand and showed them a distinct lack of bullets. "I always keep it empty to remind me of who I am now."

Roc patted him on the shoulder in a fatherly way. "I realize it may sound crazy to you, but this is how we stay alive. We work all day, worship together, and share food. We men run security, the women take garbage to the transfer stations in exchange for slices of bread."

"Every five kilos, or so, that we bring, they give us another slice." Serenity said.

"It helps supplement our diet here and keeps us relatively healthy," Abigail added.

Tanya found herself feeling very guilty for eating that slice of bread. The women had picked up garbage all day in order to earn it. "We make a great partnership and it keeps us alive."

"I have set up three other partnerships like this one," Father Roc said, "I believe that DeShawn will be ready to start taking over the spiritual leadership of this co-op soon. When he is ready to assume full leadership, I will depart to plant another."

Not only is this co-op thriving, paying people all day with nothing other than garbage, but it is appealing enough that Roc is franchising?

"But that is enough about us, it sounds like you all have quite the story as well," Roc said.

Awkward stares passed between the four of them. Tanya could tell they had no interest in telling their story. But Tanya felt compelled to share. Their new friends possessed a freedom, an openness with their lives and struggles that Tanya deeply desired. They lived on the bottom of society with nothing to lose, yet with a powerful faith so they could say anything. Perhaps if Tanya too told their story, then maybe she could move toward that freedom.

"I can tell them," she offered.

"Go ahead," Luthor said.

Tanya felt herself switch into history mode and proceeded to recount their story. Beginning with Luthor's ground-breaking invention and Eli's murder, she described their frantic escape and the rooftop showdown that had forced them to the streets. It felt like telling a story that had already been written down in textbooks but one in which only she knew the details. She left nothing out.

Their new friends listened intently. It didn't seem to bother them at all when she spoke of death and murder. They leaned in eagerly when she described their dramatic escapes. She had never spoken before to such a fantastic audience. If only her students listened so actively; instead they played with their devices, finding every possible means to waste both electricity and her time. Her new friends had no phones, no technology, nor even the energy with which to use them. They could simply appreciate a story by a campfire, something modern generations had all but lost.

"Thank you so much for sharing with us," Roc said as she concluded. "Your honesty is both refreshing and appreciated."

"You believe us? I tell you we can control gravity and you just accept it?"

"What reason do you have to lie?" asked Abigail. "Surely, even if you were lying you would not make up something so ridiculous as that. Reason then concludes that you must be telling the truth."

"Roc always tells us we are supposed to live by faith, not by sight," DeShawn said, "so I don't need to see anything to know you telling the truth."

"Well said brother. You are closer than you think to taking over for me."

"But I like having you around here. Maybe I need to have a relapse or something."

Roc laughed. "We both know that isn't going to happen."

"Knock it off, D," interrupted Thaddeus, "you ain't gonna relapse. Besides, our friends need help." His eyes burned with more intensity than the trashcan fire.

DeShawn nodded. "Yeah, anything you need. We got you." Everyone else nodded in agreement. Their eyes burned with the same hope, that maybe 126 could change things.

Free energy probably seemed like an oasis in the desert to them.

"You would help us?" Tanya asked, feeling flattered.

"*Anything,*" said Thaddeus. "If you can end hunger, I'd take a bullet for you."

"Same," said DeShawn, "I seen too many dead kids wash up in these gutters for one lifetime. Just one thing though—I ain't killing nobody. Never again."

Tanya nodded appreciatively at his conviction.

Luthor scratched his graying stubble. "Right now we are trying to find a way to Chicago. Any way you could help us get on a train? My laptop was destroyed in the explosion. We need to retrieve our backup files from my friend back home."

"Tony's is one of the most profitable restaurants in the area thanks to our services and the owner is generally glad to give us extra help when needed," Roc said. "Unfortunately, I don't know if they can help you with the train."

"Do you have anything to barter with?" Abigail asked.

"We have a gun," Vika said.

"I don't know if that's enough," Abigail said. "A gun might buy you tickets. But you'll still have to deal with the Mark scanners."

"Seebee gloves shouldn't be that hard to find," suggested Michael.

Abigail shook her head. "New York City has been upgrading its security lately. The mass transit stations have a new streamlined system to stop the use of gloves. Now that they all use overhead scanners concentrated around the ticket turnstiles, they've completely outlawed gloves."

"So a single carp could stop us in our tracks during the bottleneck," said Luthor.

Michael grinned, "you know the carps. They're like rats—"

"Where there's one, there's sure to be…" Thaddeus

stopped himself, "a poop-ton more." DeShawn patted him on the shoulder appreciatively. It was a common phrase, apart from the impromptu censorship, to refer to the patrolling habits of the carbon police.

Tanya didn't see any way around the problem. Last time they had needed to bypass security, they had used Vika's expertise to counterfeit gloves. But if gloves were illegal then it would be impossible to do the same trick again. Not that she was particularly sad about not needing to kill anyone and cut them up.

Luthor appeared to be thinking hard. "There must be an inherent flaw in the security if they have removed the individual scanning stations in favor of the overhead scanners. Would it be possible for a Markless to get on undetected if they had a ticket?"

"That might work, but not for us," Michael said. "There is no way for us to mask our damn CPI signals without cutting them out."

"I would severely caution against that," Vika replied. "In the event that we do succeed, there will be no way to prove your innocence if you destroy your identification chip."

"I don't want to cut on myself any more than the next guy. But I'll smogging do it if I have to choose between that and Sabers killing my friends again," said Michael.

Luthor rubbed his temples in frustration and looked at Abigail. "I know we can't fake them, but do you know if there is any technology that could mask an individual signal?"

"I don't know. Anything is possible, I suppose. I am just not that familiar with black market technology."

"Black market technology?"

"Sure," Abigail said. "There are a lot of really smart people who lost everything almost overnight with the new carbon regulations. And they've now had twenty years to experiment— that is, if they survived the *Culling.*"

"Do you know anyone with access to that kind of technology?"

Thaddeus frowned. "I... No, it's a bad idea."

Roc whispered something to him.

"If you know someone who can help us, please don't hold back. I assure you we can take care of ourselves," said Luthor.

He looked troubled, but Roc nodded, encouraging him. "The guy's name is Jose Ostafal, but I don't trust that rat any farther than Serenity can throw DeShawn. He tried to recruit me to do the same thing D was doing."

"I'm glad you got out of that life before it was too late," DeShawn said.

"You're the one that got me out! Introduced me to Roc. You saved my life man, I had nothing to do with it." Thaddeus continued, "anyway, Jose never lost his mark, so he used his money to open up a small convenience store on the fringe between the suburbs and the city. But that is just a front. His store is actually an outlet for every illegal product you could dream of. And anything that he doesn't have he can have custom made from his suppliers in the suburbs."

"If you see him, be careful. His wares do not come cheap, but he may be able to help you," Roc said.

"If the worst thing we have to worry about is not being able to afford his tech, then it seems like it's worth a look."

Thaddeus shook his head violently. "It's not. He's with the Dog Pound."

"The *Dog Pound?*"

"They're the most powerful and ruthless bastards in the city," DeShawn said. "They ain't people you want to mess with."

Luthor crossed his arms. "If it's a chance to get home, we have to take it. How far is it?" "It's about a two day walk from here," Thaddeus said.

"Then we leave tomorrow."

CHAPTER 17:

Eleven Years ago: Titan Dome, Antarctica

The men lay crouched on ice 4000 meters thick that stretched as far as anyone could see. Luthor re-attached his skis to his pack—he couldn't exactly ask the Chinese to wait while he unstrapped from them. Luthor switched on his infrared and the omnipresent, obscuring whiteout became nothing more than an icy canvass for heat-emitting weapons. The Chinese defensive emplacements popped up as tiny orange dots in the distance. Everyone had turned off their heating packs again so they would not similarly grace the screens of the enemy's infrared. With their pure white suits and freezing extremities, they were all but invisible.

Garcia looked at his Battlepad, waiting for the signal from command to begin the attack. Hundreds of other COs spread around the periphery of Titan Dome also waited to send their men on a massive coordinated assault. "Damn it's nice to have a few of those comm-sats back in orbit again. Let me tell you. Greedy-ass China shot down 75% of them before the first month of the war was over. Coordinating anything without them was a bitch."

The new allied satellites launched since the beginning of the war all had defensive countermeasures capable of shooting down earth-based missiles. Apparently, the cost to saturate their defenses was too high for the Chinese to bother trying any more. They were also outfitted with enough armor to withstand impacts of debris from the other destroyed satellites that still orbited the planet. Luthor was glad he hadn't been in service long enough to have experienced the communications snafus that had plagued the allies in the beginning.

"Protect Chaz until he lights up that dragon. So long as you don't shoot, nobody's going to see you."

"Jake not shooting could be a problem," Chaz said.

Garcia and Luthor laughed. It felt good to break the tension. Luthor didn't want to think about being the initial assault of the largest, riskiest offensive of the war. The front line had a tendency to impersonate ground beef. It had been that way since the invention of the machine gun.

Finally, after 90% of his body was completely numb the order came through to attack. Luthor vaguely heard a murmur from the Battlepad, "*operation Zeus is a go.*" It seemed a fitting codename for an offensive that would capture Titan Dome.

"Remember men, don't be a hero. Just do what needs to be done," Garcia said. "Move out!"

Luthor's heart rate rose like a kinetic warhead. With chilled muscles he began a crouched run. The hulking form of Marri ran next to him, Claptrap still obediently strapped to his back between his skis. The white-on-white of the landscape was broken only by measured dragons and missile defense towers; it stretched on, limited only by the very curvature of the Earth. The nearest cluster of artillery lay 300 meters ahead. Several other groups of men joined them on the right, attacking the same position.

Chaz knelt, rocket to shoulder, and fired. The explosive projectile ripped a hole through the metal carapace of the dragon; burning bodies were ejected from the wreckage like shrapnel. Luthor saw dozens other explosions down their line. It looked like their surprise attack was being executed flawlessly despite the deployment snafu.

The remaining dragons woke up and sprayed returning fire. The sheer number of bullets those things could discharge was staggering. The rounds made a pulsating bar of white-hot flame, slicing anything in its path. His ears couldn't distinguish the individual gun shots any more than he could hear the individual explosions inside the cylinders of a revving engine. The dragons were designed to be a versatile anti-armor, anti-air, anti-everything weapon, their massive bullets were impervious to stealth and countermeasures that could fool missiles. It turned out that infantry didn't like them either.

The laser beam of lead swept back across the line, rending men in half with its fury. Luthor ran flat out. The sooner he got to the nearest gun, the sooner he would be inside that arc. China hadn't expected the Coalition to be able to penetrate this deeply with mere paratroopers and so had relatively light defenses against infantry. Fox-holes and machine-gun emplacements were scarce. They had the advantage.

Jake and Garcia crouched next to the ladder to the cab of the dragon, keeping the meager Chinese defense at bay with their MX-5s. Acting on instinct, Luthor made the best of their covering fire and jumped up the ladder. He pointed his rifle in the cab and pulled the trigger. His rounds went wide as a foot kicked the gun from his hand and sent it flying to the ground.

One of the Chinese gunners appeared over the side aiming a pistol at Luthor's face. He grabbed the man's forearm and pulled it down against the ladder, and pinned it in place with his belt knife. Blood spurted up into Luthor's face as arteries severed, and the man cried out in Mandarin. Luthor jerked it free and vaulted the remaining rungs into the cockpit. He kicked out the bleeding man and leaped on the remaining gunner, who still vainly tried to shoot the infantry on the other side. He sank the knife deep into the gunner's chest.

"Die, you son of a bitch!" Luthor cried, unexpected fury rising within him. He twisted the knife cruelly. Horror and pain froze on the man's face as immutably as the Antarctic landscape. It took only a few uninterrupted beats of his heart before his eyes glassed over, the light winking out of them.

"Greedy Chinese bastards. You made me do this!" Luthor wrenched the knife free and kicked his next victim out the other side.

Luthor climbed out, not wanting to spend another second in the belly of another dragon, he had enough of that for one lifetime. He grabbed the MX-5. In minutes, Martinez had successfully demolished the radar-clad missile defense platform adjacent to it with lethal quantities of C-4. The other dragons on the line also stood silent, either destroyed or captured. Smoke rose all along the defensive line. The attack had been executed flawlessly.

Garcia walked up, Battlepad in hand. "Helluva job, men. Everyone's reported in. Phase one complete, minimal casualties. Flanking divisions are engaging enemy air support, our armor column is rolling full steam ahead."

"Now we just have to stay alive," Martinez said frowning.

"You aren't dead yet!" Garcia shouted.

"Alive and kickin!" Jake said patting his shouldered rifle, "we just shat on their guns and wiped their asses with C-4 and RPGs. We have the advantage. Besides if they want *this* gringo dead, it's going to take an army."

"I've heard the Chinese have one of those," said Chaz

Marri looked up from reloading Claptrap, "how long until the armor arrives?"

"7th Tunneling Division is supposed to reach us at the same time 3rd armor engages the Shackleton side," Garcia said.

"When is that Sarge?" asked Chaz.

"About thirty minutes. We have to hold this position till those Moles get here."

The wind paused for a moment. It might have been peaceful if not for the crackling of the smoldering weapons that sliced the silence. Luthor stared at the corpses of the dragons and freezing bodies of the Chinese soldiers. *How the hell did I get here again?* he thought. *Stuck in the basement of the world, freezing my ass off, fighting for oil scraps. Meanwhile, everyone I have ever known starves back in the States.*

Luthor stopped reading reports from home after he'd read that his mother had died of the plague and everyone he'd ever met was on the brink of starvation. All he knew now were the dystopian rumors floating around. They were calling it the *Culling.* Everyone not strong enough to survive was dying. Supposedly, the military had rationed the already scarce food and medicine and had commandeered nearly all of the oil. If reports could be trusted, far more civilians had died from starvation and sickness worldwide than soldiers had in the war. WWIII was proving to be every bit the bitch that Einstein had predicted. He had said, "I don't know what weapons would be used in World War III, but World War IV will be fought with sticks and stones." The irony was that he thought it would come out of a nuclear apocalypse born of superpower stupidity, not an energy death born of scarcity.

Silence never lasted long in Anti. A volley of American cruise missiles blasted by, crushing the sound barrier in their wake. They'd sent them in as soon as they had confirmation that the missile defenses had been destroyed. Harmonizing with the sonic boom came the Chinese reply. A barely detectable whine, whistled the prelude of the artillery strike. A deafening explosion off their left flank became the herald of the familiar battle melody like a cymbal in Luthor's ears.

Stunned from the shockwave, Luthor looked up from the ground to see Garcia waving his arms frantically, trying to give them orders to defend against the counterattack. If only Luthor could hear him over the ringing that filled his head.

#

Aurora, IL, United States of the West

"I still can't believe you're alive." Qwiz said into a computer mic attached to Luthor's old phone. His voice modulator disguised his voice so Stalker wouldn't be able to identify him. It made him sound like an overweight demon. He had also taken digital precautions so the censors wouldn't be able to find his location.

"I figure if 100 million Chinese couldn't manage it, what chance do a few guys in gelvar have?" The voice had not named itself but it could have only been Luthor. Qwiz knew if he was calling he would be worried about censors overhearing. Since Stalker's men had blown up Luthor's apartment, he had been considered a national security threat. "We also owe a great debt to our new friends."

After all the stories coming in from New York that week, it seemed all but certain he had died in the same gunfight that had killed ten others. Qwiz had agonized that he should have done more to save them. But they were alive. He hadn't failed. His honor remained.

"I called in and told them you were extremely dangerous. I hoped to get you extra protection from the Stalker."

"So that's what your Vanguard call was about! I had been wondering. But who is the Stalker?"

"I don't know his true identity. It's my codename for the diabolical man who seems to be behind everything. I think he works for the European Union."

"That's what we had assumed too. But the men who kidnapped us were definitely American."

"He had someone he was communicating with here in

the USW."

"What does that mean? I thought we weren't getting along with Europe."

"I'm still working on that one. I've only been in the system for a few days. Maybe they want to share your research to use against China."

"Keep looking into it. Hopefully we can compare notes soon. Unfortunately, we have more pressing problems."

"I thought things were going well."

"We lost the laptop in the explosion."

Qwiz smiled to himself. "I have some good news for you then. I managed to save the research and the... substance. It's in a safe place. Don't worry."

"Fantastic!" Luthor shouted something away from the phone and a few people cheered. "We weren't even sure you were alive until you called the station. You are remarkable; your father would be proud."

Qwiz blushed, he couldn't help it. His father was a great man, even if his allegiance to a country as morally bankrupt as China was misplaced. "Thank you for warning me. They arrived minutes after you called. We barely escaped with our lives."

"Now for the hard part. We have to get to you."

"What is your plan?"

"They think I'm an international terrorist remember? I'm not sure it's smart for me to say over the phone."

"*Right.* Sorry."

"I'm sure you can figure it out."

"I will do my best, but there are a lot of lies being spread about you. It is going to be hard to get any solid information to start from. The media is blaming you for everything from that New York helicopter crash to global warming."

Luthor laughed, "for once they got something right, I

did blow up the helicopter."

How on earth did you manage that? I better not ask, it would reveal too much.

"We are following up on a lead today. It's in the suburbs..."

"Is it really necessary to risk that?" Qwiz said. Nobody went to the suburbs anymore without twenty to fifty, gun-toting bodyguards to watch their back. Qwiz himself had not been to one since he had lived there as a child. carbon police didn't even bother patrolling the ghost towns unless they were on a major train or food-shipping route. The only people that frequented suburbs were the ubiquitous scavenger companies, trying to salvage everything they could from the pre-Oil Crash era—that is, everything that hadn't already been looted. And they did so with a private army. Squatters, looters, and Markless roamed the burbs in packs. The stories Qwiz had heard made him shiver. Supposedly, the rival gangs constantly hunted for food in the abandoned houses and raided other gangs' food stores. Raids were supposedly bloody and frequent. Some well-armed gangs would hunt live food. Abandoned zoos and pets had transformed the streets into a wild game preserve, there were plenty of dogs and deer to go around.

"We don't see any other options."

"Be careful. Please."

"Always. We need to be on our way. We will call in a few days with an update. If something happens, our friends live outside an Italian restaurant."

"There have got to be a lot of those in New York."

"Sorry, I can't risk the sensors finding our friends with anything more specific."

Qwiz ended the call, pulling up his email. His father had emailed again.

#

New York City, United States of the West

"The pale horse still rides," Roc said as they walked, gesturing at the poor Markless shuffling around the street. In every alley homeless clustered for warmth or companionship. They had replaced rats as the dominant species living in the gutters of New York City. They walked with the same purposeless, haunted expression Luthor had seen days before in the woman who had accosted him. Their desperation seemed to filter out into the street. Men and women held signs pleading for the smallest assistance, yet were certain they would not receive any.

"What are you talking about?" Luthor said. He didn't see any horses. The rickshaws clogging the street were all being pulled by men on foot or bicycle. There wasn't a car to be seen, so he couldn't be referring to *horse-power* either.

"The fourth horsemen of the apocalypse."

"Oh, another Bible thing," Luthor said dismissively. He enjoyed Roc's company, but Luthor could have done with less religious prattling.

"I wouldn't say it is just a 'Bible thing' any more, Luthor. At this point it is history."

Tanya sidled up between them, listening intently. He didn't know if she was waxing religious again or what, but she hung on the man's every word. "History?"

Damn it, Tanya, now he is going to start preaching.

Sure enough, Roc pulled out a little leather-bound Bible and flipped to the back of it, though he did not read. "The four horsemen of the apocalypse come from the sixth chapter of Revelation. They represent the beginning of God's judgment of humanity and are heralds of the end times. This is another point where I disagree with the Catholic Church. I believe these horsemen have already come, and that the last of them, Death—who rides the pale horse— hasn't yet left. You can see his remnants with the dying and suffering people here in the city."

"What were the other horsemen?" Michael asked, looking intrigued. Michael had never shown any interest in God before. But that was the effect Roc had on people, it was hard not to listen to him. He made too much sense and the purposefulness with which he led his life was infectious, even if misguided.

"Chapter six says the first horsemen came on a white horse, bent on conquest. The Church always believed that the horse was white to represent a conquering king. In biblical days, a victorious king would always ride home on a white horse. But I have come to think that the white actually represented Antarctica and that the conqueror was not a king, but China taking over the Titan Dome oil field. That is the event that triggered everything else."

Luthor raised an eyebrow. What the old man said *did* sound like history, not the religious blather of the bullhorn touting nut-jobs he'd heard in college—particularly since Roc disagreed with the rest of the Church. No one who disagreed with the Church could be totally wrong.

"That makes more sense than most of the poster-waving I have seen. But it still sounds like coincidence to me."

"That is what my brothers who still serve in the Church say. They hotly disagree with me, saying that the rider must conquer the whole world. They say of the many areas China conquered, that one happened to be white doesn't seem like prophesy. They say it seems like a rather generous coincidence."

"But you believe it," Tanya said.

"Yes. When taken with the rest of the horsemen and what actually happened in history, it fits perfectly."

"What's the next horseman?" Michael asked.

"That's easy," said Thaddeus, "it's War." The priest had brought him along for protection, leaving DeShawn as leader of the Tony's group. He acted as if he were trying to impress Roc with everything he said.

"Yes, the bible tells us the next horse is red. The rider —War— was given the power to take peace from the earth. It is rather hard to discount that World War III took place on a scale that would have been unimaginable to any other generation in history. I would say peace was indeed taken from the whole Earth."

Luthor nodded, he certainly could attest to that. Upwards of 300 million people were killed just from the bombs and bullets. It made World War II look like a single battle, and World War I look like a bar fight. The war had raged from the Arctic Circle to the South Pole and the location of every oil field and power station in-between. Not a single country had been able to remain neutral. Those that tried had been swallowed up by the Coalition or the Chinese Block.

Tanya prodded Roc to continue, and though Luthor said nothing, he too found himself strangely interested in hearing the rest of Roc's strange, but compelling interpretations of the Bible.

"The third horseman came riding on a black horse. This is the horse of Famine. The scripture says this rider would announce that a loaf of bread would cost a day's wages. The church has said that it was black because it is the color of death. But I believe the black represents oil. Since we had no oil, and the allied governments had outlawed all other types of fossil fuels, we didn't have sufficient energy to grow enough food. Most of it we did grow went to the war effort, leaving the rest of the population on the brink of starvation. It was simple, brutal, supply and demand. Scarcity of oil inexorably led to high prices on everything else."

"The *Culling*," Michael said. Father Roc nodded soberly.

Tanya shuddered. "I only had one loaf of bread a week."

"Poor baby," Michael said, "imagine life on the street!"

"You," Tanya's voice quivered, "you were on the street?"

"Yeah, I was." Michael said stopping in the middle of the sidewalk. Luthor had never heard him talk about his childhood before. He jabbed a long finger in Tanya's face, "my mom became a prostitute trying to feed us and then starved to death. I didn't have a Dad to help, he was just some one-night stand. Don't talk to me about how bad it was for you, Miss College. At least you had *some* food."

"How did you survive?" she asked, a tear rolling down her cheek.

"Well, after my mom died trying to keep my sister and I alive, shit got real hard. Sister got fucked for a living too. They paid her in food and she shared some with me. I spent my days wandering around the sewers hunting rats for us. I was lucky to get one, because everyone else was doing the same smogging thing."

Tanya didn't say anything more, but tears flowed freely down both sides of her face.

"When I turned 18, they held one more draft, I volunteered quick. I thought I might get some food and some warmth. Right after I finished basic, the war was over. Fine with me. I got the GI bill to pay for school even though I never fought. My sister? She died of AIDS she got from some prick who paid extra to forgo the condom."

"I'm so sorry, Michael."

Michael scowled. "What was that last horseman again Roc, wasn't it the brown horse of bullshit?"

"There is no need for that," said Roc, furrowing his brows, "just because you had a worse situation does not invalidate someone else's experience."

"I didn't know, Michael." Tanya said, "I never meant to hurt you."

Luthor decided to redirect the conversation. Even the Bible was better than bickering.

Even Michael didn't know true desperation and Luthor wasn't about to enlighten them. "Tell us about the last horseman, Roc."

They started walking again. After a long pause the priest continued. "The last horsemen, in my opinion, is the most convincing of all. His name is Death, and he rode a pale horse. It says in the Scripture he is given the power to kill by sword, famine, and plague."

"What about guns and explosives?" Luthor said.

"The sword has been a euphemism for all weapons of war for thousands of years," said Roc without a hint of sarcasm. "Tell me Luthor, how many people died in the midst of the Oil Crash, the Culling, and war? Total."

"I have heard estimates between 2 Billion and 2.5 Billion."

"Exactly. The prophesy says the pale horseman will kill one quarter of the Earth's population. Before the war the population was about 8.5 Billion. A quarter of that would be between 2 to 2.5 billion."

"And people died from the war, starvation, or the plague," Michael said, looking genuinely impressed. "I saw it. People dropping from the plague and not getting up again — smogging rat fleas. Or they would just give up looking for food and lay down to die. Priest, I have to admit, that is a compelling coincidence."

"For me, at a certain point, too many coincidences add up for them to remain mere coincidences anymore."

It was a bit hard to swallow as mere coincidence. But truthfully, if Luthor himself had predicted the end of the world, he might have predicted something similar. Of course, Roc said that Revelation was probably written almost 2000 years ago; who was to say that they would have had the same sensibilities.

They continued their walk north. After several hours Michael brought up a conversation that had been shelved the night before. "You never did tell us who you thought the Beast was. We have all day now and I'm bored. How about another sermon?"

"If you wish. What the Church never considered was that the Beast might not *be* a person. The scripture does personify the Beast, but it wouldn't be the first time the scripture did that about something that wasn't a person. For example, the Old Testament often described the entire nation of Israel as an adulterous woman."

"Okay, I'll bite. *What* is the Beast then? China? Oil? Girl Scout cookies?"

"I think the Beast isn't a group of people, or a thing. I think it is an idea." Roc said dramatically. "In today's world, we don't bow down and worship people as much as *ideas* or *philosophies*. People worship the *idea* of wealth or worldly success and spend their whole life chasing them. We worship the *idea* of romantic love and are often willing to betray our loved ones to chase after it in an affair. We worship our political philosophies to the point of demonizing anyone who doesn't share them."

"Lame Roc. The Beast is politics?" Michael said.

"No, Politics are inherently divisive. The Beast is an idea; an idea that has to be universally accepted. The scripture says almost everyone will worship it. It also has to be associated with CPI or else it wouldn't be the *Mark* of the Beast. So what idea does everyone believe that connects to the chip in your right hands?"

Realization flushed across Tanya's face. "You think the Beast is the idea of global warming."

"Yes. Or perhaps more specifically, the *fear* of man-made climate change."

"But climate change is scientifically proven!" Michael said. "The carbon regulations have saved this planet from flooding. How could something true be the Beast?"

"Who ever said that the Beast couldn't be true? It just has to be worshipped. Being true would make it more compelling to worship, don't you think?"

"But people don't worship science," Michael said.

"They don't?" Roc asked. "In ancient times, worship took the form of sacrifices. People would sacrifice animals, wealth, and sometimes even their own children to appease angry gods and stop them from destroying the Earth. Worship doesn't have to be singing hymns or bowing to a statue. Our world worshipped the Beast by sacrificing everything to stop climate change—just as if they were trying to appease an angry god. Paris 2, carbon enforcement, CPI, banning of coal and natural gas, all of it was sacrificed to fight climate change despite the hardships they imposed on people. And they did it to stop the earth from being destroyed, just like in ancient times. It sounds like worship to me."

"But those things were necessary."

"Maybe they were, maybe they weren't," Roc said. "That is irrelevant. The important thing is that each of those things set up a situation where we fought World War III in Antarctica."

"I don't see how saving the planet from destruction caused a war."

"Imagine for a moment if no scientist had ever come up with the idea of global warming."

"No one would notice that the earth was inexplicably warming?" Michael asked.

"I'm asking you to imagine. Maybe they blamed it on the natural fluctuations of the Sun. Anyway, the earth would have continued to steam along, utterly dependent on oil. Eventually, as it became scarcer and more expensive to procure, people would have looked to other sources of readily available power.

"They would have turned to coal because they would be unafraid of the carbon. They would have turned to natural gas because they wouldn't worry about methane escaping the fracking process heating up the atmosphere. In short, everyone would have had enough energy *without* needing to fight over oil in Antarctica, they probably would never have even looked for it there. It was the scarcity of energy that led inexorably to that conflict."

"Okay, I see your point," Michael said.

"I have come to believe that this fear of climate change was the Beast predicted in Revelation. Without that fanaticism, we never would have needed Marks, we never would have adopted a one-world currency, and the four horsemen never would have come to kill Billions of people with the war and the *Culling*. In short, worship of the Beast brought about all of that."

"Be careful, Priest," Luthor cautioned. "You're dangerously close to sounding like a 2180 fanatic. Take it from me, you don't want that."

"The difference between me and them, is that I don't dispute the science nor presume myself a judge."

"Or blow anybody up," Thaddeus added.

"Certainly not. I simply observe and make connections to the scripture. For me and for many others," Roc nodded to Tanya, "including your parents, these prophesies have challenged and changed us. How else could they be so true if not for the influence of God?"

"Roc, I'm a scientist," Luthor said, "as a scientist I'll always concede a good point when I hear one. Your prophesies are impressively coherent. My issue is, and always has been, with God. What sort of all-powerful being would allow *two billion* of his creatures to starve to death without stopping it? You claim he is loving, but those are not the acts of a good person. Good people do not allow evil to happen if they can prevent it. The God you believe in would certainly have the power to stop whatever he wanted. Imagine if I sat back and just sold 126 to the highest bidder, instead of working to make sure everyone could have it. I would be starting another future war.

"We will probably fail, but each of us has already risked our lives several times over trying to stop evil. God didn't even try. He just let everyone slaughter each other. So even if he did exist, I would never believe in him, because I will not follow an evil being."

"You would blame the acts of man on God?" Roc asked quietly. "It was not God who killed so many, it was us. We built bombs and missiles and guns and shot them at each other. We fought over something as frivolous as oil. Who are we to blame God for our stupidity?"

"But God did not stop it!"

"No, he did not," Roc replied. "What would it have taken for Him to stop such a war? God would have had to restrain, stop, change, and direct individuals and change their decisions. In short, He would have had to remove their free will. But free will is God's ultimate gift to us; unfortunately, many of us use it to choose evil instead of good."

"You weren't there," Luthor said, "you can't possibly understand how horrible it was. If your God exists, he should have done whatever it took to stop it."

"Let me ask you Luthor, for what would you give up your free will? What would be so valuable that you would trade it so that someone else could pull your every string? Your every thought?"

Luthor didn't respond. He sensed Roc was trying to corner him into a place he had no interest in going.

"Through his great mercy, the Lord will never take our free will. It is too important; He let His only son die to protect it. Without free will we would be robots incapable of love, goodness, or unfortunately—evil. Humanity's sin is ours alone and we are the only ones who are responsible for it. Do not blame God.

"But perhaps His greatest mercy is that He is willing to use *our* war and *our* sin to exact *His* wrath. Instead of supernaturally destroying us on top of our war—as we deserve for our millennia of wickedness—He instead accepts the war that *we chose anyway* as enough to punish us."

"You've got an answer for everything, don't you priest?" Luthor said.

"I have had almost 50 years of ministry. I took a vow of celibacy for most of that. I have had plenty of time to consider the problem of evil and the prophesies of the end times."

Luthor did not engage any more, but walked on in silence. Mercifully no one tried to talk with him. Luthor hated talking about God, religion, or faith. He didn't really know why, but it made him angry. Today he was even angrier, because for the first time in his life he had met someone who could go toe-to-toe with him in debate. Not that he had any intention of converting. Leave that to Tanya, she had kept one foot in the church even after they all fled to the country. She wouldn't move in with him, even wanted to get married in the name of a God that she sometimes claimed she didn't believe in. At least Luthor was consistent. He knew there could be no good god that allowed what happened to him in Antarctica, regardless of Roc's arguments.

CHAPTER 18:

Outskirts of New York City, United States of the West

Vika, why aren't you a Saber anymore?" Michael asked. Again. Luthor was thankful Michael hadn't shown such persistence in questioning his own past. "Why leave the coolest job in the world to be the secretary for a professor?"

"Careful, Laramy..." Vika replied.

"If you're going to punch me, then get on with it," he said defiantly, "but I'm not going to stop asking. Is it so wrong that I want to know the person who's saved my life?"

Vika softened a little. "Fine, but I will only tell you once. I don't like recalling it."

"I won't bother you again."

"That is a promise you can't keep," Vika said, "you bother everyone, everyday."

Thaddeus clapped his hands. "Oh snap. Nice burn!"

"It happened after I was recruited to the Black Sabers. Their sniper had been killed and my perfect service record made me the obvious replacement.

"We were only given the toughest assignments. We trained together constantly, usually it was a month of preparation for each op. Over time the members of our unit grew very close."

Luthor definitely didn't like where this was going. It was only a matter of time before they asked him for *his* story. Anti-Luthor rattled his cage, screaming in Luthor's mind to let him out.

"How is that bad?" Michael asked.

"Men find me beautiful," Vika said, "and I was always the only woman in our unit which made it worse. After a while Captain Jacques became… obsessed with me. But I turned down all his advances. I didn't think it would be wise to become involved with a member of my team. And he was arrogant. He thought that because he led the Black Sabers everyone should worship him, so he did not interest me."

"What happened?"

"He wasn't used to being turned down. So, one night in the shower room he cornered me," Vika said.

Luthor ground his teeth in anger. He wanted all bastards like that strung up by their balls and burned alive.

"He said if I didn't have sex with him, things would go badly for me. I rejected him anyway. Then he tried to rape me."

"That polluter deserves to die," Michael said, sounding every bit as angry as Luthor felt.

"He did," Vika said, "before he was able to…enter me, I… I killed him."

Luthor hadn't seen that coming, but was delighted to hear that the man got what he deserved and that Vika had not been violated.

"We fought. I crushed his skull against bathroom piping… then I broke both his legs… and his back, and … castrated him."

"Holy crap," Michael breathed.

"I confessed everything to his superior officer. I told him he tried to rape me. But Colonel Dimarin had been close friends with Jacques. They had worked together for years. I think Dimarin had hand-picked him to lead the Sabers. Unfortunately, he was also the one officiating my Court Martial."

"They had to see it was self-defense," Tanya said.

"No. No one believed that a woman would be capable of killing *Captain Jacques* himself in unarmed combat. Dimarin ignored the evidence and believed a made up a story that I had been plotting to kill him."

"What evidence?" Tanya asked.

"Jacques had hidden-camera videos of me in the shower that he liked to watch. One was recording when I killed him."

"Damn..." Michael said. "They saw what happened and still ignored it?"

"Dimarin liked his job too much to defend me. He sent me to prison—reduced to five years because of my 'excellent service record,' and I was dishonorably discharged. When I got out, Eli offered me a job and a place to stay."

"I'm sorry, Vika," Tanya said, giving the taller woman a hug. "Thank you for helping us." Vika stood awkwardly, as if she had no idea what exactly a hug was.

"Do you think Dimarin is still running the Sabers?" Luthor asked.

"Possibly. But it has been six years, he has probably been promoted to general by now for his *excellent service record.*"

"But he could be the one behind all of this."

"He could move the Sabers around Europe. But I do not know why he would want to steal your research."

"That's easy," Luthor said, "it's worth trillions of credits. That's trillions with a T, if he gets a monopoly on it."

"But that does not explain how he had access to your phone calls with Eli or why he would have an applied materials professor bugged in the first place."

If not for the phone tap, Dimarin seemed to be a likely candidate for who'd framed and chased them. He had access to the Sabers, and presumably, the means to deploy them. But it didn't make sense why or how he would have spied on Eli to know that Luthor had something worth stealing.

"What about those helicopter guys you shot?" Michael added. "How could a European official get *that* many people to the States? I would think there would be a *lot* of red tape to get a smogging helicopter in here."

Vika just shook her head.

"The one thing that seems clear at this point," Luthor said, "is that we really don't know enough about the Sabers, even with Vika. Hopefully, Qwiz can uncover more."

"Knowing who is irrelevant, Tenrel. Men chase us, we kill them. We stay alive."

"When you put it like that," Michael said, "it really doesn't seem to matter. Of course, when we have Queen Badass herself on our team, I like our odds."

Vika frowned in reply.

As they progressed away from the city-center the surroundings became ever dingier and unkempt. The buildings rising up around them no longer soared to astronomic heights. Brick and concrete chips littered the ground from where they had fallen off their sides as if the inhabitants of this quarter were trying to knock the buildings down with a chisel. Multicolored graffiti plastered every open wall and more than a few that weren't open. Fewer solar farms had been built over the road, meaning fewer high-end storefronts above them and fewer businesses overall.

The culture of the homeless clustering the streets changed too. The rag-clad men and women that prowled these streets began appearing feral instead of pathetic. They hunted and stalked; they were underfed and dangerous. They stopped under a solar farm for the night. It was a mercy that the theft of money had become impossible since the advent of the CPI chips or they would have all been dead by morning.

#

The next morning Vika approached Luthor. The stench of suburbians and very hard concrete had made sleep elusive. It was the worst of both worlds, his intermittent periods of unconsciousness had been pock-marked by dreams of Antarctica. He woke up more than once after seeing blood on his hands. He was tired and frustrated and not in the mood to talk.

"Tell me, Tenrel, what happened to you during the war?"

"Why do you ask?" he said carefully. He slapped another lock on Anti-Luthor just in case; he would not let that bastard out if he could help it. He didn't want to take another swing at her.

"Call it fairness, call it the soldier's code. I told you why I am broken, so now you share why you are broken."

Luthor caught Tanya listening. He couldn't tell her what happened, she was scared of him already. She'd leave him if she knew the rest. "What makes you think I am broken?"

She raised her damn eyebrow. "Don't play games with me, Tenrel. You lose control often, you are a paratrooper who is afraid of heights, and you cry out every night. Or are you going to try to tell me that is normal for Americans?"

Years ago, he had discovered that the optimum sleep ratio was about four or five hours of sleep per night. If he did that, he minimized his dream time while eliminating most effects of sleep deprivation. Of course, even a single dream could ruin his day. Luthor could only assume Vika had a similar problem which is why she knew what his cries meant.

He glanced at Tanya again, she was still eavesdropping—so was everyone else for that matter. "I don't like to talk about it." Luthor decided to study the pot-holed pavement that hadn't been replaced in twenty years intently.

"Not good enough, Tenrel."

"I'm sorry you lost your career because of some horny commando, but that doesn't mean I have to tell you about the worst smogging times of my life!" Luthor realized he was shouting and pointedly stared away from the others. Two homeless fought next to a subway entrance over a piece of edible trash.

"How many times do I have to save your life? Three, four before you will talk?"

Luthor felt like a cornered animal. *My life is my own damn it! I don't have to tell anyone about anything if they save me or not! I will not relive those goddamn memories again. If I tell anyone, I will have to hear about it for the rest of my life.* Luthor snapped yet another padlock on his Anti-Self just to make sure it didn't break out again.

"It's a bad idea to open up that part of me. You won't like what comes out."

"Everyone has baggage," Vika interjected, "the question is what you do with it."

Roc turned to them. "Indeed. I have chosen to lay mine at the cross. You might consider doing the same, Luthor."

"I will continue to carry mine," Vika said, "it makes me stronger."

Roc nodded in respect to the sturdy, determined woman.

"Jesus never showed up when we needed him in Antarctica, Priest. He isn't strong enough to handle mine," Luthor said.

#

Somewhere in the Suburbs

Water from the recent rain dripped off the rain gutters, plinking like a thousand cowbells as they emptied roofs. None of the streetlights worked in this area, but the ambient city light still glistened off the wet surfaces giving the area an ominous glow. Only a few barred windows were illuminated. Roc had assured Tanya that each of those rooms were certainly full, but if people lived out here, artificial light wasn't a luxury they could afford—not to mention it was the middle of the night. Still, she wished there were some other sign of life. No homeless were visible in this quarter, they gravitated toward downtown where there were more scraps to find.

"Jose's a broker of pretty much anything illegal," Thaddeus told them, "and none of the other gangs bother him because they don't want to mess with the Dog Pound. He's also got his own security. He'd give worse than he got if anybody crossed him."

Movement flashed in the periphery of her vision. It could have been her imagination, but it looked like a slightly darker shadow had flitted across an alley. Solitary gun shots echoed off the graffitied brick walls like thunderclaps, proclaiming the danger before the storm. Tanya shivered. Eerie didn't fully describe the feeling of being on the periphery of the city limits. She wished there were a word that described the nostalgia she felt for a lost age combined with the fear of being in the broken, dangerous form of that same place in the present. Alas, there was no such word to her knowledge, but that was the emotion that beat in her breast. Fear for her life and regret for the apostasy of oil economics.

She stuck close to Luthor as Thadd led them deeper into territory controlled ever more exclusively by gangs.

"Tread carefully, brothers and sisters," Roc said, "we're now in Dog Pound territory."

"What are they anyway?" Michael asked, "a gang or something?"

"Something like that. Just way more powerful. DeShawn used to murder people for them," Thaddeus said, "they'll kill us if they think they can get half a credit's worth of food for it."

Tanya found it ironic that the carps seemed content to let the Markless kill each other in brutal gang violence, but if anyone started burning large amounts of wood or fossil fuels for heat, well, that was a different story. *Not that anything could burn on a night like this one.* The carps could also be summoned if there were some rampant human rights violation like slavery taking place. Interestingly, they didn't consider murder a human rights violation. The USW had come a long way from the "life, liberty, and pursuit of happiness," upon which the old United States had been founded. Now they based law on "Safety, Security, and Sustainability." The death of Markless and suburban refugees affected all three of those areas positively. One less desperate person on the streets meant greater safety for both the people, better security for the state, and it meant more food and resources for everyone else, so it was overlooked.

"Right around this corner." Thaddeus led them through an archway that had once been a functioning traffic light. Now devoid of purpose it had been turned into a billboard for Ostafal's wares.

"He's going to be open this late at night?" Luthor asked.

"He *only* does business at night," Thaddeus assured them.

The large man prowled like a lion. Every muscle was tensed. His eyes darted around, looking for any danger that might threaten his beloved priest. Tanya felt safer knowing he watched out for them. Vika held her rifle as if she planned to shoot it at any moment. Thaddeus might look more intimidating, but Tanya suspected Vika's knife would be at an enemy's throat before he managed a single step.

They turned onto a street composed entirely of utilitarian concrete business space such as might have housed any number of small manufacturing companies twenty years ago. A large opening for cargo doors formed their only entrances. Now they sat dark, cold, and empty. The rolling metal doors had all been ripped off—presumably sold for scrap like everything else of value—leaving gaping rectangular mouths. Tanya didn't blame the homeless for not occupying these shelters, she wouldn't want to be eaten by those buildings either.

One mouth had light pouring out of it and a functioning door about halfway down. Three men inside waited for them.

The two larger men wielded fancy-looking machine guns. The firepower stood in sharp contrast to their unkempt, tattered clothes. The bald one in the middle—presumably Jose—bore no weapon other than a sneer that popped out of his goatee. He had a stylized "2180" tattooed across the crown of his bald head. Behind them were rows of steel shelves holding every conceivable electronic item and a wide assortment of weapons.

"Thadd!" Jose said, hands wide in mock welcome. "It's been too long."

"Not long enough," Thaddeus growled.

"To what do I owe the pleasure? Have you learned the error of your sad pathetic life yet and returned to the Pound? Or do you enjoy your new job as the priest's bodyguard too much? He has you trained well."

"I will rip out your throat and—"

Roc grabbed a fistful of Thadd's tattered shirt, "Peace," he said forcefully, "love your enemy, pray for those who persecute you."

"Let *him* pray for *me* then!" Thaddeus shouted. "I want to persecute all over his ass."

Ostafal laughed, which didn't help her large friend's temper. Tanya could see that Jose had even raised the hackles of the unflappable priest. "What is it you want? No, don't tell me. Let me guess."

Ostafal had all the makings of a first-class son of a bitch. One such quality was his enjoyment of his weaselly voice a little too much.

"If I were a wagering man—I'm not, money is much too likely to run away when you bet it on things, *math* you know—I would say you felt pity on these pathetic people," he gestured at Tanya, Luthor, Michael, and Vika. "You brought them here because they need something you can't provide. Am I getting warm?"

Tanya shifted uncomfortably.

"So that means, they are criminals, running from the law." Ostafal's eyes seemed to pierce every part of them, Tanya felt naked.

"Oh, and nice choice of bitches, got some nice asses there."

Luthor ground his teeth audibly in anger, but the Uzis trained on him seemed to stay his hand.

Vika glared at the man. "Fool. I would shoot you dead before your guards got their hands out of their pants."

Ostafal threw his head back and laughed again. "Yet you didn't shoot me, because you know that everyone else in here would die," he laughed some more.

Tanya felt like she'd had just about enough of Jose Ostafal's posturing. They hadn't come to hear him yammer. They had come for train tickets. She found her mouth running before she could stop herself.

"Congratulations. You have convinced us all you are smart. Gold star for you. Can we get down to business or do we have to put up with another soliloquy?" she turned to the others. "No, better yet, let him keep talking. Maybe he will complete this shitty Shakespeare impersonation and off himself at the end of it."

Ostafal took out a pistol from a leather hip-holster in the blink of an eye. "Best put a leash on that whore before I have to put her down."

Tanya was pretty sure she heard Luthor's teeth physically crack from the strain of restraining himself, but he feared for her life and it kept him in place.

Ostafal returned his gun to its home. His yellowing teeth flashed in the well-lit room. "To business then. What do you need?"

"Four train tickets to Chicago."

"Those are easy enough to provide. Surely, if you are getting them from me, there is something else you need too," he rubbed his pasty palms together. "Anonymity. Invisibility from the scanners perhaps?"

"Just the tickets. I am sure we can find a way through security."

"No, I am sure you cannot."

"I see what you're trying to do," Tanya said, "quit trying to up-sell us. I am sure there is a way through security without whatever it is you're trying to make us buy."

"You're right, I want to go selling my most valuable items to people I can't trust, who are clearly wanted criminals, risk having the goddamn carps track it back here and arrest my ass. Then my ass will be put in a penitentiary where it will be penetrated by polluted perps or I'll have my CPI chip privilege stripped permanently!" Ostafal abruptly finished shouting and smiled, evidently pleased with himself or his alliteration. Tanya couldn't tell which. "I'm not trying to up-sell you... I am telling you that your plan is impossible. You can't smogging do it!"

She hadn't expected such an outburst. But unfortunately, it *had* convinced her.

"Fine," said Luthor, "what do you think we need?"

"You need a signal inverter, something only *I* can provide."

"What is a *signal inverter*?" Luthor asked, though Tanya had no doubt Ostafal would have told them anyway.

"It is all *very* complicated. I don't want to confuse you," Jose replied, "there are a lot of *really smart* homeless folks from bankrupt tech companies. They take old tech, new tech, whatever, and splice it together and reprogram it. I doubt you would be able to comprehend anything that they could build."

The man was infuriating. He continually did his best to insult her intelligence, and pretty much everything else outside of her mother—though that was undoubtedly coming before long.

Luthor repeatedly shut his eyes. He looked like he was trying not to strangle Ostafal. "Try me," was all he said.

Jose folded his hands together in mockery of an elementary school teacher. "It's all simple Mathematics. My signal inverter works just like noise canceling technology except with electromagnetic radiation waves instead of sound waves. I am sure you didn't know this, but noise canceling works by emitting the exact opposite wavelength of incoming sound. As they meet, the opposite waves negate each other, eliminating the sound altogether. The signal inverter does the same thing, except with EM waves. It reads the signal produced by a given CPI chip and emits the opposite electromagnetic wave in real time. The result effectively cancels the CPI signal, by reducing the amplitude to a level undetectable by the scanners the carps use."

Regardless of what Jose claimed, it did not sound like *simple* math. It sounded like post graduate, applied trigonometry or some other smoggingly complicated thing. Though Luthor certainly would have understood it, the man had unlocked the secret of controlling gravity for God's sake. He could figure out a signally-thing.

"How many signals can this device block? What is its effective range?" Luthor asked.

Better you than me, I don't have a damn clue what to ask.

"It can block up to five signals at once. The boys tell me that its range is ten meters, but I wouldn't stretch it past five, just to be on the safe side."

"Alright. Sounds impressive. Let's deal," said Luthor.

"Is it safe to assume that you plan to barter?"

Tanya hadn't thought much about how exactly they were going to afford anything. Mark scans were off limits and therefore so was buying anything with actual money.

Vika palmed her rifle, extending it in her right hand. "What can this get us? .306 special, custom sniper scope. Laser is sighted to 300 meters."

"I don't often deal in guns. They are far too dangerous. Someone is liable to get killed you know," he smiled cruelly, "and since they're illegal to civilians, they have a way of being tracked. Every gun has a Government GPS unit to monitor its location."

"I already disabled the GPS unit."

"Maybe your friend will give you a gold star too." Tanya's face grew even hotter. Why did they have to deal with this polluter? "Regardless, there is no way for me to confirm what you are saying. You may or may not have actually disabled it and I am not inclined to take your word. Besides, I don't have any shortage of firearms at present." He gestured to the men flanking him, who smirked and brandished their Uzis.

As if we hadn't noticed them already. I swear, men and their guns... I need to have Luthor make a chart to show that the size of your gun has nothing to do with the length of your penis.

"Tell me you have something else to barter. Please."

Everyone shared an awkward glance. It quickly became evident that they did not, in fact, have anything else worth bartering. The silence stretched on interminably.

"Wonderful. Showing up to the gun fight with a slingshot," Jose rubbed his hands together, "that means the guy with the guns sets the rules."

Ostafal turned around and reached into a large plastic bin on one of the many shelves strung out behind him. He produced what was presumably the signal inverter. It wasn't very large at all. It was about the size of a wireless router with a scanning lens on the top. The exterior bristled with little antennae like an electronic porcupine.

Ostafal put his palms flat on the table on either side of the device. "Before you ask, I am going to tell you what it is going to cost: all the credits in each of your accounts and one of your CPI chips."

Luthor was incensed. "You are talking about a lot of money—"

"We both know that is a bunch of bullshit. Judging by your clothes, you've been on the run a while, which means that either you have already spent most of your money or you can't risk accessing it for fear of the carps finding you. Either way, credits are no good to you, and that is my price. You are lucky I am not charging you all of your CPI chips."

"How do you expect us to—"

Ostafal interrupted, "I expect you to barter with the only valuable thing you have or do you have something else you wish to barter?" he flashed a sinister smile at Tanya.

Tanya would rather pick the dirtiest, smelliest, most generally disgusting Markless in the city and service him than be touched by Jose. The thought of his clammy hands and his damnable 2180 tattoo staring at her... Tanya shuddered. Though for once she did not feel envy for Vika's beauty. If only Ostafal would try something on her... He would have no idea what was coming to him. She'd probably make him eat his own testicles. She would have paid to see that. She would have given up her Mark to see that.

"What do you want with our chips?" Luthor asked.

"I am afraid I am not in the habit of divulging delicate information like that for free. I'll tell you for the price of.... another of your CPI chips."

Luthor frowned.

"Your CPI chips will not be traced through this facility, as much for my security as your own. I have a very useful program, that again you wouldn't understand, that delays processing for several days. It then routes the CPI transactions through a half dozen neutral locations connected to my account."

"But they will be notified our accounts were used?" asked Michael.

"Yes, but not for three days, and then all that will be obvious is that you are somewhere in New York City, nothing more."

"That might actually help us," said Michael, "if we can get on the train to Chicago but they still think we are here, it could really throw them off."

"If it does what he says it does," Tanya corrected.

"Yes, I suspect it would be good for business for me to con convicted killers with a routing program that doesn't work. They certainly wouldn't come and kill me when the carps came looking for them," he looked pointedly at Tanya, the tattoo making a poor excuse for a haircut, "as always, good thinking, you stupid whore."

For perhaps the first time in her life, the absence of a weapon at her side was palpable.

Tanya longed for nothing more than to put a bullet hole between the 1 and the 8 on his forehead.

Luthor's face could have belonged to a drunk on a weeklong binge with how red he had turned. At least Jose was an equal opportunity asshole, he pissed off everyone.

"He can have my chip," Vika said, seeming to make the decision for the group. Luthor's bulging carotid disqualified him from making any sound decisions; Tanya's blood-pressure disqualified her.

Vika whipped out her utility knife with a flourish and placed it to her hand.

"Wait!" Ostafal said frantically. "It needs blood to soak in. Put it in here. He rushed over to hand Vika a plastic sandwich bag. She promptly sliced open her hand like she was peeling a potato. She stuck the tip of her knife in and popped out the small cylindrical device that transmitted her ID into the bag. She squeezed the wound until the requisite amount of the viscous liquid surrounded the chip.

"I require a bandage," Vika said.

Ostafal for once did not comment on the situation, instead he handed her a length of white cloth. Sterile it was not, but it seemed to suffice for her purposes. He almost looked concerned, but then he probably had not expected her to fillet her own flesh without so much as a grimace.

"The rest of you will need to scan your hands here," he gestured at the gun-like CPI scanning device on the table. "The program will not retrieve any funds for 72 hours. When it does, your undoubtedly tiny bank accounts will be emptied by numerous small transactions throughout New York City. The carps will hunt you for a week before they figure out you aren't anywhere in the tri-county area."

The word suspicious could not have been more woefully inadequate to describe her feelings. The worst part was they couldn't even screw the bastard over by spending their remaining money elsewhere—and Jose knew it. If they did, the damnable carbon police would swarm them. Their only chance was to trust him and try to get on the train in the next few days.

Tanya didn't like it, but she scanned her hand the same as Michael and Luthor. It was a rather anticlimactic way to lose every credit to their name. Thaddeus and Roc watched silently. The only potential consolation prize was the possibility the government had already frozen all of their assets and Jose wouldn't have a turd to flush when he tried to withdraw the money.

#

Having finished with their transaction with Jose Ostafal they left. No one wanted to stay one second longer than necessary. Still, they *had* accomplished what they had set to do. It was always better to look on the bright side of things.

Luthor took out the stolen phone that Vika had acquired. “Damn. The battery’s dead.”

“You shouldn’t flaunt something like that around here,” Thaddeus said, “it could be dangerous.”

“What do we have to fear?” Luthor said. “There’s six of us and Vika still has her rifle.”

“I wouldn’t put it past the Dog Pound to hit a group this size, even if they have a gun. So put that phone away. No need to give ‘em any more reason,” Luthor did as he was asked.

“What makes the Dog Pound so dangerous?” asked Tanya.

Roc and Thaddeus shared a glance, “I ran with them for a year, D got me out before I had to start killing folks. The areas they control… some bad sh—” Thadd closed his eyes deliberately, “some bad stuff goes down in those areas.”

“They aren’t just a normal gang, are they?” asked Michael.

“They’re bigger than a gang. They’re kind of like a gang, crime syndicate, and drug cartel all rolled into one. But not really any of those either. Damn, I can’t explain it. Just don’t mess with them.”

“That doesn’t sound very appealing,” Tanya said, “they deal drugs?”

“No, they undoubtedly would have been stopped long ago if they were flooding drugs into the city. They’re strong, but the carbon police are still stronger,” Roc said, “they are dealing in something far more addictive than drugs.”

Roc stopped, as if he thought his description sufficient. But Tanya didn’t have a clue. *What’s more addictive than drugs?*

“Food,” said Thaddeus, “it’s where they get their name. Back right after the war broke out and everything got all fucked sideways, a huge distribution warehouse for some big pet store chain shut down. It was too expensive to fuel the semis to deliver the goods. So, it just sat there, abandoned until it was 'liberated' by those Dog Pound bastards—at least that's what they called it; seems like stealing to me. Anyway, this was a big-ass facility, thousands of shipping containers of every type of pet crap you could imagine. But most of it was food."

"Wait," Tanya said, hardly believing her ears, "you're telling me this syndicate is based off *pet food*?"

"Yup," Thadd said as if it were the most natural thing in the world. "Why do you think they're called the *Dog Pound*?" Michael and Luthor didn't seem to be perturbed by the revelation at all either. People eating dog food? And more than that—an entire gang, syndicate, whatever, whose power was based upon dog food?

"Dog and cat food are perfect if you think about it. That… crap keeps forever— particularly the dry stuff—and it's never going to get confiscated or rationed by the government for the military. The government's not going to think to ration the left-over Kibbles and Bits, you know what I mean? So, they found themselves sitting on enough food to last fifty years."

"Son-of-a-bitch," Michael let out a low whistle, "there's a lot of power in that."

"Damn straight. And they used it too. They're the most powerful gang in New York right now. All from selling pet food to people."

"So, all they're doing is *selling food*? That doesn't sound so bad," Tanya said.

Thaddeus shook his head. "People will do some serious shit for food. And the Dog Pound knows it. They sell it cheaper than regular food, so people can afford it, but there is more to it than that. They require *favors*."

Tanya wasn't sure if she wanted to know what sort of favors they were talking about, but Thaddeus explained anyway.

"Some are pretty simple. Bartering for valuable items, sexual favors, free repair work for electronics. But sometimes it gets real polluted," he winced, "sorry. It gets *really bad.* They ask you to steal for them, sometimes even *kill* for them—rival gang members, or people who owed too much money. If you don't do what they ask, then they quit selling food to you, which puts lots of poor bastards on the street."

"That's what they asked you to do? Kill people for dog food?"

Luthor gave her a sharp stare, which stung as much as a slap. *I really don't know what this world is like*, she thought. *Everyone here seems to have gone through worse than me. I just can't imagine being so desperate that I would kill for a dog biscuit. Apparently Luthor can.*

"Yeah, I almost did it too. Lots of people would rather kill than die. I got recruited after I lost my Mark. Said they wouldn't give me any food if I didn't help them. After a year, they sent me on my first mission—that's what they called it —assassination is more like it. But, DeShawn convinced me not to go—said murder would only just kill me on the inside. Then he introduced me to Father Roc."

"I daresay that I am glad to have you both. You have good souls," Roc said.

"That's why he keeps that old gun around. Helps remind us not to ever go back."

"We aren't buying food from them, so are we in the clear?" asked Michael.

"You never know. The high-ups in the Pound are rich as gold-plated shit after selling food for this long without having any overhead, they have their own motives. But I won't feel safe until I get back to where I see some good old-fashioned suburban refugees again. These Dogs on the outskirts make me nervous. Never know when one is gonna pop up and bite you in the ass."

Tanya heard a click. It echoed like a gunshot in the

abandoned street. A man aimed a pistol against Thadd's head. "Like this?" he said.

Half a dozen other Dog Pounders appeared from the shadows in all directions, indeed resembling their namesake. Each had a gun, mismatched clothes, and lips peeled back in a snarl. Everyone froze; Tanya put her hands up, eager to show them she had no intention of fighting back.

"Welcome to the Pound, bitches," barked one juvenile, wagging his gun.

"What do you want?" said Luthor. Sounding annoyed rather than frightened. But gang bangers probably don't seem all that intimidating to a man who had survived the bloodiest parts of World War III, killed Sabers, and recently blown up a helicopter.

"We want everything," said another, "but from you, just that signal inverter."

"I don't know what you're talking about," said Luthor.

"Don't be a smart-ass, you smoggin' moron. We watched you buy it from Jose and now he wants it back."

"That son of a bitch," Vika yelled. Tanya had never seen her so angry.

Two men surrounded Vika, pistols erect.

"Show us your tits," one of them said. Tanya could smell the man's breath from two meters away. It was not pleasant.

Vika spat contemptuously. "Go fuck yourself."

"Why would we do that with you around?"

Vika gave him a look that would have killed a small animal. "Then go fuck Ostafal, you bastard."

A particularly grimy male approached Vika with his gun drawn. "Ooh, a feisty one. Me first!"

Tanya would not have believed what happened next had she not witnessed it. Something about the man's face and intentions snapped Vika's control. It was like watching a dam that held back a mountain of rage break or maybe more like a volcano erupting.

In a blur she reached out, tore the man's pistol from him and shot him in the groin. He crumpled, a bloody splotch replacing the spot where his bulge ought to have been. In the same movement she turned and shot the one behind her, also in the groin. Spinning and crouching to the ground she somehow ended up with both weapons. She discharged them several more times into the stupefied chests of the other men who had surrounded them. She whirled and fired bullets in a tempest of lead. It was as if her fury at Captain Jacques and Colonel Dimarin itself was propelling the projectiles.

Tanya flinched as blood splattered on her face when the Dog Pounder next to her swallowed a slug. He slumped, his gun clattered away on the gravel-esque pavement toward Michael's feet. Michael reached down and grabbed it. He held onto it like a life preserver. Not that he needed it, Vika had already taken care of all of them.

Not a single man managed to get a shot back in return at the force of nature ending their lives. They never expected someone—least of all a beautiful woman—to stand up to them when they all had guns. In mere seconds the stunned soldiers of the Dog Pound lay bloodied or dead on the ground, their weapons lay impotent in their cooling hands. For the first time, Tanya really saw how deadly her companion was. She did not doubt for a moment that she had the ability to kill *anyone* who tried to corner her in a shower—Black Saber or not.

Thaddeus whistled. "Smogging son-of-a-polluter... remind me never to mess with her." Vika stood over the two men who had taunted her. She didn't say a word but fired two more rounds into the place where their manhood had been moments before. The men doubled up in agony.

"Just to make sure neither of you ever reproduce," she said coldly, "never forget this day. The last day you *ever* disrespect a woman," she spat derisively.

No one spoke. Vika stalked between the bodies back toward Ostafal. No one had any doubt of her intentions. She exchanged her pistols for fully loaded ones and continued walking.

A murmur bubbled up from the ground. "You god-damn bitch." One of the men had not yet died. He held up a shaky pistol at Vika's back.

Tanya ducked as another gun-shot ripped through the street, echoing in the silence of death. Vika whipped around, but the man was already slumping back down. Michael held a trembling gun, a wisp of smoke issuing up from the barrel. He grasped it with both hands and quavered from head to toe. Shock filled his face.

Vika's face softened. She approached and placed a hand on his cheek. "Thank you. You just saved my life," she actually smiled. Her kind demeanor disappeared as quickly as a muzzle flash and she returned to her march back to Ostafal.

#

Michael followed a safe distance behind the hurricane of death marching in front of him. Vika –in all truth—frightened him. She bulls-eyed eight men in fewer seconds. Eight! She really didn't miss. Ever. And all that death didn't seem to bother her at all. That wasn't right. *She wasn't right*! He had only shot one half-dead guy and it bothered him. A lot. The heaviness of the pistol in his clammy hands, the resistance as he depressed the trigger, and the power of the explosion of Cordite that sent the ordinance flying, all played again and again in his mind. But the worst—damn was it awful—was the man's face as the bullet hit him. A light—or whatever it was in a person that made the difference between a dead-body and person—had flickered out in his eyes. Michael had actually seen it turn off. And he was the one who had flipped the switch.

There hadn't even been time for the poor bastard to contemplate his death. Vika had already messed him up, so Michael's own bullet had killed him almost instantly.

How does she do it? How does she kill without feeling this... this awfulness. Hell—how does Luthor do it? They're all certifiably, bat-shit crazy.

Sweat ran down his back despite the cold. Too many emotions. On top of everything else, Vika had thanked him. Never had she been so sincere since he had known her. That haunted him too. Her hand touching his face, he could still feel it, and that smile. *Thank you, Michael, you just saved my life... Damn, I thought I was past this! Here I am replaying a girl's touch like a middle school pubescent.* But try as he might, Michael could not stop thinking about any of it, the dead man or Vika.

Vika strode ahead, backside swaying alluringly. Not that he would ever say that—he liked having a face too much. He had trouble not watching though. Only a moron would waste a chance to appreciate the sexiness of a woman like Vika, combined with a pair of pistols she knew how to use. Michael was not a moron, so he watched during the entirety of the short trip back to Ostafal.

Roc called after her, "Are you sure you need to do this?"

Without turning around, she answered. "Ostafal tried to kill us, he lied to us, he betrayed us. How does he not deserve to die?"

"Vengeance is the Lord's. Do not do something you will regret."

She raised an eyebrow at the old man, "who's to say I am not the agent of God's wrath?"

Michael couldn't tell, but Roc might have nodded subtly at the remark.

Everyone followed at a safe distance, afraid of what Vika might do. She disappeared around the corner into the open cargo bay of Ostafal's shop. A shot rang out, echoing violently off the concrete walls. Michael froze, having no desire to go back in. Another gunshot rent the air, equally as piercing as the first. Michael peaked around the edge, still clinging to his gun. One of the two guards lay on the ground behind the table, not moving. Vika stood over the other who cradled his arm protectively. Blood leaked through his fingers. The assault rifle, sub machine gun, whatever-gun he had held sat innocently on the floor. Evidently, Vika had chosen to keep this one alive for questioning.

"Where is he?" she demanded.

"I don't know," blubbered the man.

She jammed the business end of the gun into his frontal lobe. "Tell me."

"I swear, I swear! I don't know! He got a phone call right after you guys left. Then he walked out. He doesn't tell us where his going. God! Please don't shoot me!"

Vika picked up his discarded weapon, pointedly flipped off the safety, and trained it on the pathetic excuse of a man before her.

"Last chance. Where is Ostafal?"

"Oh shit, please God, please don't kill me," he began weeping. "Please don't shoot me again. He just walked out that door. He didn't say anything. Oh no. Please!"

"Where is his computer?"

"Over there," the man pointed a bloody finger and looked suddenly hopeful. "He also has a server rack behind those crates."

Vika leveled the automatic weapon in the direction of the computer and pulled the trigger. A burst of bullets reduced the enclosed semiconductors to a smoking silicon colander. Vika yelled something in another language, then turned and emptied the remainder of the rather significant magazine into the aluminum enclosure that housed the servers. There had to be at least 50 more bullets she poured into the poor thing. It sparked and smoked and eventually sagged into the housing.

"Let Ostafal try to take our money now," she let off another string of foreign profanity directed at no one in particular.

Satisfied, she picked up a plastic bag from the table and shoved it in her pocket. It contained her CPI chip. She then searched the dead body, taking several full magazines of bullets for her pistol and what looked like a silencer. Once she relieved the other man of ammunition as well, she walked out without a word.

Michael realized far too late that he was still watching her. He had been the only one looking. The rest of them had crouched behind an ancient dumpster. Vika locked eyes with him, but said nothing. More importantly, she didn't hit him. Instead, she slapped a manila folder against his chest. "Make sure everyone gets one of these."

"What are they?"

"Too stupid to read? Look." He did look. The folder contained a pile of subway tickets.

"Subway tickets? But we need to get to Chicago," Michael said.

"Ostafal knows where we are going. We need a new approach." Apparently not finished with her gifts she threw the newly acquired weapon to Luthor. "Ever used one of these?"

Luthor's eyes widened. "This is an MX-5. This is my old gun."

"Based off the HK-436. The best assault rifle ever produced. Thought you might want it."

Michael couldn't tell if Luthor was pleased or petrified. He held the gun as if it were a poisonous snake, like it might bite him.

"Thank you Vika, but I can't. It isn't... good for me to hold this." Luthor gave no more explanation than that for his refusal of weapon.

Maybe he doesn't kill without any negative effect. Michael thought.

Vika shrugged and tossed the weapon aside. She grabbed two more pistols from the wall display then strapped her own MX-5 to her back.

"We'll have to get rid of these before we get on the subway," Luthor said.

"Don't remind me," she said.

CHAPTER 19:

Aurora, IL, United States of the West

"Help!" a woman cried. She hung from the edge of a rooftop by her wrists. Her long skirt fluttered in the high city breeze.

Justice coursed in his veins like blood, and the compulsion to save her banged in his chest like a gong. "Hang on!" Vanguard yelled back at her. His inhumanly strong muscles allowed him to leap the void between buildings with ease. His cape echoed his movement behind him. He landed in a crouch near the hanging woman.

"Fool. You will never save her," a man in jet black armor leveled a gun at him. It was Bastion. The most sinister man Vanguard had ever faced. Even in a world as fallen as theirs, he truly was a stronghold of evil.

"Bastion. Of course it would be you. Why? What do you have to gain from this?"

"What do you have to gain from trying to save her? The same thing as me. A purpose. You save people. I hurt them. Without duality, what would this world be?"

Without warning Bastion pulled the trigger. Lethal bits of metal sprayed at Vanguard. He dove to the side, ducking behind a solar battery array. Slugs impaled his custom fitted gelvar body armor, reducing each impact to a harmless pinching sensation. A hot sting from his calf alerted him that he had not successfully avoided all the bullets. Pain wasn't important. Stopping Bastion was.

A persistent beep came from underneath him. Did Bastion plant a bomb? *The beep grew louder until it seemed to be emanating from the entire city at once.*

Qwiz sat up. He had been dreaming. The eternal battle between Bastion and Vanguard raged on, perhaps he would return to them later. Desperate to stop the infernal beep, he slapped the snooze button on his alarm clock. The beeping continued. The clock read 2:47. His alarm wasn't set to go off for another four hours. He scrambled out of bed and rushed to his computer.

He muted the beep and expanded a browser window running in the background. He had written an extension to track the communications of the Stalker. He had been so silent in the last week that Qwiz had coded an alarm mechanism to alert him if any communications were taking place. It beeped loudly and automatically recorded the message or conversation.

He would listen to the message in its entirety later, but he was wide awake by now and needed to hear what was going on.

He clicked an icon and the message poured out of his speakers.

It was clearly the Southerner speaking "...from the most influential dealer in the area."

"At least you are capable of some semi-competent work." Stalker's voice was as icy as ever, but it was angrier than Qwiz had heard it before.

"Semi-smogging-competent? You're the one who let him get away when we still had the element of surprise!"

"And you lost most of your team and a fully loaded Cherokee. Not to mention you let the two escape in Chicago —"

"But I was given the *Omega* abort code! I had them at gunpoint when I received the order."

"You should have known better."

"Known better than to obey my smogging orders?

Don't give me that shit. Face it, Tenrel is good, and there's someone on the inside helping him."

Qwiz still didn't know who had saved his life that night by calling the Texan off, but he hoped that whoever had helped was still looking out for him—for all of them.

"I don't want any more excuses. Allow me to be perfectly clear. I have the *Lancing Protocol* in place for you on this mission. If you fail this time... Well, you won't have to worry about failing again."

"You son of a bitch."

"Admittedly. If you wanted someone sensitive, you should have found a job with a military therapist."

Qwiz wondered what the *Lancing Protocol* entailed. But whatever it was, Texas didn't like it.

"I do hope you feel strongly about your plan," Stalker said.

"It's solid. Their copy of the research was destroyed in the carp car. They won't have a pot to piss in without it."

"Good. So that means the two men who escaped in Chicago have the only copy we haven't already secured."

"Yeah. Tenrel will have to try to meet up with those smoggers to retrieve it. That means he'll try to get to Chicago."

"Go on."

"They won't risk a 3 month walk through the suburbs with these post-war winters, and they just bought four Acela train tickets and a signal inverter from my contact. I know their likely departure point and have men stationed there. It won't be long before one of their chips pops up on a scanner or they try to sneak on that train."

"I hope for your sake it works. I would hate to have to kill you because you can't handle his gravity tricks again."

So, the Lancing Protocol means he's going to kill you if you fail. Qwiz realized. *Like lancing an infectious boil.*

"Ah, but that's the thing. Tenrel isn't the only one with

gravity tricks anymore."

"Good. You will need every advantage possible, because no one is coming to reinforce you."

"Throw me a smogging bone here, I've only got 4 men left. And I have to have two of them at other Acela stations!"

"Recruit then. Find a hired gun or two to bolster your team."

"This is ridiculous. We have Saber units in 8 cities across America. Send one of them!"

"The White House has personally barred the transfer of Sabers from any other region."

"Why?"

"Jimenez loves to make life difficult for me, and you parking that Cherokee helicopter in the street did not put me in his good graces."

The Texan swore, he seemed to do that a lot. "Why not just send them in anyway?"

"I did. They are already en route from Atlanta, but it will be two days before they can arrive. They have to navigate the suburbs to dodge all CPI scanning stations."

"They will be too late!"

"I can't move assets any quicker."

"At least tip off the authorities to put some drug sniffing dogs patrolling the Acela stations."

"Why?"

"Let's just say I found out that Tenrel's shit has some unexpected results with animals. He won't know what hit him."

"It's done. Do not screw this up."

"I won't. *Lancing,* remember?"

The message terminated leaving Qwiz with a pit in his stomach. He still had no consistent contact with Luthor. He didn't bother replaying the beginning of the message. He had to alert Luthor before he walked into a trap. He called the phone back that had contacted him before. A kindly automated woman informed him he needed to leave a message.

Qwiz mashed his finger on the end button. If only cell-phones had the ancient functionality of being able to hang up. Then he could have slammed the phone back hard on the receiver and relieved a bit of stress. It was imperative that he get a hold of Luthor's new friends. Maybe they could help.

Luthor had mentioned an Italian Restaurant. Qwiz began searching the internet for every Italian restaurant in a multi-kilometer radius around the site of the helicopter crash. He quickly compiled a list of possible candidates. It was not a short list.

He called Bill. It was now 3:00 in the morning. "Were you planning on sleeping tonight?"

"Hell no! Rest is for pussies and hippies. I can sleep when I'm dead."

#

They decided to try the signal inverter on the subway first. In all likelihood a standard subway terminal wouldn't be *crawling* with carbon police, it would hopefully only be *saturated* with them. Michael would have put money down that they had a better chance to escape from a mere subway than from a major rail depot if the damn thing didn't work.

The inverter looked a lot like most of the other individual scanners he had seen in his life, only this one had a spiky tumor on its ass. Luthor pressed a few buttons then put the device over his own Chip. It beeped conclusively.

"Let's hope this actually does what the bastard says it does," he said.

"How do we know?" Michael said, giving voice to his concerns. "Who's to say that he hasn't double crossed us with this thing too?"

"I doubt he would have tried to kill us to get it back, if it didn't work," Luthor replied. "And I don't see many other options for getting back to Chicago—unless you really like to walk."

"If we walk, can I keep the HK?" Vika said hopefully.

"Hell yes," Michael responded. "Only, I'm not real excited about walking 1500 kilometers in the winter. It's already September, and with winter beginning earlier and earlier, there's a chance we'll be caked in snow before we get out of New York."

The world's combined efforts at carbon reduction seemed to be working. Global temperatures had been falling appreciably for the last twenty years, though most scientists attributed it to vastly increased dust in the atmosphere after the war. Unfortunately, lower temps meant longer, colder winters, making overland travel much more difficult.

Luthor nodded in agreement. "Let's face it. If we want to clear our names, then we need that data. It's all in Chicago. That means the train."

A half hour later the guns had been ditched in a pile of refuse in an alley. The bullets—at Roc's request—were dumped down the sewer. Vika's expression called to mind a child who had just lost a pet. She'd wanted to keep that assault rifle. Despite protests she had kept a single pistol—just in case. Not that Michael objected to it. He liked the security of knowing she had access to a gun. Having an ally who didn't miss and could kill without remorse had its advantages. Particularly when one was being pursued around the world by the European government or Sabers or whoever-the-smog this Pain guy worked for.

Guns disposed, each of them scanned their hands under the inverter. Only three of them had chips any more now that Vika had removed her own; hopefully that would be well within the parameters of the device.

That was the only weakness of the CPI system. In situations of mass transit, or anywhere else that required large numbers of people to pass through with a minimum of delay, the overhead scanners rendered a Markless effectively invisible—so long as they managed to get their hands on a ticket. They couldn't be detected since they weren't broadcasting a signal. If everything worked right, in a few minutes they would all be just as undetectable as any Markless. As they were about to descend the stairs to the subway, they said goodbye to Roc and Thaddeus. It proved more emotional than Michael expected. They had been invaluable companions, and had proved that at least a small fraction of the homeless population weren't the mindless zombies or bloodthirsty savages he'd encountered as a kid. They were civilized, generous, and kind. Nothing he could have anticipated.

Tanya gave each a long embrace. Luthor and Michael received a warm handshake. Even Vika seemed sorry to see them leave.

"Don't give up, my friends," Roc said. "May the Lord be with you."

"So you can kick some ass," Thaddeus added.

As they left Michael wondered if they would ever see them again.

The predawn lavender sky began to push back the blackness overhead, but it exaggerated the looming skyscrapers. The occasional un-vandalized streetlight illuminated the dreary atmosphere.

They flowed into the hoard of morning commuters, following the stream downstairs. The moment of truth was upon them. Would the inverter work? It currently was tucked into the top of the duffel bag, broadcasting the exact opposite signal of each of their chips.

Signage made it abundantly clear that no gloves would be tolerated in the station. They each slipped their tickets into the turnstiles, the digital reader removing the requisite funds, then spitting the tickets out the other side. Michael glanced up at the row of unassuming scanners overhead and could almost see the electromagnetic signals being transmitted and received. He prayed his had been effectively obscured. Not prayed exactly—as much as he liked Roc, he hadn't developed any desire to convert —more like he thought really hard at the scanners.

Michael winced, fearing the dreaded squeal of the alarm. It didn't sound. He had made it through! He waited for the others, making sure he stood close enough for the inverter to do its work. Luthor walked through, no siren. Tanya followed, no siren. Vika came last, no siren. Michael realized he had been holding his breath, and took a deep one. Tanya was grinning broadly, excited to not be heading back to carbon police custody.

Suddenly one of the carps blew his whistle. A red light flashed over the top of the scanners. The turnstiles locked up and everyone who had not yet made it through found themselves stuck. He approached them. "Ma'am, you are going to need to come with me," he said gesturing toward Vika.

#

Vika protested of course. She just wished she could have protested properly. Words were so inadequate. There were inflections to consider, reactions to calculate, not to mention facial expressions or body language. Trying to effectively communicate her intended meaning with all the variables vying for dominance approached impossibility. She was particularly fond of the American saying "actions speak louder than words." They did. In this particular situation a fist in the proper place could tell him exactly how much she wanted to accompany him. Against her wont, and her better judgment—she attempted a diplomatic solution instead.

"Is there a problem officer?" she said in her kindest tone. Michael, who had stayed within earshot of their conversation, winced. Apparently, her vocal calculations were off, again.

"Ma'am, in this state, we do not allow hand coverings through scanning terminals." His eyes struggled to extricate themselves from her chest, but he finally managed to glance at her right hand. It was still wrapped in bandages from her asinine encounter with Ostafal.

One of the great disappointments in their current adventure were Ostafal's lungs. They were still breathing. She longed to make them cease doing so. Unfortunately, the coward ran off as soon as they were out of sight, so she had to content herself with killing one of his lackeys and shooting the other in the hand. She didn't even get to keep that beautiful HK-436.

I liked that gun, she thought.

The stunning weapon played through her mind. Its special-forces custom-built ergonomic mag easily held 90 rounds, making its impressive fire-rate monstrously effective. Yet even in full-auto it boasted scalpel-like accuracy thanks to a next-gen inertial-dampener that independently countered each bullet's recoil. The standard coalition rounds it fired had such gorgeous stopping power, and the way the stock fit so nicely in the crook of her shoulder... Vika sighed. It was beauty perfected. Now it was in a dumpster. *That's a shame, a smogging shame.*

"Ma'am, I am going to need you to scan your hand over here," he directed her over to a tiny Plexiglas cabinet of an office. She followed him. A lot of good it would do him. She didn't have a CPI chip for the machine to read. What she did have was a pistol. A sig-Sauer .40, custom grip, stainless steel finish. Another beautiful gun. She didn't need a caliber that large, 9mm was sufficient for anyone with decent aim, but there was something innately satisfying about the feel of a .40 discharge that made her love it. The gun's blunt metal exterior felt painfully obvious tucked into her pants. She needed a holster. Only rookies, or the very desperate, thought that a waistband was a good place for a sidearm.

Even if the CPI reader didn't work, a simple pat down would suffice to find the illegal weapon.

"Here you are," he said, eyes lingering in ways she didn't appreciate. At least the bulges he focused on were not caused by her concealed sidearm.

Damn men. You're all the same. If only more women would discover that you all have a weak spot, you bastards might just change. Or go extinct. Yes, extinct would be better. The thought of kicking this carbon cop's weak spot was appealing, but Vika again restrained herself.

"You won't find much."

The guard stiffened. She had messed up the intonation again. Still too terse.

"You are aware it is illegal to travel without proper identification. I can escort you to the nearest CPI clinic for a replacement if you'd like."

It was unlikely that carbon regulations would permit an officer to leave his post to escort anyone anywhere. But the man looked hopeful. If she agreed he would no-doubt take the longest possible route in order to spend more time with her. Or more accurately, more time mentally fondling her. There was no way she would be able to restrain herself from killing him for more than another minute, let alone a thirty-minute walk.

She needed a lie. And she needed it now. "Negative," she shook her head. That was the wrong word. "That is not necessary." Vika tried not to throw up at the sound of her own voice. Michael smirked in the background.

"I insist. What happened to your hand anyway, miss?"

Vika's mind raced. This whole talking thing needed to go. Leave it to Tanya. She was far better at pretending to be a moron. "I had surgery. The doctor had to remove my chip. I won't be able to have it re-implanted until it heals."

"Wow. Sounds serious. What was wrong with it?"

Smog these imbecilic conversations! Go away! After a moment of hesitation she responded, "Cancer... I had a tumor removed." Not her best lie, but this guy would probably have believed anything, so long as she kept talking. *I had an alien tentacle growing off my arm. The doctors had to remove it. It had a tendency to decapitate men who spend too long looking at my breasts.*

"That sounds serious. Was it malignant?"

"No," she tried not to scowl. It didn't work. She produced a small plastic bag with her very inactive CPI unit. "Here it is. Can I go? I might miss my train."

"Oh, of course miss," he said apologetically. "Sorry to bother you. Please be safe."

"Thank you," she quickly left the carp's company, aware that his eyes were fondling her ass continually as she left. Hopefully, he didn't notice the extra curve from the Sig.

The other three stood against an advertisement, feigning nonchalance as they waited for her. Tanya looked relieved, Luthor implacable and serious, but Michael seemed to barely be able to contain his laughter.

"Is there a problem officer?" Michael said in a faux female voice, as he pretended to twirl his hair.

"Shut up," Vika said. She meant it. Fists might be the perfect solution here.

"What happened to your one rule? 'You hit on me, I hit you,' something like that?" he laughed some more.

"I thought I would pass on his punishment to you. My rule doesn't specify *who*, so long as *someone* gets punched."

Michael deflated like a balloon. *Better.* Unexpectedly, a pang of guilt popped as she saw his reaction. She never expected to feel pity, much less guilt, as a result of a man, least of all Michael. But there it was, squeezing her innards like a vice-wrench. He *had* saved her life after all. Maybe he deserved some pity. Only a little.

"But, since you saved my life, you get another pass."

"Wait. Really?" Michael relaxed. "Thanks, I was only

kidding you know."

"I know," she said.

Later, as they boarded the subway, Tanya grabbed her by the arm so they were the last two through the automatic doors. "You're starting to actually like him, aren't you?"

"Don't be stupid," she said, utterly offended. "Why would you say that?"

"You didn't hit him," Tanya said simply, "and you smiled. I have almost never seen you smile."

"When?"

"Just now, when you were talking with him."

"I didn't smile," she said, though suddenly uncertain if it was true.

"If you say so," Tanya said wending her way through the seated and standing passengers.

"It wouldn't be the worst thing in the world if you had smiled, you know."

She grabbed an overhead rail next to Luthor, leaving the seat next to Michael open. Vika stood awkwardly indecisive about where to sit. The rational choice would be to take the open seat. It was open. Sitting required less energy than standing, leaving more energy in reserve for a potential fight. But there were those damn social implications again. So much more difficult than action! *If only there were a way to solve this problem with a punch, or a bullet. Yes, a bullet.* If she sat, he would likely attempt more conversation with her, and she could possibly be put in another situation to unintentionally smile. If she didn't sit, there would be questions as to *why.* Questions she was not particularly interested in answering. *Damn it all! If I punched them all hard enough…* she clenched her fists until her knuckles turned white, then purple.

She did not punch anyone. Though she did kick herself for getting into this mess. In one swift motion she sat down next to Michael and concentrated on *not* smiling.

Vika paid so much attention to her facial expressions, or rather lack thereof, that a large, disheveled man, slipped onto the train without being detected. Normally, he would have stood out to her like a smiley face sticker on the Mona Lisa. His muscular bulk was impossible to hide with tattered clothes, and he prowled rather than walked, a symptom of extensive combat training.

He stood ten meters away watching Michael chat with Vika, occasionally speaking into a mic hidden under his tattered hood. He undoubtedly saw her smile at least once.

CHAPTER 20:

Eleven Years Ago: Titan Dome, Antarctica

Jake blasted away with one of the captured dragons against the Chinese counterattack. It had an entire shipping container of ammunition. Jake had used three fourths of it in twenty minutes against a line of Chinese infantry that had managed to advance to a defensive trench a hundred meters back. They fired intermittently, mostly depending on the artillery and missiles to accomplish damage. Luthor and Garcia were almost out of ammo, and Chaz had no rockets. Claptrap patrolled the sky, but failed miserably to counter the missile strikes that continued to bombard their position.

"Where the hell is the goddamned armor?" Jake bellowed. "This thing is so hot, its gotta look like a searchlight to those missiles. I don't want to be a popsicle, Sarge."

"Just keep shooting. We have to hold out a few more minutes." Garcia said.

"You'd better be right," the dragon roared some more, Jake along with it. "Die you greedy bastards!" he yelled as if it would help the bullets find more skulls. He sprayed the trench for any infantry stupid enough to poke their heads out.

The shells kept falling. All around, the ice vaporized to steam and smoke as shells landed, refreezing to snow before hitting the ground. All Luthor could do was pray that none of them would find the gun he defended. At least the Chinese hadn't sent in their armor. They wouldn't have lasted long against that.

What are they waiting for?

The ground began to shake. With a rumble and a crash, a team of Moles burrowed up through the ice behind them. The 7th tunneling division had arrived. Luthor cheered with the rest of the men at the tank-like machines. They were mounted with a massive drill on the front that melted and drilled through solid ice, shunting the slough behind them through giant hoses. The military used them to drill temporary shelters underneath the ice sheet for the men and create safe, undetectable paths to move men and materiel. They were essential for war to be possible in such extreme conditions. It was still unclear if the Chinese had developed a comparable technology.

The cheers grew as the impressive M1A2 Abrams tanks followed the Moles. Perhaps nothing could be more intimidating than a twin-cannoned Abrams in pristine Antarctic camo, Luthor's personal favorite configuration. A traffic jam followed composed of Bradleys, Strykers, mobile defense stations, and the venerable M1A1 Abrams. More missiles buzzed overhead, clearing the way ahead for the sudden surge of allied armor. The Chinese had no answer to stop them. Evidently, the other paratroopers had successfully harried Asian air support. Enemy missiles exploded overhead harmlessly as the mobile defense stations fulfilled their purpose.

Luthor sighed and slumped down on the ground away from the dragons. Finally, it was over. He could let the grunts take it from here. The machines kept rumbling past, burning an almost unfathomable amount of fuel to do so. They seemed to rattle the entire continent with their power. The Chinese would fall before their might.

The rumble of the passing armor column abruptly grew to a violent shaking. Luthor was thrown to the ground. The ice shrieked and began to crack and splinter in spidery slivers in every direction. With a boom, a geyser of steam and smoke erupted from one of the cracks, enveloping Jake's dragon, and completely obscuring it from view. Luthor stumbled frantically away from the frightening scene. More eruptions burst forth from the ice, jutting jagged pillars of smoke high into the air. It was like someone had instantly vaporized all the ice underneath the surface, forcing the steam violently to the surface to release the pressure. Luthor watched in horror as the cracks spread, in a terrifying line parallel to the defenses as far as he could see in either direction.

The ground shook again. The individual pillars paused, as if taking a deep breath. Then all at once, the entire line exploded in a great wall of steam and fire. The explosion swallowed Luthor, stealing his breath. He couldn't see, his tinted goggles were completely blinded. The ice cracked and huge chunks fell into an unseen chasm below. He tried to escape, but it was too late. The ice beneath him broke and he fell, sliding into a newly formed canyon.

Like everything else in Antarctica, Luthor's vision whited out and he lost consciousness.

#

Hudson River Station, NY, United States of the West

It didn't take long to arrive at the Acela transfer station. The subway was decidedly faster than walking. It also happened to be on the same line. Luthor had no desire to switch trains and risk more forays with the carps. Vika had since removed her bandage to reveal a grisly, but no longer bleeding wound. Hopefully getting on the Acela to Chicago would not be a problem. The squeal of the train's brakes indicated they were approaching their stop. The annoyingly soothing female voice declared they had arrived at 207th street station— the closest one that intersected with the high-speed railway.

The city had become so dense that it had been nearly impossible to find a location for the high-speed rail station.

So engineers had built out onto the water and created an additional bridge to accommodate the East West travel. The whole project had been ludicrously expensive but had kept the life blood of travel flowing in a zagging line between New York and Chicago and the few surviving cities in between. They exited the subway into the newly made station that issued out of high rises ringing Inwood Park Farms and out onto the water.

Luthor entered the utilitarian, concrete structure with more confidence than the subway. It was like the last half mile of PT from his training days. If he could just push through a few more minutes then they would be out of this damnable city. He could do anything for a few more minutes. There would still be the terrorist label to shed, but invincibility from Mark scanners and a new city would be a nice start.

Hundreds of people crowded the tiled foyer, buying tickets, waiting for trains, or meeting passengers. They contrasted sharply with the homeless clientele he had been associating with as of late. The suits, ties and briefcases stank of credits every bit as much as the rickshaws and other human-powered forms of transportation reeked of sweat and were just as repulsive. Some were even fat. *Fat!*

A particularly rotund man waddled by in a tailored suit. An artificially beautiful woman held his arm and glared at Luthor. With food this scarce, obesity equated wealth, and this man wanted to show it off. In contrast, the slim woman seemed more intent on showing the largest percentage of her legs possible while still technically wearing shorts. "I wonder how many weeks his daily food intake would feed Father Roc's group?" Tanya muttered under her breath.

"He's got to be packing in four thousand calories a day to maintain that shape," Michael said.

Not everyone tried to imitate a beach ball, but many still offered disapproving glances to Luthor's unkempt band. Eyes seemed to bore into him from everywhere even though he strained to blend in.

"Why are they all staring at us?" he asked.

"We haven't showered or changed in a week, we look like Markless."

"Shit. We are never going to make it. We stick out like a sore thumb."

"Be quiet," Vika said sternly. "Act like you *aren't* committing a crime. Quit whispering."

Luthor stood up a little straighter, they would surely have the eye of security, but their scans would be clean. No reason to act strange and draw even more attention to themselves.

"I'm used to seeing people stare at you Vika, but not with *that* look," said Tanya.

"Like they say, every guy's either got a dick or a wallet in his hand," said Michael.

"Which one do you have?" Vika quipped. "Last I checked, Ostafal took all your credits."

Luthor could have sworn that Michael blushed. Of course, the lucky bastard's dark skin hid it too well to be noticed.

"Well, it *was* a figure of speech," Michael replied, "I mean, nobody's carried a wallet in years. Even credit cards are digital."

"That would explain a lot about men today," Vika said.

"Damn it, that's not what I meant!"

Luthor laughed like taking the Acela to Chicago was the most normal thing in the world for him, but the stares still made him uncomfortable.

As they moved along the line the distribution of people became increasingly skewed toward the carp side. It seemed like every third person wore the green and black of the carbon police. Luthor had never seen so many in one place. One of them was bound to notice that his face was the same as the image gilding the top of the Most-Wanted list.

The 126 around his belt made it worse. Luthor never could tell what the subtle change in gravity did to others. *He* noticed it, but he knew to expect it. Garcia hadn't seemed to notice anything different until Luthor had floated him to the ceiling. Everyone reacted differently to the odd distortions it caused in the inner ear. Who could know if subtle changes magnetically drew their attention or caused them to focus inwardly on their own endeavors?

Luthor moved forward, sneaking glances to evaluate the situation. Unlike the subway, each line had its own dedicated carbon cop ensuring rule compliance.

"Qwiz knows to meet us at the station in Chicago?" Tanya asked.

"We can only hope, otherwise we'll have a bit of a walk," said Luthor.

"Where are we going to stay?" Michael said.

"Street living will be sufficient," Vika said.

"No, seriously. We have to find something else," Michael replied. It was the first time Luthor had ever seen him openly contradict Vika. She raised an eyebrow. "I'm not just saying that because I want a bed. I don't care about a bed. We have been spending so much time just trying to smogging stay alive that we have forgotten the whole point of getting to Chicago. Those damn bastards blew up our computer and we need to get our research back. And the whole point of getting our research back was to publicly announce our findings. I don't see how we are going to be able to do that if we are homeless, look like Markless, and have no goddamn resources."

"He is right," Vika said, looking as surprised to be saying it as Luthor was to hearing it. "We need connections. Resources. We need to fight back."

"Yes, fight back!"

"So let's figure out what we have to work with," Luthor said. Things became so much simpler when they were broken down to their elements and analyzed. "We have Qwiz, who has both our data and the rest of the 126. There's our primary resource. But apart from him, we also have the best sniper on earth," Luthor hoped Vika would appreciate the compliment, but that didn't make it any less true, "and we have our brains, and whatever connections we can bring to the table."

"Speaking of the best sniper on earth," Tanya said, "Vika still hasn't ditched her pistol, that thing is going to light up the metal detectors like a—"

"I will," Vika snapped, "but not before I have to." Vika paused, looking intently into the distance. "Look over there." She pointed at the periphery of the chamber. A police dog strained against its master's leash as it prowled, sniffing out lawbreakers. Another K-9 duo appeared on the other side of the hall.

"What are they doing here?" Tanya asked.

"Probably just standard drug sniffing dogs," Luthor said, "most smuggling between cities is going to come by train."

"It isn't that simple," Vika said tersely. "In Europe they have been trying to train dogs to smell out CPI chips, and more importantly the lack of CPI chips."

"There is no way it could *smell* that you've had yours removed," Michael said.

"It is a possibility. Perhaps American dogs have mastered that task."

"Let's hope they haven't," Luthor said.

"There is no need to panic," Tanya said. "Vika got her chip back, and ours haven't been removed. Even if the carp brings the dog right by here, we'll be fine. And CPI chips can't have *that* obvious an odor. And it will be trying to tell the difference between one inside the skin versus one outside the skin. If Vika just heads to the bathroom as the dogs approach, she shouldn't have any problem."

"I can't think of any better solution," Vika said, striding away without a second look. She leaned against the restroom wall, while the rest of them continued to wait in the security line.

One of the dogs passed within 4 meters of her, but didn't seem to notice. The carp began meandering in their direction, letting the dog sniff wherever it desired.

"It isn't going to smell that our Marks are being blocked, will it?" Tanya asked.

"Dogs can smell lots of things, but I doubt they are ever going to be able to smell variations in electromagnetic radiation," Luthor said. Tanya seemed to relax.

Across the room Vika took a sip of water from a fountain to justify her continued presence against the wall. Meanwhile, a businessman tried vainly to make conversation with her. It wasn't hard to imagine the conversation. A rich white man offering to lift up a poor, pathetic, but beautiful suburban refugee to higher status in return for certain services. *Watch your balls buddy, they're liable to get stomped. Mental note: overhear next such conversation for comedic entertainment.*

The dog slowly sniffed its way farther from Vika, it hadn't seemed to notice her. Luthor relaxed. *We just need to hold out a little longer. Then we're home free.* It continued to wander the grounds casually, its simple steps belying the powerful muscles underneath the fur.

A minute later, the shepherd's casual sniffing became more insistent. It did a nice impression of a bloodhound as it smashed its nose to the floor, following unseen olfactory trails. Probably the scent of some illicit substance. Luthor would not want to be the poor soul who tried to smuggle drugs through today, with that animal on the hunt. He also had a sadistic desire to see someone get busted that *wasn't him* for once. Yes, that would be nice.

The dog sniffed incessantly, drawing ever closer to where they stood. No one around them looked much like a drug dealer, at least in the stereotypical sense. Luthor never would have suspected the suits and briefcases to be hiding cocaine and heroin. But that was likely what they counted on for their success. The carps probably wouldn't suspect them either.

The dog suddenly lifted its head from the ground, its lips peeled back, and it growled. It snarled and foamed, people backed away in fear. It dragged the carp straight at Luthor.

What the hell is going on? Vika isn't here! What is the dog yammering about?

It reached them and barked ferociously and continually. The carbon cop's expression quickly morphed from startled, to suspicious, to downright angry.

The carp reached down and said something to the dog. It stopped barking, but did not relent its straining on the leash. Its canine lips peeled back in a snarl. "I'm going to need to scan you and search your bags." Another dog farther away started barking too. It leaped against its master's grip up on its hind legs.

Luthor's mind sprinted like a greyhound. He had no idea what to do. Should he surrender? Would the inverter work if they did? If they ran for it, he doubted they could get away from these dogs. They could get to the door, maybe, but outside in the open they would be run down like foxes. And why were the dogs flipping out anyway? It didn't make any sense, they didn't have any drugs. Vika looked on, alert and ready for action.

Suddenly, the second dog snapped the leash of the carp holding it, and closed the distance between the three of them with blistering speed. Its jaws snapped like it intended to break bones. Adrenal glands quickly took over and erased any doubt as to the correct course of action. Thankfully, PTSD had not impaired those instincts. A rabid dog going for the throat reliably produces the same response in all humans, PTSD or not: *run.*

In a split second, Luthor dodged a pillar and sprinted back through the crowd. Judging by the startled yells around him, Tanya and Michael had followed suit. Chancing a glance back, the dog slithered through the crowds, chasing only them. The other one now pursued them as well, only meters behind. *Why?* Luthor thought frantically. He tried to figure out what they might be smelling to set them off like that. Luthor vaulted the turnstiles leading to the subway and pushed through the lines, legs pumping as fast as he could make them go. The mass of humanity slowed down the dogs too, maintaining his narrow lead.

Slamming through the breakaway doors, Luthor leaned into his sprint as he made for the street, hoping to jump the high fence that guarded a plush farm across the street. He dodged an old woman with a cane, hobbling down the sidewalk. As he passed her, she fell over as helplessly as only a geriatric can. He had gotten close, but hadn't touched her at all. Why did she fall?

In a flash of epiphany, Luthor's brain went into overdrive. *The 126!* Its subtle effect on gravity wouldn't be perceptible to most people, but would be obvious to someone as unstable as the old woman. It would be noticeable to anyone sensitive to a change in equilibrium. And dogs had far more acute senses than humans.

That's what happened in the Geneva terminal with the stupid purse dog! These dogs aren't chasing me, they are chasing my 126 because they sense the gravity distortion!

In the same moment, Tanya and Michael burst through the doors. The dogs were right on their heels. Luthor ran toward them, quickly taking all three of his BOGs and smashing them together. The gravity increased exponentially around it. He hurled the wad as far as he could toward the river. He lost his balance as the gravity dimple raced away from him.

The dogs leaped over the fallen Luthor, ignoring him completely and bolted away after the offending 126. The BOGs sailed down the sheer slope into the water. The dogs stopped on the shore, barking continuously at the murky New York water. Tanya and Michael stood by the fence, bewilderment plastered on their faces. It only took a moment for Luthor to explain that he had discovered another of 126's properties: dogs—and presumably other animals— absolutely hated the stuff.

Vika appeared next to them. "Quick, blend in with other refugees!"

They melded into the crowd, all but disappearing into the sea of other homeless.

"With any luck they will think we jumped in," Michael said.

"Luck?" Luthor roared. "This whole thing is completely *fubar*! They had to have seen us, they know we're trying to get on the train," Luthor noticed that Michael no longer held the duffle. Luthor stabbed a finger violently into his sternum, "and you managed to lose the smogging inverter!"

Michael didn't back down, but shouted back centimeters from Luthor's face. "Sorry if I wanted to stay alive! I doubt you would have had the presence of mind to pick up the bag either!"

"I had the presence of mind to save your ass!"

"Yeah and you lost, what, three more of beads of 126? Great job asshole. You just sacrificed a month of synthesis work."

"Maybe I should have sacrificed you in—"

"Both of you shut up!" Tanya yelled. "You want the carps to find us?"

Sure enough, both of the carps were standing by the

river talking on their phones. They hadn't kept up with their dogs long enough to see them flee the station. It was clear they believed their perps had gone for a swim.

"We just need another plan," Tanya continued. "We don't need you two doing their job for them. What about the whole saving the world thing? It's going to be pretty dang tough to do that with you two strangling each other. It's going to be alright."

"No, its not," Vika said, staring off blankly. Her voice cut through the city noise like a diamond blade. "Get down. Now."

She shoved them roughly behind a bus.

"What is it?" Tanya asked.

"It's Pain," Luthor and Vika said at the same time.

Michael let loose a string of curse words.

Luthor stared into the reflection of the windshield of a stopped electric car. If Vika said to get down, it meant Pain was out there somewhere. It took several moments, but he finally found what Vika had instantly seen. Several hundred meters away a figure perched unnaturally behind a billboard mounted on the side of an office building. To the untrained eye, it would have looked like a decorative gargoyle.

"How did you possibly spot him?" Luthor asked.

"Because I was looking," Vika said. "He is waiting for a clear shot. Don't give him one." She brandished her gun. It only held twelve bullets. They didn't have a spare magazine.

"We all have to make a run for it at the same time or we'll get picked off," said Luthor.

Directly across the sidewalk Luthor noticed that there was an oddly empty alleyway between two buildings. The perfect place to get the hell out of the sniper's sights and lose the carps.

As passengers filed off and onto the busy bus stop, they ducked and sprinted for the alley. Luthor didn't hear any shots, but a sniper bullet well exceeded the speed of sound, Luthor knew it would hit before he heard anything. He didn't hear the shot. Just as they entered the alley a huge chunk of pavement exploded right behind them.

He took a deep breath, but realized there was a reason the alley had been deserted. The unmistakable hulking mass of human flesh who called himself Pain stood between the aging brick walls with a submachine gun trained on them. On his left flank stood an equally intimidating man in black fatigues. To his right lounged a shorter, bald-headed man with a 2180 tattoo on his head. All three wore gelvar.

They dove behind an abandoned suburban dumpster that probably slept four every night. Strangely, no bullets plinked around them.

"Ostafal," Vika breathed. Her face bled loathing.

"Forget about Ostafal," Luthor said, "how the hell are we going to get out of this alive? They have three armed men and we have twelve smogging bullets."

"Oh, and there is a sniper that will shoot us if we leave," Michael offered.

"Why aren't they shooting?" Tanya asked.

"They would rather shove us out into the street and let their sniper pick us off," Luthor said.

"We will lose a gun fight and they know it," said Vika. "With their sniper, we can't do a damn thing. It's exactly how I would have set up an ambush."

Luthor had to admire Pain's plan. They had the choice of facing down three armed soldiers in body armor, or running unprotected into the open. That sniper would probably have one of the high-end semi-automatic sniper rifles deployed by the seals in Antarctica. Those things were accurate beyond 1000 meters and could shoot as fast as a sniper could pull the trigger. A single seal sniper could take out an entire unit of Chinese soldiers if he managed to set up in the right spot.

Even if one of them did manage to elude those bullets,

it wouldn't be hard for Pain to run them down to finish the job. "I don't like our odds with that sniper," Luthor said.

Vika reached around the dumpster and fired one of their precious rounds. It echoed off the brick like a cathedral.

Vika grunted angrily, "hit him in the chest. They are coming closer."

The last vestiges of the gun shot faded off the walls leaving a pregnant silence. Luthor knew he had only minutes to live, if they were lucky. Even the grim determination on Vika's face looked more like the attitude of a Texan defending the Alamo, than one who expects to walk away. Luthor tried not to give into despair, but his brain didn't seem to offer much in the way of hopeful ideas.

"You just stay alive," Tanya said, "I will handle the sniper."

What did you just say? Luthor thought.

"How?" Michael asked.

"Just shut up and give me all your BOGs. I'm going to need about ten minutes, I think."

"I can't give you the gun," Vika said, "it would be suicide for us."

"I don't need it. Just give me your 126. Now."

Luthor had used his to escape the dogs, but Vika and Michael handed her two each. She picked up a tattered cloth some suburbian had tossed in their hurry to escape the alley, and she picked up a trash bag. She slung the bag over her shoulder and began limping out of the alley. She was careful to keep the dumpster between her and Pain to hide from his sight.

"He will be looking for four people, particularly men," she said. "He won't suspect a single pathetic, Markless woman."

Luthor looked at her a long moment. "Be safe," he said. "Please."

"I know what I'm doing."

Luthor hoped she did. Otherwise, she would be splattered all over the sidewalk in a matter of seconds.

#

I'd better know what I'm doing. Tanya thought as she exited the alley. She kept her face down lest the sniper recognize her in his scope. She also intentionally did *not* act as if she were hiding. The sniper would be keying on people who ran out into the street, people who looked like they were going for cover, or anyone who seemed to be trying to avoid someone with enough firepower to turn them into ground beef. She limped slowly across the blasted pavement out in the open, careful not to hide behind the ramshackle, human-powered vehicles that transported passengers to the train station.

Every slow, agonizing, deceptive step she expected to feel a bullet pierce her flesh. *What the hell am I doing?* She wondered, but suddenly found herself praying with a fervency she hadn't felt since church camp. *Dear God, please keep me safe. There is an evil man who wants to kill me. He has the power and skill to do so. Lord, blind him so he doesn't see me.* Tears leaked down her dirty cheeks. *Keep Luthor safe too, Lord. I love him. I really do. I know we haven't been living according to your will, but I promise that will change if you get us out of this. Just please save us.*

Then her foot slammed into the curb. She had made it across the street, free of any extra holes. A quick glance revealed the others were still alive for the moment. Pain hadn't seemed to notice her either.

"Thank you, Jesus," she breathed.

Safely out of the sniper's focus, she quickened her step. There wasn't much time, and a lot of building to climb.

#

Vika leaned around and fired another shot. Still no return fire echoed off the walls.

"Damn," she said again.

"I thought you *didn't* miss," Michael said.

Vika gritted her teeth. "Gelvar gets in the way." The infuriating man had no idea that this was the *worst* possible time to make jokes. She glared at him. Accidentally smiling was *not* a problem this time.

Strangely, his face softened. "I'm sorry. I'll shut up. Kill the bastards for me."

An apology? From the most self-absorbed, annoying man in history? The temptation to smile reared its ugly head again. Despite her all but guaranteed death, she found a sliver of joy in the change he seemed to be showing as of late. He truly wasn't the same man that had drooled over her just weeks before. He learned—at least a little—and now tried to be less infuriating. There was something strangely endearing about a man who realized he was a worthless sack of excrement but tried to change.

She heard shuffling as Pain advanced a few more steps to hide behind the next pile of garbage. Heaped trash piles made unexpectedly effective cover.

"I've got eight bullets left," Vika said in a hushed voice.

"They still aren't firing," Luthor replied.

"The carps will only take notice if they hear automatic fire."

"This *is* New York City," Michael said, "who are they to care about a couple of gunshots?"

"They are bleeding me dry," Vika said, "they keep getting closer every time I don't fire. Soon it's going to be too late to escape even if Tanya gets rid of that sniper."

"Then keep shooting," Luthor said, "keep them away

long enough to get out of here."

"I've got a better idea. Save your bullets," Michael said. He cupped his hands over his mouth and called over the dumpster.

"Hey Jose! Good to see you again. I haven't seen any pussy since the last time we talked."

"Shut the fuck up," Jose called back, "you're a dead man."

"If I'm a dead man, why are you so scared of me?"

Vika nodded approvingly. She didn't know if it was intentional or not, but his strategy was sound. Attack the weak link of the enemy and get him to make a mistake. The old teaching of Sun Tzu popped into her mind. "*Never interrupt your enemy when he is making a mistake.*" Of the three in front of them, Ostafal certainly had to be the weak link, and if Michael could rile him up enough, maybe he would do something stupid. If nothing else, it might buy them a few more minutes so Tanya could complete whatever task she believed could neutralize the sniper. Besides, it felt good to piss off Ostafal.

"Sorry I had to kill your lover, Ostafal, he said he missed you," she called out. Not as pithy as Michael, but coming from her it had to sting.

"Keep talking when I shove this gun up your smogging cunt!"

Vika smiled. She would be dead in a few minutes, but at least she would have a little fun in the process. A good way to go out.

#

What the hell was I thinking? Tanya thought as she placed another double-BOG above her. She felt gravity shift with the 126 as she crawled forward another few feet. Straight up the side of the sniper's building.

She tried not to look down as she retrieved the BOG below her. She had only climbed seven or eight stories and probably had at least another ten to reach the sniper. But already she felt the queasiness in the pit of her stomach that comes from standing a little too near a sheer ledge. She had never been particularly afraid of heights, but when she was suspended against a wall only by artificial gravity, she could empathize with Luthor's own trepidation.

She didn't know where the idea to use 126 to climb up a building came from, but it seemed an obvious extension of the technology. If she could increase gravity enough to outweigh earth's pull, and then fasten that gravity to a fixed point above her with Eli's polymer, she could theoretically climb anything. She basically just built a ladder of gravity and climbed up it. The only difficulty lay in trying to move in double strength gravity. The earth neutralized some of the power of 126, but her body felt like it weighed more than it ought and every movement taxed her a little too much. In spite of her growing fatigue, she still crawled forward, positioned just on the other side of the building to remain out of sight of the sniper.

She accidentally looked down. It didn't *feel* like down, but down it was nonetheless. *Disconcerting* was a shadow of the word she really needed to describe the experience. If it could be mixed with *unearthly* it would be about right. She never could have imagined being in this position even a month ago. Fifteen stories off the ground, climbing to try to stop a sniper bent on killing all of them.

Killing. It seemed like all that she had seen since Geneva. Each death was etched into the living stone of her mind. It seemed like only yesterday when Vika had sliced open the agent's throat on the seabus. Sometimes all she could think about was the blood spurting out the poor man's neck. She had watched men shot in front of her, next to her, all around her. Sometimes managing any thought but those deaths became a chore.

And for what? What is the purpose for all this death? She answered her own question. *Because everyone wants the 126 for themselves. Smogging energy. Why does there have to be so little of it?* She knew as intimately as anyone the causative series of events that led the world to its current state. The world designed itself around a reckless use of oil and oil-based products. The entire American society would never have developed without access to a gas-powered car. The suburban ghost towns around the country stood as a testament to the folly of their blindness to decreasing oil reserves. It had become impossible to live in a place that required a car to do anything. Then to make matters worse, scientists discovered that many of the viable alternatives to oil—as well as oil itself—were steering the earth toward ecological disaster via global warming. Coal was subsequently banned out of a fear of its carbon output. Mining for natural gas followed soon after, because harvesting it out of the ground released too many greenhouse gases far worse than carbon. This artificially limited energy possibilities, decreasing supply of energy—and increasing demand of oil. It was only a matter of time before the oil bubble burst, and all society crashed. World War III made for a very sharp pin.

Now that a quarter of the world starved to death because there wasn't enough energy to produce crops, electricity and the means to generate it, dominated the new carbon economy. Something as powerful as element 126 looked like a fresh water oasis to a desert wanderer. Control of 126 meant control of the world and unimaginable wealth.

At least that's what Luthor believed. But at what cost? How many deaths were justified by his crusade to release it publicly? Starvation had run its course already, the world population had downshifted to compensate for lower energy, thus lower food supply. Hadn't it? Most of the lives that 126 could have saved were already lost. So why kill more?

A crowd gathered below her, watching her climb the glassy exterior of the office like Spiderman, albeit a slow, female Spiderman sans spandex. All members of the crowd were scraggily, starving, pathetic wretches. Most had undoubtedly come from the now-extinct suburbs. They came to major cities around the world in the hundreds of millions in hope of jobs, food, and security from the rampant crime. Most found none of the above and were now stuck here with no jobs, no food, and even less hope. Tanya, defying gravity, as they understood it, broke up the monotony of their abject squalor. She tried to ignore them. An audience made climbing more difficult, whether the watchers were starving or not.

Roc's voice seemed to echo in her mind "*the pale horse still rides.*" Revelation predicted that the fourth horseman would take the lives of a quarter of the world with his tools of scarcity and war. But Roc believed the Culling had not yet reached its conclusion. He had a point; the remnant of the earth certainly still struggled to feed themselves. Dozens of the horsemen's future victims watched her climb, none of them knowing where their next meal would come from. She felt their eyes on her. She climbed higher. The sniper loomed nearer.

But what options do they have really? They could work all day and deliver kilos of trash in exchange for single slices of bread at the transfer stations, they can hunt rats to cook, beg for handouts, or join the Dog Pound.

The Dog Pound. That one still boggled Tanya's mind. She understood how hard it could be for Markless to survive in this economy, but something about being reduced to a diet of dog food jarred her academic sensibilities like a kidney-punch. She wished there were a word or two to describe the *wrongness* she felt when thinking about grown men and women living on such a diet. She had heard all about the resurgence of the Black Plague stemming from over exposure to rats among the homeless. But hunting—even if it meant hunting rodents—still felt like an inherently human activity. It required strength, speed, or intelligence to accomplish. Begging too, while demeaning, at least had all of human history as a precedent to justify it. Even becoming human garbage trucks in exchange for bread felt like a façade of an honest day's work. But being reduced to eating pet food? It was *dehumanizing.* Yes, that was the right word. Mental images of men and women on hands and knees eating from a dish scarred her every bit as badly as blood from a dying man's throat.

That was the world. Too many people, not enough food. Not enough energy to grow it or to ship it to where it was needed. People did what they had to do in order to survive. Sure, the war had ended and the Oil Crash had finished crashing. Even the world economy had adjusted and started to climb again, providing the possibility for a decent standard of living and the hope of a real middle class at some indeterminate point in the future. But there were still too many starving. Millions upon millions, just in this one city. The most powerful gang in New York City reigned with the power they wielded through stolen dog food.

Insidious thoughts infected her mind. *Maybe this crazy crusade* is *worth killing for. How many people could we really save if we provide energy to the world again? How many lives could we improve?*

She crawled up another few feet, gravity firmly fastening her to the side of the building. Judging she had reached her desired altitude, she peeked around the concrete corner. The sniper crouched on a slim walkway behind the billboard about 4 meters above her. He didn't notice her.

Damn it. Luthor was right. This guy needs to die. There was no turning back, the others were counting on her and stopping the sniper without killing him would be extremely hard. If she did nothing, then they were as good as dead. *Time to face the music. Time to kill. I've got a chance to save those poor bastards down there, or else let the world rot.*

Tanya removed the rest of her BOGs. She hoped four would be enough. She mashed them together and slapped them around the corner. Multiple Gs flattened her against the wall. She prayed that her gravity, combined with the earth's own power would be enough to dislodge the sniper from his perfect vantage point. It was certainly enough to give her a headache.

An ear-crushing gunshot cracked above her. Tanya hoped her gravity alteration had caused it to be off-mark. An instant later the slender barrel of a sniper rifle tumbled down, accelerating toward the new center of gravity. It bounced off the wall and its inertia pushed it passed the BOG's influence until it plummeted to the street.

The sniper himself evidently had not fallen. Now he was at least weaponless. Tanya mustered the courage to peek around the corner, but barely had the strength to do so. The gravity made each limb feel like an extra 20 kilograms of dead weight were strapped to it. Sure enough, the sniper hadn't fallen. He dangled from the narrow architectural lip around one of the windows.

He grunted and strained as his fingertips tried to support the weight of a half dozen men his size. His grunts became the roar of a straining body-builder, until his voice echoed off the adjacent apartments. Then he fell. He shot down unnaturally quickly, like he had been ripped off by a tow rope. A terrified shriek tore from his vocal chords. He, like his gun before, bounced awkwardly as he slowed through Tanya's gravity well. His momentum pushed him through the gravity dimple. She quickly split up the 126 just to make sure he kept falling. He bounced off the wall, spinning to the street below.

Tanya did not look to see the splatter at the street level. She had no desire to witness her handiwork. She climbed higher. It would be better to descend on another side of the building to avoid attracting attention.

With all the commotion on the front of the building, few noticed her painstaking decent on the opposite side. If anyone did, no one would have believed them.

#

Vika measured her lifespan in terms of bullets. She had four bullets left to live. Not very long. She just couldn't get a clean enough shot to get by the gelvar.

"Ostafal is going to snap. Let's hope your lady has done her job," said Michael. "We have to make a run for it."

His words were prophetic. Their constant badgering of Jose Smogging Ostafal – Vika's new favorite name for him —indeed caused him to snap.

"I'm so goddamn tired of this bitch!" Ostafal yelled. He stood up and sprayed a burst of ammunition against their cover. It plinked harmlessly off of the sturdy dumpster they used for cover."

"What the hell are you doing?"

"She needs to die, enough stalling. They don't have a chance."

"Get back you fool. Let them waste the rest of their ammo—"

Vika knew she had one chance. She leaned out, drew aim, and pulled the trigger at the temporarily exposed man.

Crack. Her solitary gunshot rang out.

Ostafal dropped his gun to the ground, blood oozing up from his hand. His arms had been outstretched and the gun had blocked her bullet from improving his face. Not ideal, but destroying his ability to shoot back was a start.

Pain quickly returned fire. He had a better angle and forced her more tightly against the dumpster. His burst finished, she immediately reached around again and fired another shot. It struck Ostafal square in the right hamstring. He doubled over with a cry of pain and limped out of the alley.

Ostafal was defenseless and within her grasp. She only had two bullets left now, not enough to save their lives. She might fail her intended mission, but at least with her dying breath she could accomplish one last good deed: ridding the universe of Jose Smogging Ostafal.

Tanya, you had better eliminated that sniper. Otherwise, I'm a dead woman, and far more importantly, Ostafal lives.

She shared a look with the others and ducked into the street. With any luck, the dumpster would block Pain's view long enough for her to escape. Luthor and Michael followed wordlessly. Suddenly another chunk of sidewalk directly in front of her splintered violently up into their air. Half a second later, she heard the discharge of a Force Multiplier X8, a Seal-issue Semiautomatic Sniper rifle firing the 8.6 x 70mm Lapua magnum round. It sang like an aria off the streets of New York. Vika didn't stop. Strangely, no more bullets fired. Even more strangely, the sniper had missed.

She dodged pedestrians, shoving them away haphazardly. She took the next alley hoping to cut Ostafal off. Thousands of hours of training and conditioning allowed her body to efficiently shunt away the lactic acid buildup in her muscles. Running flat out, she jumped, planted a foot on the side wall, vaulted a tall chain link fence, and landed without missing a step.

She turned, twisting through a back-alley maze, intent on her prey. Ostafal's trail of blood left little doubt as to his path. She found him cornered against a fence he was now powerless to climb.

"I swore to myself if I ever saw you again, I would put a bullet in your head," she said.

"And I swore to myself, if I ever saw you again, you would be on your back, chained to a bed. I guess neither of us will get our wish today."

"Guess again. You still die." He needed to die, a lot.

"This is your only chance to escape. Let me live, I will lead the others in the wrong direction."

"Like hell you will. You are a liar, Ostafal."

"Right now, I am in a generous mood."

"Me too. I think I will give you another piercing, free of charge."

Ostafal abruptly reached for a handgun he had secreted in his side pocket.

Vika didn't give him the chance to retrieve it. She aimed quickly but carefully and pulled the trigger with joy. The bullet slammed Ostafal square above the left eye. He dropped immediately. Killing had become part of her job description normally providing no more emotional reaction than a desk worker might get after successfully filing a large stack of paper. But this kill felt good. Like the very hand of God patted her on the back for ending that asshole's miserable life. She went to inspect the body and found that he did not actually have another gun. He had reached for a cellphone. The little rat had been trying to give away his position.

Luthor and Michael finally finished climbing the fence. Did they have to look for a ladder or something?

"We are so screwed," Michael said.

"They are right behind us!" yelled Luthor.

And I only have one bullet, for two of them. A strange compulsion came over her as she saw her imminent death approaching. The urge to free herself and have no regrets became overpowering.

"Michael, you made me smile," she blurted.

"What?"

"No man has made me smile in ten years. Thank you." There it was. Out in the open. For another ten seconds or so.

Michael scrunched up his face in confusion, as his inferior, male brain struggled to make sense of her statement.

Then, as if he had been slapped by a massive hand, his body slammed up against the brick wall.

She had noticed it too late. Gravity had shifted. She too fell against the wall and the unexpected jerk of gravity yanked the pistol out of her hand. It bounced away toward Luthor. She found herself pinned, four meters in the air against the sheer brick wall of the adjacent building.

The side door of the building opened. Pain stepped out followed closely by the other soldier. Both held P110 sub-machine guns. "I never knew how effective gravity could be in a pinch," Pain said. "Turns out, drug-sniffing dogs hate the stuff. And it works almost as well as handcuffs." He must have found Luthor's 126 in the stairwell. Vika felt like she weighed twice as much as usual. Judging from how they were pinned, he must have placed it against the inside of the wall, she wouldn't be able to move it. "It doesn't matter how trained you are, Agent Veronika. You just never see a change in gravity coming."

Vika didn't stop to ponder how the man knew her name, focusing instead on getting out of the gravity dimple. She slowly scooted toward the door. Since Pain had walked out of it, that meant gravity was normal there.

Luthor reached for Vika's gun.

A blast from the sub-machine gun stopped him cold. "I don't think so, Tenrel." Luthor obediently put up his hands in surrender. "So, here's the deal. You give me the name of your friend who took your research and the key to the encryption on your lab's hard-drive and I'll let you all live."

Vika scooted some more.

"Why would I believe you'd let us just walk away from this?"

"Oh, you aren't walking away. No chance of that. But I will take you into custody, and if you're really good, I'm sure I can arrange for your cell to have a mattress."

"I don't have the key. It was inside the carp car you blew up."

"Then the name. We'll figure out the files on our own."

"We'd destroy the research before we'd give it to you!" Michael yelled.

"I guess we won't get it then," Pain said with a sneer. "Of course, retrieving any actual data isn't really all that important in the end."

"*It's not all that important*?" Luthor yelled. "Then why the hell are you trying to kill us?"

Pain smirked. There might have even been some genuine mirth behind it. "Good question Tenrel, struck right to the smogging heart of it. But I ain't—" He was cut off abruptly as an enormous man slammed into him.

"Run you retards!" the man shouted. He was as tall as Pain but with tattered clothes and tangled red hair.

"Thadd!" Luthor shouted in recognition.

Vika did not heed the sage advice of her Markless friend, not when there was a bullet left in the chamber. She finished sliding out of Pain's BOG and leaped off the wall. She landed, rolling to soften the impact of a four-meter fall and snatched her gun from the ground. The other soldier had whirled to face Thaddeus and leveled his sub-machine gun at him. Vika exhaled, then inserted her last bullet in a charming spot just right of his left ear. The slug rammed through his skull, and he collapsed.

Only one man left standing. If only she had another round. Nothing left for it but to get in there and engage. Her reflexes took over, the utility knife appeared in her hand, far more deadly than a bullet in close quarters. But she had to get inside a meter. Two quick slashes is all it would take. One to the back of Pain's knee would destroy his leg tendons ability to contract and thus move. The second slice could go to any of several spots on his arm. The wrist would stop him from being able to grab anything, below the bicep or tricep and his arm would dangle like a cooked noodle—a very muscular noodle. Then he would answer all of the questions they could think of before she dispatched him. Thaddeus just had to keep him occupied a moment longer.

Her long legs closed the distance quickly, but not

quickly enough. Thaddeus might have been a large man, but he held little chance against a seasoned special-forces soldier like Pain. He flipped Thaddeus on his back like a French omelet. A second later the P110 reared its ugly muzzle again.

"Not a good idea," Pain said to her.

Vika froze, only three meters from doing her second good deed of the day. She itched to sink her knife into him, but had no desire to have a friend as brave as Thaddeus die for her recklessness.

Pain spat at Thaddeus' supine form. "You will pay for that. I am going to shoot off every single one of your limbs. One at a time, until you smogging die."

Thaddeus wiped the dangling sputum from his forehead. "You shouldn't swear so much."

Pain's eyes narrowed in confusion. It was the last expression his face ever bore. The next instant, the side of his head exploded outward. It looked as if someone had detonated a focused charge inside his brain. He fell sideways, lifeless. The residual bang of a large caliber gunshot hung in the air.

Thaddeus turned toward the street where he himself had come from. Vika stared around the corner to see where the shot had originated. DeShawn stood thirty paces away, his massive handgun trembling in both hands.

CHAPTER 21:

One Hour Ago: New York City, NY

DeShawn stirred on his mat, his old back injury ached. It needed an adjustment, but it had needed an adjustment for ten years. Chiropractors remained outside his disposable income by a considerable margin; for that matter, so was a stick of gum.

The phone in Tony's continued to ring periodically. For some reason it was more incessant than the rest of the growing background noise produced by the city in the early morning. Like a mosquito buzzing in his ear, it kept him awake. Not that he had slept much at all that night.

He rolled on his side. Something stabbed him in the side. He rolled back and removed the offending object. He turned a single, brass-encased .50 caliber bullet over in his hands. It fit his pistol like a glove.

Shame stabbed him sharper than the bullet. He had lied to everyone about the bullet's existence. Father Roc didn't know, not even Thadd knew about it. None of them could understand. They hadn't done what he'd done. Seen what he'd seen. More than that, they had no idea what it felt like to be a killer, a murderer. The Lord had forgiven him, he knew that, and he had been given a new purpose. But the Lord was more benevolent than DeShawn himself was. He might be able to look at any sin and see the blood of Christ instead, but most of the time all DeShawn could see was the blood on his own hands. Dozens of dead men and women, even a few still young enough to be called children, crying out for justice.

All the killing had been for what? So he could eat dry dog food? There had been no meaning, purpose, or justification for anything he had done. At least Luthor had killed people in a war. DeShawn had killed to eat Purina out of a dog dish. They always made him eat it out of a smog—a *stupid* dog dish. He hated that. It was so humiliating. It would have been better for him to have just starved to death. At least then the rest of his victims wouldn't have needlessly lost their lives.

He turned the projectile over in his hands as he did every time sleep eluded him. It would be so easy just to end all the shame. He didn't keep the gun as a reminder of what he had been. That was a bold-faced lie. He kept the gun for protection. To protect the world from DeShawnte Martin, in case he ever got a little too hungry again. He could just slide it into the chamber, load it into place, and pull the trigger then... No more killer D. No more danger to the world. The fifty-caliber slug would blow a hole in his sinful brain big enough for Serenity to climb through.

He mulled it over in his head until dawn slithered up between the structures of the urban jungle. The ringing phone had kept him up all night, it gave him lots of time to think. Several times the temptation grew so strong that he actually loaded the gun. Each time he pushed it away, removing the bullet.

DeShawn lay on his side in the shadows of their fizzling fire, the gun resting against his head. His finger caressed the trigger, like a crack addict fondling a pipe.

"What the hell are you doing?" Thadd asked. He kicked him in the ribs, hard.

He hadn't heard him return with Roc. He was light on his feet for such a big man.

"You gonna shoot yourself or something?" Thadd said again, "because I will smogging kill you if you commit suicide."

DeShawn flushed and lowered his gun. The bullet resting in the open chamber clattered out and pinged on the concrete. He hurriedly snatched it, but Thaddeus slammed a foot on his arm. He could feel Thadd's callused skin through the holes in his boot.

"Where'd you get a bullet?" Thadd said quietly.

"I ain't got no bullet," said DeShawn.

"Don't shit up my ass. I've seen enough bullets today to know what one looks like. Open your hand."

Reluctantly, DeShawn opened his hand. The .50 cal rolled out.

"I can explain."

"You better, because it looked like you were about to blow your brains out with this little *reminder* of yours."

DeShawn sat up and looked at his best friend with pleading eyes. "You *don't understand* what it's like. I done so much evil in this world. I killed so many people. Even as messed up as this world is, it would be better off without me."

"You want to know *why* I don't understand? Because of you. *You,* damn it! Before I got into all that pollution, you saved my ass."

"How can that outweigh all the murders I done? I had to kill 20 people a year just to survive."

"Who knows how many people I would have killed? Maybe you saved hundreds."

"Or maybe not. You don't know! All I know is, everything I done is a sin."

"Aren't you the one always telling me about how we don't know God's plan for us? Maybe He still has something really important for you to do. Maybe it's something no one else could do. Maybe He saved you cuz He has an important job. Who are you to question God?"

"You are starting to sound like father Roc. Stop it. You're making too much sense."

"Want me to curse a few more times? Maybe that would help," Thadd cleared his throat. "Quit being such a pathetic smogger! Pull your ass out of the shit and drop that damn gun. You ain't the same polluting son of a bitch you used to be. Now get your head in the smogging game."

DeShawn smiled weakly. "Yeah. That's better. Thanks."

"Any time."

The door into Tony's opened. Tony himself poked his head out; he was usually in early prepping for the day's customers. He was a kindly balding man with a huge snout and a volume any true Italian would envy. "Hey, I got a phone call here for one of you guys, from somebody calling himself 'Vanguard.' Says he needs to talk to anybody who knows a guy named Luthor. Says it's *really* important."

Thadd rushed to the door and took the phone. He nodded a few times into the receiver and exchanged a few terse words. He handed the phone back to Tony and hurried to DeShawn.

"Grab your gun—*and* the bullet. I think I know what God is planning for you after all."

#

Michael couldn't believe it. His life had flashed before his eyes only to be replaced with utter relief and joy. Not only was he not going to be imprisoned forever by whatever unknown entity employed Pain, but he wasn't going to die either.

Still in a daze, he glanced down at Ostafal's corpse. Blood and gore circumnavigated his head wound, coagulating in grotesque lumps. Michael found himself becoming increasingly desensitized to death—so long as he wasn't personally causing it. They already retrieved Pain's two BOGs and went to search through the dead merchant's pockets.

Apart from an expensive looking 20th century wristwatch, there was little of interest. His phone was clutched in his cold, rigid hands, and it took some effort to pry it free. After a moment, Ostafal was flopped on his back and Michael had the phone. Maybe it would come in useful.

The dead man stared up blankly at them. The bloody entry wound was clearly off-center, somewhat unusual for Vika.

He turned to Luthor, “Well at least we know that Vika is human, she missed.”

“What do you mean? Ostafal looks dead to me.”

“What is this about me missing?” Vika scowled at them.

Michael smiled. “Look here,” he pointed to Ostafal, “you hit him on the left side of the forehead, not square between the eyes. You missed.”

“That was intentional.”

“You’re just saying that.”

“No trust me. If I ever wanted a man dead, it was him.”

Michael grinned, it was just like Vika to have a reason for everything— including a slightly off bull’s-eye shot. He wanted the explanation. “Okay Vika. Tell me.”

“Kill shots are based in probabilities. I gave myself the best probability for him to die. You should know about this.”

“You of all people should know how stupid I can be.”

Vika raised an eyebrow, and damn was it ever sexy. “Since this was a small caliber pistol and I did not have hollow point shells, a perfect dead center shot was not the best place to shoot. There was a very small chance that a dead center bullet will enter and exit relatively cleanly, severing his corpus callosum, but not killing him. And Ostafal probably had more hot air in his skull than brain, so it was probably a fifty percent chance it would miss gray matter altogether.” She kicked the dead body.

"If you really want somebody dead, put a round through one whole side of his brain. There is no way for a bullet to travel nicely through that much. It's a probability of zero that he gets back up."

Michael nodded. She *did* have a good reason. That didn't make it true, but if it wasn't, she was one hell of a liar. *She's one hell of a ... Everything else. I suppose lying would be the least surprising of them.*

They turned back to investigate Pain. He gave that corpse a wide birth. He wasn't *afraid* exactly, more like justifiably cautious. Yes, that was it. Michael did not fear dead men. Of course not. Fortunately, he had nothing to fear. Pain's head had been blown almost completely off. Whatever gun DeShawn had used was *much* larger than Vika's.

Michael almost laughed as he saw the body of Pain's associate. The wound was identical to Ostafal's, except he had been shot from behind. *Son of a Bitch—she was telling the truth. She doesn't ever smogging miss.*

Thaddeus embraced his large companion. It made sense; the two of them seemed to be best friends. DeShawn's limbs hung at his sides and he seemed content to simply be hugged. Thaddeus rocked him back and forth as if he were comforting a frail old woman. *Two men that size shouldn't hug like that,* Michael thought. Still, there was something pure about it. Tears streamed down DeShawn's cheeks and his chest heaved in big, pathetic man-sobs. *Men that size shouldn't cry either.* Even so, Michael felt a pang of pity for him. Whatever was making him cry wasn't anything to laugh about.

Fifty meters away, he saw Tanya. *She is alive too! This couldn't get any better.* Luthor shouted at her, and the two ran and embraced. Luthor twirled her around as they hugged. Michael suddenly felt very alone. Was he really jealous of two overgrown hulks of humanity— which were both men —and a couple who had been together since he was in diapers?

Yes. Yes, he was.

He turned and looked at Vika, the only other person there who was not currently locked in an embrace. She also happened to be the most beautiful woman he had ever seen, that didn't hurt. *Worth a shot,* he thought. He smiled faintly at her.

"Don't even think about it," she said.

Michael lowered his head. He'd hoped for the briefest on instants, that she might have actually been interested. *No. Impossible, this is "Agent Veronika." I must have imagined what she said about smiling.*

He thought he basically understood women. True, they were still confusing as hell, and way more contradictory than the quantum world could ever hope to be. But over the years he had figured out some of the basics and had consistent success as a result. Vika was another animal altogether. She didn't react to him right. His smile softened women, turned them into putty. If he wanted, he could mold that putty. Even lesbians didn't mind his smile. They might give a mildly confused look, but were often still grateful for the gesture. Vika was like smiling at a stone, it just bounced off, or punched you.

The embraces ended and the awkward moment subsided. Tanya ran up and hugged Thaddeus and DeShawn. Michael could feel the faint shift in gravity she caused as she approached. "How did you two get here?"

Thaddeus quickly explained the call from a man claiming to know Luthor. He and DeShawn had followed on foot and had arrived just in time to save all their lives.

"Qwiz," Luthor said, "I owe that guy a beer. No, make that a case of mountain dew."

"That is once we can smogging use our credits again," Michael corrected.

"Touché."

"I hate to break this up guys," Tanya said, "but the

carps are swarming everywhere."

"How did you get by them?"

"I convinced the sniper he could fly—I'm afraid it didn't go too well for him. I suspect he— and his gun— might be more interesting than a Markless woman wandering by."

Vika threw her head back and laughed. It was a weird noise. "Well done!" she said, clapping her on the back.

"They thought that rifle of his had been the source of the gun shots. But I doubt they will be convinced for long."

"Don't worry guys, we got this," Thaddeus said.

"Yeah, we will steer them away from you," echoed DeShawn.

"But what if the carps think you did it?" said Michael.

Thaddeus wagged his massive hand at them, "sure, a couple of homeless bums could take down dudes with gelvar? I don't even have a Mark. I hope they arrest me!"

DeShawn smiled, large yellowing teeth squeezed out between his lips. "And if they get mad and shoot me, it's what I deserve. I'm just glad I was able to get one good deed done in my life. I saved you guys."

Thadd patted his friend on the back. "You might have just saved the whole world. Maybe in a few years they can even feed our fat asses."

"Go with God, friends," DeShawn said.

They turned and started walking toward the carps. Tanya looked like she had more tears blooming.

"And if you ever get back to this shit hole again, look us up!" Thaddeus called after them.

DeShawn punched him in the arm.

"Sorry Jesus!"

#

Luthor couldn't have been more surprised with his long-time girlfriend. Not only had she discovered yet another use of 126, but had killed a man. Her attitude had been so negative toward any violence whatsoever; it defied reason that she could possibly take a life herself.

She had been distant since the boat. Not that he could blame her for her attitude, in the past month she had discovered that PTSD was a cold-blooded ghost haunting him. Obviously, she knew that he had been in the war, but he very seldom mentioned it and *never* discussed the details. His familiarity with death and killing must have come as a painful surprise.

But now it was different. She acted warmly toward him, she had run forward to embrace him. She had changed. She didn't make him feel like a monster any more. He still was, nothing could change that, but it felt good not to have her think of him as one. Hopefully, she wouldn't discover the rest and change her mind.

After they'd put a block between themselves and the carps, Michael stopped them. "Um, sorry to pollute everything, but we now don't have any way to get to Chicago."

"We certainly can't go in the front door," Tanya said. "There had to have been some carp who saw our faces."

"Or a video feed that recorded us," Luthor added.

"Don't be dumb," Michael chided. "Nobody is going to pay the electricity bill to run a live video feed when there are CPI scanners everywhere. The only places worth filming anymore are the food markets. You know that."

"Could the signal inverter still be in the terminal?" Luthor asked.

"I don't know, but it's a helluva risk to find out. If it is still there, it'd be by the bathroom where I dropped it."

"It hasn't been *that* long," Tanya said, "maybe no one picked it up."

"We should search for it," Vika said. "We didn't use our tickets yet, and I do not think anyone will recognize us."

"Why not?"

"Before you made friends with the dogs, I made friends with an Acela engineer."

Luthor recalled wanting to overhear her conversation with the man by the bathroom. Perhaps it had been more productive than he expected.

"You? Making friends?" asked Michael.

Vika gave him a flat look. "Men treat me as a confessional booth. He told me his whole life story. Including the duty schedules of the station. The next shift of carps is transitioning in as we speak."

"As long as we don't look like the pictures they have of us, that should work." Tanya said.

"And we need the scanner," Luthor added.

"Do we look different enough to be safe?" Michael asked.

Luthor stopped and looked at himself in the window of passing storefront. This dyed hair looked nothing like any he'd ever had. His face was partially obscured by the stubble of half a week of street living and he was dirty enough to look a slightly darker race than he actually was. Tanya looked equally different, with short black hair instead of her normal long auburn locks, and Vika was grungier than Luthor had realized. Michael, who looked the most like himself, was still doing a great imitation of a suburban refugee. Luthor began to hope they might still sneak out of there.

"I think we should give it a shot," Luthor said, "but I am out of there if there are any more dogs. They *hate* 126."

No passengers exited the doors, but that didn't stop the menagerie of various forms of human-powered taxi to wait impatiently at the curbside. A few well-dressed people milled around, presumably also waiting for passengers. The carbon police were divided between the river and the sniper with a mouthful of pavement. He didn't see any in the terminal.

"Again, well done, Tanya," said Vika.

"Thanks. I'm sorry I was such an ass about.... everything."

Down in the terminal they did see a lonely carbon cop. He was examining a non-descript duffle bag by the bathroom. "Shit," Michael said.

That pretty much summed up Luthor's feelings about it as well. While they watched, he picked up the bag and carried it to a nearby office, similar to where Vika had been questioned in the subway.

"I think it's time we do things my way," said Vika.

Tanya sighed, "I am willing, but Vika? It doesn't mean I want you blasting everyone."

"Sure, no killing."

Luthor didn't want to think about the latitude contained in *not killing.*

"We sneak down the rail, eliminate any carps in our way and use whatever 126 is left to break onto the train before it is moving too fast."

Luthor did not like the sound of *Vika's way* one bit.

"Wait," Michael said, "what did Jose say about the effective range of the inverter?"

Luthor thought for a moment. "He said it was 10 meters, but not to risk more than 5."

"Look where the carp put it. That baby is sitting in his office maybe 7 or 8 meters from the security checkpoint and it can't be more than five from the first train entrance. It could still work."

Luthor hadn't noticed, but Michael was right. If they hurried before the carps had a chance to examine the contents of the bag, it might still mask their CPI chips.

#

Five minutes later they walked into the rear door of the train. The inverter had worked. It was lost to the bowels of whatever bureaucracy carbon contraband was sent to, but who cared. They had made it out of the city, Pain was dead, and things were looking up.

Rows of comfortable seats flanked a center aisle. They sat down into a set of four seats that faced each other. Luthor sank into the leather cushion. He realized that it had been the first comfortable seat he had experienced since he had been dragged out of the carp car.

Tanya leaned her head on Luthor's shoulder. That felt good too. A fine change indeed.

After a few moments, the train doors shut and the high-speed Acela began its slow acceleration West across the bridge.

#

Acela Train, Somewhere in Indiana

In the hours since they had last stopped Michael had finally been given enough quiet to try and dig out the truth underneath Vika's strange behavior. *"You made me smile."* The stupid phrase stuck to him like Eli's polymer. What exactly did that mean? Was she actually interested in something romantic? Fat chance at that. She hated all men thanks to Dimarin and Jacques. More likely, she found Michael a humorous commodity, like a late-night comedian. Only he didn't get paid.

The train continued hurtling toward Chicago. He was quickly running out of time. He nodded at Vika indicating he wanted her to accompany him. They stood up and walked toward the front of the train. Green countryside whizzed by the windows at 300 kilometers per hour.

"What do you want?" asked Vika in her predictably terse tone.

"A word," he replied.

"You may have your word, just remember my rule."

How could I forget? 'you hit on me, I hit you.'

"I remember."

They stopped at the bar where wealthy—or alcoholic—patrons waited for drinks. They didn't order anything. A few people glared at the dirty couple, but otherwise didn't bother them.

"What was that in the alley in New York? Remember, right before we were all about to get shot and die?"

The immutable Vika-stare suddenly became mutable. He'd touched a nerve. Maybe there *was* something to it after all. The bartender crushed ice in a blender behind them.

"Don't concern yourself with it."

"Too late, I already have. You know what it sounded like Vika? It sounded like you were unburdening."

She shifted uncomfortably. "Perhaps I was."

"What exactly were you trying to get off your chest? Why, as you stared death in the face, would you mention how I made you smile?"

She hesitated, glancing sideways at the bartender as he delayed picking up the ringing bar phone.

After a moment she looked at him square in the face. It was like trying to stare down a tiger. "I did not want to die having any regrets, Laramy," she paused, uncertainty spilling into her facial expressions. "I did not want you to believe that I—"

The bartender loudly answered the phone.

"That you what?"

"—That I did not *appreciate* your company lately."

Michael wasn't sure what to think. The woman was infuriatingly unclear.

"Thanks. Coming from you," he stuttered, "that is quite the compliment. But I still don't understand why that was so important. I mean, why choose *that* as your final statement before you die?"

She raised an eyebrow. Michael worried for a moment

that he had gone too far. But she wasn't looking at him. Her focus had trained back on the bartender. Michael had been so intently focused on Vika's every twitch looking for hidden meaning that he hadn't noticed the man's conversation. Bad move.

He picked up the tail end of it. "Are you certain that's really necessary?" he paused waiting for an answer that Michael could not hear, "but it would be great for business... That's at least another half-hour that thirsty folks could be spending money here, why should they have to spend all that time in their seats...Are you serious? How can there be a security threat? .... How are you just finding this out now?... This train started in *Boston* for smog's sake." The bartender grimaced. "Fine. But it's such a waste." He mashed his finger on the end button.

Vika and Michael shared a glance that spoke volumes. They were stuck on a train traveling at three hundred kilometers per hour and the carps were going to do a systematic scan of everyone's CPI chips. No place to run, no place to hide.

"Move," Vika said.

"But—"

"Bar's closing people. I'm sorry," the bartender shouted, "not my call on this one. You'll have to finish your drinks and head back to your seats."

The many patrons of the moving alcohol repository blustered their protest. Vika walked quickly out of the bar, Michael stayed on her heels.

"Vika! You didn't ever answer my—"

She grabbed a fistful of his grimy shirt and slammed him into a bathroom door. She was deceptively strong. "Don't press your luck," she said, but let go of his shirt and patted him softly on the cheek. "I have become fond of you, okay?"

Michael tried to speak but nothing intelligible came

out.

"Don't let it go to your head," she walked away.

#

Vika mentally added the prerequisite of actually being shot to any future unburdening. She shouldn't have said anything at all. Words. So ineffective. They *always* made things more complicated than they needed to be. All she had wanted was a clean conscience. Now, because she had opened her polluted mouth, Michael had all sorts of other ideas as to her real purpose. She balled up her fist and told herself again that she had no interest in him *that* way. Definitely not.

The train had slowed noticeably. They could make their move soon. The speakers instructed them to remain in their seats, an instruction she had no intention of following. She wasn't even going to remain on the train.

"Please tell me there is another option," Luthor pleaded when she had told them her plan.

"Join the Phylum Chordata, Luthor. Grow a backbone," Michael said.

"This is the best way," Tanya added, "we can escape the train, and nobody needs to die in order to do it."

"I might," Luthor replied.

Vika shook her head. "Don't hesitate."

"Seriously, I'm not sure I can do this."

Luthor and his fear of heights. Actions were the only form of communication that would suffice to deal with him. She grabbed the red emergency bar on the window and pulled. The window popped out and the wind howled through the cabin. Alarms sounded shrilly enough for her to hear over the gale. Other passengers stared openly at them. A few witnesses would hardly matter, their faces were already all over the news. It could place them firmly in the Chicago metro area, but Chicago was a big place.

Tanya already had her BOGs out. Leave it to a woman to know how to take charge. Simultaneously, both of them slapped 126 up on the side of the train. They climbed out.

The enhanced gravity made the climb out of the train surprisingly simple. In moments they were up top, wind violently whipping their faces. Vika reached inside and pulled Luthor kicking and screaming outside. At least the altered gravity meant she didn't have to lift his full weight. They lay down to minimize the effect of the howling air-stream.

Ahead the skyscrapers had grown from meager three-story tenements to horrific hundred story monstrosities. From a distance, the skyline resembled a pyramid or a volcano made of steel and concrete.

The massive breaking system of the Acela shrieked. As their speed slowed to a manageable level, communication became possible.

Michael shouted over the wind, "we need to jump before the station!"

Rising to a knee, Tanya looked over the crest of the train. The wind blew her hair in a trail behind her. She pointed ahead. "Let's jump onto the edge of that building."

A utilitarian structure approached rapidly. It's long flat, concrete sides not looking particularly soft for the inevitable failure of the men to land properly. The train slowed and they stood up, BOGs in hand. Luthor visibly shook from fear, but at least he didn't completely shut down like he had on the seabus. He was improving. Sort of.

In one motion Vika threw her 126 at the wall and jumped toward it. She reoriented instinctively, landing perpendicular to the wall next to the orange BOG. Michael's body tumbled sideways and slammed pathetically against the vertical surface. He grunted as the air was knocked from his lungs. Luthor landed equally awkwardly while Tanya landed with a catlike grace. She looked like she had been born jumping off trains into altered gravity wells. She impressed Vika. Killing that sniper had saved their lives and in the process she had learned the folly of pacifism. Sometimes people just needed to die and you needed to be the one to kill them. It was as simple as that. Tanya had finally grasped that concept and had grown into the woman they needed her to be.

Michael squatted on his haunches and rubbed his knee. "It must be a woman thing, I suck at this," he said. There was something strangely endearing about him being in pain. *No.* She pushed the thought away. *Nothing is endearing about him.*

"You're just coming up with excuses," replied Tanya.

"Then why is it easy for both of you, and hard for me and Luthor?"

"It's just easier for you to blame your ineptitude on a genetic problem rather than a personal one."

"I helped discover 126!" Michael yelled. "If anyone knows how it works, it's me!"

"You'd think," she said with a grin, "but this time it was simple."

"You call that simple?" he asked, "we just jumped off a moving train!"

"Like Vika says, you just have to think of the wall as down. The rest *falls* into place—so to speak."

From the way the boys landed, they obviously hadn't been cogitating much about their orientation. At least Luthor hadn't crapped himself this time.

Michael glared at Tanya, who seemed to be enjoying the experience. "You want to try something hard, Michael? Try climbing twenty stories and killing a sniper without him seeing you."

If Vika had been wearing a hat, she would have tipped it to her.

They dismounted the building, landing outside the

high wall protecting the tracks and casually made their way back to the street.

Almost immediately, a dilapidated truck picked its way through the hoard of human chariots outside the Acela station and stopped at the curb next to them.

"You look like you could use a lift."

Vika saw a soft-looking Asian leaning out of the window of the truck. Probably the "Qwiz" person who had been helping them.

"How did you know we would be here?" Luthor asked.

The man driving the truck shook his white mane. "You kiddin me, son? This is Quency, the computer whiz. That boy could find anything, anywhere. You could bet your dick on it." Vika had no idea who the man was, but she liked him instantly. His vulgar, yet positive demeanor, implied a man of action. This was a man who could get things done.

"They are searching the train for us as we speak. Was that a fluke that you found us or are we that easy to track?" Luthor asked.

"I knew what you guys were trying to do, so I could see a pattern where they might not," the Asian replied. "The carbon police seem to think you went for a swim, they decided to scout the train as a precaution."

"They know where we are now."

"At least we'll have a head start," Michael added.

"Are you going to actually get in the truck or just keep playing with yourselves?" the old man yelled.

"A man after my own heart," said Vika, and she swung herself onto the truck.

END OF PART II

PART III:

CHICAGO

CHAPTER 22:

Eleven Years Ago: The Great Crevasse, Antarctica

"Damn it, Tenrel. Not you too!"

Someone was shaking him. Luthor's eyes popped open. His tinted goggles painted the white backdrop into a yellow red. Garcia's masked face loomed above him.

"Get up." It sounded like a plea, rather than an order.

Luthor tried to move his muscles, and to his surprise, found they responded to him. His suit was warm. Garcia must have turned it on. "What happened?"

Garcia closed his eyes slowly, like it was too painful to remember.

"Damn you, Sarge. Tell me!" Luthor's voice echoed strangely. Normal Antarctica didn't echo, it absorbed voices like a sponge; the wind whisked them away immediately. He looked around, wherever he was it wasn't the flat plane of Titan Dome. A steep canyon of jagged ice rose dozens of meters into the air around him. The light that made its way down refracted off the walls giving them a blue, gem-like hue.

Chaz appeared next to Garcia. "Can't you see? An hour ago, this place didn't exist. The Chinese planted enough napalm along this trench to burn every tree in Vietnam. They waited until half of our armor was through and lit it up."

"They what?" Luthor couldn't believe his ears. "They could have destabilized the whole continent!"

"For all we know, that's exactly what they did." Garcia said. "I haven't had any communication since I fell down here."

"I can't believe they would risk something so stupid."

"Neither did command, or we would have never launched this offensive."

"They could have flooded the planet!"

"Yes. My best guess is that this was a failsafe. In case we ever managed to break through their perimeter with overwhelming force, they could light it –"

"And cut off our escape and reinforcements."

"Exactly, operation Zeus is totally fubar. They launched a counter offensive the minute this thing blew. If the battle isn't over yet, it soon will be. They will have killed or captured 7th tunneling and our entire 3rd armor division."

"Son of a bitch." It was all that needed to be said.

"Come on, we need to move. If we can't find transport or power, our heating cells will give out within the day."

Luthor remembered what Jake had said, "*I don't want to be a popsicle, Sarge,*" and heartily agreed with the sentiment. He groaned and got to his feet.

Garcia grabbed his knee in pain. "That fall fucked up my knee."

Luthor wondered again what had allowed him to remain uninjured and alive when everyone else was dropping like flies. Garcia leaned on him and led him down the ice-canyon. The floor was uneven, glossy, and covered in debris and chunks of ice. They passed a mangled Dragon, gun impaled into the ground like a spade. Chaz hunted around the wreckage. Luthor passed a tangled mess of wire and metal half the size of a man. On the side, a few hand-painted letters in blood red were still visible. They read: Claptrap. Luthor felt a tear freeze on his cheek for his mechanical companion.

"I found him," Chaz said, his voice deader than the landscape. He pointed. Several meters away the unmistakable form of a crumpled paratrooper lay unmoving on the ice. The bottom of the dragon seemed to salute the dead man.

Chaz handed a dog tag to Garcia. "You should have this."

Luthor caught a glimpse of the imprint as it passed him. It read: Jacob M. Eugene.

Garcia clenched his fist around the metal, but said nothing. Jake was dead. Thudding in the distance bespoke continuing violence on the surface.

#

Aurora, IL

Back safely in Bill's apartment, Qwiz brought them up to date on his own brushes with death and proudly produced the research he and Bill had saved.

"Well done buddy," Michael said, "our copy took a bath and then sort of...blew up."

"Thank you!" Luthor said. "Without the risk you took in saving this, our research would be lost. For the first time since Eli died, I feel like we actually have a chance to get ourselves out of this mess. By saving this, you saved all our lives."

Qwiz bowed as humbly as he could manage, accepting the gracious words. Qwiz might not be the Vanguard or any real hero, but he'd risked his life and helped keep his friends alive. He was sure his father would agree that all of those things mattered.

Then the debate began. How to proceed? There were lots of varying opinions between the four valiant friends, but Qwiz didn't feel particularly qualified to add much to their discussion. What they'd gone through made his chase with Stalker's cronies seem like a game of patty cake.

Out of the corner of his eye, Qwiz saw little beads of

sweat had formed on either side of Bill's retreating hairline. The man might have been brave when the bullets were flying, but less so with people. Something about the discussion was bothering him, but he didn't know how to address it.

"There has to be a way to do a mass email or post this to a website or something," Michael was saying.

"We have gone over this before, it can't work." Luthor's face was taut with frustration. Qwiz had imagined the Vanguard with the very same expression when dealing with corrupt authorities. "It would be censored and taken exclusively by the USW before anyone could read it. That's the reason I never risked saving it to the cloud. Anything online will be taken."

Michael turned toward Qwiz, "with him here, we can hack around all that."

Qwiz bowed again. "I apologize, but Luthor is right. This isn't something I can fix."

"Why not, didn't you hack into the European network?"

"Actually, no. Remember that email I told you about? Somebody gave me a username and a password to go with it. That's how I got in. And anything I did access had already made it past the sensors and screeners. Uploading is a totally different beast, different protocols, different security."

"But you *can* get around it right? I mean the law isn't exactly something we have been worried about following the last couple of weeks."

Tanya grinned, "we haven't even been obeying the laws of physics."

Qwiz laughed, but stopped himself quickly. What they were suggesting wasn't funny, unless it meant that they were funny in the head. Hacking the current system to upload data was such an absurd notion that even the Vanguard would have regarded it as impossible.

Qwiz folded his hands in front of himself calmly,

they didn't possess even a rudimentary understanding of the nationalized computer network. "I am telling you it is totally impossible. The USW has completely rerouted all network connections through central locations in the major cities, all hard lines end up there, all wireless connections are routed through their towers, so any attempt to upload something ends up in their hands first. The censors can scan, read, confiscate it, or delete it altogether before it ever gets to the public."

"So there is no possible way to do this?" Luthor asked, the first one of them sounding reasonable.

"No," Qwiz said, trying to be polite but also allow no room for debate. "Let me ink a comic for you: In Chicago, the main screening center is in the USNN Tower. It houses both the USNN and the Censor Bureau and is something like 90 stories tall. All the upper stories are covered in Satellite dishes and cell towers. We would have to climb up the outside to those floors, and tap directly into one of the satellite dishes. That's the only way to bypass all of the screeners and physically get around their firewall." Tanya looked intrigued for some reason, she did realize that climbing something that tall would be impossible, right?

He had to turn on the heat, show them how stupid the idea was. "Even if by some miracle we did get up there and access the network, they would still see our activity. They would *know* they'd been hacked. They'd automatically get a copy of anything we send. And probably shut us down as soon as we did anything. Plus, that place is going to have a gazillion guards. We would have *minutes* before they arrest us."

"Damn," Luthor ground his teeth audibly, "are there are other transmission towers in the area?"

They still weren't getting the point. "There are a lot of them in an area the size of Chicago. But they are all subnetworks."

"What does that mean?" asked Tanya.

"Basically, the USNN Tower is the king, they are all serfs. They all do the work delegated by the king."

"But they might have less security, right?"

"We wouldn't have to climb so many stories, but because the building is smaller, that means the swat team would get there faster. We're still talking *minutes* of time before they arrest us. And they would still see our activity! Which means after our first upload, we'd get shut down."

"So, basically, trying to upload this through the internet is a dead end," Michael summarized. "We can't do it, and even if we do, we'll get caught before anything happens."

Qwiz nodded. They had finally figured out how impossible—and how stupid— trying something like that really was.

"What about the USNN itself?" Michael asked. "What if we broke into the newsroom instead? We could record an interview and broadcast a special report or something about 126."

"The only way to do anything like what you're talking about—sending a global message—is to steal whatever authorization codes the USNN has for their news. Which, by the way, are probably guarded with extreme security; think nuclear launch codes. They might even require some sort of activation. A CPI scan. Something like that. Then whoever got those codes would still have to tap directly into the satellite uplink on the roof so they would be able to bypass the censors in the building," Qwiz sighed. "We might as well be trying to steal an ICBM."

"Then we should steal a missile and threaten to launch it at the capital unless they publish the research," Vika said matter-of-factly.

Michael laughed, but abruptly stopped after Vika scowled at him.

"Do you know what sort of security would be around the actual codes themselves?" Luthor asked.

"I'm more familiar with digital security. I haven't ever come across anything regarding USNN codes, which means they are probably transported non-digitally, hand to hand."

"Like the briefcase with the nuclear launch codes?" Michael asked.

"I doubt that they are *that* well protected, but whoever has access to them probably has their own security."

"And you're sure we can't do a special report without those codes? What if we just hacked the USNN thing on the roof?" Tanya asked.

"Without the codes we can't do much. Anything unapproved through the USNN dish would probably trigger an immediate shut down. Essentially, it would be like if we'd hacked into the other satellite dishes. It would allow us to upload a single uncensored file—like an email or something — before they noticed the hack and cut the hard lines. It would be the same as the other uplinks. We just wouldn't have enough time to do anything. I am talking enough time to send one file. *One* email to *one* person. I doubt one email is going to do much."

Luthor lowered his head. "So we're back to square one."

"I have a plan," Bill said tentatively.

Everyone turned to him expectantly. Surprisingly, Bill hadn't blathered anything about the government putting sedatives in the water or that global warming was just a made-up conspiracy created by politicians as an excuse to grab more power. In fact, he hadn't spoken a single word the entire conversation, an exceptional feat for him.

"My son was recently promoted to reporter for USNN Chicago. I bet my beard that he'd love an exclusive with you."

"Why didn't you mention this before?" asked Tanya, not unkindly.

Because his son hates his guts, disagrees with everything

he thinks and says, and won't speak with him. Qwiz thought.

"My son and I don't exactly see eye to eye on..." Bill hesitated. "Well, on a goddamn thing. He might not want to help us because of me. In fact, that nuke might be easier to steal than getting him to talk to me."

"But he'd have no problem meeting in secret with a bunch of international terrorists?" Michael asked.

"He might. He's the one who did the special report on the explosion in Luthor's apartment."

Michael whistled.

"On the other hand, it would make for an interesting angle for him. He probably wouldn't be shy about a miracle energy story. He could get you on the news all safe and legal-like."

"You're saying if he helps us, we don't need to sneak anywhere and we don't kill anybody?" Tanya asked. "What are we waiting for?"

"Hell yeah. Let's give it a shot," Michael agreed.

"I will see if I can find him tomorrow."

"Find him? Why not call him?" asked Tanya.

"He won't answer my calls, ma'am. So I got a job as a janitor at the USNN building hoping maybe he would talk to me then. My plan hasn't worked so good, but I run into him occasionally and we ... exchange words."

#

Bill managed to "run into" his son at work. Apparently, it hadn't been easy, but he convinced him to come meet them under the condition that he not report it to the authorities.

Tanya felt bad for the old man. She had certainly had her share of rows with her father too—particularly when they decided to leave society rather than be marked—but she didn't hate him. She loved him. It sounded like William legitimately detested Bill, despite all of the efforts that Bill made to try to restore the relationship with him. *Poor guy, all he wants is to know his son.*

They waited for him in a small park that had once been a large park. The vast majority of it was now an exclusive, fenced off garden for the super-wealthy. The fraction left as a park made for a fairly anonymous meeting point. It lay off a nondescript street lined with nondescript apartment buildings. Descript refugees roamed the park, enjoying the sunshine or else hunting any birds stupid enough to land near the starving humans.

William was late and Bill looked nervous. He paced next to a tree. "Where is he?" Tanya put a kindly hand on his shoulder. "Stone, it'll be okay."

"You think so?" his bushy white eyebrows rose in hopeful expectation. If only Luthor was this easy to comfort.

"Maybe he will finally see how much you care for him."

"I appreciate it Tanya, but there is a better chance that global warming isn't a load of shit than my son forgiving me. And we all know how big a pile of shit that is. How is it that no one thinks that variations in the goddamn *sun* might have something to do with how warm our planet is?"

"Keep your hopes up." *And keep your ridiculous conspiracy theories to yourself. I didn't think there were any climate change deniers outside of 2180.*

Qwiz made a face and vehemently shook his head, evidently she made a good decision not to vocalize her thoughts.

A few minutes later a well-dressed young man with flowing blond hair walked across the grass from the parking lot. He stood out like a sore thumb among the shabby suburbians. Tanya recognized him as the reporter who had done the initial story on Luthor's apartment. She didn't know how she felt about turning to him for help. Bill ducked behind the tree out of sight.

"Are you Dr. Tenrel?" he asked.

Luthor nodded. "Thank you for coming."

"How do we know we can trust you?" Tanya blurted. "You're the one who originally reported Luthor as a terrorist."

William raised his hands as if that would make it all better. "Yes I did, but I'm here now, still willing to meet with you. That should tell you how much I buy into the stories I'm given. I just read the words on the page, I don't have to believe them."

Tanya remained unpersuaded, but Bill jumped out from behind the tree before she could respond. "You can trust him. He's as legit as my pecker."

William raked his hands through his hair, "Smog-it. I swear *Stone,* if this is just another one of your elaborate ploys, I'm leaving. You did *not* tell me you would be here."

Luthor looked desperate as he held up his hand. "Please don't go, I believe you. I swear this will be worth your time."

"Frankly, I'm already risking my life to meet with a wanted terrorist. If I have to put up with *his* bullshit too, I'm gone."

"Son," Bill blurted, "will you just give me a chance, just one damn time?"

"Sorry, *Stone,* I am a reporter now. We report on *news,* not asinine conspiracy theories. Has he told you about his alien abduction yet?"

"It really happened! I woke up in the middle of a field with burn marks on my—"

William laughed derisively, interrupting his father. "Have you told them your *theory* about how climate change is a giant government plot to control the masses?"

"Goddamn it! That isn't a theory! How can you not see —"

"And you expect me to sit here and listen to what you're saying?" William stopped shouting and turned politely to Luthor. "I am sorry, Dr. Tenrel, you might have been framed for that bombing, maybe not. But I can't deal with this. And yes at least *I* keep my word; I won't turn you in."

Luthor held up a hand. "Please don't leave before you see a demonstration. If this research doesn't get out, we will all probably be dead within the week."

"I will give you the name of another reporter. I just can't be the one to deal with scum like *Stone*."

"William, please!" Bill pleaded. "I give up. I won't say anything if only you will just stay and talk with us."

"Sorry, but they don't pay me enough to put up with drunken, lying, sons of bitches who leave their families for dead."

"You got that right. I doubt any amount of money would be enough to cover what I did to you."

William did a double-take.

Stone continued. "You're right about what I was! That's why I left."

William's scowl deepened, but he said nothing.

"I have tried to tell you this a hundred times, son, but you would never listen. I left because I didn't want to hurt you or your mother. My sanity was shot to hell coming home from the war. I only wanted to do two things: drink and beat the shit out of something. I didn't want that to be either of you. So, I left."

"You took all of your pension. We had nothing."

"You would have traded your safety for a new Lidius Phone? Material things aren't worth dick if you ain't safe William, I of all people, know that."

"Well having a place to live and enough food to eat would have been nice too."

"Get it out, say what you need to say, I deserve it."

"You're just lucky that the Culling didn't happen before I had enough money to be able to support mom. Not that it mattered anyway, she still died. Goddamn pneumonia, nobody had antibiotics with the rationing."

"Son, I'm so sorry. I made the best choice I knew how to make. I didn't want you to turn out like me."

"Damn you."

Bill didn't respond, just maintained an open posture, receptive to whatever beating his son fit to throw at him.

"Damn you for trying to rob me of my hatred for you."

"You don't have to stop hating me. You don't have to change anything, I just want you to understand. And know that I'm sorry."

William turned back. "I promise nothing. I will only listen if he keeps his mouth shut."

True to his word, Bill said nothing. Not a single curse throughout their recount of their time since Geneva, nor whisper of conspiracy.

William was understandably skeptical about 126's properties. But the demonstration quickly changed that. Luthor was careful not to do anything too dramatic with 126 that a circle of people couldn't obscure from prying eyes. But a floating stick, combined with a strange feeling of down was pretty convincing. It didn't take long before the young reporter was chomping at the bit to broadcast everything. The excitement of telling their tale seemed to have overridden his anger at his father. Any hesitation he felt over being with a supposed terrorist had evaporated as well.

"I'm telling you, my producer is going to love this idea. She has been around long enough, that she knows when to let a reporter run with a story."

"You think this is really going to work?"

"Are you kidding me? This is the single biggest story—I mean *globally*—since the end of the war. Think of the headlines, instead of things like "WAR ENDED" we could have something like "ENERGY CRISIS ENDED."

"I like the sound of that."

"Me too; breaking the story of the decade is generally good for one's career in the news business. I also have the personal touch of being the one to break the story on Tenrel's apartment. If this goes like it should, I might even have to give *him* another chance not to be a dumbass."

"Stone struggles with that, so don't get your hopes too high." Qwiz said.

"Was that *sarcasm* I just heard?" Stone clapped Qwiz on the back, "damn fine job boy, you're learning!"

"Everyone calls you that now?" William asked.

Stone blushed. "That's another thing I didn't tell you. After I left, I told people to call me my army nickname. I didn't want there to be a warm fart's chance in Anti that people would connect you with me, I thought it might hurt your career. Bill Jr. might lead to questions about who Sr. was."

William didn't say anything, but for the first time he didn't look quite so harshly at the man.

Luthor continued, "you should know that this is dangerous information."

"I gathered that from the murders, explosions and general destruction that has followed you across the Atlantic. And the fact that it is completely illegal for me to be meeting with you right now."

"Do not underestimate our enemies," Vika said.

"Or us," Michael said brightly, "bad guys tend to die when we're around."

Vika gave him a withering eyebrow, "you mean when I'm around." She turned back to William. "Tell *no one* about this, not even your producer, if possible."

"Sorry, producers have to give the thumbs-up to any story. No way around that one."

"Then watch your back."

"Believe it or not, I know how to take care of myself. I've had some nasty dirt on politicians and massive corporations before and stayed safe. Don't worry. I got this."

"I could come along and scare them off," Bill said.

"I think stealth is a better defense than bad breath *Dad*, but thanks for the offer."

Bill's white hair swayed with belly laughter. Tanya realized it was the first time William had used a father-pronoun since he'd arrived.

William continued, "I think there is a great chance we can have this up on the evening news tomorrow night."

Luthor handed him a memory stick. "Here is a copy of our research data, complete with the synthesis method. Above all else, that must get out. 126 is worthless if no one knows how to make it."

William shook hands with Luthor, Michael, the women, and then to Tanya's surprise, Bill's hand as well.

"This is awkward, but, thanks Dad. Thanks for the chance to do this story."

"I'm glad I can do something right in my life."

William smiled. "I will contact my producer immediately, and just as a heads-up, she will probably want to do a live interview."

Vika shook her head. "Not safe. You never know where they will have planted bugs."

"There is a secret location the station has set up to do high-risk interviews. If we do it from there, we can remotely broadcast a full interview with only her and me. No cameramen, sound techs or anything. You will be safe."

"That sounds good," Luthor said, "when and where?"

"I'm afraid I can't tell you that until I get the go-ahead."

#

They waited for William's call the rest of the evening at Bill's apartment. He finally called a few minutes before midnight and gave them directions to a very poor area southwest of downtown. He instructed them to meet at 1:00 pm the next day so it could be edited in time for the evening news.

As they left, Vika handed each of them a pistol. Luthor had the good sense not to ask where she had found them. All he knew was that she had gone out the night before and came back with enough pistols for everyone. Luthor, in turn, insisted that each of them wear some 126. Thankfully, Qwiz had saved all the 126 from his old apartment which meant they had plenty despite the beads they had lost in New York.

The warm day meant the solar panels on Bill's truck had managed to charge the battery. Luthor sat in the bed while they circumnavigated Chicago. The formerly labeled Willis Tower— its name had been auctioned off so often that no one kept track of it any more—rose prominently in the distance. It remained the tallest structure in the city by law, if only by five meters. Its baroque features were outshined by other, more modern buildings whose exteriors glittered with photovoltaic cells and whose roofs buzzed with wind turbines and crops. Some had entire floors in the middle of their steel lattices devoted to rotating turbines.

Chicago had been one of the few Midwestern cities to prosper in the midst of the scarcity of the modern world. It was ideally placed around a network of rail systems, fertile farm land, and water transport. It also had a pre-existing system of nuclear power plants combined with high yield wind farms and an effective mass transportation system to move people around. There were even many of the suburbs that hadn't completely eroded into chaos, which was why Fermilab still existed and why Luthor had been able to pursue an experiment as energy-intensive as new element creation.

They hopped out of the truck in a section of the

city that had once housed Chicago's Midway airport—not that anything flew anymore. The terminal itself had been converted into housing with the open airstrips now dense gardens for the residents. Outside the airport, the slums had descended into a disgusting level of disrepair. Windows were rare, roofs had been cobbled together with rusty sheet-metal or plywood, and bullet-holes seemed to be the decoration of choice. The two and three-story apartments housed some of the more notorious gangs in the city along with hundreds of thousands of Markless, homeless, and suburban refugees. Bill's truck was the only automobile they had seen in several kilometers.

Luthor was certain they'd come to the wrong place until William's smiling face popped out of the front door of a cracked, brick apartment. He waved them inside.

They dodged piles of refuse and ignored the Markless on the street corner begging for food. The rickety wooden door squeaked loudly as it opened. The door was a farce. Affixed to the inside of the moldy wood was a 2 cm thick steel door. William shut it behind them, locking enough deadbolts to stop a missile.

"Sorry for that, in this community, we need *a lot* of extra security to maintain a place like this."

Luthor instantly realized the need for such security. Polished wood floors covered the ground, adorned by intermittent plush carpets. A room to his right housed thick-cushioned couches, a pool table and a large TV. A powder room lined with well-lit mirrors flanked it. The windows which had appeared cracked from the outside, were lined with metal bars and had another layer of security glass inside. They followed William upstairs where the equipment to run an entire broadcast was installed. Computers, mixing boards, and a server rack greeted them. He led them to a smaller room with a green screen and a sophisticated camera. More armored windows covered the walls and a sturdy access hatch was mounted in the ceiling.

"William, I think you have outdone yourself," Michael said, clearly in awe of the facility.

"Don't think I put this together," he said quickly. "Remember, we are well-funded by the government," he opened a small refrigerator with a grin. "Care for a beverage?" Not one of them would pass up a luxury like a soda.

"I don't suppose you have a mountain dew?" Qwiz asked tentatively.

"Sorry, but no. The government only owns shares of Coke," Qwiz humbly accepted a Sprite instead, lament on his face as he sipped the carbonated concoction sans caffeine.

"Why put such a high-tech place in the middle of the ghetto?" Bill asked.

"Remember the Chinese defector from a few years back? The USNN constructed this as an offsite location to film the interview. It was supposed to keep him safe from the Chinese government and snipers or something. Apparently, money was no object."

"Damn, I'll say," said Michael, admiring the mixing board.

"They put it in this neighborhood so it would be impossible to find," William looked at his watch, "have a seat, when my producer gets here we can get started." He scrunched his eyebrows, "actually, I thought she would be here already."

They all sat down in comfortable chairs of the type seen in interviews. "Why would she be late?"

"I don't know; it is possible she got lost. She's probably never been here before. Not a lot of people even know this place exists."

Vika raised an eyebrow. "How many exactly?"

"I don't know. The producers and executives mostly, and a few of the field reporters like me who have actually filmed here. Why?"

Vika's hand hovered over her pistol. "How does someone find out about it?"

William glanced at the weapon. "You only find out if you do a story here. The producers just have to submit a request to film here with their team.

"You're telling me that your producer had to get permission to come here?"

"Of course. They aren't going to let just anyone walk in."

Vika cursed in French, or maybe Russian. Luthor couldn't tell. "Your producer is late because she is probably dead."

William did a double-take. "What? I just talked—"

"Agent Veronika is right. I killed her myself," said a cold, accented voice from the doorway.

Before Luthor could process the significance of the mysterious man who knew Vika's name, she had already reacted. She fired her pistol in a rapid burst. Shots streamed toward the intruder, blurring the line between semi and fully automatic. The man ducked his head behind the doorway. Most of the bullets connected with the wooden frame, two struck his thick gelvar body armor, which shunted their impact in ripples around his body. He laughed from behind the door.

Suddenly, the security windows and ceiling hatch mechanically snapped open and men in full shock gear poured in via ropes. Luthor jumped behind the chair and managed to get several rounds off. He heard gunfire from Bill as well.

"Put your weapons down," said the accented man, "you are surrounded. Don't make me kill you all. It would make my job more... annoying."

To Luthor's surprise, Vika raised her hands above her head and dropped her gun, "don't be stupid, Tenrel," she said. Luthor found himself also raising his hands, his gun falling to the floor. They leveled their sub-machine guns at him while one of them snatched the discarded pistols and dropped them out the window.

"Better," said the man, "now, the rest of you." One by one, each of them were stripped of their side arms.

Qwiz boldly refused to give up his gun. "I know your voice," he said, eyes narrowing even more than was typical for a man of his heritage.

"Excellent," the man walked forward and kicked Qwiz hard in the gut.

Qwiz doubled over and the man slammed the butt of his assault rifle into his back. Qwiz cried out in pain and crashed to the floor. The man sneered over his prominent nose as Qwiz writhed. His greying hair and bushy eyebrows obscured his black eyes.

Hurt, but not yet broken, Qwiz looked up from the ground. "You're the one who was behind this all along!"

"The Stalker!" Bill said, the shock of realization on his face. Luthor remembered the hacked conversations between two men Qwiz had described. One of which he referred to as the Stalker.

"Stalker?" said the man, "I like the sound of that. That makes you the mole." He kicked him hard in the side again. "You made communication *difficult*."

Qwiz wheezed defiantly.

"Do you think you're some kind of hero then?" another kick. Qwiz curled up in the fetal position, moaning. With each blow, Vika turned an angrier shade of red. "You've covered your tracks well. Very convenient for you to reveal yourself to me now."

The man—Stalker—casually removed Qwiz's weapon from his pants and tossed it out the window. Luthor's mind raced, searching for an escape, anything. But they were completely surrounded and they had no guns. The Sabers—Luthor assumed that's who they were—wore gelvar and riot helmets. Pistols would have been all but useless on them anyway. If only Luthor had his MX-5 loaded with High-Impact rounds... they could slice through all but JDU compound armor plating.

But he didn't have HI-rounds—or an assault rifle. Luthor mentally switched focus and began trying to analyze the enemy and, perhaps, find a weakness. The windows and ceiling hatch remained open, which provided a potential escape route, but they would have to wade through a fire hose of bullets to get there. The Saber-swat team showed no weakness whatsoever, with the possible exception of taking their cues from Stalker.

Vika fumed next to him like a stick of dynamite.

"His name isn't Stalker," she said, "it's Franco Dimarin. The man who imprisoned me for five years."

"It would have been life, if I had my way," Stalker-Dimarin said.

"The bastard tried to rape me!"

"It's what you deserved for refusing him."

Vika threw her head back and yelled. She shrieked as if she thought she could kill Dimarin by tearing out her vocal chords and strangling him with them.

The armed men gripped their weapons tighter.

"Scream if you want," Dimarin said, "but you're trapped and there's nothing you can do about it."

"Tell your Sabers to put down their guns and we'll see what happens," Vika growled.

"No!" He punched her across the face. She collapsed next to the couch. "We'll see what happens when I start asking questions."

William raised his hands in surrender. "There has got to be some mistake. I have nothing to do with this."

"There is no mistake," Stalker said coldly. "I have been chasing these fugitives across two continents, do not think for a moment I have mistaken my quarry."

"Then what do you want? I work for powerful people,

they can double whatever you're making!"

"Does it look like I need money?" If Stalker needed anything, it most certainly was not money. Luthor couldn't help but be impressed by the quality of their gear. The carbon it took to outfit his unit could have purchased a transatlantic flight with a fighter escort.

"I'll tell you what he wants," said Qwiz quietly. "He wants to steal all of the research on producing 126, to let the EU have a monopoly on free energy."

To Luthor's surprise Stalker laughed derisively, full of genuine mirth. "And I thought you were some sort of hyper-genius. Even after listening to my conversations you still don't know anything," he laughed again. "I told you, I don't need money." Luthor couldn't think of what they had wrong. What other possible motivation could this man have, other than stealing the technology for himself? *Unless...*

"You forgot one thing, Qwiz," Michael said. "In order for him to have a true monopoly, he has to kill everyone who knows how to make it. That means us."

"At least you have that part correct. You will all be dead as soon as you give me the information I am looking for."

"You son of bitch," Bill spat. "We won't tell you anything."

"Very well," said Stalker, the corner of his mouth curling in a sneer, "I am not above torture. Of course, I could be persuaded to forgo it..." he let the implication hang in the air. *He won't torture us if we tell him everything.*

William threw up his hands. "Either way we are going to die, whether we resist or not. We might as well not die with all our fingernails pulled out and our lungs full of water."

Stalker smiled. He knew he was in control. The trouble was, Luthor had no idea how to retake any semblance of it back from him. His only chance was to draw things out as long as possible and hope for an opening.

"Let's start with an easy question. Who else have you told about 126?"

Michael stood up. "Suck my dick." He spat on the floor. "We aren't telling you shit." The nearest guard hit him brutally with the butt of his gun in the back of the knees. Michael cried out and collapsed next to Vika, who hadn't bothered to get up after Dimarin's punch.

"Why are you so stupid?" William asked to the groaning, crumpled Michael. He turned to Stalker. "*I will* talk. Just answer one question first and I will spill my guts on 126."

"Ask."

"How did you find my producer?" he asked.

Damn it, William, you wasted it. She's already dead. Luthor realized, even as he thought it, that William wouldn't have his perspective. He'd never been in a situation where he'd had friends and team members killed. Her death was probably more traumatic for him then his own imminent death.

"She made a phone call yesterday that was recorded. She asked a USNN executive for permission to film here. We heard the call, tracked her to her home, shot her, and then waited for you here. Now, who have you told?"

William's voice quavered. "I haven't told anyone else. They said it would be too dangerous."

"And they were right," Dimarin said. "Luckily, I believe you. Now, give me the research data. I know you have it."

William closed his eyes. After a pregnant moment, he opened them again and tossed Stalker the memory stick with Luthor's research. He turned back to the rest of them, pain written all over his face. "At least we know *someone* has the technology."

"No!" Luthor yelled. "Does this look like a man who's

going to do *anything* good with it? Don't you see? He doesn't want money, he wants war!"

It was blindingly obvious. Dimarin didn't care about money. A man like him wanted power. Someone who organized military strikes would gain incalculably more power during a war with China. A war they would certainly win with the help of 126. Only hundreds of millions more innocent people would die in the process. It would be Antarctica all over again. It was all Luthor's fault. If he'd never discovered the damn synthesis method, no one would ever know the properties of 126. He hadn't avenged Jake and Martinez. He hadn't atoned for Chaz's life and Garcia's leg. He'd betrayed them all.

Dimarin hefted the memory stick in his hand. "I don't think these men here would be prone to follow orders if they knew it would lead to another war. Men like them tend to die in wars."

Luthor heard one Saber next to him chuckle behind his helmet.

Inexplicably, Dimarin then dropped the memory stick on the ground and crushed it with his boot.

"What are you doing?"

"The same thing I will do to every other copy of your research. I'm destroying it."

"What! Why?" Luthor shouted. "The world needs this. Don't throw it away!"

"What the world needs is *stability*, Tenrel. Surely you of all people can understand that. The stability the Sabers provide would be threatened if the world were suddenly flooded with free energy."

"That isn't your decision to make."

"I can make any decision I desire. I answer to no one; I am outside of the jurisdiction of any country."

Vika looked up from the ground and glared at Dimarin. "Once the EU discovers this insanity, they will execute you."

"I love that even after years with us, you still believe that we work for Europe. If Jacques were still alive, I would give him a raise for managing to conceal our true nature so completely."

"What? That you have agents stationed in America?"

"Why wouldn't we? America is part of our Charter."

"What Charter?"

"The CPI Charter. The Sabers were written right into the Paris 2 agreement. We are the ultimate enforcement arm of the Carbon Enforcement Coalition. Unlike the carbon police or conventional militaries, we were intentionally kept neutral to keep everyone in line. We're the check to keep world powers from violating carbon protocols."

"If the Sabers were so global, why were we always stationed in Europe?"

"Because that's where carbon enforcement is headquartered and where the CPI databases are."

"You're lying," Vika insisted, "I did not kill for the sake of carbon!"

Dimarin seemed to be enjoying himself. "Think about it, Veronika, why else would we only bomb energy sources? We destroy the ones that emit carbon."

"Now I know you are lying. We bombed plenty of green energy too," Vika said.

"We can't have any one area becoming energy independent. That would be bad for carbon enforcement and erode our influence."

"This is bullshit," Vika said. Michael slapped her arm as if trying to get her to shut up.

Dimarin sneered, "we keep the world's energy supply low because it keeps people docile and keeps us in power. Nothing threatens that more than you, Tenrel. If the EU or US applies your technology, it would eliminate the need for CPI, carbon regulation, and thus the Sabers, overnight. Why monitor carbon output, if everyone has unlimited carbon-free energy? It must be destroyed, along with everyone who knows about it."

"At least give it to *someone,*" Luthor pleaded. "America, the EU, I don't care!"

"But you were right about what that would do," Dimarin replied. "If I give it to one of them it *will* start a war. China does not have a monopoly on greed. The Coalition is just as capable of trying to dominate the world. I do not want to send my men into another war. Eliminating 126 is my only choice."

"So you are just going to kill *everyone* who's even heard of 126, just to protect your power?" William said.

"Yes. A single loose end would ruin everything. I have Tenrel's friend Garcia in custody already. Other Sabers are tracking down the Markless who helped you in New York. It is only a matter of time until the rest of you tell me who else knows about 126. Once we get you back to the compound, you won't last long."

"You'd be surprised how long I can last," Bill said.

Dimarin took out a large pistol from a shoulder holster built into his body armor. "I look forward to finding out. But for now, a promise is a promise. No torture for you, reporter." He pointed the weapon at William.

Images flashed in Luthor's mind of everyone who had been killed in the war. His friends, his enemies, the Culling, all of it had been for the sake of man's greed. Now William sat before a one-man firing range for the same reason. Luthor couldn't stand it. He refused to let one more innocent person die for energy, or lack thereof. *I will not let Antarctica happen here. This is where I draw the line!*

Luthor threw himself at William, trying to get in between the gun and his head. Several gun shots discharged as he tumbled to the ground, William in his arms.

When he looked up, Stalker and his entire team had

been thrown against the nearest walls.

They stuck there, struggling to escape. That's when Luthor noticed a radical change in gravity, it no longer was down, it was up. He fell upward, William in tow, and slammed hard against the ceiling. Hands reached down through the ceiling hatch and pulled the two of them through it. Once on the roof, Luthor rolled away from the hole, panting. He weighed several times more than normal. Vika reached her wiry arm back inside. Bursts of gunfire greeted her. In a moment she withdrew her arm again; it bled freely, amorphous BOGs were clasped firmly in her fist. She separated them, and Luthor felt gravity return to normal. The rattle of automatic weapons echoed up from the inside.

"Luthor, give me all your 126!" Michael shouted.

Now weighing only 75 kilos instead of 200 he stood and did as was requested. "I hope you know what you're doing!" Michael had 15 BOGs.

"Just get off this building."

"Over here." Vika held one of the ropes Stalker's team had used to climb into the windows. The braided nylon was tethered firmly to a post on the edge of the roof. Tanya dropped off the side. Bill helped his wounded son.

Luthor sprinted to the edge, hoping not to feel the sting of bullets. Michael handed Luthor the rope, his eyes were wide with adrenaline. "Remember the gravity bomb? We're going to try one. Now go!"

Luthor shoved down his fear of high places, refusing to let it control him. He gripped the rope firmly, shuddered in fear and backed to the edge.

"Now!" Vika yelled.

Michael braced himself against one of the rooftop air conditioning units and smashed his hands together. Even halfway across the roof, Luthor felt the violent shift in gravity. It was even more intense than when he had crashed the helicopter. Michael lobbed the makeshift grenade into the ceiling hatch just as Luthor jumped off the roof. The new gravity well was so massive that he was able to walk down the side of the wall 30 meters away barely needing the rope. The fringe benefit was that the wall felt like down, his brain told him it was down, and so the heights didn't bother him.

Luthor stepped off the wall awkwardly onto the gravel. He fought against the 126 to get away from the building. Tanya grabbed one of the guns Stalker had thrown out of the window and handed another to Luthor. Vika landed lithely next to him.

"I don't know what's going to happen in there, but we shouldn't be here when it does," Luthor said. They sprinted to the truck. William limped badly, and a full quarter of his fine shirt had been stained dark red. Luthor helped him into the truck-bed.

Luthor felt the gravity continually growing as the BOGs that had pinned Stalker's team to the wall coalesced with Michael's massive concentration of 126. An ear-splitting shriek rent the air and the building shuddered on its foundations. A huge chunk of the left wall crunched in on itself like a discarded aluminum can.

"Where is Michael? Did he get sucked in?" Luthor asked.

"He will make it," Vika said quietly "...please make it."

A second later, Michael leapt off the roof; he held no rope. He ran down the wall, even as it cracked underneath him, pieces of brick and mortar sucked inward toward the terrifying new gravity well at the center of the building. He strained like he was carrying a 200-kilogram pack. Three meters from the ground he leapt forward desperately, crumpling onto the concrete walkway.

"Run!" Vika shouted.

Michael struggled, his arms were riveted with road rash, and his legs pumped awkwardly against the competing gravity wells. But he ran. The building's windows shattered behind him as the bomb sucked in the steel restraints.

He rolled ingloriously onto the bed of the truck. “Floor it!”

Two figures forced themselves out of broken bottom windows. One was unmistakably Stalker. Luthor emptied the entire magazine at him as he rolled out. Ripples in the black gelvar spread from several shots, but none found flesh.

The truck’s ancient batteries attempted to accelerate, but only managed a slow roll away from the implosion. Stalker managed to get to the street. He dropped to a knee and returned fire in 3-round bursts from his assault rifle. Luthor ducked, praying the frail frame of the truck bed would withstand the force of the gunshots. It didn’t. They ripped through the aluminum body like tissue paper. Luthor covered his head as holes popped up all around the rim of the bed. Images of huddling against a frozen wall against a Chinese assault flooded his mind.

William cried out in pain, as a projectile struck him square in the leg. Luthor shook his head violently, trying to rattle the memories loose from his conscious mind. With a grunt, Luthor forced them down to their prison and jolted back to the present. This was no time to shut down and get stuck in the past.

The shooting stopped. Luthor chanced a peak. The building groaned like a dying giant and crashed in on itself, resembling a reverse explosion in slow motion. The brick walls folded over the wreckage like paper mâché, creating a red-brown sphere with a ten-meter radius where the building had been. The only remnant of the structure were the steel I-beams, firmly secured into the foundation. They formed a rounded cage as they were slowly bent around the debris ball at the center. Stalker stood impassively next to the disturbing scene, oblivious of the gravitational phenomenon next to him. His goal seemed to be reloading as fast as humanly possible.

Less than a second after the initial volley, more bullets erupted from the gun, the muzzle flash appearing in the characteristic starburst pattern of an MX-5. Just as Luthor heard the plink of more bullet impacts, Bill wheeled the truck in a sharp turn onto a different street. Luthor heaved a sigh of relief.

No time for relief, William's hit. For once, Luthor was glad for the memories that pounced him; they reminded him of how to care for a wounded man. Having no proper bandages, he stripped off his shirt, and tore long strips from the threadbare cotton fabric. Vika had already done the same, she was already tying them around the wound on his side. Luthor avoided staring at Vika's lean torso and full breasts. Instead, he focused on the task at hand, stopping William's bleeding. Michael failed to focus on anything other than Vika.

Luthor ripped the frayed pant leg to see the wound better. Blood gushed from the hole in his thigh. Luthor blotted it away with one of the strips to try to see if the bullet had lodged itself in the leg or not. It looked like it had gone clean through. Luthor hoped the round hadn't severed the femoral artery, if it had, the kid would definitely lose the leg —if he survived at all.

Luthor didn't like tying tourniquets, in Antarctica they had been a death sentence for whatever limb they were tied to. It wrenched his heart every time he'd seen a friend lose a limb. *Garcia.* Too bad he would never get to walk on his prosthetic again now that Dimarin had him.

Luthor blotted some more, trying to see the wound clearly. "What do you think?" he asked Vika.

William moaned softly in pain as she held pressure on his side.

"Tie it," she said simply.

"Smog-it." Luthor wasted no time. He cinched the blood-restricting knot just above the wound and William bit off another cry of pain.

"It's all right, kid. You're going to make it," Luthor

said.

"Are you sure?" asked Michael. "He looks like he's lost a ton of blood."

"I'm sure," Luthor said definitively, though his infused confidence was more for William's sake than for his own surety. For some reason men tended to be far more likely to survive if they believed they were going to live. William was much closer to that fine line between life and death than Luthor wanted to admit. The kid could use every advantage he could get.

"For God's sake, man," Luthor said, interrupting Michael's pathetic attempt to stare without getting caught, "give the lady your shirt."

CHAPTER 23:

Eleven years ago: Titan Dome, Antarctica

Luthor jumped over another gaping crack that splintered the floor of the artificial ice-canyon. It fell to unknowable depths in the multi-mile thick ice. His stomach fell in each time he traversed one. The feeling became worse each time. How easy would it be for him to slip and fall forever into one of them? He would almost rather be stuck down here than jump over another one. It was just so *deep.* He and Chaz helped the very gimpy Garcia make the same leap.

"I still just can't believe they would do this," Chaz said in his never-ending diatribe against the Asian Axis.

"Believe it," said Garcia. "The greedy bastards were the only major power to oppose Paris 2. We both know they couldn't give a shit about the earth, so long as they can profit from it."

"Paris 2 and blowing a goddamn hole in Anti are a little different, don't you think? Seriously, why don't they just launch their nukes and call it a day? *That* would end the world even faster than flooding it."

"The Chinese wouldn't dare. They know their arsenal can't match ours. Even if only one in ten missiles hits, we would nuke them into the stone age."

"It doesn't look like they care too much about that. Fucking failsafe my ass," he muttered. "Besides if we do nuke them, *we* will also *nuke ourselves* into the stone age."

"Will you two shut up?" shouted Luthor. "I don't really care right now about the environment, nuclear winter, or this bullshit war. I want to get out of here before my heat cells are gone. Or before I slip into one of those goddamn cracks!"

They walked on in silence.

After searching the endless stretch of ice-trench, they found a jagged path to the surface and were finally able to use their skis.

Luthor's heating coil expired an hour later on the windswept plateau. The others' winked out soon after. No one had spoken since their batteries died. It was too hard to hear anything without a functioning communicator. His shivering was all that kept him awake. He knew it wouldn't be long before he collapsed and became a permanent fixture of the landscape.

In Antarctica, shelter was preeminent above all other needs. Not only the coldest place on earth, but the high glacial plateau of Titan was one of the windiest. The combination of the two could sap a man's heat in hours without a heating coil. And they weren't dressed for a long deployment, they were dressed for agility, for attack. They needed to find the shelter they had built when they'd rendezvoused before the assault, and soon.

"Damn, its hot," mumbled Chaz. He started to take off his mask.

"No, you idiot! No!" Luthor screamed, restraining his friend.

"But it's so hot! Just let me get some fresh air," Chaz fought him, but Luthor restrained his arms and forced him to keep skiing.

Chaz had entered the last, most dangerous stage of hypothermia before he froze to death. His body had begun to give up on the extremities and used all its blood and heat to keep the vital organs from freezing. The result was a wave of heat to the chest and head, which drove men to delirium and the uncontrollable urge to strip and cool down. Many men who froze to death in Anti were found in nothing but their skivvies. It was imperative that he keep his clothes on and conserve his warmth.

Luthor grabbed either side of his best friend's mask and yelled into his face. "Focus! Exposed skin will freeze. Get a hold of yourself!"

His eyes abruptly rolled back in his head and he fell backward onto the windswept ice.

Luthor tried vainly to rouse him, but he wouldn't budge. *Not another one. Not you. No more good men should die on this damned continent.*

He quickly strapped Chaz to his skis and started pulling him like a sled. Luthor knew with his injured leg, Garcia couldn't help. He needed to keep going to save Chaz before it was too late. But this was Titan; they were on top of a three-mile thick slab of ice and 13,000 ft above sea level. The air was very thin here. Luthor started huffing immediately. Garcia grabbed the gun and skied ahead to scout.

Interminable minutes passed as Luthor lugged his unconscious friend across the frozen landscape. Garcia had disappeared into the distance. Luthor found himself mumbling through his heaving breaths. "Don't give up on up me now buddy. We're almost there. Don't die on me. Please." Luthor didn't know if was talking to Chaz or himself.

Garcia began shouting. All Luthor heard was a mumbled gasp in the wind, but skied forward as fast as he could manage and found Garcia pointing to a green flag, the rallying sign.

Luthor couldn't believe his eyes. They had found shelter Foxtrot.

Luthor sprinted the last few hundred yards to the flag and heaved Chaz inside the ice shelter. A few dozen paratroopers huddled around a command cube. Two meters to a side, it was little more than a massive air-dropped battery. Men used it to charge their suits and power the equipment used to create a shelter.

Upon seeing the unconscious Chaz, they rushed into action running charging cables from the cube to his suit's heating unit. They rubbed his arms and legs to promote circulation. The newly recharged AED in the suit then began its work informing the men to begin compressions.

Luthor tried to catch his breath and could only watch as the men cared for his oldest friend.

It wasn't looking good. The AED could only send the requisite volts to shock his heart back into rhythm, if it *had* a rhythm. The screen showed nothing. No quantity of electricity could change that. Other men rotated in to continue compressions. Luthor knelt next to Chaz's head and heard Garcia take charge.

"Anyone have a battle pad?" he barked.

A timid man produced one. "I found it on the lieutenant... he didn't make it... after the explosion. I thought it would be important."

"Good work, soldier."

"We didn't have the codes to operate it," another added.

Garcia did. He punched in the codes and dialed command.

The battle pad crunched through the encryption protocols. After Garcia explained the situation to a staff sergeant, a blocky man with crew-cut white hair pixilated on the screen. It was General Stutsman.

"Lieutenant Hopkins?"

"Sergeant Garcia, sir. Hopkins is KIA."

"Goddamn it man, it's good to see somebody that ain't been blown up yet. Tell me some good news to brighten up this clusterfuck," Luthor leaned in to watch the broadcast.

Garcia glanced around, "sir we have 50 paratroopers that have retreated to staging area Foxtrot in need of evac. A number are wounded and most of us have some level of frostbite.”

Stutsman spat from a large dip of chewing tobacco. “You want evac for fifty men?”

“Yessir. But I believe more will be arriving.”

“You’ve got to be out of your goddamned mind.”

Luthor’s mouth fell open. Garcia stared at the screen. “Sir?”

“Did I stutter sergeant?” Stutsman spat.

“Sir, our men will die here without rescue. It’s a thousand kilometers to the Shackleton Base and we only have a few unbroken skis. Even if we had enough, with our gear and provisions we wouldn’t survive two days out in the elements. It’s the dead of winter! There are injured—”

“Sergeant. Strap on some balls and figure it out.”

“With all due respect sir, we just air dropped behind enemy lines, assaulted a heavy defensive line, and eliminated Chinese air support. Don’t you think that warrants an expenditure of resources to help us?"

It might have been the most politically correct tongue lashing Luthor had ever heard. He began his turn at compressions. 1, 2, 3, 4 stayin alive. Stayin alive. Come on Chaz!

Stutsman shouted through the pad. “Our biggest offensive of the war just went to shit. I mean totally fubar. We lost our entire third armor, 7th tunneling has been captured! We don’t have any goddamn resources, and if we did, I wouldn't spend them to rescue a handful of stranded paratroopers.”

“Sir, please—”

“Make peace with whatever god you like. There’s no help coming.”

“Damn you, General!” Garcia yelled. “You can’t do this!”

“I just did,” he said with a straight face, “and I would do it again.”

"You just sentenced us all to death! Because you won't spend the fucking oil?!"

"Bingo. All of your lives combined aren't worth the tank of gas it would take to save you. This conversation is over. Good luck."

The battle pad winked out, displaying "Session Terminated" in red letters.

Luthor continued his compressions. The medic tried to tell him it was too late. Chaz was already dead. Luthor didn't listen.

#

Bill's Apartment, Chicago, United States of the West

To Tanya, it felt like they were back in New York: insurmountable odds, everything going wrong. Like nothing they had done mattered. Their only chance at breaking free of this mess was now being scraped off the pavement with a shovel.

At least everything finally made sense. They hadn't been fighting some rogue splinter cell, they had been fighting against the carbon enforcement itself. So naturally they would have access to Eli's phone call with Luthor, because they had access to *every* phone call. They could easily manipulate the media if they wanted. Of course they could send Sabers to America; they were in *every* country.

They were screwed.

The man who wanted to destroy Luthor's research and kill all of them had the entire resources of CPI at his disposal. They might as well be fighting against God himself.

Vika brooded even more deeply than her usual wont. Dimarin's revelations about the Saber's connection to CPI seemed to have sapped her usual composure. She paced the small apartment shouting intermittently, alternating between her several languages. "How could I have been so stupid?" she yelled, having now switched to English.

"How were you supposed to know?" Michael asked. "They tried to hide it from everyone. Not just you."

"I served for years! I thought I was protecting people, not working to keep carbon enforcement in power. All those years I was just another carp, I just had a bigger gun and more permission to use it." She then let loose a string of obscenities in French which Tanya had no desire to translate. Michael smiled at her, though she didn't seem to notice, while flexing his abs. *Do you think we can't tell what you're doing?* Tanya thought. *You aren't impressing anyone. Go put on a smogging shirt.*

"You protected us today," he said, "without your help we never would have escaped." It didn't exactly cheer her up, but Vika brooded with slightly less intensity.

"I don't even know how we did escape," Tanya asked. "When Luthor dove on William, the Sabers all just smashed against the wall."

"It was Michael's idea. We both threw our BOGs against opposite walls simultaneously, but saved two to get us to the ceiling hatch."

Michael seemed pleased with himself. "But ducking down behind the couch and whispering would have looked pretty damn suspicious, don't you think? But if I could get them to hit me and knock me down next to her, they wouldn't think twice."

"The Sabers were closer to the walls, so they were trapped there," Vika added. "The rest of us were in the middle of the room so we fell up."

"The gravity on each wall cancelled out in the middle, so we were only affected by our BOGs on the ceiling."

"I appreciate you volunteering to be their punching bag," William said weakly.

Bill chuckled and ruffled William's hair. The man watched over his wounded son as diligently as the most meticulous nurse. Fortunately, the gunshot to his side hadn't been deep enough to graze any organs. On the other hand, his leg wouldn't be long for this world without care. In spite of that, William insisted on staying out of the hospital. Being admitted always required a Mark scan and since Dimarin undoubtedly had access to the whole CPI system, the poor kid knew he would be shot on sight.

William squeezed Bill's hand as he eased his head back on the couch. He might lose a leg, but it looked like he had gained a father.

"Getting hit didn't feel too great, but it worked. I knew we would need at least two of us to be throwing BOGs at the same time for us to have a chance. And I have to thank you for the idea of the gravity bomb," he said to Luthor.

"You used 126 to kill people," Luthor said flatly.

Tanya offered a weak smile, "but it saved all our lives."

"What does it matter?"

"Try to stay positive, maybe a building that got wadded up like a piece of paper will make the news."

"It did," William said pointing, "the news is already on."

Allen Wilcox sat with his hands folded over his notes, somber and sober as ever and continued the broadcast "... bright spots in this city. A new artist-turned-architect has begun trying to revitalize the Midway neighborhood. Using condemned buildings, Aaron Lichtenhaus is creating works of art." The camera panned around the now roughly spherical structure that had been the USNN safe-house hours before. A reporter began to interview the man who supposedly created the 'work of art.'

"Those bastards," Michael breathed. "They even found somebody to act like it was their idea."

"Somebody has to notice the gravity around that thing," Luthor said.

"One phone call from Dimarin will get a hoard of carbon agents to keep people away," Vika said. "The only people that will notice it are the few Markless who saw it happen."

"And who's going to believe a Markless?" Bill said. "Just one more conspiracy theory that everyone but me will discount. I'm telling you, the things that this government has covered up... It would make your skin crawl."

The anchor continued. "... tragic news tonight that hits very close to home for us here in at USNN Chicago. One of our longest tenured producers, Cathy Bernal was found murdered in her home tonight. She was dead before emergency crews arrived. Cathy has been working for USNN since it was founded, nearly 20 years ago."

Images of carps and emergency workers combing through the aftermath of the gruesome crime played across the screen. "We now go to the scene, with Tom Bishop."

A man about William's age held a microphone in slightly wavering hands, apparently shaken by the events. The high-rise where Bernal lived loomed behind him. "This is a terrible tragedy for anyone who has relied on USNN for their news. Early this afternoon, Bernal appeared to be the victim of a robbery gone wrong. The perpetrators broke into her home while she was still there. After a struggle, she wound up dead, but there are two other blood samples recovered by Chicago's finest. After cross-referencing with the CPI database, it should be possible to identify her assailants."

He paused and dabbed his eye with a handkerchief.

"Somebody needs to punch that guy in the balls," Bill said.

"Why?" asked Qwiz.

"So he'd have some real tears to sop up. My son would never fake something so badly for the camera."

"Many expensive items were stolen and her apartment was ransacked. Unexpectedly, 2180 was found tagged on her door. The investigators suggested it is likely a retaliatory strike by terrorist Luthor Tenrel for the USNN exposè on his crimes earlier this week."

Luthor threw up his hands. "I have no words."

"Stalker thought of everything, didn't he?" Qwiz said.

"He managed to murder my boss and get the carps to blame it on 2180." William grabbed his side in pain, "it's all my fault! If I had been more careful, she wouldn't have died."

"It wasn't your fault," Tanya said. "She is the one who made the call, not you."

"But it was *my* story she was getting permission for! If I hadn't told her, she would still be alive. And for that matter, I wouldn't have been shot!"

"I'm sorry," Bill said, a tear leaking down his cheek, "I should have never gotten you involved."

Tanya felt for the strangely loveable old man. He had been trying for years to reunite with his son and right when things were beginning to turn around in their relationship, William's leg did an unwilling impersonation of William Tell's apple. It had been one polluted day.

"Dad, believe it or not, I don't think a whole bunch of Sabers breaking into our safehouse is your fault." Bill patted his son on the arm.

"No, it's my fault," Luthor said.

"Don't say that—" Tanya began, but Luthor cut her off.

"If you want to trace this back to its inception, and assign real blame, then it has to go to me. You see, I didn't die in Antarctica like I was supposed to."

"Damn it, Tenrel. Don't talk nonsense," Bill said.

"Not nonsense. You see, if I had died like smogging General Stutzman intended, I wouldn't have been alive to discover how to make 126. And I sure as hell wouldn't have the motivation to give it away to the world."

"Fault is irrelevant," Vika said, "this is pointless."

"You're right, it is pointless," Luthor said, "all of this,

pointless! I thought that whoever had been chasing us would at least want to *use* our research. They might use it selfishly, but at least if we failed it would still get out there. But Dimarin wants to destroy it. He's going to kill us all and burn every hard-drive to ashes."

"Don't be a fool, Tenrel," Vika snapped. "It's time to fight back, not roll over and die."

"What can we do? You of all people should know how hopeless this is. You were a Saber for carbon's sake! He isn't just going to let us escape. As soon as he finds this apartment he'll just bomb the entire block just to make sure we're dead."

"But Luthor—" Qwiz said.

Luthor shouted, bowling right over the diminutive Asian. "Probably blame that on my ass post mortem as well. I can just see the headlines. 'Luthor Tenrel, the mother fucking terrorist, accidentally blows himself up!'"

"Luthor!"

"Goodbye peace, goodbye hope, goodbye every smogging good thing left in this world because it is all over now. Game over."

"*We* still have the research," Qwiz squeezed in.

"So what? We'll be alive for another day before they find us and kill everyone we've ever known. Maybe you want to jump another train? They'll never expect that!"

Tanya had never seen him so furious. His face was beet-red and he was yelling at the top of his lungs. It frightened her.

Bill stepped uncomfortably close to Luthor. "William's been shot, Vika's busted up too, and the goddamn Sabers are hunting us along with every carp from here to China. I don't see how this situation can get much worse. The last thing we need is for you to go *trying* to make it worse!"

"You don't know the first thing about *worse,*" Luthor said, his voice suddenly cold and quiet.

"I did not have to help you!" he yelled through gritted teeth.

"I thought you were a marine. All you are is a pathetic old has-been."

Bill turned away, visibly shaking with anger.

"Coward."

Tanya couldn't help it. She reached back and slapped Luthor harder than she had ever slapped anyone, hoping it would slap some control back into him. "What's wrong with you?"

Luthor gripped her wrist so hard that her hand started turning white. It hurt. She strained against him, but he didn't budge. "What's wrong with me? You really want to know what's wrong with me?" Luthor shoved her arm away. "Antarctica! That's what's wrong with me! I fought and killed in that frozen cemetery for a country who valued a few liters of crude more than my life. What did any of you do? Were you forced to kill other men and watch them freeze to death before they bled out?"

Vika glared at him. "That doesn't give you the right to —"

"I don't have the right?" Luthor yelled as if he were trying to tear a hole in his larynx. "What gives *you*—any of you—the right to tell *me* anything? Have you had a general tell you to your face that he was going to let your whole unit die because diesel was too expensive? NO!"

"Luthor, please stop…" Tanya pleaded, tears running down her cheeks.

"I can't stop now. *You* always wanted to know what's wrong with me," Luthor's eyes bulged with a manic intensity. Tanya stepped back unconsciously.

Tanya thought she knew him. They had dated for years. He was an adorable, focused scientist with a past that scarred him too deeply to mention. Even when she'd seen the full scope of his ability to kill, he hadn't lost the core of the man she loved. But this tirading, frightening lunatic before her couldn't have been more foreign. It was as if the war itself had indwelt him and was intent on spewing its horrors through Luthor's mouth. Whatever monster he had locked up inside so carefully had finally gotten out.

"Every night when I go to sleep, *every time* I shut my eyes, I see that bastard general condemning us to a slow death by Antarctican winter. You want to know why? He said we weren't worth it. The diesel to rescue us was more valuable than all our injured and freezing men put together.

"This is how your life could get worse. Imagine if you were starving in the middle of the smogging South Pole. Then you had to watch your best friend die only to realize the only way to survive is *to eat him*. That's right. Me, and the fifty-three other survivors of Titan, turned into cannibals. I still see those picked-over skeletons. I see the meat from Chaz's body." Luthor shut his eyes slowly and deliberately as if to make a point. "Every time I shut my eyes."

No one tried interrupting him now.

"Your son is going to lose his leg? Imagine having to chop it off and then eat it! Garcia gave his broken leg to us to eat before it got infected. Why don't you just go chomp on William's calf there, Stone? That might make this all *worse!*

"Vika, you feel bad because you were working for the bad guys? Imagine finding out that your whole goddamn country is the bad guys!

"So don't tell me about worse. Don't tell me it's going to be *alright* after my only chance to prevent that from ever happening again is ripped from my hands by some polluted piece of greedy shit who wants to keep his power. We're going to be dead tomorrow, and all of my suffering—all of *their* suffering— will have been for nothing."

Luthor turned and left the room, shoulders slumped. He looked deflated, like whatever fire had been driving him all the years since the war had just been snuffed out. He was deeply broken, but for the first time, he made sense.

CHAPTER 24:

Eleven Years Ago: Titan Dome Antarctica.

It had been a month. A Month of freezing cold; the command cube providing just enough warmth to keep them alive. He'd lost three toes to frostbite already. The medic had amputated and cauterized them. The worst part was those toes had been added to their daily rations. Men had *eaten* the meager meat on those toes to help stave off starvation another day.

The interminable cold, the omnipresent wind, the isolation without hope of rescue, all of it would have been bearable if not for the insatiable, ravenous hunger that plagued Luthor every second of every day. He could think of nothing else. If only he could fill his belly, then it would all be okay—if only for a minute. It hadn't taken long for them to resort to cannibalism. They hadn't been able to parachute in with much, and the reinforcements that had been captured in the battle of Titan had held the rest of their supplies. They had arrived at Foxtrot with nothing more than a few frost-protected protein bars. Those hadn't lasted long. An amputated limb meant a handful of men could live for another week.

Garcia had been so courageous. He'd voluntarily given his injured leg to the men. He worried it would get infected and they'd have to amputate anyway. They knocked him out with the last of the morphine and removed it. Luthor had eaten it. What else was there to say? It was awful, unforgivable, but Luthor had survived. What Luthor really wished is that both of Garcia's legs had been injured. Then he'd have more food. A good calf muscle was hard to beat. Cooked to medium over the command cube's coils... Maybe he could just cut Garcia's leg off and—

NO! Luthor shook himself back to humanity. He'd been consumed more and more by dark thoughts driven by hunger—manic, insatiable hunger. He tried to push them away, but it was just so hard to do when there was nothing to do all day but sit together and huddle for warmth with other emaciated men equally oppressed by their starving bellies. That and wait for the last team they'd sent out on recon to return.

He hadn't asked about where his food came from; he hadn't wanted to know. He only asked once.

One time.

Chaz.

Chaz had died. No amount of CPR could cajole his heart into rhythm, and no number of volts from the AED could resuscitate the lifeless muscle. Luthor had wished the damn electrodes worked like the paddles did in the hospital TV shows and brought him back to life. But they didn't. That was fiction. Electricity wasn't magic. If a heart had no rhythm, shocking it was useless.

A piece of Chaz stayed with Luthor even after he died. There it was in his pocket. Luthor had been given half his tibia to gnaw on. He'd saved it. He hadn't eaten it. How could he eat his best friend? He'd known Chaz since they were 18 and met at Western.

Luthor shivered. Of all the horrors he expected to encounter in war—killing, death, gore, imprisonment, torture—he'd never imagined he would be so desperate that he would be forced to turn to cannibalism. But here he was, starving and freezing to death, a cooked piece of his friend in his pocket. He knew when he got desperate enough, he would give in and eat it. It had just been so long since he'd eaten. He didn't know how long he could resist.

Chaz's cleaned skeleton stared out of the corner of the shelter with the rest of the picked-over bones. His vacant orbital sockets seemed to call out to Luthor. *Why? Why would you do this to me? I was your friend. How could you eat me?*

When you were freezing and starving in the basement of the world—that's how.

Luthor pulled out the bone with the dried meat and looked at it again. He needed it… He hadn't had so much as a nibble in a week. He would die without it… Chaz wouldn't mind…

Luthor's brain finally disengaged completely and he grabbed the bone out of his pocket and started gnawing on Chaz's calf. He didn't even think about it. He was consumed by his hunger. He *needed* food. There it had been in his pocket for weeks, taunting him. He ripped the flesh with his teeth as fast as he could. He didn't consider the consequences. When you were starving, sometimes the forbidden could be ignored.

Luthor barely noticed the frenzy of activity as starving men began running around. *What was going on?*

Luthor turned to ask Garcia.

"They… they've returned…" Garcia said. He was sick. Luthor had trouble understanding him. His severely sunken cheeks seemed to impede his speech.

"What?"

Garcia just pointed at the door to the ice shelter, he didn't have the energy to vocalize again.

Luthor stood up with a groan. He dropped Chaz's tibia in horror as he realized what he'd just done.

How could you Luthor? Chaz's skeleton said again. *We were brothers. This is how you treat me?*

He went to the door of the ice shelter, trying not to look at those haunted eye sockets.

"We did it!" men we shouting.

"We can escape!" men crowded around and their voices mixed together unintelligibly.

"Finally!"

Luthor looked out into the windswept Antarctican desert and saw that the recon team had captured a massive Chinese troop transport. Equipped with tank treads and a hybrid gas-electric battery, it looked as if it could carry two dozen men.

"We'll hook up the command cube!"

"It'll get us at least 500 miles toward Shackleton base!"

"We can drag skis for anyone that won't fit!"

"Fuck Stutsman!"

"Fuck oil prices! We'll get home anyway!"

Luthor had trouble processing what they were saying. All he could think to do was to wipe his mouth.

#

Aurora, IL, United States of the West

Luthor slumped against the wall of the stairwell to Bill's floor. He had never told anyone about that event—no one but the worthless VA therapist who had prodded him like a lab rat. *What will happen to the hopeless soldier if I poke him here?* Now he had shouted his most desperate secret at the top of his lungs in front of six people.

He was a cannibal.

He felt naked, like his tri-fold science fair experiment in fourth grade, exposed for anyone to scrutinize and grade. He wouldn't be awarded any blue ribbon for this. He shut his eyes, but the sight of Chaz's half eaten calf forced them open again.

He had eaten his best friend.

At least he would be dead soon. It's what he deserved. He half expected to feel the heat of a missile irradiating him in a high explosive baptism. Perhaps it would be painless, like Doyle in Alaska. Then he wouldn't need to worry about the fate of the world, he would be dead after all. That was it.

He wouldn't be looking down from any cloud city of gold or up from a dungeon of fire and torture. The only bright light he would see would be the ignition system of a warhead.

Strangely, despite the fact that he knew his life was over, he felt lighter somehow. Like a literal weight had been lifted from his shoulders. He might be naked for all to see, but at least he didn't have to carry such heavy clothes on his back any longer.

He was just thankful that whatever part of him was still good had kept him from hitting Tanya. No man should ever hit a woman. Tanya would leave him. That was a scientific certitude. Her Christian tendencies made it inevitable. He was quite certain that the Bible forbade cannibalism at least 400 times.

It didn't matter that he had stayed alive and had helped the recon team who captured that Chinese transport get them all back to Shackleton base. He had *eaten* his best friend.

There could be no forgiveness for that.

At least Tanya finally knows why I am broken. She deserves that much.

Then there was Bill. The man selflessly had risked his life, watched his only son maimed, and Luthor had called him a coward. *Why did I do that*? Even in the moment, Luthor knew it had been horribly wrong, disgusting and cruel. PTSD had the power to make compulsions overwhelming, irresistible. But the worst part was that the calculating, science-side of his brain still functioned. It quietly took notes on the outburst and passed judgment, while simultaneously being impotent to affect his behavior. Luthor hated himself for it, he hated that he couldn't control his temper, even though he never lost his rationality in the process. What did Aristotle say, "to know the good is to do the good"? Aristotle didn't have PTSD.

The door to the stairwell opened. It was Bill.

Luthor noted that his heart increased its pace. Bill

might have thirty years on him, but he was not a man Luthor ever wanted to meet in a death match. Luthor waited for him to pull a gun and end his misery early, but he just stood there. Watching, reasoning. If he'd had a pad of paper, he might have made a good observational scientist.

"Are you going to kill me or what?" Luthor said impatiently. "Now everyone knows I deserve it." He would be dead soon, he might as well die to a good man with a just cause, rather than a bureaucrat with a hard-on for power.

Bill scrutinized some more.

Luthor wished he would just make up his mind and do whatever he planned to do.

"You *are* broken."

What the hell does that mean? Luthor thought.

"I'm such a dumbass. Should've noticed it right away," Bill didn't sound angry. A good sign. Luthor knew he should apologize. But his anger hadn't yet abated enough.

Bill continued in his smoke-stained voice. "You know, I really oughtta rip your balls outta your sac and make you eat them."

Luthor nodded. That would be a fair punishment for a cannibal. "But the truth is, I've been there too," he continued.

"I don't really think—"

"Shut up, Luthor. You got yourself calmed down now, don't go smogging up your chance to make it right."

Luthor shut up.

"I'm telling you that *I've been broken too*. Diagnosing PTSD wasn't as common during Iraq and Afghanistan as it is now, but we all had it. Only a few in a hundred can go through real combat and not come out as polluted as the other side of my ass."

"And they're often the ones who weren't right in the first place," Luthor said, remembering his own learning on the subject. A high percentage of people who came out of war without any measurable PTSD were hypothesized to be psychopaths—in the sense that they didn't have normal emotions. "The ones who could have just as easily been serial killers if they hadn't been in the military."

"Bingo. Only you aren't a serial killer."

"That's debatable."

"You're just an asshole."

Maybe this wasn't going as well as he'd hoped. He liked it better when Bill was describing how Luthor should take communion with his own testicles, rather than outright insulting him. Punishments implied restitution was possible. Insults? They implied something worse.

Bill let his comment sink in before he continued. "But an asshole is someone I can relate with. I came back an asshole too, you know. I drank myself stupid for years. Gambled away my family's money. Shouted at anyone whose shoes I didn't like, punched anyone who rooted for the wrong team. I can relate, Tenrel. Hearing yourself curse out your own kid, throwing things, all the while knowing its wrong but you just can't stop yourself."

"How did you deal with it?" Luthor asked, surprised at Bill's level of empathy for his condition; Luthor didn't think anyone else besides Garcia understood. Not only that, he certainly looked pretty collected and in control—apart from the conspiracy theories. He didn't seem to struggle to contain the bad memories from leaking out.

"I didn't want to beat my kid and my wife, I was afraid I might kill them. So I left. I was too afraid of reliving Iraq with my own family."

Luthor had often found himself making the same choice with Tanya. So many nights in the lab... Sometimes being alone was the only good choice he had the power to make.

"I drank myself homeless, took a long time to get straight again. By then my wife was dead, and my kid hated me. I had just never been able to get over what I had done in Iraq."

"What did you do?" Luthor found himself asking. It was easier to ask now that Bill knew Luthor's own past.

"It's not just one thing. You know how it is. Every time you make somebody die, a little part of you dies too. But sometimes it's a bigger part than others. The one that pushed me over the edge was when we were chasing these terrorists through the city; they had just blown up a medical supply truck, killed eight civilians, and destroyed life-saving antibiotics bound for an orphanage. Real sons of bitches, you know? The cowards were dressed up in women's Burqas and blended in with the civis. I followed one of those goddamned jihadists and when I got a clear shot, I took it. Put a three-round burst in his back.

"Only it wasn't a terrorist. It actually *was* a civilian. A woman holding her baby. The bullets penetrated enough to kill the kid too. I shot an innocent mother and murdered an infant. That ain't so good for your sanity. Every time I saw my wife or my son, I saw that poor woman and her baby... Every time."

Luthor felt another pang of guilt for Bill. He might not have endured the horrors of Antarctica, but he had nightmares of his own. Bad ones. Luthor had never killed a kid, just lots of oil-hungry Chinese. He wasn't sure if he would have been able to be functional after a mistake like that either.

"From what Quency has said, and from what I've seen of you in person, I know you aren't that man I saw in there. The man in there was born in Anti; he don't have to be you."

"But he *is* me. We are the same. I am the one who lived that life."

"Son," Bill said seriously, "you aren't. The problem you have right now is that you are just sharing the same body."

Bill's gruff metaphor made a kind of simple sense to

Luthor. He really had been there too; he understood. And he had successfully moved beyond it. "So how do I get rid of him? How did you do it? Or is that even possible?"

"The problem is you're both in the same place. If you want to be free of him, you have to let him out."

"No, I can't do that! I've spent the last ten years working to lock that part of me away. It's dangerous when he gets loose—you saw what I'm like. I try not to let him take over. Tanya deserves better than a broken, bitter, abusive man."

"Listen to me; you have to let him go."

"You just witnessed what happens when I lose control! I have to be stronger, so I don't call honorable men cowards and curse at the people who saved my life." Luthor hung his head, the full weight of his shame palpable on his shoulders.

"Then why, after the son of a bitch is out, would you let him back in? He's out right now Tenrel! Don't welcome his ass back into his cage. I don't care if you have a maximum-security prison in there, he *will* get out again. Trust me. I tried that. I lost my wife and my son trying to control it. But you can't control it. You have to get rid of it."

"I would do anything not to lose Tanya. I love her."

"Luthor, the only way to keep her is to stay sane. Shove all those memories out every time they come in. Tell her your story Luthor—the whole damn thing—and anyone else who will listen. Be honest about having shit for temper control and goddamn PTSD. Just keep pushing *that guy* out so he can never make a mess again."

"Why are you trying to help me?" Luthor asked quietly. "I insulted you— and your honor—after you helped me. Nobody in their right mind would do that after what happened to William."

"I think you just answered your own question. I *ain't in my right mind.* If I hadn't been like you 30 years ago, I wouldn't have to regret never knowing my own son, and not being there told hold my wife as she died. Maybe if I help you, this won't hurt so damn much."

Luthor closed his eyes and hung his head again. He couldn't have been more wrong about the kindhearted, veteran before him. The guy deserved the Medal of Valor, not a bastard who tore him down. "I'm sorry Stone. You are anything but a coward."

Bill nodded, accepting the apology. "So, what are you going to do now, Tenrel?" he said, reminding Luthor of a football coach. "You just spilled your guts all over the room. Your secret's out. That asshole from Anti is out. Are you going to let him back in just to take over your life again, or do you have the courage to tell your story and keep that fucker out for good?"

Luthor felt his heart surge. He wanted to try again. He wanted a fresh start at life. Maybe Bill's idea would work. Maybe Luthor had tried the wrong strategy all along. Only... there wasn't any time left.

"What difference does it make at this point? I am going to be dead soon, along with the love of my life. Why bother starting over?"

Tanya suddenly appeared around the corner, she had a tear in her eye. "Because I want you to. I don't care if we only have one day left. I want you to try."

"How long have you been listening?"

"The whole time. Bill told me to come along. He said I would hear what sort of man you are."

Emotions bubbled up Luthor hadn't experienced properly in years. His atrophied tear ducts struggled to express his feelings with mere saline. Tanya stepped forward, cupped his face in her hands, and kissed him gently on the forehead.

"Why would you want to be with me? You're going to die because of me, and now you know what I really am. It doesn't make sense."

"You're the one who likes to say that women don't

make sense," she said with a twinkle in her eye that was deeper than the tears. "I still love you Luthor, Antarctica and all. I don't care how horrible you think you are. I want to be with you. For however long we have left."

The tears broke and Luthor began sobbing. He heaved and cried, and Tanya knelt next to and held him. It was as if the giant dam of locks and cages that stored all the times he had been unable to cry had suddenly collapsed. Years of pain and regret, joy and sadness, all roared forth at once in a deluge of emotion.

Long minutes passed where no one said anything, no one dared. Finally, as the reservoir slowly drained, Luthor managed to collect himself. Everyone else stood around, no one looking with judgment, some even smiled at him. None of it made much sense.

Answering his unasked question, Tanya spoke, "Bill and Vika explained it to us. We know that wasn't really you back there."

Luthor shook his head. "Thank you so much, but please, go. They are going to come kill us. Dimarin is going to hunt us down and kill everyone who even knows my name."

Bill raised a very Vika-like eyebrow. "You giving up now, Tenrel?"

"Doesn't seem like I have much choice, we've already lost. Dimarin controls the media, he has worldwide carbon enforcement resources, and has access to the CPI databases. We can't get our message out. And anyone we tell about 126 we will just be sentencing to death."

"I am not sure you heard me earlier," Qwiz said without a hint of resentment. "*We* still have the research. And we still have a bit of your element left too."

"I still don't see how that can help us. You of all people should know that. You saw what they did to my entire apartment just to cover their tracks. Dimarin will bomb whatever he has to, to ensure he's destroyed us and the research. We will be dead tomorrow."

"Then we act tonight," Vika said.

Michael grinned again. "If we are going to share this with the world, we've got about twelve hours."

"It's impossible," Luthor said bitterly.

"My old brain's got a few more cobwebs than it used to," Bill began, "but I seem to recall Quency over here already having an impossible plan."

"You mean we are going to steal the nuclear missile?" Vika asked hopefully.

"I was thinking more along the lines of hacking the USNN broadcast," Bill said. "But maybe next time we can steal a nuke." Vika looked like she just found out that she wasn't really going to receive a rifle for her birthday.

"You're insane," Luthor said.

"I believe we have already established that." said Bill, "but then we've had a chance to see that you're a few farts short of a turd yourself."

Luthor shook his head vigorously. They didn't understand the danger. "You should be running. Not signing up for a suicide mission."

"What else have I got to live for?' Bill said simply. "Might as well bust some commie skulls as I go."

Qwiz gave a sidelong glance to the old man, tactfully ignoring that they were, in fact, in the USW and not, in fact, communist. "And you won't be able crack into the USNN uplink on the roof without me.

Luthor couldn't believe what he was hearing. "Qwiz, don't be a fool. Dimarin doesn't know your name yet. You can still escape. Why would you risk your life for a bunch of condemned fugitives? You have so much to lose."

"My father always told me 'courage isn't defined by what you do, but by what you are willing to lose.' If I were going to die anyway, helping you would be logical, but now I have the opportunity to do something truly honorable."

Qwiz and his honor; it would be the death of him.

Luthor turned to Vika and Michael. Michael was several standard deviations closer to her than she would have allowed an average person—Vika had an exceptionally large personal space bubble. He nodded to Luthor, "what the hell. Like Qwiz said, what have I got to lose? We're going to be dead tomorrow either way, right? He can't let the ones who actually worked with the research live."

Luthor turned to Vika, "I'm sorry for what I said to you too. We would all be dead many times over if it weren't for you."

"I am bad with words too, Tenrel," Vika actually smiled, at least what passed for a smile from her "so forget the apologies. Let us kick Dimarin's ass." Michael nodded approvingly.

Bill rubbed his hands together cheerfully. "Looks like everyone's in. Let's get cracking."

Luthor blinked. He must be dreaming. No. He couldn't be dreaming: no one had died, there was no blood, no cold, explosions, or cannibalism. This was real. He smiled, shaking his head.

"Thank you. All of you. I... I don't deserve this kind of friendship."

"Knock it off, Tenrel," Bill said. "We're with you."

"We all hate how messed up this world is," said Qwiz. "This plan is our best chance to fix it."

Luthor smiled. It felt strange.

"Getting to the rooftop is easy, we have enough 126 to send someone up there," Luthor said, "but how are we going to get a team inside to steal the transmission codes?"

"That's even easier," stated Stone. "My job as janitor. I have a keycard and my Mark is on file. After what Stalker's put him through, William might be willing to lend us his knowledge of the building too."

Luthor couldn't help himself; he actually believed

that their crazy plan might just work.

CHAPTER 25:

Outside the USNN Tower, Chicago, United States of the West

"If I have to sneak into another secured area with a Mark scanner, I am going to cut somebody's balls off," said Vika tugging at her janitorial overalls.

"Unfortunately, mine are already spoken for," said Luthor, nodding at Bill. "But I believe Michael's are ripe."

"So they are," Vika said turning to a green dumpster and giving it a kick. Muffled cursing came from the receptacle.

Tanya climbed into another green garbage can. "At least you don't have to be stuffed in this damn thing."

"At least you have an identity."

"Touché."

"All of you, shut your pie-holes, "said Bill. "This ain't gonna work at all if somebody hears you. Don't forget your Seebees either."

Luthor shut the lid of his own dumpster and said nothing more. The absence of light highlighted the stench accumulated from years of waste removal. Luthor covered his nose with the scanner-jamming glove. It effectively protected him from the inevitable scanners at every entrance to the government building, but was somewhat less effective at protecting him from the smell.

Two swift knocks on the lid were the only prelude to Bill rolling the dumpster forward. Vika rolled Tanya in; Michael had to wait. Thanks to Ostafal, Vika was now impervious to the CPI security protocols; she also had no identity nor could legally own anything. Ever. A rough tradeoff. A mechanical beep followed by a series of clicks indicated that Bill had unlocked the steel security door using his keycard and CPI chip. A slight bump on the threshold indicated he had passed through the overhead scanners and made it inside.

The plan was relatively simple. Disguised as janitors they had to infiltrate the building, find the security codes, and send them to Qwiz. Qwiz, who had left earlier and hopefully was already close to the roof, had to tap into the hard line feeding the primary USNN satellite dish. Once they sent him the codes, he could transmit an interview they had recorded earlier with William's help, thereby transmitting a special report to the world. *Right, simple. Simple as quantum mechanics.*

The only flaw in their hastily devised scheme lay in actually finding the codes. William told them they would be somewhere between the 60th and 65th floors. These floors were where the executives and producers worked.

After about fifteen minutes, Bill and Vika had rolled each of them into Bill's janitor closet. Luthor gratefully climbed out of the olfactory torture device. He too wore janitorial overalls.

"I bet William my truck that the codes are going to be somewhere on the 63rd floor," Bill put a few spray bottles of disinfectant on a cart and started to wheel it out the door. Luthor stopped him, "so you're certain they'll be there?"

"Nope," Bill said brightly, "I just wouldn't mind losing that smogging pile-of-crap truck. But it'll be somewhere close. I mostly clean on the lower levels, but I know you need a special access card on a different elevator to even get to the 60th through the 65th floor. If they have anything worth hiding, they'd put it where I couldn't find it."

"Smart of them," said Vika.

"All I know is they don't take much liking to anyone

poking around on the 59th, if you know what I'm saying."

"But that's where the maintenance hatch is?" Tanya asked.

A building bristling with that much communication equipment needed a way to repair it. Bill had informed them of hatches throughout the building leading to the outside for just such a purpose. If they could find the hatch on the 59th, they could use it to exit the building and then climb the exterior to the 60th through 65th floors using 126.

"Like I said, I ain't seen it. But if my boy says it's there, then I'd believe him."

Luthor put an arm around the old man and patted his shoulder. "Thank you for coming. We couldn't do this without you."

#

What have I gotten myself into? Qwiz thought as he looked down, or rather sideways. He knew it was down, but it felt very different. To him the vertical face of the skyscraper was down. He was about 40 stories up, and the contrast had become highly disconcerting. It scared him that he didn't feel afraid. Heights were supposed to give butterflies to all but the most fearless of men. He knew for a fact that he wasn't fearless. But for all the world it felt like he was crawling unbearably slowly on flat ground.

He placed another wad of their element above his head and felt gravity subtly shift in that direction. *This is going to take some getting used to. Oh well, I have another 50 floors of crawling to figure it out.* He crawled forward half a meter and the repeated the painstaking process.

He felt naked up on the side of the building. Who knew who would randomly look up from the street and see a small Asian man scaling the massive edifice? He pushed it out of his mind; now was not the time for second-guessing, it was the time for courage. Cognitively, he knew he was all but invisible on the side of the structure, it was just hard to remember that this high up. He wore all black and was fully obscured by the jungle-like lattice of communication equipment girding the outside of the building.

The building was the main hub for all the communications in the entire Chicago area, and therefore needed an absurd quantity of cell towers, satellite dishes, and communication arrays. It looked like a man-made millipede with all its protrusions. Qwiz desperately wanted to see the cabling connecting into the subbasement. It boggled his mind the amount of bandwidth the building would require. Millions of people's internet usage, all eventually funneled through this place. Qwiz could almost feel the electromagnetic buzz in his skull with all that information shooting around. He couldn't wait to get his claws on that rooftop satellite array.

This is so boring, Qwiz thought, *I'm never going to get there.* He sidestepped, or rather side-crawled, a cell array mounted directly in his path. He passed quietly over a dark window and heard a thump from the inside of the glass.

Qwiz froze. He hardly dared breathe, someone had caught him. It had only been a matter of time, he just hadn't expected it this soon. *Curse my ineptitude, I have ruined everything. I am sorry Luthor, I hope you can forgive me from whatever dark dungeon they'll send you to.*

Then he saw what had made the noise. A lowly stapler, firmly stuck against the inside pane of the window. By placing the 126, he had changed the gravity *inside* the office as well. The stapler obediently fell toward the new orientation of gravity defined for it by Qwiz.

He rolled over on his back and took a deep breath. *Crisis averted.* A poke jabbing him in the back reminded him of the gun Vika had made him stuff back there. Hopefully, he would never be put in a situation to use it. Realizing he couldn't sit on the outside of the building forever, he shuffled forward, up and away from the window. He had to find a way to go faster, or he wouldn't be ready when the others recovered the transmission codes.

#

Tanya sighed. The 59th floor had quickly become a depressing place. It contained nothing more than a bunch of cubicles with computer terminals. Even at this time of night, hundreds of men and women sat and mechanically clicked through other people's emails and listened to recorded conversations all in the name of national security. Tanya had known that the government still monitored and censored communications, but she honestly had not ever imagined it would be on this scale. It had been ten years since the war had ended, when would they terminate this stupid practice? There hadn't been much national tension with China in years—not that there had exactly been much communication either. Still, seeing the entire floor dedicated to nothing but censorship helped her understand the scale of their monitoring. And each floor of the 90-story building had equally large numbers of people doing the same thing. Their sole purpose was to double-check anything flagged by their AI algorithms. And there were *dozens* of other buildings in the area filled with the sensors who screened less-critical data. *Excessive* would be putting it mildly.

Tanya pushed her cleaning cart around awkwardly, trying not to look too suspicious as she searched for the maintenance hatch. Bill's old grey Carhartts didn't fit her well. A balding, heavily bespectacled man turned from his typing to stare awkwardly at her. The lenses were so thick his eyes appeared many times their normal size. She smiled politely back. He quickly turned away upon being noticed. She just hoped that he had been admiring her and not the fact that she obviously wasn't supposed to be there.

She turned her cart around the corner and noticed a slightly different-looking cubicle near the corner. Instead of a walk-in opening, a locked door completely sealed the contents of the inside. The door read *Caution, Maintenance Only.*

I wonder if lock-picking is in Vika's repertoire? Tanya wondered

#

Qwiz's muscles ached. He hadn't thought about the consequences of climbing using gravity before. You couldn't just stick to the wall with a small manipulation of gravity; you needed a significant change in gravity. Qwiz felt like he weighed twice as much as he normally did and even crawling had become exhausting. He estimated he was near the 70th floor. He rolled over and rested again. No wonder Tanya told me to leave early. This is hard work. He wished he could have used the elevators with the others, but it was just too risky to get through the detectors with all his equipment, they might have metal detectors embedded in the security.

But heroes didn't give up when they got tired. They didn't give up when they got scared. Heroes acted in the moment, doing the right thing no matter the cost or difficulty. Qwiz knew he was no hero, but it was what he had always striven to be. *Live a life of courage and honor,* his father had told him. But there wasn't a lot of honor to be gained in fixing computers. And as exciting and fun as gaming was, it didn't take a lot of courage to complete a digital quest or stand firm in the face of insurmountable 0's and 1's. But climbing the USNN Tower, striving to give the world a source of energy that could eliminate scarcity... that was different. For the first time in his life, Qwiz felt like what he was doing something that might make a real difference, might be worthy of honor. Qwiz had finally found the task that was worth risking his life over.

If only I could go faster. Maybe he could walk. It was

worth a try at least. He felt as securely planted on the wall as he could be, walking could rest his arms and chunk the distance. Carefully, he rose to his feet. He could feel the regular Earth gravity pulling him toward the street, but the 126 overwhelmed it. The combination of the two gave him the sensation of walking steeply uphill, nothing he couldn't handle. He rose to his full height, standing perpendicular to the wall.

His head became dizzy. Standing up straight, he couldn't tell which direction was down. He took an experimental step, placing another BOG in front of him. Gravity shifted as the BOG moved. So did his insides. Qwiz realized the problem immediately. The well of altered gravity was too small for standing, his feet were pulled toward the wall but his skull wanted to fall to the street. The distortion curdled his stomach.

He quickly threw himself back down to the safety of his hands and knees. Instantly his queasiness subsided. But the jolt of crashing back against the wall combined with the shifting gravity field jostled his pack. In the scrum, the pistol popped loose from his pants. Artificial gravity pulled it down against the wall. Qwiz frantically reached for it, but it skittered away from his hand, just out of reach. As it slid away from the gravity dimple, the pull of the earth began to compete with Qwiz's 126 for dominance.

Qwiz watched in horror, as the gun floated slowly away from the wall, almost perfectly suspended between the two gravity wells. It hung in the air twisting slowly, appearing frozen. He grabbed for it again, but a sudden gust of wind pushed it the rest of the way into the influence of Earth's gravity. It slowly accelerated out of Qwiz's reach until it began hurtling toward the ground according to Newton's laws.

It smashed the pavement several seconds later. Qwiz winced as people around it scanned the skyline, looking for storm clouds that rained Glocks. They probably wouldn't have seen anything, but even the stupidest suburban refugee would know that illegal guns just didn't drop from the sky. Hopefully, none of them would call the carbon police… now he really had to hurry.

#

Luthor closed his eyes against a blast of wind that blew through the maintenance hatch opening. *I am actually going to climb out of this hole,* Luthor thought—*sane and in my right mind?* He steeled his reserve. He had been here before; he had beaten this before. He *would* do it again. *At least there's no jumping required this time,* he reminded himself. He still felt the fear that haunted him for a decade trying to shut down his muscles and paralyze his mind, but now he felt the power within himself to choose to ignore it. The stomach churning remained, the dizziness remained, yet Luthor simply chose to not to be bound by the whims of his fear any longer.

Straining against his every instinct, Luthor reached outside and stuck a BOG firmly against the wall above the hole. Gravity shifted, adding to the terror-inducing sensation that he was about to fall. He added another below the hole, making sure if anyone slipped, they would be firmly anchored. Luthor reached out with a tentative leg; a shiver shot up it like a bolt of electricity. Luthor set his face firmly. *No. Not this time.* He stepped outside.

The sensation was extremely odd, it was more like climbing out through a hole in the ceiling than anything else. His hands naturally stuck against the wall. Bracing either side of the opening he pushed the rest of his body up and out. He breathed deep, pressing his face against the reinforced concrete. Luthor didn't dare look around and stayed strictly prone. *No need to mess with a good thing, right?*

"Remember you are not sideways on the wall," Vika said, turning to Bill as she joined Luthor outside, "we just changed gravity. The wall is now down." She leapt out and clung to the wall like a panther. Tanya followed, looking more housecat than predator, but no less graceful.

Bill's furry face popped out of the opening like a whack-a-mole. "Starting to wish I was old enough to need diapers because I'm about to piss myself. You people *are* crazy. Are you sure I'm going to stick?"

"The gravity seems to be a property of the element itself," Michael said, from the shaft. "So quantum-ly speaking, there is a nonzero chance that the 126 will fail."

"You're saying I could fall?"

"Yes."

"He's also saying you could randomly burst into flames or teleport across the room," Luthor added.

"Technically, yes. There are also nonzero chances of those things occurring."

"Michael?" Luthor said.

"Yes?"

"Shut up."

"Okay."

Tanya offered him a hand. "Stone, I promise, you aren't going to fall."

Bill took it with minimal hesitation and joined them. He looked around wonderingly. "This is amazing, it really is down!"

"Your inner ear can't distinguish between regular and artificial gravity," Luthor said. "Whichever pulls harder is what you think of as the ground."

When Michael had joined them, they started the arduous climb up to the next floor. It didn't take long before Luthor began to feel sorry for Qwiz; he had to climb the whole thing.

"Wait," Michael said, "what if the other maintenance hatch is locked? What are we going to do then?"

"Blast a hole in a window and break in the hard way,"

Vika produced her handgun, almost caressing it, like she *needed* to shoot it.

"Why don't we hold off shooting until we get there?" Tanya suggested. "Alarms won't give us *or* Qwiz much time."

The hatch itself was a steel door about half the size of a standard door. The passage had been designed to fit seamlessly in the space between the acoustical ceiling grid of floor below and the carpet of the floor above. The handle reminded Luthor of the latch that had secured the doors to the airplanes. He shivered, thankful he was only 60 stories up, and not 16,000 meters.

Standing perpendicular to the wall, Vika grasped it with both hands. Luthor held his breath. The handle turned 90 degrees and the door swung open. In moments they were inside.

Bill's phone beeped. It was Qwiz.

#

Qwiz peered over the top ledge. Three men stood on the roof. One hung from straps on a giant antenna while the other two stood around not doing much of anything. Qwiz figured that the minimum number of supervisors per worker on any government project was two, leading to their current ratio. With only one guy working, odds were bad that they would complete the repair any time soon. Making matters worse, the two that weren't climbing both had side arms.

Why two guards were on the roof assisting a mechanic, Qwiz could not ascertain. Regardless, Qwiz had the unfortunate predicament of trying to hack into the very equipment that the guards leaned on. And now he had no gun—not that he had proven particularly proficient at its use in the past. He had no reason to suspect his aim from altered gravity would be superior to his aim from a moving truck. Nor did any of the three men seem like they had done anything worthy of a death sentence, therefore a gun was the wrong tool anyway.

Qwiz rummaged through his bag of equipment to find his phone. He found it, but realized he didn't have his voice modulator, there would be no way to disguise his identity from the sensors. He couldn't exactly say, "please help me, I'm planning to hack past the USNN firewall, but there are guards in the way". Stalker would be using all his resources to track them down and eliminate them, which meant he would have access to phone conversations.

After crawling down two levels so his voice wouldn't carry, he called Bill. He took a deep breath and hit speed dial 1.

Bill picked up on the first ring. "You all set?"

"No. I am having trouble on *the last level, right before the boss*." Bill would understand, but the censors would think he was talking about a video game.

"Oh right," he said, "So ah, what seems to be the problem?"

"I don't know how to sneak into the base. I am out of *mana* and the orcs took my *sword*. And there are guards at the top."

"Shit," Bill said. Qwiz heard intense, muffled conversation behind the earpiece.

"No ... ah *Sword?* How in the name of Jesus H. Christ did you lose that?"

"I was *climbing those cliffs*. An orc used a spell, it made me drop it."

More muffled conversation, all Qwiz could make out was an occasional curse word that slipped through the receiver.

"I will *log in* and come to help you."

"What about the others?"

"Don't worry about them, none of this will work if you

can't *beat the level.*"

The call terminated from Bill's end. Qwiz laid on his back, waiting. Hopefully Bill would have a better clue to get rid of them than he did.

#

"We should send someone else. You know this building better than us," Luthor said.

"I've never been on this floor either. Not sure why my eyes can search better than yours," Bill replied.

Michael nodded, now that the old man had gotten them in the front door, he'd become much more decorative.

"I can't just leave the boy," Bill continued, furrowing his brows with worry, "with William thinking… what he thinks of me, Qwency has been as true of a son as I ever had. I can't leave him up there alone. This has to be me."

Michael gave him his best manly clap on the back. "Good luck, Stone."

"I know how to climb with this stuff now, I don't need no luck." In a moment he was back outside, using half of their remaining eight BOGs to meet Qwiz.

Unfortunately, that left them to finish the far more tenuous task of finding the mythical transmission codes. William said they would be in an office of someone called the *Transmission Security Director,* but didn't have a damn clue where that office could be found.

"Should we go door to door threatening important looking people?" Michael offered. "If somebody waved a gun at me, I'd point them in the right direction."

"No, you wouldn't," Vika said, "you'd just soil yourself."

"Trust me, I would." Michael replied, not backing down. Usually, she could intimidate him, but she didn't understand what it had been like to watch them shoot Eli.

Not because he hadn't told the truth, but just because he hadn't told it fast enough. "I really don't like it when my friends die on my account."

"Let's hope no one dies," Tanya said.

"Spread out and look for that office, and meet back here in 15 minutes," said Luthor.

Michael found nothing. In fact, the 60th, 61st, and 62nd floors hadn't looked an atom different than any of the other floors in the polluted building—though the average beauty of his company had increased markedly once Vika had replaced Bill. Bored looking censors stuffed into matte grey cubicles filled every crevice of the open area. Their night was filled with the same monotony as the décor, reading other people's emails, texts, and transcripts of phone calls. The edges of each floor were pock-marked with real offices made with actual walls and stuffed with slightly more well-paid censors.

The whole damn thing felt like a waste of time.

A text message popped up on the cell phone he'd "borrowed" from Ostafal. It was from Luthor, "better look like you're working. Guard incoming."

"Should we clean or something?" Michael asked Vika.

"The bathroom would be the safest location."

"I was afraid you'd say that."

Minutes later Michael wiped a rag across the bathroom mirror. It took a few extra to get all the streaks off. "This is the single most boring heist ever," he said.

"Are you actually trying to give us away?" Vika responded, looking up from a urinal.

"It's just that this should be more… exciting."

"Do you really want someone to shoot at you?"

"No. But I am not cleaning the toilets. I refuse to clean up a rich man's shit."

"Why not?"

"I spent too many years on the street looking up

at those high-rise smoggers with their suits and thousand credit shoes. During the Culling things got so bad I had to roam the sewers, wading through their excrement to hunt rats. Their crap literally covered me for years of my life. You see, only the rich had enough money to afford a sewer bill. I didn't get all the shit cleaned off until I got drafted. I'm not voluntarily going to get back in it.

Michael paused and then added, "I wouldn't ask you to flirt with a Saber. Don't make me do this."

Vika nodded. She finished her urinal and went into the first stall. She closed the door to have enough room to work. Michael squirted a blue cleaner onto another gold embossed mirror. *Damn these smoggers and their expensive bathrooms.* The bathroom was beautiful by anyone's standard. Pristine, black marble countertops flowed seamlessly into sinks, girded with polished gold faucets. They even had automatic soap and paper towel dispensers. *Is anyone so lazy that they can't be bothered to press a button to get soap? What a waste of electricity.* It was lavish, and it made him sick.

Vika flushed the toilet and moved to the next stall. "They are not even dirty." "I

"I don't care," Michael said stubbornly. "Their shit stinks." She didn't understand. The Culling had permanently etched things into his brain. One of those things was the smell of rich poo.

Just then the bathroom door opened. A gigantic man in dark blue security fatigues strode in. He was nearly a head taller than Michael and easily twice as wide. The man bent the laws of physics to fit his massive arms into his rolled-up sleeves. A pistol hung in a holster on one side of his waist, a walkie-talkie and a mag-light on the other. Michael dropped his rag in spite of himself.

"I don't remember seeing you before," said the man in a voice befitting his size.

"Oh, that would make sense," Michael said, trying to

sound both genuine and smooth, but unsure if he'd managed either. "I just started."

The man narrowed his eyes. "Is that a fact? When did you start? I am here every night, and I haven't seen you cleaning."

Michael felt like the guard was staring into his soul. He wanted to run. Unfortunately, the imposing man filled almost the entire doorway. He would have to ask the man to move just to squeeze around him.

Michael forced himself to smile. "I started on Tuesday, but they have been training me during the day. This is my first night shift."

It had felt like a believable lie, but the man continued to press. "Who trained you?"

Michael could feel sweat beading on his forehead. "Oh, different people, I honestly don't remember, I'm not very good with names."

"Is that a fact?"

"Yes sir." Michael gulped, but stuck out his hand. "Uh, what's your name? I'm Michael."

The man took his hand and shook it. "Well Michael, it just so happens that *I am* good with names." He didn't release Michael's hand. "I also happen to be the head of security of these floors. I interview *every* new custodian who works here and am responsible for conducting their background check. I know a lot about anyone before they scrub their first toilet."

He backed Michael against the countertop and squeezed his hand painfully. "And *I* have never seen you before."

Michael was bent so far backward his head bumped against the mirror. "I am going to need to get a CPI scan from you, *Michael*; and then," he smiled, "then you are under arrest."

Michael began to panic, stammering his protest.

"Honestly, it isn't what you think, I swear I—"

"Move a muscle and you die."

The man's eyes widened as Vika jammed her suppressed pistol to his occipital lobe. Unfortunately, he quickly regained control of his emotions. He didn't even look afraid. Vika used the mirror to gesture for him to slowly back away.

He did just as she asked. Then a step away from the mirror he jerked violently, whipping his hand around to bat the gun away. He fell in a bloodied heap before he came close to disarming her.

Vika's Glock smoked. Wisps of smoke curled from it like a lit cigarette.

"What about moving a muscle didn't you understand?" she said to the corpse.

Michael breathed heavily. "Where the hell did you find a silencer?"

"I kept the one from Ostafal. I thought it might come in handy."

Vika patted him kindly with the weapon. It felt very strange to be comforted by the muzzle of a gun that had just killed someone. "How many times is it that I have saved your life now?" she asked nonchalantly.

"Only five."

"You aren't counting the USNN safehouse."

"That was a team effort."

"Five and half then."

"Fine," Michael said grudgingly. "Thanks."

Vika smiled. Michael wished she would do it more often. Her beautiful white teeth bloomed before his eyes like a time-lapsed flower. "You're welcome," she said.

Michael smiled back reflexively. It was frighteningly easy to ignore the dead giant on the floor with Vika staring at him. "You do realize this is all totally backwards. It's the guy who is supposed to be saving the beautiful girl."

She smiled even more broadly, a twinkling appeared in her eyes. "Get used to it. There's probably a lot of things backward about *us*."

"Us?" Michael stammered.

"Us," Vika said, leaning in. "Thank you for being pathetic."

"What is that supposed to mean—"

Vika cut him off. She pressed her body firmly against his and kissed him.

Michael felt his eyes roll back in his head as her lips enveloped his. It was as if everything else in the world had disappeared. All he could think of was the feel of her arms around his back, her succulent lips caressing his, her hair lightly brushing his face. Firecrackers exploded in every single one of his nerve centers. He had imagined kissing her since the moment they met, but the feeling surpassed his wildest dreams. He didn't ever remember a kiss that consumed him so completely. All other kisses in his life had been a means to an end—and he knew that going for *that* with Vika would be a death sentence. This kiss was an end in itself—the best end he'd ever experienced.

She pulled away, his bottom lip still gently in her teeth. "Help me with this body."

Michael couldn't think straight, he simply grabbed an arm and pulled. The guy had to weigh 150 kilograms. They struggled, but managed to drag him to the far back stall and stuffed him into the corner.

"Let me get this straight," Michael said, "of all the places you choose to kiss me, you pick the men's restroom on top of a dead guy?"

Vika raised an eyebrow.

"Don't get me wrong..." Michael stuttered, "It was fantastic. I mean *really* fantastic. But I guess... what I'm trying to ask is why? What about *this*," he waved his hand at the dead security guard, "made you want to kiss me?"

"You think too much. I like saving your life. Now we need to clean that floor again."

#

Bill peered over the edge. Two guards were helping a single engineer repair one of the rooftop antennas. Just like the government to overwork a couple of underpaid employees so that the bureaucrats could do less and make more. Guards should be guarding, not holding a ladder and the safety rope. Damned cheapskates.

Not that they deserve to live either. Bill thought. *Helping to keep the people oppressed and misinformed should be an automatic death sentence.*

"Please don't kill them," Qwiz said, seeming to read his mind.

Bill stared at him in shock.

"I know that look. You get the same look in Devolution when you are planning to charge in stupidly and try to kill everything."

"It's your job to protect me," Bill said grinning.

"You usually die when you try that."

"Because you don't heal me enough."

"This isn't a game. I don't have aphotic shield. And these men didn't do anything wrong."

"The hell they didn't. They protect an agency whose sole job is to spread lies."

"Stone, I don't think they see it that way."

"But I do. They've done such a good job that even *you* believe in global warming."

"And *everyone else* besides you," Qwiz said, a touch of irritation in his voice. "The computer models and simulations are irrefutable. Even you have to see that."

"Have you ever seen the code for the programs that run those worthless simulations?" Qwiz was probably the only person on earth that knew that Bill had actually studied computer science.

"No."

"Guess what the retards left out?" Bill didn't wait for Qwiz to respond, "the SUN. Don't you think changes in the goddamned sun would be more important to temperature than how much you exhale? Or did you know that they give carbon dioxide six times the impact the actual data shows? But you never hear about that shit because it's never reported."

"Bill, this isn't the time," Qwiz said.

Bill frowned, it was never the time for anyone to hear about the truth. But they were the ones who drank unfiltered water, drinking all those sedatives every day kept them docile, less prone to revolt. Or maybe Qwiz was right —about the part that they didn't have time to discuss it.

"Remember the plan," Bill said as he scuttled around the edge of the building.

Bill couldn't see him, but knew Qwiz was climbing over the edge. *Any moment now. Just wait for it...* Bill heard shouting.

"Wait! Who are you?"

"Another engineer, they sent me to help."

"Did you ever hear about them sending another one?" the guard asked to his partner.

"No," the other man replied. "Why did you come up over the edge? Why not through the door?"

"I, ah, was already working up here, it seemed easier just to climb up," Qwiz stammered. The boy was an awful liar. Not that Bill had any desire to change that; he loved Qwiz's honesty.

"I'm going to need to get a CPI scan and confirm it," the guard said.

Bill's turn. He climbed up over the edge, carefully counterbalancing against the 126 on the lip of the building, pulling him backward. He stepped up silently on the roof—right behind the unsuspecting guards. Bill's arms shot out, gripping the nearest man in his best sleeper hold. The guard began to thrash wildly, but Bill's grip was locked in, there was nothing the man could do about it.

The other guard who had been advancing on Qwiz wheeled around at the sound. He drew his pistol. "Stop right there! Let him go."

Bill had no intention of doing any such thing. Besides the guard had no shot, he would more likely hit his partner in the head or chest than hit Bill. The struggling continued within Bill's vice-grip, but the guard was quickly weakening.

"Drop your gun, and I let him go."

"Drop Mason, and I let you live," the guard replied.

Bill shuffled toward the edge, dragging the expiring guard with him. "New deal," Bill said casually, "you drop the gun or I drop your buddy."

The second man froze, gun wavering in his hands. After a moment of indecision, the weapon fell from his fingers to the roof. Qwiz snatched it, albeit awkwardly. *I definitely need to teach him about gun-safety* Bill thought. *He's holding that thing like it's a rabid hamster.*

"Thank you," Bill said to the unarmed guard. "Now over this way, no sense in gettin' dead tonight." The guard obliged, slowly shuffling toward Bill.

Bill jerked the man in his sleeper hold brutally, choking the last breath from his lungs. He spasmed, and then slumped limply in his arms. Bill had done that enough times to know he wasn't faking. He dropped the unconscious guard and grabbed the end of the safety rope. "I'm going to tie you up. So long as you don't resist, I won't shoot you."

Bill grabbed the yellow cord and began to wrap it around the conscious man's hands.

Before Bill finished the first loop, he jerked free, grabbed Bill's arm and flipped him over his shoulder. Bill's back slammed painfully against the hard roof. Bill reached for his gun.

"No, Stone! He doesn't need to die!" Qwiz shouted.

Bill froze, trying to make the right decision. During his hesitation, the guard kicked at the gun, sending it tumbling away.

Bill cursed, but reacted quicker than the man expected. He grabbed the man's foot with his other hand and twisted brutally. The guard flipped to the ground, giving Bill a chance to stand back up.

The other man bounced back up dexterously. He threw a quick punch, knocking Bill in the jaw. Bill returned fire, with a blow to the gut, comboing into a haymaker to the face. The man spun, but didn't go down. They exchanged more punches, Bill wasn't fast enough to dodge most of them. Bill had never been very good at dodging or blocking, but happened to be excellent at taking a punch. Most men exposed themselves right after they connected; no one ever seemed to suspect a guy to ignore the pain and immediately strike back. His current opponent was no exception. Every time the guard landed a punch, Bill got at least one back in return.

They circled each other, a meter from the edge of the building. The guard slammed him hard in the kidney. Bill ducked and crushed the man's chin with an uppercut. He stumbled backward and Bill kicked him hard in the stomach, hoping to knock him over enough to get a choke hold on him. But the man left his feet completely, as if kicked by the Vanguard himself. He sailed through the air for several meters until his feet clipped the lip of the building. He flipped erratically head-over-heels over the edge, screaming as he flew. Bill ran, but could only watch the helplessly flipping man as he plummeted to the street below. His screams grew fainter as he gained speed. Bill winced as he saw a tiny red splatter appear where he met the illuminated concrete.

Qwiz approached quietly, and Bill hung his head. "I didn't mean to kick him that hard Quence, honestly. I don't know where my strength came from."

"I think I do," Qwiz reached over the lip of the building. He came up with the orange BOGs Bill had used minutes earlier to violate Earth's gravity. "You kicked him into this thing's influence," Qwiz said softly. "It's what sent him off the edge. Not you."

"I'm sorry, I didn't even think about it. I know you didn't want anyone to die."

"It's not your fault. You did your best."

"Thanks," Bill picked up his phone and dialed Luthor. "Hurry, it won't take them long to figure out where we are... A guard thought he could fly."

A weak voice unexpectedly spoke from above them. "What are you going to do with me?" It was the engineer, still clipped into the mast of the antenna he had been working on all along.

Bill moved the extension ladder away and laid it on the ground. "You can just sit tight, unless you'd prefer getting tied up." The man squeaked an assent Bill didn't understand, and gripped his safety carabineers a little tighter.

"We promise not to hurt you," Qwiz assured him, "and we won't be long."

"What are you doing up here?" asked the helpless man.

Qwiz looked up with the same honest expression he always had. "Saving the world," he said.

#

After cleaning up Vika's mess, they rejoined Luthor and Tanya. Michael could tell from their expressions that they'd found something. Tanya led them to the secure lift. The elevator ratcheted them up to the 65th.

"What do you think "TSD" means?" Tanya asked holding up a paper with office numbers on it. "That someone has dyslexia?" Michael offered.

After a moment, Tanya gave him a satisfyingly flat stare, exactly the reaction he'd hoped for. Vika mirrored the expression, but it was so much sexier coming from her with those full lips.

"Even if he does not have the code," Vika said in her unbelievably arousing accent, "I can make him tell us who does." Michael didn't doubt she could still brow-beat just about anyone into doing just about anything, shot-up arm or not.

The four fake janitors exited the elevator as casually as possible. Instantly, they all knew they were out of place. The 65th had a very different feel than all the other floors. Rich oak and mahogany desks were scattered around various offices with permanent walls instead of portable cubicles. There were far fewer people, but the ones who braved the late hour were dressed in tailored suits and sat in executive swivel chairs. Michael could almost smell the money in the room—that is, if the digitized units of one's carbon allotment could have a smell. It had a palpable air of importance, he could tell this was where big decisions were decided, the difficult choices chosen. He picked at his overalls, trying not to stand out.

Tannya led them to the windowless office she had mentioned. Sure enough, blazoned in gilded lettering across the door read, "Transmission Security Director."

Upon receiving nods from the women as well, Luthor carefully turned the knob. The well-oiled door opened silently into a spacious office replete with custom wooden cabinets, plush carpet and a luxurious matching corner desk. Framed degrees and awards dotted the walls and a high-backed leather chair faced a half-meter monitor that even Qwiz would have envied. A quick glance at a framed degree told him the woman's name was Shawna H. Kerchoff. Luthor quietly shut and locked the door behind them.

The chair turned around.

CHAPTER 26:

USNN Tower, Chicago, United States of the West

Qwiz wasted no time and began physically circumventing the firewall on the USNN broadcast dish. It had been more laborious than difficult, given the hardware at his disposal. Normally fiber-optics were annoyingly difficult to splice into, but Qwiz had a handy little gadget that automatically did the work for him. With that in place, the hack was quite simple since he had physically circumvented the firewall.

Bill watched the restrained guard and the stranded engineer, allowing Qwiz to focus without being disturbed. It looked odd to see a man, with purpling facial bruises, guarding two relatively unharmed men.

"Stone, do you think Stalker really wants to destroy all Luthor's research?" Qwiz asked.

Stone scratched his beard. "I didn't see that one coming. This whole time I thought it was the dirty French trying to bend us over."

"But is he telling the truth?"

"Maybe, he didn't have any reason to lie to us till we crumpled up his panties along with the rest of that safehouse," Bill said, "but from my experience, the real truth is a couple steps removed from the first place you look."

"What else could it be?" asked Qwiz.

"I haven't had time to do any good research, so I'm just pissin' in the smog right now."

Qwiz had absolutely no idea what that meant. "Well, could you take a guess?"

"Let's look at the possibilities," Bill said, doing a passable impersonation of Luthor. "Maybe he told the truth. Maybe he wants to blow up China. Or it could be something else entirely."

"Any of those possibilities not involve aliens?"

"Damn it boy, if you go asking for my theories don't go putting restrictions on them!"

Qwiz laughed. "Whatever Stalker wants, it won't matter in a few minutes. The hack's complete."

Qwiz readied the prerecorded interview and the research data, ready to send it off as one file. If Luthor could get him those codes, then with the push of a button he could instantly send a special report all over the globe. Every TV in the world watching USNN would be given the data about element 126, how to synthesize it, and how to use it to create unlimited energy. It would set in motion a worldwide change more radical than any since the industrial revolution. Qwiz's fingers quivered with expectation, never before had he held so much power at his fingertips. No more hiding in the dark, behind aliases and IP scramblers, to do tiny quanta of good. Now, as soon as he got those codes, he—Qwiz—could literally save the world.

But there was of course, the other outcome. No codes. No saving the world. The logical half of Qwiz imagined that was a far more likely scenario. The combined forces of the world's carbon enforcement were being leveled at them through Stalker. If it became known what they were trying to do before Luthor stole the codes... Qwiz knew he would probably never see the outside of a cell again—if he was lucky. All of the amazing power coursing through his laptop would be reduced to a single, pathetic uncensored email without those codes. They would start cutting it off as soon as the first packet of information was sent.

So, he waited.

#

Luthor froze as a middle-aged woman regarded them. She had short, styled hair with flecks of grey, a lean build, and the expression of one who is used to being in charge.

"And who might you be?" said the woman.

Tanya, never missing a beat, took a step forward. "We are the new janitorial team for this section of the building. We came to introduce ourselves," she said with a smile.

"And you did so without knocking," said the woman. "Curious. How do you intend to make a good impression on your new boss whilst barging into her study uninvited?"

"Oh my, how stupid of us," Tanya said, trying to salvage the immanent debacle. "I apologize sincerely. It must have slipped our mind. It is our first day on the job you know."

"No, it isn't," the woman said evenly.

Tanya's eyes widened.

"I am always notified of new hires."

"There must have been some mistake," Tanya said.

"No there wasn't. I think I would have been told of four new janitors who bear a striking resemblance to a group of four terrorists on the Most Wanted list. One of whom has a clear bullet wound on her arm."

Vika said nothing, but held her bandaged arm closer.

"A coincidence—" The woman cut Tanya off.

"Don't be stupid, and beware the mistake of assuming I am. I know you are here with another purpose entirely," she paused, folding her hands on her rich desk. Luthor felt the strong temptation to hide, this woman still felt in control, despite being alone, against four armed people attempting to take highly classified codes. "You intend to steal something from me and as such I notified the building security 30 seconds ago. They will be here in five minutes."

"Then you have one minute," Vika said, taking charge. "Tell us where the transmission codes are for the satellite dish."

"See how easy that was?" the woman said, condescendingly. "Do be honest next time." Luthor could palpably sense the power struggle between the two massive personalities. Luthor stepped to the side fearing that the sheer force of their wills would crush him if he got too close.

Vika leaned across the desk and brandished her gun in her good hand "Where are the codes? Tell me now."

"Better, you are improving," said the woman in the same irritating tone; she appeared oblivious to the gun in her face. "The codes are right here," she patted an unassuming fire-safe designed to hold documents.

"It seems we have two options," Luthor said, trying his best to sound reasonable; he doubted force or intimidation would work on this particular adversary. "Either you can co-operate and open the safe, or we can just kill you and force it open. Honestly, it's your choice, and either way we get the codes. But I don't really like killing people."

"I do," Vika said. She cocked her pistol unnecessarily as if to make a point. Still the woman remained immutable. She appeared frustratingly impervious to their attempts to get her to capitulate.

Tanya's mental clock ticked off the seconds. They didn't have much time.

"It seems we are at an impasse," the woman replied. "You see, I don't really want to die, but I'm also not inclined to help you."

"I don't see any impasse," Vika growled.

Then the door exploded open.

Luthor fired off shots at the men pouring in as he ducked into a corner. He would not let them enter that room without riot gear.

"It's only been one minute!" Vika shouted, taking

cover behind the desk. "How did they get up here so quickly?"

"Strange that I would notice a member of my security team falling off the roof and another shot in my bathroom," said the woman from under her desk. Luthor fired off another round, deterring anyone from entering.

"I called for security 15 minutes ago. They were already here."

"Keep her alive long enough to get the codes and send them to Qwiz. That's all that matters now."

The safe sat innocently under the desk. Return fire splintered the expensive wood finish.

"I don't suppose you're going to give up because we're so dangerous!" Michael yelled at the attackers while huddling behind a cabinet on the opposite end of the room.

The security did not respond verbally, but they did put a few more bullets in the glass, inches from Michael's hiding place.

"Not surrendering, huh? Too bad." Just as he finished, Michael threw all the remaining 126 through the open door. The next instant five men had crashed on top of each other against the side of a desk where the BOGs had stuck. They struggled to reorient themselves, trying to figure out what had happened.

Tanya yelled and fired through the door at the pile of men. Luthor leaned back in surprise. She'd emptied her entire magazine. None of the five men moved.

"I told you, I'm all in, Luthor. You were right. Some things are worth killing for, some are worth dying for."

For the first time, the Kerchoff woman looked frightened. "You can't kill me," she said.

"Watch me," Vika growled.

"It requires a CPI scan to open." The woman was breathing hard, sweat beaded up on her forehead.

Tanya grunted and plopped the small safe on the desk

and Vika forced the woman's right hand over the scanner.

It beeped angrily.

"What the hell?" Tanya said.

The screen read "Owner under duress. Five minute lockdown enabled."

Kerchoff smiled. "It senses my pulse is too fast. It won't open."

"I know how to lower your pulse." Vika flipped her pistol around and hit her hard across the head. The woman slumped, unconscious.

"Can't we shoot this thing open?" Michael asked.

"With a 9mm?" Vika raised an eyebrow. "On a safe sophisticated enough to have a lockdown contingency? Not a chance. We will have to wait."

#

Qwiz had known he would probably beat the others to the roof, but this felt like they were waiting too long. Had they been captured? Qwiz had everything ready. It would only take a few keystrokes to send the special report. It would take no time at all.

If they didn't get the codes, at least he could send an email to a company somewhere and hope that they might be able to use it. At least then the research wouldn't be lost forever. The USW would be able to see a copy of whatever he sent. They'd be able to use it, as well as the company.

Then again… maybe it would be better not to send it at all. With the way that Stalker had pursued them, what would make a company any different? Why wouldn't he just flatten a company just as completely? He was outside the law, he could do whatever he wanted. The Vanguard would not sentence an entire group of people to death just because he failed his mission. It would be better to not send it at all.

Qwiz hoped it wouldn't come to that. He tried his best

to think positively, fighting the urges welling up in his gut that told him to panic.

He heard a soft buzz. Instantly, he clicked his phone. "I think I just got the codes, Stone!" Bill came rushing over to look. A message from Vika's phone appeared.

Qwiz cheered, pumping his fist only momentarily. He wanted to get this thing sent. He clicked the message. It read: *Wait five minutes.*

"Dang it!" Qwiz shouted. He was frustrated at himself for swearing, but he couldn't help it, they hadn't sent him the codes! He realized the soft buzzing from his phone hadn't stopped. Strangely, his phone remained blank. The buzzing wasn't coming from his phone.

"Is that your phone?" he asked.

Bill shrugged and began looking around. The buzzing persisted, getting louder by the second. Soon, it differentiated into a sort of beat. Too loud for a buzz, it became a fast, rhythmic thumping. The noise continually grew until it had crested the threshold of what Qwiz considered loud.

"That is definitely *not a phone*, Quency," Bill said staring over the skyline. "*That* is a helicopter."

#

Luthor and Vika fanned out looking for more security. The huge floor with its intermittent desks and permanent walls formed a make-shift maze of offices. It took a while to search. The only positive was that all the civilians fled as soon as the first shots were fired. They didn't have to worry about unnecessary casualties.

Civilians? Luthor thought. *Unnecessary casualties? I haven't thought of people in those terms since the war. But I guess that's what this is now, isn't it? War.*

Suddenly Tanya shrieked from the other end of the room. "Everybody get down!"

The entire eastern wall of windows suddenly shattered. Glass sprayed everywhere, and bullets poured into the building as if out of a fire hose.

A helicopter appeared 30 meters from the building, raining bullets through a pair of mini-guns mounted on its flanks.

I guess they've learned to keep their aircraft out of reach of our gravity wells, Luthor thought. He ducked down under a desk while images of Chinese dragons popped into his mind. He shivered subconsciously. *Bullets. Cold. Death. Fire. Blood. Pain.*

The guns sawed off everything in an even line a meter off the floor. Smoke and woodchips splintered in a shower of shrapnel as the relentless guns did their grisly work. Luthor kept his head covered with his hands, knowing it would do no good if any of the bullets penetrated far enough through the rubble to hit him.

After the longest seconds of his life since Antarctica, the bullets stopped. Ears ringing, Luthor's flattened stereocilia struggled to interpret any noise other than gunfire. He hesitated a moment and looked around. Sawed-off office partitions were strewn everywhere, papers fluttered lazily from the outside breeze, everything was obscured by drywall dust.

"Is everyone okay?" Luthor shouted, his voice muted in his own ears.

"I'm okay," called Tanya.

"I'm hit," Vika said.

This is war, now we're taking casualties. For the thousandth time, Luthor wondered why it was never him who was hit, why it wasn't him that died. In the whole war he had never received a single gunshot wound. It was so much worse to come through something unscathed than to be hit. The injuries to the brain often lasted far longer than those to the body.

"I'm coming!" Luthor shouted back. He had to help her.

"No! Stay down!"

"I am not leaving you behind!"

"Protect Kerchoff. She has to open that safe!"

Michael yelled from the office. "Which piece of her are you planning to protect?"

Luthor swore loudly.

"She woke up and made a run for it. Those guns cut her in half."

Luthor army crawled back to the office. Kerchoff's legs stuck out of a pile of rubble and gore. Her top half was nowhere to be found.

"Try her Mark. Maybe it hasn't shut down yet," Luthor said.

Michael found her arm under what was left of the cabinets. It was drenched in blood and a bone poked out at a grisly angle. He slid her hand over the scanner and shook his head.

"Apparently, she's still under duress."

"They aren't reloading," called Tanya, "the helicopter is flying up."

"Oh no." Luthor breathed. He began to panic, fearing for the life of his friends on the roof. He fired five rounds into the safe. They barely dented the opening mechanism. They weren't going to get codes to Qwiz before that helicopter arrived.

#

The helicopter approached but stayed well away from the edge. Qwiz had just watched it pour bullets into the building 25 stories below, and it looked like it was preparing to unload on him as well. Qwiz grabbed his laptop and huddled under the rim of one of the many satellite dishes, trying to keep it in between himself and the gunship. Qwiz prayed that they wouldn't risk damaging the multi-million credit equipment. Bill had also guessed as much and crouched behind a raised electronics box.

As the helicopter moved, so did they, keeping themselves carefully out of sight.

"Do you think Luthor and the others are alive?" Qwiz asked tentatively. It hadn't looked good from their vantage point.

"He's one hardy son of a bitch. Just like me. And it would take more than a couple of mini-guns to bring *me* down."

The helicopter circled some more, playing a dangerous game of cat and mouse.

"I don't really want to wait for these bastards to run out of fuel," Bill growled. He popped his head out from behind the steel box and began firing at the hovering aircraft.

"That isn't going to do anything!" Qwiz yelled.

"Sure it will," Bill shouted back. "It'll make me feel better!" He pulled the trigger twice more. "Maybe if I'm lucky I drop one of those gunners inside." Two more shots.

A single, loud crack rang out in reply from the helicopter. To Qwiz, it sounded just as loud as Bill's gun right next to him despite being 50 meters away.

Bill cried out and fell backward. Blood and flesh splattered grotesquely away from his shoulder.

"Goddamn sniper," Bill groaned, putting pressure on his wound, "not supposed to have a smogging sniper on a chopper.'

The aircraft advanced, stopping to hover above the roof. Ropes rolled out of the side and men began belaying down them.

Will you please hurry up, Luthor? Qwiz thought. *I have about thirty seconds.*

#

Luthor watched helplessly as Vika leaned against a pile of debris, bleeding. She'd fended off the first wave of security with the last of their 126. They couldn't handle the gravity and had been dispatched.

Another group of men began pouring out of the emergency stairwell. Vika fired off a few shots but these men were better equipped. They wore helmets, shouldered submachine guns, and a few were equipped with gelvar, like Stalker's men. Luthor knew she wouldn't last long against those kinds of odds. He could see the wound in her side had bled through her janitorial garb, and her face paled by the minute. Luthor and Michael remained pinned down across from her, they could do little but provide occasional covering fire.

She leaned over a broken chair and fired again. Her aim was off, she hadn't killed a single man. She reloaded, signaling that it was her last magazine.

"Damn it, Luthor. We have to do something!" Michael's eyes were wide with concern.

"If we move, we die. I've counted ten men."

"I am not going to let her die," Michael said over the gunfire.

"Michael, listen to me," Luthor said earnestly, "in war, sometimes people die. Sometimes you can't save them."

To Luthor's surprise a tear appeared in Michael's eye. "I'm sorry. I know it sounds harsh, but if we try to save her, we will both be committing suicide." Garcia's old mantra came to mind. It seemed appropriate. "Don't be a hero. Just do what needs to be done."

"I'm not a soldier," Michael said.

"You don't have a choice. This *is* war."

One of Stalker's men began inching around to flank

Vika. In moments, he would be in position to have a clear shot. Luthor couldn't even deter him, shooting would draw the fire from at least three other men. Michael saw it too. Luthor could feel his friend charging up his willpower to do something stupid. Luthor put a warning hand on his chest.

"I'm sorry, Luthor," Michael put a second hand on the grip of his gun, "sometimes people *do* have to be the hero." He leapt across the open ground, gun shots following in his wake. In the middle of his sprint, Luthor shot at the man repeatedly. The gelvar absorbed most of the bullets, but one landed square in the man's leg and he slumped to his knees.

At the same time, Vika leaned over and shot one of the men in the face. The bullet penetrated the plexiglass of his riot helmet, killing him instantly. Michael safely reached cover by Vika. But there were just too many. Luthor knew all he had done was postpone the inevitable.

#

Six men descended the ropes and encircled Qwiz, guns drawn, though they stayed a safe distance from him. He wasn't sure why they didn't just gun him down on sight, but didn't argue with them. If they were going to let him live, he planned to make the most of it. He sat with his computer on his lap, huddled in a corner made by the main satellite dish and several massive enclosures.

He wished he had his 126, but it lay next to Bill. Not that he would know what to do with it precisely, but it seemed to help everyone else get away from impossible odds. Having some couldn't hurt his chances.

One last man swooped down from the hovering chopper. Qwiz recognized him even in the dark. Stalker.

Stalker strode forward menacingly. "Give up, Mole."

"Make me," Qwiz realized he sounded more like a petulant 7-year-old than a defiant superhero.

"I intend to. Unfortunately, I still need you alive. I need to know whom you have told about 126."

"I won't tell you anything."

"I did not expect you to tell me *here*," Stalker said, a smile playing on the corner of his lips. "But I suspect that after a little *aggressive questioning*, you will become more cooperative."

Qwiz frowned. He had hoped that he would be able to be brave. But torture wasn't something he expected he would be very good at enduring. Supposedly anyone, regardless of training, could be broken—given enough time. And Qwiz had no training, and Stalker had plenty of time. His father would have said that the only honorable course of action would have been to kill himself. It was the only way to ensure the safety of those he loved. Qwiz's palms began to sweat as he grasped his gun tentatively.

"I would caution you against trying anything," Stalker said. "We have learned from our previous mistakes. Our men are spread out too far to be influenced by your gravity tricks, and our air support remains out of range. You cannot escape."

"You goddamn fascist," Bill growled, the pain of his shoulder obvious in his voice.

"You will regret that before the end of the week."

Qwiz felt his trigger finger itching. He knew what he needed to do. His mother, his coworkers, and anyone he had ever called or texted were in danger. If he did the right thing, he could protect everyone he loved. He needed to kill himself. But he was running out of time to work up the courage to do so.

Bill didn't have a gun either. He would have to murder his best friend first then commit suicide. His father's voice mingled with his dark thoughts: *courage isn't defined by what you do, but by what you are willing to lose.* He'd been willing to lose it all. Was he now willing to sacrifice it all? Could he take his own life, along with the life of his best friend for the greater good?

"Do it, Quence," Bill breathed.

Qwiz took a deep breath, the grip of the gun sweaty in his hand. He'd never thought it would come to this.

"We have a pretty good idea where Tenrel and his team have been," Stalker continued, the man certainly did enjoy the sound of his own voice. "Questioning them is a luxury. If a few of them die it won't matter. I only need one alive to eliminate any other acquaintances who know about 126. But you two have been off the radar until now. Who knows who you have told?"

Qwiz turned back to his nemesis, "think of what you're giving up." Maybe he could talk some sense into him. It occasionally worked in the comics, the bad guy would sometimes give up and repent of his evil ways when confronted with the truth. "If you let this broadcast through, it will change the world."

"But I like the world the way it is."

"What about everyone who can benefit from cheap energy? So many people are suffering because there isn't enough to go around. Others are starving. There's a hundred million homeless in North America alone! You can change all that."

Stalker sneered. "You don't get it. I have everything I want. I can do anything I please to whomever I wish. I want this world to remain as is."

This wasn't working. Why didn't anything ever happen the way it was supposed to? He should be crying, repenting, pleading for forgiveness and a chance to change his ways.

"Mr. Dimarin, please. Whatever else you do, don't destroy this. You'd be destroying the world's best chance at a future."

"Don't worry. I will keep one copy. It would be foolish to throw away something so powerful. It will go into a vault, never to be used or touched, but not completely destroyed."

"But that's as good destroying it!" Qwiz yelled. He felt desperation rising in him like bile.

"Yes, it is."

The horror of Stalker's intentions began to sink in a little deeper. They planned to completely purge the world of its knowledge of 126's power. It was one thing to maintain a monopoly on the synthesis of 126, and therefore the applications, but another entirely to permanently erase all knowledge of it. The Sabers were going to systematically murder everyone who had ever heard the innocent numbers 1-2-6. Stalker didn't want to use it at all, in any way. Using it granted back to the people an incredible freedom that scarcity and carbon-policy had taken: the freedom of cheap energy.

Stalker, nor any of his minions, had the desire to give up a single iota of the power that the CPI, carbon-credit system gave them. With it, the Carbon Coalition wielded total control over the masses, and the Sabers were its almighty enforcers. Everyone's location was constantly being recorded every time they bought anything or used a government service. Their activities were stored in a giant database and everything bought was tracked. Qwiz couldn't believe he had never thought of it in those terms before, but the CPI chips allowed the Government to effectively spy on every man, woman, and child in the world continuously. At least that part of Bill's conspiracy was right.

And the censorship system, in the name of national security, rounded out the surveillance. They could see every electronic form of communication deciding what to allow and what to ban. They had prevented him from communicating freely with his father since before the war. They'd tracked Luthor's phone calls and murdered Eli. Combined with control of the carbon monetary system, it allowed them to completely control every aspect of the economy and every aspect of people's lives in the name of saving the planet from global warming.

Releasing 126 would corrode the foundation of their whole system. People would have access to unlimited, zero-carbon energy. CPI couldn't control something that was free and limitless. It would be like regulating oxygen intake. Without scarce energy, they had no means of control. Stalker's whole objective was to protect that control.

Stalker put his hand to his ear, his focus shifting to his headset. He nodded repeatedly and a cruel smile played across his pale face. "Excellent, be certain to remove any element 126 you can find on their bodies—check their belts. Then take them to the compound. Try to keep the girls alive, we will need them when we are questioning Tenrel and Laramy.

Stalker removed his headset and regarded Qwiz with mock pity. "Your friends have been captured."

Qwiz interrupted, fear and desperation straining his voice. He would not be receiving any codes, "How can you be satisfied with our world, when it could be so much more? You could have so much more!"

"You have a lot to learn about greed. If I *already have* everything I want, the only thing left is to safeguard my desires. I intend to set them in concrete." Stalker motioned to his team to move in toward Qwiz. They moved forward slowly and methodically, carefully watching for sudden movements.

Qwiz found himself gripping his gun tighter. He would have to use it after all. He had to protect the one's he loved. "Then you aren't greedy enough!" he shouted.

Stalker laughed and began walking forward.

Something else in Qwiz's head clicked. *Not greedy enough… that's it!* Qwiz suddenly realized what he had to do. He had only one chance. He had to send the research to someone *greedier* than Stalker. Greedy enough to use it. Fingers flying with speed that came with a lifetime of computer work he opened his email and began typing.

"Stop him!" Stalker shouted. The only man with a clear shot fired his weapon.

Qwiz turned his body to protect the computer and a bullet tore into his bicep. Searing, white-hot pain burned through his flesh.

"Cut the hard line!" Stalker screamed into his headset. "I don't care if the whole damned *region* goes dark. Cut it!"

Qwiz clacked a few more familiar characters, while two more men sprinted to get an angle. Another shot impaled his shoulder blade. A worse pain than any Qwiz remembered wracked his body, but his adrenaline pushed him onward. He had to complete his task.

With a desperate click he jammed the enter button, and fell backward in surrender. A single email went out. One file. One recipient. Without the codes, that's all he could send. But at least for once in his life, he completely circumvented the American censors.

CHAPTER 27:

Thirty Minutes Later: The Whitehouse

President Jimenez looked up from his desk as a man hurried into the oval office. He muted the two monitors on his desk to hide the classified material displayed on them. Jimenez was the first president to place monitors permanently on the Resolute desk. It had earned him some mild public criticism, but he found it incalculably improved his efficiency and so he felt the political trade-off was worth it.

The way the man entered spoke volumes about the message he carried. Most people, even those familiar with the office, entered timidly. The gravity of the space seemed to make each person question the importance of their errand that brought them inside. That is, unless that bearer's purpose was clearly important enough to disturb the President. In that case they came in, looking scared, harried, and in a rush. This man entered in the latter manner.

Jimenez braced himself. "Yes?"

"Sir, a half an hour ago, insurgents broke into the USNN Tower in Chicago."

"What did they steal?" Jimenez asked. The tower was the hub for all communications traffic in the region. It also held the regional censorship station and the electronic counterterrorism division for Chicago.

"They didn't steal anything sir. It appears they circumnavigated the firewall and sent an unprotected transmission."

Jimenez frowned, an uncensored message was hardly

something to bother him about, they had safeguards to shut down any hacks almost immediately. Let the censors deal with it. "Do you know the content of the message?"

"The Satellite Protocols automatically saved a copy, sir. We will know within the hour what it contained."

"If you don't know anything yet, then why are you bothering me with it?"

"Because sir, the message was sent to *China*."

Jimenez blanched. He reflexively restrained any change in his facial features out of political habit, but this was bad. Anyone willing to risk their life to send a message to China without being censored wouldn't be sending a Christmas card.

"Where are they know? Have the insurgents been captured?"

"It seems the Sabers have already apprehended them sir, they shut down the hack after a single file was sent."

Jimenez hated the Sabers. They were a stupid, poorly planned and maintained idea. But he couldn't fight them either. They were like the bully at school whose mom was the principal, and she refused to believe her kid could do any wrong no matter how many times he was sent to the office.

"I don't yet have confirmation of this, but it seems that one of the men captured was Luthor Tenrel."

"Really?" The situation just kept getting more interesting, "where are they taking him?"

"They have a secret compound somewhere North of the city."

"Find it. If Tenrel and the Chinese are involved then this has become a matter of national security, *not* carbon policy, so the Sabers no longer have jurisdiction. I want those terrorists in *American* custody within the hour."

"Sir, a word of caution, it has not been confirmed that it's Tenrel. If it isn't, we would be breaking international law by interfering."

"Then *get* confirmation. Find where they were holding him, tail every Saber in the country if you have to. And figure out what that transmission was; I want a copy on this screen the second it's decoded. Do you understand?

"Yes sir."

"If Tenrel was involved, I want him and any other insurgents in federal custody ASAP."

The man left the office in an even bigger hurry than he'd entered.

"Your move Dimarin." Jimenez said to the empty room. He picked up the phone and dialed JSOC; he had a feeling that Dimarin might not be so willing to give up his prisoners without a fight.

#

Eight Hours Later: Somewhere in the Suburbs

Qwiz didn't remember being knocked unconscious, but woke up to the harsh buzzing of florescent bulbs. Adorned only with a steel table with straps and a squat toilet in the corner, Qwiz knew this room had to be inside the "compound" Stalker had mentioned. Strangely, they had bandaged his gun-shot wounds. His arm was fixed in a sling and he could feel restrictive brace winding his torso like a bear-hug. They still ached in sharp waves of pain, but at least he had survived them. Perhaps torture worked better when there were more healthy body parts to injure. He prayed that he would have the courage to endure and not betray anyone.

Something rumbled above him, like rocks falling in the distance. Qwiz shrank into the corner despite himself as fear overloaded his mental RAM. He tried to imagine Stone's steadfast endurance and attempted to emulate it.

Qwiz figured he would probably never know if his plan had worked or not. It had been a desperate gamble at best, suicidal and borderline-traitorous at worst. Maybe the history books would remember what he had done, but in truth it seemed more likely that they would never even notice a simple email, let alone see the courage and insight it had taken to send it. The important thing was that he had tried. He had shown honor in fighting evil and tyranny. Qwiz hoped his father would learn of his actions and call him courageous. He had risked everything without compulsion; he had done it simply because it was right. *Courage isn't what you do, but what you are willing to lose.* Qwiz again regarded his cramped cell. *Well, at least I got one part of that right. I managed to lose everything.*

More rumbles from above; they were louder this time and accompanied by a faint rattling. Maybe they were already torturing Bill. Qwiz didn't even know how many of the others had survived to be brought here. That helicopter had used more ammunition than should have fit in the entire vehicle if it had held nothing but bullets. He hoped none of them would have to be scraped off the sides of office cubicles.

Qwiz identified the rattle as the sound of bullets issuing from a machine-gun and found himself wishing for an extra helping of courage. Just as Qwiz began to contemplate the mystery of automatic weapons being used inside Stalker's compound, the steel door burst open.

A man in all black appeared. His face was painted varying degrees of grey stripes and he held a gun that looked like it had come from *Devolution.* "Hurry, come with me!" he said.

Qwiz didn't know if he should trust the man or not, but wasn't about to argue with a guy like that when he had his arm in a sling. Actually, he wouldn't have argued with him at any point.

Qwiz got up, and the man grabbed him by his good arm and hustled him down a concrete hallway. Two other similarly dressed men wearing gelvar moved to flank him. They pushed him down the hallway, screening him with their bodies.

The raging cacophony of a full-on firefight accosted him. Men yelled to each other and blasts of light exploding from their weapons were the only illumination in the dark corridor.

His body guards yanked him away from the battle and up a flight of stairs. Qwiz's unhealed wounds protested at the violent movement, but the men forcibly carried him when he couldn't walk fast enough. The tempest continued. The ground underneath them shuddered and chunks of rubble blasted out from the wall next to them. The soldier on Qwiz's right immediately began firing shots through the new hole.

Qwiz didn't know what to think, who to trust. It was all happening so fast. But these men seemed to be taking him *out of* Stalker's compound, so that made them the good guys. Right? There was too much happening to concentrate. Without warning his two handlers quit shooting and led him farther up the steps.

A moment later the stairs disgorged them into a parking lot. Outside, the earsplitting shockwaves of exploding propellant all but vanished leaving only the eerie silence of a vacant suburban strip mall. An old gasoline filling station had dedicated itself to becoming a full-time bird-nest collector. All the other stores of the shopping center lay just as abandoned, their smashed windows and burned exteriors standing as grim historians, forever describing the horrors wrought by the Culling in the suburbs of the world. The only sign that human life persisted were the half dozen military vehicles stationed in the parking lot. Bill would have a hayday when he found out that Stalker's secret base was actually in the basement of a TJ-Maxx.

The men encouraged him, rather strongly, to enter the belly of a nearby Humvee. "If you want to live, stay here," one of them said before he slammed the door.

The two men charged back in immediately, like kids who had been given the permission to play in the pool for five more minutes. Qwiz didn't understand why anyone could possibly want to re-enter a battle. Qwiz had not particularly enjoyed being shot.

I guess that's what it means to be brave. Qwiz thought. *To risk your life to accomplish your mission.* Qwiz suddenly smiled to himself as he realized he too had been brave. He had sacrificed his body, preventing the shooters from damaging his laptop before he had accomplished his own mission.

More men sprinted out the door, carrying another heavily bandaged man. As he was shoved into another vehicle Qwiz recognized his old friend. They had rescued Bill! They *were* the good guys!

Qwiz pounded his hand on the window. "Put him in here!" he shouted. No one heard him. Qwiz saw more soldiers pouring out of the stairwell, several other bandaged people in their care. He couldn't tell if they were his friends or not.

Bullets began pinging against the armored hull of the Hummer. Qwiz saw Sabers firing from the broken windows of the TJ-Maxx. A round dented the thick glass right in front of Qwiz's face. He flinched. The men who rescued him ducked behind vehicles and fired back. The bright flash of a grenade erupted out from the building. Another explosion violently lifted the Humvee next to Qwiz half a meter off the ground. Fear paralyzed him. He didn't want his to be next. The battle raged on for interminable minutes. Bullets flew, hot and thick. Smoke and debris clogged the air. Grenades blasted around him.

Abruptly, the fighting stopped.

The Sabers walked out with their hands in the air and the remaining good-guys slapped cuffs on them. Eight were able to walk under their own power, but Qwiz saw medics tending to other Sabers sprawled on the pavement. Qwiz mentally applauded men who were noble enough to tend to the wounds of those who had just been trying to kill them.

They really were the good guys.

The door to the hummer opened and a man climbed into the driver seat. He began wiping off his face-paint with a cloth.

Qwiz's mind flooded with questions. But his questions shouted over the top of each other so loudly he couldn't make many of them out. His mental CPU wasn't fast enough to process all of the things he wanted to ask his new companion. When he'd finally buffered all the data, he heard himself ask probably the most inane question of the jumble vying for attention.

"Who are you guys?"

The man picked up a clipboard from the dash and examined it. After a moment he nodded, "Mr. Quency Park is it? We are Delta Force, United States Army."

"What's happening?"

He looked at the clipboard again. "You and your friends are being transferred to a more... suitable location."

Qwiz's heart sank. They were being shipped off to a different prison, this one run by the USW instead of the Sabers. This wasn't a rescue, it was a prisoner transfer. His email had been considered treason after all.

"Why are you driving me then?"

"Would you prefer a horse?" the man asked with a chuckle.

"I...just didn't think you would waste a car for a prisoner. Don't you usually make us walk?"

"If Dimarin were to transfer you—though after our incursion I didn't get the impression people ever actually *left* his compound—you would walk," he said conversationally, "but I'm happy to say that his compound is now under new management."

"Then where are you taking me?"

He finally put down the clipboard and turned to meet Qwiz's eyes, "to the Whitehouse."

#

Clipboard drove the Hummer in relative silence for the better part of a half hour. Qwiz was amazed that a vehicle powered by small, repeated explosions could be so quiet. He had never ridden in a gas-powered vehicle before.

Clipboard decelerated and drove out onto a massive open strip of pavement, with only blocky sections devoted to solar power. He pulled up to other camouflaged trucks parked there. The door unlocked, and Qwiz leapt out of the car as fast as his useless left arm allowed. A man in fatigues with an automatic rifle appeared at Qwiz's side. Like the men who had extracted him from the compound, he pointed the gun away from Qwiz in a posture of protection.

Without warning a dozen hands mobbed him, ruffling his hair, patting him on the back, and generally attempting to touch any available place on his body. Qwiz huddled in the fetal position as he tried to make out any of the voices bombarding him.

After a few seconds one of the competing audio files resolved to clarity in his mind.

"Damn fine work Qwency! If I had another arm, I'd hug your Asian ass."

"Stone!" Bill's shoulder bulged with bandages.

Luthor, Michael, Tanya and Vika were all there as well, each one of them beaming as broadly as if they'd just built their first computer.

"So, it's true?" Qwiz asked tentatively. "Are they really transferring me to the Whitehouse?"

"Transferring?" Michael asked laughing. "Buddy, you are a free man. They are *escorting you*."

Qwiz carefully modulated the joy threatening to burst from his pores. It took effort. If he'd run off electricity instead of ATP, he surely would have overloaded a number of his capacitors. It just felt too good to be true. "How can you be so sure that this is for real?"

"It took a video-call from the President himself to convince us," Michael said. "Yeah, it's for real."

"Wait. You actually talked with President Jimenez?"

"I'd swear it was real," Luthor said. "He called us by name and responded to our questions. He says *you* have changed everything."

"By the way, what did you do exactly?" Michael asked. "We were sort of getting shot and forgot to send you the codes."

Just as Qwiz began to explain his desperate gambit to them, the roar of jet engines overloaded his ears. Luthor ducked instinctively as if he expected bullets to fill the air. Vika took cover behind the nearest vehicle.

Clipboard raised his hands. "Don't worry, this is a civilian plane."

"Then why is it here?" Luthor growled.

"This *is* an airport. Occasionally, they land here."

For the first time since he arrived, Qwiz inspected his surroundings. Having never been on a flying machine in his memory, it hadn't occurred to him that airports even existed any more. A small white passenger jet landed gracefully a short distance away. He had never seen a working aircraft this close before. It was beautiful. Two jet-engines flanked a stately tail, broad wings shadowed the hot pavement. As it slowed to manageable speeds, it turned toward them and parked nearby.

"This used to be O'Hare International. Now it is mostly expensive apartments for government employees. We just occasionally use the airstrip. You really have nothing to fear."

In the distance, Qwiz noticed four men in black, wielding machine-guns and escorting a single prisoner toward the Terminal. The prisoner's hands were cuffed securely behind his back.

"Who is that?" Tanya asked.

"Franco Dimarin," Clipboard replied.

Quiz's biological pixels confirmed without question that it was Stalker.

"I will see you in hell, you Chinese bastard!" he yelled at Qwiz.

"Actually, I'm Korean," Qwiz replied calmly. However often Qwiz had wished for it, the world seldom was a place of justice and truth. But in this instance the stars had aligned, and a very evil man was getting what he deserved. The Vanguard himself couldn't have engineered a more appropriate result.

Luthor began laughing. "I stand corrected, once and for all. Tanya, there *is a God!*"

Stalker seethed, lurching to get at Luthor.

"Move," one of the guards said restraining him. Another prodded him in the back with his rifle. Stalker strained against them so hard he lost his balance, tripped and fell forward. Hands bound behind his back, Stalker's only option was to break his fall with his face. Vika knelt next to him. The guards moved to intercept, but Clipboard motioned for them to give her space. She clenched a clove of his graying hair and yanked his head back.

She whispered something in his ear. His eyes widened in surprise, just before she slammed her fist brutally against the back of his skull. His head bounced off the pavement. After getting up, he complied with his captors without another word. They shoved him toward a non-descript utilitarian building behind them.

"Did that feel good?" Michael asked.

"You have no idea."

"Come, please follow me," Clipboard said, "you have a date with the President tonight." He led them up the steps into the plane.

#

"I still can't believe this. We're flying!" Michael said as if waking from a particularly immersive daydream. He had done nothing but stare out the window their entire flight. Qwiz had never been on a plane either, but he'd managed to control his awe. Strangely, after the beautiful, long acceleration and the spectacular vistas had passed, the ride had become easy, almost routine. The placid white blanket of puffy clouds passed peacefully below, and Qwiz could almost see how men and women of the 20th century had taken flight for granted. Almost. Michael, however, had no such empathy. He had stared out the porthole like Qwiz stared at a monitor.

Clipboard, whose name was actually Bryce Jameson, had been explaining exactly how they had come to be freed. "Once the President saw the interview you transmitted and it became clear what Dimarin's motivations were," he suddenly smiled, "turns out that he had an even better force than the Sabers at his disposal."

"You're telling me he didn't know what was going on before Quiz's email?" Bill asked. "That's a mighty big pill to swallow."

Jameson turned to Bill, "the carbon enforcement system enacted by the Paris 2 agreement required the Sabers to be independent of the Coalition nations. That way they would be free of outside influence and enforce some very strict laws. By that same law, the President couldn't know what Dimarin was up to."

"He didn't have ways of spying on the organization?" Vika said.

"I couldn't speculate. But the Sabers do need permission to do certain things in our borders, which the President would know about, and in some cases, have to approve. From what I've heard the President and Dimarin shared some...words. The result was the Joint Special Operations Command tasking my Deltas to clean house—God, Dimarin had some ugly things in there—and you know the rest."

"You kicked that commie's ass!" Bill declared.

"I've been waiting ten years to finally see if the Sabers really were better than Delta Force like everyone said. They knew we were coming and we still stomped them."

"And thank you for rescuing us," Tanya added. "We would have died in there if not for you."

"You're welcome ma'am. It's why we serve. Bill, I wanted to tell you in person that we recovered your son."

"Are you bringing him too?" Bill asked.

"I'm afraid that's not possible. His leg was in terrible shape. We took him to our best doctor and she had to... had to amputate. I'm sorry. He is recovering, and it will probably be weeks before he is able to travel."

Bill hung his head.

Jameson placed a comforting hand on Bill's shoulder. "He recorded a message before the surgery. Would you like to see it?"

Bill nodded and Jameson produced a tablet with the pre-recorded message. Michael peaked over Bill's head to see the recording.

William sat in a hospital bed, a bandage on his ribs bulged from under his gown, and an IV dripped fluid into his arm. He was smiling. "Hey Dad. I'm sorry I can't join you; they said my leg is 'septic.' I guess that's a bad thing." William gave a half-hearted laugh. "I want you to know something. This *isn't your fault.* Tell Luthor it isn't his fault either. I wish it didn't have to be this way, but I'm glad that I know you're going to be there for me this time."

"You're damn right about that," Bill said to the screen as he wiped a tear from his eye.

"Tell everyone that I'm proud of what you all did up there last night. Oh crap, I just said I'm proud of you! Don't let that go to your head okay, Dad? I hope to see you soon."

The message ended.

"He's doing well in recovery," Jameson said.

"Thank you," Bill said, "I mean it, damn it! Thank you so much." The old man wrapped Jameson in bear hug.

"I think the truth is that we should thank you. You all risked your lives so that my kids will grow up in a better world. As we speak, your research is being sent all over the globe, in preparation to begin mass production of 126."

Tanya smiled. "Except we didn't have much to do with it, apparently, we owe it all to Qwiz."

"I thought you had this planned all along," Jameson asked.

"Our plan was transmit a special report through the USNN satellite dish. But we never did get him the codes," Luthor grinned conspiratorially, "you *did* figure out how to hack that satellite, didn't you?"

Every eye on the plane locked on Qwiz, even the beautiful flight attendant stopped to listen. "No, Luthor. I didn't," Qwiz said somberly, he had not been looking forward to recounting the event. It felt too much like boasting, something completely antithetical to honor. "I told you it was impossible to hack in polynomial time. I had minutes."

Luthor furrowed his brow, "but you said that without the codes all you could do was to send a single email before they detected the intrusion and shut you down."

"I only sent one email."

Luthor frowned in thought, Vika mirroring his look. Tanya rubbed her chin. Qwiz turned to Luthor, searching for a way to explain what he had done without coming across as arrogant.

"I don't understand," Tanya said. "I thought we succeeded in getting the research to the world; how is that possible with one message?"

"I only had the one uncensored email, I just had

to figure out how to spread 126 as far as possible. Since Stalker wanted to eliminate the research altogether, anyone I emailed would be hunted down and killed just like us. Your work would still end up lost forever, but lots more innocent people would die. I couldn't let that happen."

Clipboard—Jameson, showed them Stalker's tablet. "That's what I've been reading from Dimarin's communications last week. He was chasing everyone who'd heard of the stuff. I still can't tell if he planned to keep a copy for a rainy day or not."

"Can't oppress the people much, if they all have free energy, cheap travel, and enough goddamned food to eat," Bill said. "That's all I'm sayin."

"Qwiz, continue," Vika ordered.

Michael shot her a chastising look.

"*Please* continue."

Qwiz smiled. "The problem was that Dimarin wasn't *greedy* enough. Any normal man would have used 126 to get rich. Any country would have used it to dominate—like Luthor thought. But Dimarin didn't care about any of that. He didn't want to use it at all. He just wanted to protect his power and his station. He had to eliminate your research to do so. He wasn't greedy enough to use it.

"I needed to find someone *greedier* than him, someone who *would* use it. So, I naturally thought of China. They were so greedy they started World War III, greedy enough they still use coal. They would certainly put it into production."

"Wait," Michael blurted. "Really? China?"

Qwiz blushed slightly. "Actually, I sent it to my father. He works in the government there. I think. It was the first uncensored communication I have had with him since before the war."

"What were you thinking?" Michael said. "What have you done?"

Qwiz began to feel that the cabin of the Gulfstream

was shrinking around him.

"No," Luthor held both hands to his lips, interrupting the silence. "It was brilliant."

Everyone waited for him to expound. He did.

"You're a smogging brilliant madman! By sending it to China you made sure that the world—everyone under CPI anyway—*has* to use it. It's the only way we could keep up! Using our synthesis method, China could literally have unlimited energy within a year or two, and therefore production, food, and pretty much everything the rest of the world doesn't have enough of. But, the Coalition would *have* a copy of your email since you sent it through their system! We would have the research too!" Qwiz blushed as Luthor got up and slapped him on the back.

"With one email, you really did get it to the whole world," Tanya said in amazement. Luthor started pacing in excitement. "But in the same move you saved us from another war! If only the Coalition got it, or only the Chinese, war would be inevitable. But now everyone's got it, the world finally will have energy parity, and maybe we can have lasting peace!"

"And he didn't mention he was getting shot while sending it!" Bill said, waving his club-like bandage around as if he were a father cheering at a pee-wee football game.

"Wow!" Michael said. "Did it hurt?"

"Yeah," Qwiz replied, "a lot."

Bill's boisterous laugh filled the cabin.

Clipboard smiled too, "once they traced the location of the email, it became a national security threat, and went up the food-chain pretty quickly. Once it landed on the President's desk it was game over."

"Damn fine work," Bill said.

Before he realized what was happening, Qwiz found himself being pummeled with exultant cheers and congratulations. He beamed as everyone tried to hug him at once.

“Qwiz,” someone said, “you are a hero.”

CHAPTER 28:

The Whitehouse, United States of the West

The Gulfstream landed at what was left of Reagan International Airport, which like O'Hare, was mostly apartments and dense, urban farms. A single landing strip was maintained for government emergencies. They boarded an armored limousine and rushed with an escort straight to the Whitehouse.

It didn't seem possible that they had actually succeeded. Luthor had Qwiz to thank for that, of course. The quiet, quirky, lovable computer tech who'd risked everything. He did so not because his life was forfeit—like Luthor's had been—but simply because it was right. The kid was a hero.

Luthor blinked and found himself standing outside the door of the oval office. Hulking secret service agents in sterling black suits checked every orifice for the faintest whiff of a weapon. Luthor winced as a large black man's hand went in places he preferred it not go. They scanned them each with a wand that buzzed with electromagnetic pulses, designed to scan for listening bugs and instantly fry the micro-circuitry that ran them. They passed, and the doors opened.

The President sat behind the desk with his graying swath of black hair just visible behind the two large monitors arranged in front of him. Rolled up shirt sleeves and loosened tie bespoke a busy day in which he expected no media interruptions. Manuel Jimenez rose as they entered the room and greeted them with the warm smile that had won him the election over the war-hero incumbent that had preceded him. His genuine-seeming charm combined with his Mexican heritage had created a perfect storm among peacetime voters who hoped for a brighter future than had been possible in the dark years of World War III.

Sergeant Garcia stood next to him.

"Sarge!" Luthor exclaimed, "and um… Mr. President."

"Come, sit down," Jimenez said warmly, indicating chairs arranged in a circle in front of the Resolute Desk. Garcia embraced Luthor and sat down next to him.

"You're alive!"

"Yeah," Garcia replied quietly. "Survived again. I'm glad this time they didn't mind spending the carbon to save me—goddamn Stutsman… The Sabers captured my whole team and locked us up after we met you. The Deltas came in and rescued us last night."

"And Jimenez invited you here?"

"Yeah, says my experience with you and unlawful imprisonment earned me a 'seat at the table.'"

The agents fanned around behind them, two flanking the president, the others behind Luthor and his cohorts as they seated themselves. It was claustrophobic.

The President smiled again, his teeth as white as any toothpaste model's. "You, my friends, have gone through quite an ordeal."

"That's putting it nicely," Luthor muttered. Secret Service men and women loomed behind him.

Surprisingly, Jimenez didn't seem to object to his tone, instead he nodded. "You'll have to forgive me. Politics has conditioned me to mute all statements to bland, inoffensive, sound bites that can be repeated out of context; it's a hard habit to break, but I will try. Your friend Stone over there would probably say, 'it's been a son-of-a-bitch'?"

Bill did a double take. "How did you know what I was

thinking?"

"If our government does anything well, it is keeping unnecessarily accurate records of its citizens. I read each of yours before you arrived," he added, smiling again.

The agents shuffled nervously. Luthor glanced behind him to see a trigger-happy woman fingering her sidearm.

Again, Jimenez seemed to understand what he was thinking. "I am sorry, Dr. Tenrel, the Secret Service can be a bit overwhelming," he turned to the agents, "would you kindly have a seat, you are bothering our guests."

"But sir—"

"They obviously have no weapons; you made sure of that. I am also quite certain if they try to strangle me you would be more than capable of shooting them from across the room," he turned back to Luthor with another smile, "do try not to strangle me, will you?"

The agents slowly backed away from the circle of chairs.

"Back to the matter at hand," he continued, "this country, and the world, for that matter, owes each of you a remarkable debt. If not for you, not only would we not have any knowledge of the relevance of the 126th element, but any remnant of it would have been locked away in the bowels of a corrupt organization. As such, I am officially granting all of you a full pardon from any and all crimes incurred over the last month. I also spoke with Prime Minister Pollock today, and you will also receive pardons for any actions in the European Union."

Smiles and high-fives were shared between Luthor's weary friends. Bill couldn't high-five anyone, with his hand looking like a club, and the rest of them had at least one gauze-wrapped wound. Their victory had not come without considerable personal cost.

"I don't mean to sound ungrateful, Mr. President," Luthor said, "but if you are so thankful, why didn't you help us? Our entire time in North America we were alone, being hounded by carbon enforcement and the Sabers."

Jimenez closed his eyes, "unfortunately there are limits to my power. Even with all my advisors I simply didn't know what was going on. I am truly sorry." He spoke with a note of sincerity Luthor rarely heard in political discourse.

Luthor studied the man. His face, his serious expression, his earnest eyes all gave the impression of an honest man, giving an honest response. Luthor could not help it, he believed him.

"Then it wasn't you who sent that log-in code for the EU?" Qwiz asked.

Jimenez suddenly smiled. "Ah yes, that. You are correct, I didn't send it. But I do know who did."

Qwiz looked like he could barely contain himself. "Who?"

Jimenez glanced at his watch. "Actually, I hoped he would be here already. But he's had a bit of a *longer* trip than you did." At that moment an aid entered the room and whispered something in the President's ear. "It appears he has just arrived."

The Secret Service all took out weapons. They seemed to be even more on edge than when Luthor had first entered the room.

"Please understand," Jimenez said, "this is a historic occasion. It's the first time an ambassador from the Chinese block has been welcomed onto American soil since before World War III."

Qwiz stood up, "The Chinese Block—"

"Allow me to introduce, Ambassador Hyeon Park."

"DAD!" Qwiz sprinted to embrace him.

Luthor found himself grinning ear to ear. Joyful laughter filled the room. Qwiz began to introduce everyone to his father.

Luthor stood in respect to shake Hyeon's hand. He

looked to be in his 60s and wore a finely tailored suit with a striped green tie. He was balding badly, but what was left of his combed-over hair was still mostly black. Overly large glasses sat on a face that had a striking resemblance to Qwiz. Hyeon bowed, "it is a pleasure to meet you, Dr. Tenrel." His English was flawless, though noticeably accented.

"You were an ambassador!" Qwiz said, "after all these years, I'd never been able to figure out what your job was."

"Actually, until we received your final email, I was the Director of International Counter-terrorism. Given my relationship with you, the leadership thought I would make the perfect choice for the new Ambassador."

"One of Hyeon's spies sent you the EU login information," The President said.

"Thank you! It saved my friends' lives."

"You're welcome, my son," Qwiz's father replied, "I only wish I could have been there with you. You have acted with honor and courage. I am proud of you."

Qwiz beamed.

"So, sir, Mr. Ambassador, sir," Bill said. "How long you been watching Quency?"

"I've had an agent keeping tabs on him and my wife for almost ten years."

Bill whistled. "That means you saw us that first night when Stalker had us cornered like… like…" Bill struggled to find a non-vulgar metaphor.

"Yes. I had an agent there."

"*You* called them off!" Bill pumped his good fist. "Ha! Thank you! I owe you a pint for that. No. Make that a lifetime of pints!"

The Ambassador smiled.

"I'd always wondered why they just wandered off when they had uzis shoved up our peck—I mean our ass—in our *faces*. How'd you do it?"

Hyeon shared a look with Jimenez. Jimenez nodded. "Mr. Ambassador, we too have our own spy secrets, if you choose to share how you saved your son's life with him, I will not pry into the details. I am too concerned with reuniting families and countries to jeopardize that with lust over proprietary technology."

Hyeon bowed. "Then it appears you are a man worthy of leadership and of friendship. Yes, my agent intervened. We have a... *method* of emergency covert communication while in other nations, which my agent used to save your life. I will simply say that the... *method* is dangerous and can only be used once by any agent."

"Does that mean he died?" Qwiz asked.

Hyeon hesitated. "I do not think so. He was alive when he sent the normal communique that you needed access to the EU. That was the last time I heard from him. He took a terrible risk in exposing himself to the Sabers. I beg leniency on behalf of your government if he is found."

"I have never cared for an independent force that can operate on American soil with impunity," Jimenez said. "If he is an enemy of the Sabers, then as far as I'm concerned, he's an ally."

Qwiz cleared his throat. "Mr. President," he began respectfully, "how is it that an agency you help pay for has a goal so completely opposite your own?"

"I never said I supported the Sabers' creation," Jimenez said, "I was a Congressman in New Mexico at the time. They didn't exactly ask my permission or my input. They just acted on fear. Fear of rebellion against such an economically restrictive law. They needed a way to enforce the law, so they created the Sabers."

"Somebody to stop the mafia from flooding the world with illegal carbon," Michael summarized.

"More like an entire nation from circumventing carbon restrictions to improve their employment rate or GDP. They created an international agency that operated outside the jurisdiction of any other law enforcement or government."

"Giving any group that much power isn't a good idea," Vika said.

"Certainly not. I am sorry Miss Veronika that you had to experience so much of it firsthand."

Vika nodded. "Even I didn't know their true purpose."

"Before the war, only people at the top levels of government knew they existed. They were top secret in the first few years of CPI as they rooted out black market smuggling rings, secret coal burning factories, that sort of thing. They brought rogue states into line. When the war broke out, the Sabers had been hardened into the perfect tool to handle the most difficult missions. The Coalition used them like a scalpel to take out impossible targets, and word of their existence spread through the military.

"By the time the war ended, they had gained the reputation as the most lethal special forces group in the world. But without a war and wide-spread compliance with Paris 2, they fell out of notice and simply became a subheading line-item in the international budget."

"Where did Dimarin fit in?" Vika asked, coldly emphasizing the past tense of his role.

"Franco Dimarin was appointed head of the Sabers during the last year of the war, making him officially responsible for any special actions they took globally. A position he held until today, actually."

"126's potential to eliminate the need of carbon enforcement altogether might piss a group like that off a bit," Garcia said.

The President nodded. "It seems he viewed your promise of free energy for everyone as a threat to his power."

"He said as much when he had us trapped," Luthor said.

"You couldn't do *anything* to stop him?" Tanya asked.

"That's the nature of the carbon enforcement law. They didn't answer to me. Or the Prime Minister. That was the point. How could they be independent if I could stop them? My interference with the Sabers is strictly limited to political red-tape. I can direct the oversight committee to not approve major actions, I can hike up prices for their munitions, or impede their transportation. But anything else is illegal; direct opposition would be tantamount to declaring war on the rest of the carbon-restricted world—something congress would never approve."

"So Dimarin could freely do whatever he wanted?"

"Essentially, yes. As long as he could tie his actions in some way to enforcing carbon regulation. However, now that he's impeded *our* national security, and broken *our* laws—and for that matter, directly worked against his own charter— we can lock him away."

Vika almost smiled. "I enjoyed seeing him in handcuffs," she turned to Jimenez, "I hope he never sees the outside of a cell again"

"If I have anything to say about it, he won't. And now that he's locked away, perhaps together we can end the energy crisis."

Bill spoke up. "Yeah, you can say that now that Qwiz's brought you 126. But if you really wanted to end the energy crisis there *has been* another option for you," he looked the younger, but infinitely more powerful man in the eye, "we are sitting on enough energy to feed and heat this country for another 150 years." Tanya gasped, but Bill trudged stridently on into the traitorous 2180 rhetoric. "You could have legalized coal and natural gas; within a few years starvation would be a thing of the past."

The President bored holes into Bill's head with his eyes. The moment froze as everyone awaited his judgement. To utter such a thing in public was a felony.

"You have lived up to your nickname, Stone." Jimenez said. "Except it feels like it's not strong enough. Your manhood has got to be made of tougher stuff than mere stone.

They should have called you Steel."

The bushy mass of white hair on Bill's face shifted into a smile.

"You do know that you have just committed a felony. And you have just done so in the presence of the President?"

"I know what I said. You had the power to save millions of lives and you didn't because you were afraid of the carbon boogeyman."

Like a popping LED bulb, the secret service surrounded both Bill and the President.

Pistols trained on Bill's bandaged chest.

"Get back, you retards!" Bill snapped at the agents, "I've waited over 20 years to tell that to the guy with the big chair. I've said my peace and now I'm done."

Jimenez raised a hand. "It's okay."

"It is *not* okay!" an agent growled.

"Is Climate-Denial really a worse crime than all those they've been pardoned for already? On a list of crimes that includes terrorism and murder?"

The agent backed off.

"I think we can add it to your list, Stone; it'll save you a minimum ten years in prison."

"Thank you."

"Pardon me if this is not the time for such questions," Hyeon began, "but as this is China's first official contact in decades, am I to understand that your country made it *illegal* to question climate change?"

"Yes, of course," The President replied. "Such rhetoric was too toxic and too dangerous to allow. In order for the Paris 2 protocols to successfully curb carbon use, we needed a people united against it. We couldn't allow such obvious lies to divide us in such a critical time."

The Korean ambassador stroked his chin in thought. "Again, I apologize for my brashness. If you wish to discuss matters of international relations in private, I understand."

"You would not be here today if not for the courage of these people. Whatever you have on your mind, you can share with all of us."

Luthor was again impressed with Jimenez. He couldn't tell if it was pure political gamesmanship or if his statement was genuine, but by including them he clearly had won over everyone in the room, including Qwiz's father.

"Perhaps, the differences in our countries are finally coming into focus for me. And I suspect it will be very important for our countries to understand each other if we truly seek reconciliation."

"Nothing would make me happier than to help reknit this world together." Jimenez said. "Please help us understand one another, Mr. Ambassador."

"I believe that all our differences come down to one thing. Mr. Benyard would have had no need of a pardon had he uttered those words in China."

"How do you see such a minor change making such a big difference?" Jimenez asked.

"It makes all the difference! In China, our officials were able to ask the most important questions without being thrown in Jail."

"What questions?" Qwiz asked.

"The question that might have prevented the Culling altogether, had it been legal to ask in your Coalition. It was the question which defined Chinese policy for the last 20 years: 'which is more dangerous: the prospect of a gradually warming planet or the governmental policies designed to prevent it?' By never asking such a question, you condemned yourselves and everyone under your law to starvation. It was illegal to even suggest an alternative."

It was a very valid point. Much more cogent than Luthor would have expected.

"With all due respect Ambassador, what right do you have to criticize our country's policy when yours incited

World War III?"

Both men had valid points. Luthor hoped that these peace talks wouldn't break down before they started.

"It seems likely that you have as many misconceptions about us as we do about you. Why do you think we attacked?"

There was a pause as the President tried to find the nicest way of saying '*you're greedy climate-denying bastards bent on destroying the earth,*' as possible.

"Your country wanted to secure the Antarctican oil to have a strategic advantage in the global economy."

"You thought we were greedy." Hyeon summarized, cutting through the politically correct answer. "But the truth is, we were afraid of you."

"Afraid?"

"Afraid of you and the EU. The Carbon Coalition appeared to us at the time to be uncaring and ruthless."

"You thought we were the ruthless ones? Your country attacked us. Unprovoked!"

"Yes, we did. Ask yourself *why* Mr. President. It had appeared to us that your countries were so heartless that you were willing to sacrifice tens of millions of your own citizens to poverty and starvation, all in your zeal to 'protect the Earth.' How would you treat a country that disagreed with you? And we certainly disagreed. It seemed it was only a matter of time before you came for us, in order to *force* us into compliance.

"Attacking you was a risk, but it was our only chance. If we could keep you from getting the fuel to run your war-machine, we thought we could protect our people from your reckless destruction of the world's economy. At the bottom of it, we were defending ourselves. Defending ourselves from a people who wouldn't allow a question to be asked: which is worse, global warming or government intervention?"

The room fell silent. Luthor had never considered the Chinese perspective before. What if—in their minds—the USW was the real greedy juggernaut and they were the ones trying desperately to stave off destruction? It would certainly require some extended reflection. What if the true villains where the members of the Coalition this whole time?

Luthor found himself speaking, he knew he was out of turn in the company of world leaders, but couldn't help it. Of all them he truly understood the consequences of the war better than any of them. He had *lived* it.

"You feared our entire country would act like Dimarin did," he said.

"In short, yes." Hyeon replied. "All of your actions pointed that way."

The divide between the two powers felt as stark as the crack across Titan Dome. How was it possible to find common ground between two such radically different views on the world? To the credit of the two most powerful men in the room, neither seemed interested in expanding that rift.

"Then what would you have had us do? Let our climate turn into Venus?"

Hyeon continued. "Please don't misunderstand me, we in China also knew that something had to change.

"The Chinese Government simply wasn't willing to risk the lives of their people on the mere chance that carbon restrictions might impact the climate or that the computer model predictions were even accurate. You were.

"We foresaw the Culling as the bigger danger than global warming. The whole world's food supply was based on oil, we knew we needed to replace it before we ran out. If we could find a viable replacement, we would be able to cut carbon emissions without destroying civilization to do it, so we focused all our efforts on discovery and innovation rather than restriction."

"But in the end, the ultimate discovery to end reliance on carbon ended up happening here anyway," Jimenez said indicating toward Luthor.

"Ironic, that it was our own people who tried to suppress it," Tanya said.

"Indeed." Qwiz's father said, "but we have made great leaps of our own and are rapidly replacing our infrastructure with effective green sources of electricity. As a sign of good faith, and our attempt to begin mending our relations, my government has given me permission to share all of that innovation of the last twenty years with you."

"That is a *very* generous offer, Mr. Ambassador. And thank you," Jimenez replied. "Though I would be interested to know how useful it would be in a world where we have 126."

"You have covered large portions of your cities in solar panels, ours are 20% more efficient than your best. I suspect they will remain useful for the foreseeable future. But more importantly, after studying the details of Qwency's files, it is clear that there are some very real limitations to 126."

"What limitations?" Luthor asked.

"It requires something that can be difficult near large cities: space. It requires space for the powerplant to be installed as well as room around it where gravity is being oscillated. China has a better solution within those requirements."

"Really?" Michael asked, "a *clean* source?"

Hyeon smiled. "Did you know that China now has three operational Fusion generators, each producing 2 gigawatts?"

"Impressive." Luthor said. Fusion had long been seen as the holy grail of energy, but despite almost 100 years of trying, no one had ever been able to create an economically viable one—that is, get more power out than you put in—or so Luthor had thought. "Have you thought about utilizing 126 to improve the containment of the plasma? If it works, it could dramatically lower the temperature threshold for fusion!"

"Dr. Tenrel, it is clear I am not as knowledgeable about plasma physics as you are, but I would very much like to begin a discussion between our two countries on alternate uses for the gravitational properties of 126."

Luthor looked toward Jimenez for guidance. Who would have thought after all he'd been through that he would want to collaborate with the Chinese on anything. "Mr. President, what do you think?"

Jimenez paused for a long moment, "I think our countries have some very real differences, and it will take more than one meeting to wash over the pain we have caused each other."

"I can speak for the Chinese Alliance. We are willing to try, if you are."

"I am."

"Then I believe together we could usher in a new golden age of abundance and prosperity for the world."

"I agree. But we need to be careful." Jimenez turned to Luthor. "I will need a group that I can trust in charge of this country's management and implementation of 126. No one else on the planet knows more about 126 and its potential for energy generation than you. I would like to offer you all a collective position on my new committee in charge of 126."

"Will we get a cool acronym?" Qwiz asked.

"Absolutely," Jimenez replied with a laugh, "one of you would be required to sit on my cabinet as well, reporting directly to me. Dr. Tenrel, I would like that person to be you."

Luthor felt a knot tighten in his stomach. He had no desire to get involved with the government ever again. He had been betrayed and forgotten in Antarctica, he'd been harried and hunted by Stalker and carbon enforcement. Now Jimenez wanted him to sign up again, another tour of service. He found Tanya's eye. She wore the same knowing smile that always made him feel a little better even when he never would admit it to her.

"Dr. Tenrel?" the President prodded.

Slowly, resignedly, Luthor nodded his head, "I'll do it."

"Then let's get to work."

EPILOGUE

Luthor looked over a massive facility humming with activity. Cyclotrons, old and new, were producing 126 at a break-neck pace. Every hour this complex was producing as much 126 as Luthor and his team had in their entire first year. It still strained his imagination at times to understand the scope of what the USW was doing. In a spree of scientific production, unheard of since the Manhattan project, they had dedicated every resource to producing 126. Facilities like this one were popping up all over the hemisphere, so many in fact, thousands of highly skilled Markless had been recruited to ease the workload. Formerly forlorn, hopeless, and homeless, they jumped at the unprecedented opportunity to hold a job and re-enter society.

Luthor had even pulled some strings and been able to recruit Father Roc's little band to help run security at this particular plant. Thaddeus, DeShawn, Abigail, and Serenity had gladly joined up. Roc himself insisted on staying behind, declaring there were "more lost sheep to find." The four friends had done an admirable job of protecting the newly minted element as it was fused together from smaller atoms.

Other massive projects were sprouting up everywhere to actually utilize 126 being created. Every unused hill near a population center was being used to build self-contained hydroelectric dams. Massive pipes funneled water down through turbines and then 126 pulled the water back up to the top to run it through again. Every city in the world could have the power of the Hoover-dam in their back yard without blocking up a single river.

The main limitation was the amount of 126 available. Fortunately, its components were not difficult to come by. Stored waste from nuclear reactors was ample, it just needed to be dug up and refined, and depleted Uranium was almost as ubiquitous as steel after the war. Shoved into a cyclotron, tuned to Luthor's specifications, the refined Krypton bombarded Uranium targets and produced reliable quantities of the remarkable element.

The biggest problem was providing enough electricity for the production process. New generators, solar and wind farms were sprouting around the facilities like a corn field in the spring. Wind and solar companies struggled to meet the demand. Ironic that the production of the very element that would make their best products obsolete currently boosted their sales.

Tanya squeezed his hand and smiled at him. He still hadn't acclimated to the strange pinch on his ring-finger every time he held Tanya's hand. *Small price to pay,* Luthor thought. *Mental note: advocate marriage to friends. It far exceeds its reputation.*

Luthor smiled broadly at her; he found himself doing that a lot more lately. Falling asleep next to Tanya every night seemed to soothe his depressive spells as a massage soothed a sore back. He readily admitted to anyone who asked that he had been wrong; marriage as it turned out, was wonderful. The best thing about being married to Tanya was the lack of worry. Throughout their long dating relationship, Luthor had fretted about Tanya realizing how messed up he was and leaving him. Now, she had promised before her God that she never would, for better or for worse. As strange as it sounded, he believed her. Marriages used to end in divorce all the time, but in the modern world, few got married. To do so was a strange, and therefore serious, undertaking. It made their covenant together feel real, even sacred somehow. He never doubted for an instant any more that she would remain by his side. She knew all of him, even the worst, most broken parts of his cannibalized soul, and had promised to stay with him anyway.

The freedom not to worry about Tanya combined with Bill's advice, helped to unchain his soul just a little bit more every day, keeping Anti-Luthor from returning to his home. The old man's continued influence had helped immeasurably more than any Army-paid shrink ever had to help his PTSD. Bill had lived in the darkness as he had and had emerged again. It was possible. Luthor continued to talk about his experiences, and though painful, he sensed the pain was like surgery: it hurt, but ultimately healed. Bill had even roped him into speaking at a veteran's convention next month. That would be a test of his newfound resolve.

His phone buzzed in his pocket. He picked it up. It was nice to have one again.

"Dr. Tenrel speaking."

"You know who this is, old fart. It says on your screen. Can't you just say 'hi Michael,' like a normal person?"

Luthor laughed, "we are important people now, a certain amount of decorum is required."

Michael was currently overseeing a gargantuan new facility being constructed in Tennessee that would produce 126 by an entirely new method. He and Luthor had collaborated with dozens of PhD's from both China and the USW and developed the radically new synthesis method that didn't require an accelerator. If successful, it would generate ten times more 126 atoms than their current cyclotron farms while using less energy to do so.

"Well, boss, I just got off the phone with Fermilab, and I have some news you might want to hear about."

"Shoot," Luthor said. Tanya leaned in to hear the call as well.

"The big wigs at IUPAC are discussing the official name

of the element."

"Oh no..."

"Oh yes. Support is strong for naming it *Tenrelium*, in honor of you."

"Smogging son of—" Tanya slapped his arm and he bit off the epithet. He heard Michael laughing on the other end of the line. "What about you? You helped! And you saved my life at least twice."

Luthor had *not* wanted the element named after him. It didn't feel right somehow, but that had egged Michael on, making him the chief advocate of the name 'Tenrelium' in academic circles. It seemed to bring him joy to no end to have it named after Luthor.

"I was an intern," he laughed again, "*you* discovered it. Besides, it sounds good. *Tenrelium.*"

"It sounds terrible."

Tanya squeezed his arm and he smiled in spite of himself.

"Well, I just thought you should know. The panel is voting on it tomorrow."

Luthor hung his head. As if Michael could see the reaction, he heard more chuckling from the other end of the phone. "Ouch," Michael said, abruptly cutting off his laughter.

A new voice appeared on the line. It had a slightly Russian accent to it. "You deserve congratulations, Tenrel, and more respect than this fool gives you."

"Thank you, Vika," Luthor said, but still heard Michael cackling in the background.

Tanya grabbed the phone, "Vika, its Tanya. Smack him around a little bit more, will you? Since that tour to China with Qwiz and his father, Michael thinks he's a rock star. Somebody needs to deflate that boy's ego while he can still fit through doorways."

"Jimenez had it written into my job description. I

kick his ass every night whether he needs it or not," Luthor and Tanya shared a glance. Given Vika's new *official* romance with Michael, Luthor didn't want to imagine what other connotations that comment might mean.

"We'll see you next week," Tanya said, ending the call.

"I fear for his life if he is ever unfaithful," Luthor said.

"I know. But honestly, she is perfect for him, exactly what he needs in a woman. She'll whip him into shape in no time."

"I have a hard time imagining him as a polite, faithful gentleman."

"Believe it. Before the year is out, he will be a new man."

"If you say so."

"It seems to me, that if we can change the world and give it enough energy to thrive again, then nothing is impossible."

THE END

Made in the USA
Middletown, DE
20 September 2019